Mist in the Willows

The Spirit Fleet Chronicles
Volume 1

Lucy Linne

lucylinne.com

Author's Copy
For review
Sent by
Lucy Linne

First published in 2025 by Skulls&Cupcakes

Copyright © Lucy Linne 2025.

Lucy Linne asserts her right to be identified as the author of this Work.

Cover art and illustrations by Lucy Linne.

A CIP catalogue record for this book is available from the British Library.

ISBN: 978-1-0682757-0-8

I miss the Girlguiding songs you hummed as I fell asleep,
And waking up to open windows
and the sound of your kitchen radio
softly filling every room of our sunny city-flat with
Seventies and eighties songs...
I miss coming home from school straight to your
little bookshop at the top of the hill,
Homework in the loft among literal ceiling-high towers
Beautiful towers of dusty books.
Done! Running down the twisted narrow ladder,
"Which one will you go for next?" you'd ask,
"Oh, maybe that one... or that one?" I'd point
to the display shelves.
That's a tough choice, let's make a coffee, you'd smile.
And even now when I re-read a classic I remember
how you told it.
I heard so many of those stories in your voice
before I read them...
And we kept the bookshop open long into the evening,
the street grew dark,
Sitting there with our giant mugs and miniscule
square biscuits,
around the old writing desk with the heavy ancient till
by the store window. Talking about books to read,
books read, books to read again.
The shop was tiny and you could never afford gifts,
so every time: "Choose a book, and it's yours!"
And I don't remember if I ever did thank you
...That all my childhood gifts were books.
Thank you, mum.
You'll never get to read it, but
this one's for you.

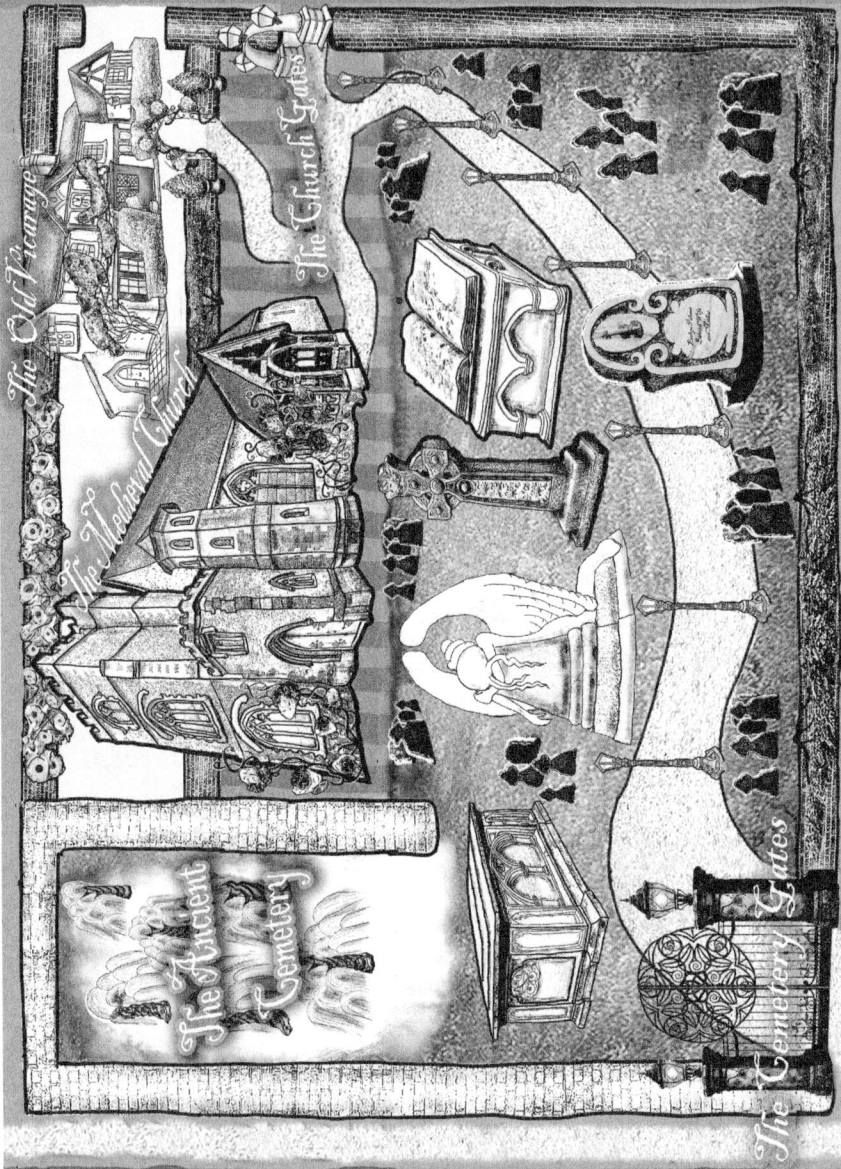

The Old Vicarage

The Church Gates

The Medieval Church

The Ancient Cemetery

The Cemetery Gates

The River Thames

Contents

Chapter One

The First Night Home

The first time I heard that chilling whisper call my name, it came from Grandad's old analogue radio.

I was unpacking the five sad-looking boxes containing all my worldly belongings and didn't pay much attention. Dad stored them in his basement, and spiders were crawling out of every corner.

When I picked up my phone to check for messages, a mega-arachnid scuttled on eight hairy legs along my fingers. It had blended in, quite insidiously, with the black case of my mobile and became invisible. Now it took up most of the screen. I dropped my phone on the coffee table and spotted its mate, the same incredible size, scampering across the floor and under the couch. At least Grandad went to bed early and didn't see this infestation I'd brought to his cherished houseboat.

I ran from the lounge to the open plan kitchen and grabbed a glass to trap the intruders.

As I passed by, the radio on the windowsill abruptly switched to a hoarse, faltering static.

The music returned as I shook the glass out of the barge door, tossing the eight-legged giant into the grass by the river path. The other one, nowhere to be found. I regretted trying to trap and release them. I would have rather squashed them with my hiking boot. But cleaning bug goo off the floor is a task I'll always avoid where possible. A flamethrower *would* be ideal but I'm out of those since I'm back home. So, the spider got to live another day.

As I rinsed that glass to put it away, I noticed it.

Wait a minute? What's going on with the radio?

I stood beside the little radio, in the same spot it had sat since my childhood, gathering dust on the windowsill, and listened to the static.

It had a quality about it that I found almost obscene. It sounded alive, fluctuating from deep cavernous whispers to a strange whistling. I fled the kitchen when it pitched that abominable screech of steak knives against dinner plates.

The static immediately faded away, returning to Grandad's favourite sixties rock radio station. Back in the lounge, I punched a pile of empty boxes flat to bin them. Not that I wasn't glad the static stopped. But something about the way it had switched so fast bothered me, as if it *knew* I had moved away from the radio.

Moments later I returned to the kitchen. The music shifted to static in an instant. I stood next to Grandad's ancient kettle, plugging in my coffee maker, a survivor since my student years in the dorms.

How could it be so loud and not wake up Alan?

Its pulsing tones surged, like the call of a bottomless pit, then lulled to a sinister hum at the very edge of hearing. Every time it came, I cringed, as if plunging into neck deep water with ice cubes bobbing all around me.

Before I knew it, I had crossed the room and stood with one hand on my dog's collar.

"You don't like it either, huh? Good boy," I said, as Cannelloni sat back down among the window seat cushions. The static melted away behind me, the music replacing it. Cannelloni tucked his head in his paws again with a huff.

I glanced back at the old radio. Had it sounded a bit like whispers in some guttural language? Surely, I was over thinking it. It could be nothing but static.

I headed for the desk to start my Wi-Fi set up, hoping to stream a movie and chill after the gruelling day, moving in with Grandad. And most importantly, to make sure her messages would come through on a stronger signal.

I reached and patted my cargos' pocket, the little one with the zip on my hip. It was still there: I felt the round shape of her compact mirror. The only thing I have of her, until we meet again.

I felt better. There are good things in the world, and good days ahead.

As I pulled up the lid of my laptop, in the split second before the dark screen lit up, your face flashed at me.

It's only been happening in the last few years or so, that my reflection startles me, looking like you. I've always had your impossibly thick and straight, dirty blonde hair. And your bushy brows over cobalt blue eyes. But most of all, in my late thirties, I'm now your age. The way I remember you. You would be much older today but if we could somehow meet, across death and time, both aged 38, we'd look like twins. Anyway, it only lasted a fraction of a second, and then the desktop lit up and I was looking for a movie right away.

Ten minutes later, I glanced suspiciously at the radio. Nothing.

Twenty minutes later, nothing.

Halfway through an outbreak of a superbly gruesome zombie apocalypse, I still couldn't stop thinking about the static. Was I causing it? It only happened when I neared the radio.

Run a test?

I hesitated. So many other things to worry about at this moment. Why did I even care if the songs were interrupted a few times?

Because of how freakin weird this noise sounded.

I paused the movie, resigned to my curiosity. I edged along the back of the loveseat towards the kitchen. The music staggered as I reached the counter. Just to pretend to myself I didn't come to test the radio, I reached out and grabbed a handful of cookies from the doggie jar.

The static soared.

Sounded like a cold gust whistling savagely out of a black chasm. Then dulled to the throaty whisper of an unsettling breeze through dead leaves. That did it. I got the hell out of the kitchen.

Joining Cannelloni at the window seat, I felt an unreasonable amount of relief that the music returned on the radio. Cannelloni thought so too. He gave such a profound growl he even startled me a bit. He bared his teeth at the kitchen. Not like him at all.

"Don't worry, just a funny noise!" I said, letting him slurp the cookies on the palm of my hand. My gaze wandered back to the spot I had been standing.

A funny noise that comes only when I'm close to the radio. But how close, exactly?

I stood up, arms crossed and edged to the back of the couch marking the end of the lounge, not quite entering the kitchen.

"Ok Cannelloni let's see, one step. Two steps, three..."

The music faltered. I stopped moving.

I leaned back as far as I could go without shifting my feet. The music flowed. I chuckled.

Not because I wasn't scared. More like, because I was getting *too* scared.

Then I leaned forward.

The music faltered.

I tried to hold my balance, bent as far as I could reach like some demented yoga teacher who forgot which warrior pose they were demonstrating. A sudden fear, out of nowhere.

Rivulets of crimson streaking dry sand. Something solid in the blood. Glistening strips of sinew. Twitching on the red mud. Not again!

The gaps in the music, for some reason, flashed images from my nightmares in my mind.

I straightened up. This wasn't funny anymore.

I'm good at pushing the memory of the nightmares away during the day and focusing on my work and everything else I have to worry about. This bloody radio thing was getting on my nerves.

I jumped with a yelp as a sharp pinch came from behind my left knee.

"Cannelloni! What are you doing?"

The dog had bitten hard into my trouser leg and was pulling at it. As if he wanted me to leave the kitchen.

"Aren't you clever," I said, disentangling myself and coming to sit with him by the window seat. "It's ok, I'm staying here, you can snooze again!" I scratched under his ears until he turned around full circle on his cushions and plopped in the comfiest spot.

At least I know. It's about four steps into the kitchen.

That would mean I can't reach the counter without setting off the weird.

But I was done experimenting. Hated the way the static made me feel, and what it did to my dog too.

This boy, the only good thing about this new, civilian life, was normally a big bundle of cuddles. At the moment he looked perturbed, ears twitching. Cannelloni's natural state was passed out, belly up, and fast asleep on his giant plushie bed. Ever since I brought him here from the shelter after Easter, he acted as if Grandad 's houseboat has always been his rightful kingdom, where he reigned supreme and absolute. Yet now he kept sitting up, fretting, scanning the room with anxious eyes. Tiny whimpers squeaking at the back of his throat. I sensed danger too. But I couldn't understand why.

I cast my gaze around the empty room.

I felt watched.

The dark water of the Thames sparkled under the moonlit sky from every side of the semi-circular cabin. I hated the glass, U shaped wall of the main cabin, but that's what you get when living in a wide beam Dutch barge. The lounge was basically an open balcony. Anyone could be watching me from the dark river paths on either side of the banks, and I had zero visibility at night. Meanwhile, I lived and breathed in full view, unless I went to hide in my cabin at the back of the houseboat.

I went around lowering the window blinds post-haste.

Better. Only the kitchen window remained. I hesitated. I wanted to close those blinds too, but that would get me in the vicinity of the radio.

Pressing my hand to my brow, I felt sweat droplets at the root of my hair.

I took two steps forward. I was nearing the invisible mark I'd noted mentally, on the kitchen floor.

Two steps more. The music was faltering. Maybe if I went really fast it wouldn't happen.

I dashed to the cord hanging at the casement, leaning in, real quick, my hand reaching out to the blind. The static came loud.

Flustered, I backed into the lounge again, and the songs came back on.

I sat down onto the couch, feeling like a coward.

The radio on the sill kept singing its quiet and perpetual song.

Grandad never changes station or switches the music off. He turns the sound up when he is around, which isn't often. He doesn't think the kitchen is a man's place, he only comes to fill the water can when he looks after Grandma's flowerpots. He treasures her little terrace garden in the front of the barge. He lowers the volume when he heads for his berth to watch his shows, the music from the radio playing quietly through the days and nights in the main cabin.

I wanted to close the kitchen shades but an irrational fear of going near the radio pinned me to the spot.

"Don't be a twat, this happens all the time. People moving around a device can mess up the signal. Just fucking go," I thought.

I moved to the window directly and lowered the blinds to the sound of loud static. It seemed eerily similar to fast, angry whispers.

And this time I could not deny it.

The radio called my name.

Jade... JADE!

OK, I hadn't imagined that.

I ran back to the lounge to grab Cannelloni by the collar. He growled at the radio, irritated. I led him to my berth, shutting the door. We never went near the kitchen for the rest of that night.

Quite annoying, because the Wi-Fi signal is terrible in my cabin, so I had to go stand at the door every ten minutes to check for her messages.

None came.

Seemed ungrateful to complain. Grandma's bedroom: Hands down the biggest room I had ever called my own. Walk in wardrobe. En suite bathroom. A recliner armchair, proper Victorian style. Fancy letter writing desk, with the miniature drawers to put in useless shit like ink bottles. Good to store the USB cables I keep losing. Queen bed. Four memory foam pillows. An army of multi shaped squishy cushions on a crochet throw. Fluffy duvet and matching dog blanket for Cannelloni (that's store bought, I got it so my dog feels like he fits in). Lush. But still, I couldn't chill enough to finish my movie.

I kept thinking about the radio saying my name.

In the cosy safety of my berth, it all seemed ridiculous. Of course, the radio didn't say my name.

Probably someone spoke from outside, maybe someone else called Jade. Walking past with a friend.

I pressed play in my movie for the umpteenth time, getting comfy on the bed.

Lost cause. I couldn't pay attention. Not even when the hordes of undead swarmed down the streets towards the hapless group of survivors hiding in the rubble. I was absolutely unable to stop wondering who had called my name outside the boat, in the dark.

That voice spoke to *me*.

Unwelcome memories from a few of hours earlier made my teeth grind as my jaw tightened.

"You're staying with Alan then? How you gonna get yourself a nice man if you're living with your Grandfather?" Their old man cackles, phlegmy snarling that ended in ugly coughs, had resounded across the river. Grandad 's friends sailed by leisurely, at a speed easy for him to jump over from their boat on to our deck. They wiped sweaty foreheads with beefy hands and stared at me while Grandad hopped on board.

"I'm not looking for nice," I said, and watched their confusion halt their sneers. They'd thought I'd say I'm not looking for a *man*. All three of them took a gulp of their cans of lager, manspreading their knees a little wider as their boat bench creaked under their weight.

"What you looking for then?"

"None of your business."

"Don't be a smart ass," Grandad told me under his breath, as he waved goodbye to the six seater rental sailing on. His friends don't own a boat. And they take up two seats each.

"You look after your Grandfather now!" one of them called back to me.

"I will." *But I won't be doing the kind of looking after that* you *lot expect of me.*

"Your Grandma kept the Lady Thomasine spotless!" said another, looking over his shoulder.

"She had cinnamon buns hot from the oven every morning!" called the third over the growing distance between the boats.

Which meant that Alan had already complained to them about me. I only just moved in today for fuck's sake.

"Grandad, can you please not discuss me with your friends?" I said. All I got in return, was a scowl in the direction of his laundry basket, parked in front of the washing machine. And a loud slam of his cabin door.

As if.

"Adults wash their own clothes," I called after him. "And the bakery in the village has excellent cinnamon buns."

Distant calls from the river bend reached me, and more guffawing. Something along the lines of 'get in that kitchen, woman!'

I was used to their banter devolving, from barely friendly to openly woman-bashing, in T minus half a can of lager; I didn't reply.

"They don't mean anything, just joking!" shouted another one of them, as I turned around to look at them. Their shoulders were shaking from laughter; they found the women in the kitchen comment hilarious.

"Watch out for my high school mate Caden at the Lock today," I called back.

"Why, you gonna marry the new Lock keeper?"

"No. His wife's with the Port of London Authority, she has the power to breathalyse those suspected of boating under the influence." I grinned as they choked on their snorts. "Have a nice evening now." As they glowered wordlessly at me, I slammed the deck door behind me.

I generally never met Grandad's friends, apart from on their river pub crawl weekends, when they picked him up and dropped him off. It's an aspect of life back home, that I'm *not* looking forward to: seeing the three bigots Alan calls my 'uncles'. Since I was a girl, they spent every moment of our brief weekly meetings cracking jokes at me, because apparently, I'm doing girlhood wrong.

I'm great at fixing the plumbing and maintaining the generator around the boat, every time I visited. Who cares if I don't know how to operate the oven; when shit kept breaking after Alan tried to repair them three and four times over, Grandma called me; and I got the job done. Grandad hated it. Called me an odd ball ever since I was young. When I grew up, he and his friends took the piss every time I pulled out my toolbox. Which, incidentally, is bigger than any of theirs.

So, it had to be them, they probably came for a walk down the river path, calling my name outside the boat in the night. Stupid of me to buy it.

I turned to sleep, a tight knot in my stomach. Grandad's friends are arseholes. Not the best first night back home.

But I guess this is not really home. Just where I stay for now.

Cannelloni's soft fur felt warm against my side, as he plopped down and curled up with a happy blink.

"Our first real night together, huh? I'm so glad to have you, boy," I said, throwing an arm around him. The way he acted towards me with complete trust, as if we'd known each other out whole lives; it was amazing.

But as the dog fell fast asleep, I stayed wide awake in the dark. So, you see, Mum, it's not been fun moving in with Grandad.

Jade paused and took a sip from her beer bottle. Her short ponytail waved in the breeze and brushed against the tombstone. The sun hung heavy on the horizon. Darkness draped more than half the graveyard. The thousand-year-old church, nestled among the graves and willow trees, cast a long and wide shadow over the grounds. The gust that blew from those darker tombs under its shadow, brought a chill to where Jade sat. She hugged her knees and shivered.

The golden disc of the sun vanished behind the treetops. As the world darkened around her and the evening birdsong gave away to silence, her blue eyes were vague, lost in thought.

The screen of her phone flashed, and she snatched it up. She looked at the message, but it wasn't the one she wanted. She rolled her eyes.

"Leela won't quit," she muttered and threw the phone on the grass beside her again.

She turned to the grave and looked at the violin carved there. "Only thing I'm glad about is getting to chat with you whenever I like, now, Mum. I missed this when I had to be away all the time. But the shitty thing is I've never had a real, grownup civilian job in my life. I need one, to afford a place of my own. Clearing Grandad's friends' laptops from viruses is not going to get me a deposit for a flat."

Taking another sip of her beer, she gazed at the tall-stemmed glass that stood, untouched, at the step of the gravestone, full to the brim with red wine.

"Sorry for the cheap bubbly, Mum, I can't afford your posh vino at the moment. I'll bring you better soon. Everything's gone to hell right now. I never planned to retire from the Corps, but those nightmares! They just fucked everything up. Got a *diagnonsense* now. No more tours for me. And typical Dad, he refused to let me stay with them. What a great way to welcome me home at the airport! At least he said he will pay for therapy to sort out the nightmares. But only because I'll never hold down a job if I can't sleep through the night. Not that he cares, other than making sure I'll never again ask him to stay in my childhood bedroom. *She's* turned it into a jewellery crafts studio." Jade rolled her eyes and chuckled. "I honestly don't mind living on the boat. Really. Easier to get here from the mooring on my bike. Just hope that weird stuff with the radio will stop so I can get some work done and get some money saved. To move out as soon as possible."

She finished her beer in one last sip. Blond locks had come loose from her ponytail and fallen over her face as she put her bottle away in her backpack. The tips of her hair were sun-bleached to almost white by nearly two decades in the desert sun; in contrast to her once fair skin, now tanned to a deep bronze.

Movement among the distant graves made her look up. Someone had crossed the cemetery gates in the twilight. Jade instinctively hid behind her mother's tombstone and watched him follow the winding path among the tombs.

"That's a bit late for visiting this place," she muttered. She waited to see which grave he would visit, ready to make a mental note of its location and check the tombstone later on. He looked young, even hunched as he was, with his face in the shadows; his gait was light and his pace swift. Jade guessed someone that age was probably not here for a partner; more likely, like herself, for his mum or dad...

Her curiosity slowly turned into a frown of surprise. He'd kept going. He crossed the path into the grove of the willows. And still he walked on.

"Why *that* way, that side is the old burial ground." She crouched deeper and leaned to peer from the other side of her mother's tombstone. He crossed to the pitch-black darkness at the back of the old church. No matter how hard she tried, she couldn't see any details of his face or clothing; it was too dark on that side. The ancient burial ground was off the path and the light of the lampposts didn't reach it. Only the dim pearly starlight granted some shapes to the vista of mossy headstones crumbling there. No one had been buried there in the last two hundred years; the latest dates on those stones were in the eighteen hundreds. No fresh flower bouquets were left on those graves, and moss grew on the stone unchecked, deepening the cracks and eating away at the skull symbols etched there. No one ever cleared away the ivy growing over those names.

Why would anyone go there?

A clink of glass alerted her that she had almost knocked over the wine sitting at the front of the tombstone. Jade lost all interest in the stranger.

"Sorry Mum." Making sure the wine was safe, Jade picked up her phone once again.

"No new messages."

She sighed.

"I keep re-reading the old messages: *No dates yet, but everything is short notice. People get told to pack at noon and fly out before sunset. It could happen any minute. I know it will be my turn soon.* Ami wrote that three days ago. I replied: *I miss you. I can't believe it's taking so long. It looks like chaos over there, it's on the news every day. Are you ok.* One day later, without getting a reply, I texted again: *I haven't heard your actual voice in four weeks. I can't stand it.*" She paused.

"That text was so embarrassing," Jade muttered. "Throwing my own pity party while I'm back home, and meanwhile she is in the desert, her deployment extended and she's dealing with the madness of the evacuation. I wish I had deleted it." She bit her lip.

"Thirty-two hours later, came a reply: *I know, I miss you too. Don't worry about me, I'm fine. I just never imagined anything like this. How are you? How is Cannelloni? Is he settling in? Happy to have a new family?*"

A chuckle. Then Jade got serious again looking at her screen.

"That's the last I've heard from her. I replied: *Cannelloni 's the best! He's with Grandad for a few weeks already, I dropped him off first. You'd think he's been living on the boat all his life! Grandad sent me photos.* I wrote this on the last days of packing back on the base," Jade murmured wistfully. "*That dog is so cute I'm actually looking forward to moving day so I can see him. I guess your plan worked. I'm not 100% devastated to be leaving. There's this teeny, tiny part of me that can't help being happy. So damn happy about a stupid dog.*"

Jade sighed.

"There's been no reply since." She fidgeted with the phone in her hands. "I've been sending her photos of Cannelloni nonstop since I arrived at the boat, but they haven't been delivered. I wish I could tell her how awesome he is! I was worried he'd have forgotten me over the few weeks I had to leave him with Grandad and go back to base to pack and check out of the accommodation. But he remembered me right away! Fell in my arms like we are best friends. Maybe he'll always know I'm the human who came and took him out of the dog charity, I guess. Maybe that's why he likes me so well. I'm so glad I got him, Mum. These feel like the worst days of my life and yet he makes me smile all the time. Ami was so right telling me to get a dog."

The night chill made her shudder.

"I think I'll head home, Mum. Love you always." She picked up the glass and poured the wine slowly on the grass covering the grave. She finished the silent goodbye by brushing a kiss on her own fingertips and pressing them for a heartbeat on the stone, where the name Evelyn could just be discerned carved in silver against the darkness.

"See you soon, Mum."

Jade stood.

"Hang on, hang on. Where the hell did *he* go?"

She was alone in the cemetery. The stranger was no longer among the Celtic crosses and gothic inscriptions of the ancient tombs, nor had he come back down the path.

"There's nowhere to go from that side," Jade said, puzzled. She scanned the ivy-covered wall surrounding the churchyard. It was too tall to climb over. And yet the man had somehow managed to get out.

"Ok Mum, I think next time I'll bring a ginger beer. Clearly, alcohol doesn't go well with late evening chats in the cemetery."

She scanned the darkness one last time.

The only thing moving where the stranger had been was a veil of pearly white mist, flowing over the grass like wisps of coiling tongues licking the gravestones.

She shrugged.

"Whatever. Bye, Mum."

She walked briskly down the solitary path and through the cemetery gates, where her bike stood tied to a railing. Just like Jade's trainers and backpack, the bike was well used, but pristinely clean. She welcomed the sounds of laughter and clinking cutlery that came from the garden of the village pub down the road. It was always too quiet inside the cemetery, once you crossed through those gates.

She'd often wondered how the ancient stone wall around the churchyard blocked all auditory evidence of life—no voices at all, even though the riverside path was often busy with couples or families deep in conversation as they strolled by the Thames. No crunching of footfalls, no dogs barking, no bubbling cavitation of boats zooming past, no music, no clicking of bicycles' wheels—but the burble and swoosh of the river was ever present. It made the cemetery feel like an isolated world of its own.

Like it somehow cancelled out all living sound.

Chapter Two

The First Storm

S orry, it's been a minute, Mum. Six days is too long not to visit, now that I'm back home. But I got a job! And I made a discovery.

The mysterious static follows specific rules. Doesn't come at random.

Sure, it only happens when I'm near the radio, but there is a second condition.

The first morning after the night we talked, I tiptoed into the kitchen, worried and ready to flee. Pounding headache, from next to no sleep. Nightmares non-stop. Well, no, really, it's the same nightmare. Over and over again.

I walked in, prepared to justify the five quid it would cost to buy coffee at the bakery that morning, if the radio tried anything while I caffeinated in the kitchen.

But nothing happened.

Then I promptly forgot about the radio because I stupidly attempted and failed to call her. The network over there can't hold data for video or voice calls. Hardly any telecoms left. Not even pictures or long messages get through anymore. The briefest texts are all we have to stay in touch now that the evacuation has begun.

It's not enough, I'm dying with worry about her.

Then Cannelloni came and asked for his walk. He knows exactly when I need to get out of my head. Where would I be without this dog? Anyway, there were no voices from the radio, and no static happened, so I just simply forgot about it.

I never even saw the radio the next few nights. I was out late every evening, repairing senior citizens' computers. Turns out there is a ridiculous number of people around here, naïve enough, to click OK to all kinds of pop-up windows. Get slammed with the most laughable bloatware. I had to go back to that one house six times. A dentist kept calling me to check why his 80-year-old Dad's computer wouldn't be rid of some, very specific types of sites. I *did* get rid of them. Squeaky clean, all six times I visited. Then it was back again. Someone in that house kept at it. The dentist didn't live there, he bought his father the computer so he could videocall his parents from his own house, with his kids. He seemed genuinely appalled to look at it, so I knew it was not him. I assumed it was his father, but the old man could hardly see the screen to answer a skype call. The dentist insisted someone was 'hacking into the laptop' to put it there, I had to stop myself from laughing in his face. In the end I took the dentist's seven-ty-six-year-old mum aside. I slipped her the passwords to a discreet subscription I hid as a shortcut in her knitting pictures file, so her husband and son will never know. Much safer site than what she was going for before. Not *my* cup of tea, mind you. But a couple of mates I was with on my third tour, swore that this was pure class for male gay porn.

Never heard from the dentist about his father's laptop since. And more power to his mum.

But all that going on, meant no radio static happened for days. I came in exhausted and went straight to bed and at breakfast, though I peered at it wearily, it never made a peep. A few days of this, and I wondered if I had imagined the whole thing.

Then I realised.

Since the day I moved in, almost a week ago, I'd never set foot in the kitchen at night.

"What do you recon, Cannelloni? Is that it? Are you thinking what I'm thinking?" I said yesterday morning. The dog barked in joyful assent, but then— I *was* opening his tin of meat after all.

But I had to find out.

I got home at sunset. Going into the kitchen, I propped my phone up on the counter, so I could keep an eye for messages while staying close to the radio. The music, as I expected, continued uninterrupted.

As I waited for the sun to disappear across the fields, I locked Cannelloni away with Alan, so they could watch shows together. I didn't want him upset like last time. Whatever was coming, it wasn't getting my dog.

Then I returned to the radio. Nothing changed. To pass the time, I searched news videos of the armed conflict on my phone to pass the time. The embassy was now operating from a hotel by the airport. The hotel is barricaded. Unreasonably, I looked for her in the crowds, and I looked for her among the armed soldiers. But of course, I couldn't see her, because that's not where she was.

The radio sat innocently playing its old ballads, framed in the lilac twilight of the late evening. The river view is always stunning from the Lady Thomasine's windows, and I could see why he and Gran loved living in a boat so much. The Thames turns a hundred shades of crimson-gold and midnight-purple at dusk, now the days are longer and sunny. Still, the radio perfectly behaved itself.

Did it have to be pitch black outside for the static to come? That could take a while.

I have work to do.

Finally landed a contract job, cyber security for a website. It was strangely exciting, not having a boss. My first real project as a civilian. I've been proud to wear the uniform all my life; but this whole working for myself, somehow it felt very fulfilling. I was eager to start. Putting a pin on the radio experiment till nightfall, when something might happen, I moved to the monitors that I'd set up on the desk, at the very front of the boat.

The second I opened that site and saw the mess I had to fix, my mind went into hyper focus. Cyber security for a small online company is not half as complicated as the shit I did for the RAF. But it's always rewarding to catch so many holes in technology and plug the gaps. I get happily lost in that kind of productivity.

It was hours later, when I glanced up again. The world had turned monochrome and moody, black skies rolling past with mesmerising speed. Splatters of white smoky clouds travelled higher up, but grey syphoned down into the thick cloud masses hanging low over the river. A potent summer storm was brewing.

I kept typing, with the kitchen behind me and the radio singing softly into the night.

A loud growl. I looked up to see if Cannelloni had snuck back out, but it was just my stomach. Time for a break. I headed to fix a bowl of porridge forgetting about the spooky experiment I had going on.

Yawning sleepily, I stirred the silky oats as they softened in the hazelnut milk. Growing ever hungrier as they turned into a pudding of creamy goodness, I tapped impatiently on the floor. The soft sensation of the old sleeper booties on my feet made me smile. Grandma Tamsin had crocheted them for me many Christmases ago; I'd found them unpacking my boxes and I was so happy: There's nothing like comfy feet on a chilly summer night. Did I want my bowl sweet? I pondered. But that would mean chopping bananas and pears. Oh, and vanilla extract! But I couldn't be bothered peeling fruit right now.

"Savoury porridge it is," I muttered, reaching for the soy sauce, the garlic flakes and a glass jar of button mushrooms.

Finally, my steaming bowl of absolute creamy deliciousness was ready, the salty sweet fragrance of umami from the smooth grains making my mouth water. Just as I scooped a spoonful topped with a single juicy mushroom, lemon drizzled to perfection—

Static.

I jumped like I'd been electrocuted, and the hissing immediately subsided.

I looked around, taking in my position and surroundings. The blackest night had descended outside. Zero starlight. The sky hung ominously overhead, I could see it through the oval windows as if it was pressing down on the boat. Angry and laden with a chaos of twisting clouds that slithered into each other like a knot of giant smoke serpents.

And the radio played its innocuous music, as I stood, breathless, one step away from where I'd leaned against the counter a moment ago, to eat my porridge: completely forgetting my invisible demarcation lines across the kitchen.

So yeah, the static had two conditions to appear:

I needed to be near the radio.

And it needed to be night-time.

I'd forgotten to breathe. Images of gooey, dark red paddles flashed in my mind. Those combat boots splashing around in the gore. The suffocating sound had resurrected my nightmares.

A coughing fit hit me out of nowhere. It forced my lungs to function, and I gasped, gulping down air. Then I pushed away the haunting images from my dreams and focused on the problem at hand.

Why doesn't the static come in the daylight? Why doesn't it happen when Grandad is around the radio? Why has it never happened in the many summer and Christmas holidays I've stayed here before?

The coughing dissipated but left a metallic taste in my mouth. And my hands were rigid from the cold.

I took a step forward, pressing my bowl so hard between my hands my fingertips turned white.

The static screeched.

I didn't retreat. I listened, even though my breathing came as fast as if I was running.

I didn't understand this senseless dread. Why did the sound of static make the little hairs on my arm stand on end? Like a cat fluffing up to twice its size when she senses danger. I've been in firefights, for fuck's sake; surrounded on all sides and praying for support but never feeling an adrenaline rush like this. This was a chilling, bleak fear.

I had an urge to throw the radio in the sink and set it on fire. The antique oakwood case and fabric speaker would burn nicely into ash. But Alan had it since before my father was born, he'd probably sooner get rid of me than his radio.

Speaking of Alan, how come he didn't hear it? Why wasn't he up, storming out here to tell me to keep it down?

Is it only audible to me?

I tried to steer clear of unreasonable fears and stick with the facts, but I couldn't shake the feeling that something was very, very wrong.

I stood my ground.

I ate my bowl of porridge leaning against the counter, trying to focus on the taste, to calm this mysterious anxiety. The soy was deliciously salty, the mushrooms gorgeously meaty; but I couldn't enjoy it. I listened carefully, studying what I heard.

The mysterious static continued relentlessly. Burrowing like wisps of vaporous fingers reaching through my flesh to the bones of my spine. I wriggled at the bizarre sensation and focused my will to ward off the revolting noise: I refused to be frightened.

This is my actual job for crying out loud. If I had heard this in the desert, I would know exactly what the answer was. Hostiles would be jamming our signal. Or in this case, someone's pirating the radio station frequency modulation. Child's play.

The radio spoke.

A suppressed; grotesque voice.

"Jade. JadeJade. Jade!"

They were rapid, staccato sounds, like a computerized voice reading letters in the right order but failing to form comprehensive words. And the question burned in the back of my mind: Who is calling me?

This time there was no doubt the voice came from the radio. This was not a drunk, yelling from outside. The ancient speaker spoke my name.

The bowl shook in my hands.

The static continued. That odd fluctuation from shrill whistle gusting out of a black chasm, into the rasp of an unnerving breeze though dead leaves and pitching to the atrocious scream of the dentist's drill.

Fighting the urge to run out of the kitchen, I gulped down the knot in my throat. That creeping kind of fear made me nauseous. I forced myself to think logically: Some tosser out there had used a jammer to block the radio signal. This was what created the static, and they'd brought a transmitter, to broadcast my name.

That would be a tidy explanation, but it didn't fit. My name had come out mechanical and strange, not like a human had spoken it. And nothing about the static resembled regular white noise. This sound was especially unsettling and peculiar.

Why does this bring up so much fear?

I listened.

Somewhere inside the radio static, whispered a voice.

It had an unnatural cadence. Shocking gasps interrupted the dark flow. Then whispers poured fast again a moment later with sickening, miserable urgency.

OK, fine, if it's a whisper, what is it saying?

The rasping message continued, obscured under the static's irregular outbursts. Now I was sure I could hear words; but could not understand them. It sounded like a foreign, guttural language.

I flicked through my phone for a translation app— And that's when the radio spoke in English.

"Are they close? Are they coming?"

Almost dropped my bowl.

It was the same rapid, distorted voice that had called my name; could very well be the same voice as the hidden whisper. Although, when speaking words I understood, it sounded sharper.

I waited for more, but none came. The relentless static went on. It swelled like a cry from some dark abyss, then stilled to an ominous whine, so quiet I wasn't sure I was hearing it or imagining it. Every time it soared, I still cringed. The feeling of being pushed into an ice plunge pool did not ease with time, but it became more overwhelming.

In a desperate bid for mental self-defence, I thought about what the therapist would say— Dad pays her a fortune after all. She'd insist it was an anxiety attack from my PTSD.

Maybe I should stop resenting my diagnosis.

Or maybe it wasn't me, but Alan's stupid friends. Out there, playing a prank. They could be doing all of those creepy sounds on purpose. And by sitting here giving it all this thought, I let them win.

That voice isn't human.

This notion kept returning in my mind unbidden, from some unknowable depth of my consciousness. Cold like the darkest hour before dawn. I couldn't shake the feeling that it was right. The voice in the static had an irregular rhythm, a timbre too dark and breathy. One moment it reverberated implausibly low with searing rage, and then grew wretchedly shrill, shifting too fast for vocal cords.

"Be reasonable," I mumbled to myself. "It *is* a human voice, what else would it be? Bad signal is distorting it. Those idiots are doing it."

With that thought I took a deep calming breath and felt stronger. I wanted to leave the kitchen to let the songs return, but I stood my ground. Let's see if they get bored and give up. I've got all night.

It was the longest I had ever allowed the noise to go on for.

The insistent static continued and the more I forced myself to listen, the more unbearable it was.

The agonising urgency of the underlying whisper was disturbing, and a sense of mortal danger overtook me. Instinctively needing to locate the danger, I scanned my surroundings: cosy couches, my Gran's crochet cushions and soft woolly throws- and that bloody radio.

There was no threat here. I took a step closer to rinse my empty bowl in the sink. And that's when I saw the figure. It stood on the opposite banks, among the grim outlines of the trees lining the river path. Just a shorter shadow with a head, shoulders, legs. Some knobber watching my boat in the dark.

So there they are, jamming the signal. And that's how they know when I'm near the radio.

They could *see* me.

Something was wrong about this, something didn't add up. Alan's friends were all his age and standing out in the wilderness in the middle of the night, for hours, just to prank me, was not their thing. Sure, they'd crack vicious jokes when they happen to see me, but not at this level of commitment. And they were far too old to be up at this hour.

The slender figure didn't look like any of them. They were all heavier, wider, slouching.

This shadow was tall, and his posture had the virility of youth.

OK, if he was a stranger, he could be a teenager out there pranking people randomly.

But then, how did he know my name?

I guess he could have easily heard Grandad call me.

Alan has been shouting at me to put the kettle on, about three times a day, because I never do it. It's code for 'make me tea and toast'. Always the same:

"Make it yourself Alan, I'm working."

Scorching glowering shoots through, from the open door of his cabin.

"Your Grandmother always had my tea and slice ready when came in from work!"

"It's the twenty-first century, Grandad."

"It's disrespectful is what it is."

"How about you make *me* a nice cup of tea? Seeing as you're retired and I'm the one working?"

To which he grumbles that no man will marry me if I don't change my tune.

Then I get the silent treatment until dinner time when I cycle to the chippy at the next village and buy him supper. When I hand him the heavy box wrapped in oily newspaper he likes me again.

Until the next day, when he wants his tea and slice, and it all starts over.

Which is funny, because he doesn't realise, I found a vegan fish and chip shop. He has been eating beer-battered tofu seasoned with seaweed since I moved in. Says that's the best fish supper he's ever had.

Anyway, there are plenty of opportunities in a day for people to hear my name yelled around this mooring.

Jade took a sip of her ginger beer, smiling at the tombstone with the wine glass standing full before it, as if the grave had nodded along to her story. The quiet cemetery was warm on this fragrant summer night. The skies above were streaked with magenta and violet as the sun vanished behind the treetops. She took another sip and continued.

I was so angry with this prick, I reached out and did the thing Grandad never does, I switched the radio off.

I glanced at the distant observer on the opposite banks.

"Bugger off," I mouthed, giving him the finger.

He didn't move.

The radio turned back on.

That shook me a bit. It being an old analogue device, with a dial that needs to move until it clicks to switch the power on.

Somehow it'd come on without the dial turning.

Had he broken into the boat and fitted some remote-control function inside the radio? Should I open it up and check that? I could feel the gaze of the stranger on me and I didn't want to give him the satisfaction of knowing that he'd spooked me. The more attention you pay people like that, the more they feed off you. He still stood across the river, still watching, absolutely motionless. Freak.

I reached to the socket and unplugged the radio.

Remote control that, ya dobber.

I headed to my desk, but in the semicircle of the lounge windows, I felt exposed. My own reflection blazed bright back at me, the room glowing as the windows that had turned to mirrors; and it showed me what someone would see from outside the boat. I went and stood with my face right to the glass, so my reflection vanished. The dark countryside, the riverbanks and fields, all silently watched me. The figure still there.

I went around pulling down all the blinds.

Then I sat down and tried to concentrate on the night's work. I failed. When I wasn't trying to resist the urge to check if the guy was still there, my mind went to Ami. What was she doing right now? There was only one thing she could be doing. Same thing she'd been doing for days.

The thought of her working with all that chaos at the embassy, the crowds so desperate and the guarding soldiers so overwhelmed, it just upset me. Ami just doesn't belong there. Sure, we met in the service, but she was different. She was an English Lit major who won poetry competitions and showed everyone pictures of her pet chinchillas in the tiny hats her mum embroidered. A translator should not have to go through this, she isn't equipped for it. And she's all alone. When her message buzzed, I jumped so hard I almost fell off my chair.

"On my feet 19 hours," her text said. "Back for 3 hours rack time, then rinse and repeat. Situation here insane."

"I miss you so much!" I wrote immediately. It wasn't much of an answer, but I hoped that if I spent no time typing, I had a chance to catch the window of signal.

Didn't work. The message was sent but not delivered. Just like every other message. It might take days again to reach her. Clenching my fists, I wanted to scream but Grandpa was sleeping.

Although how he slept through that ear piercing static earlier, was beyond me.

A hammering sound made me look up. The low wooden ceiling of the entire boat erupted in a thunderous clatter, like a thousand fists pounding on the flat roof.

It took me a moment to figure out it was rain.

The skies had finally opened, discharging the rainclouds that had been swelling up all evening. Solid sheets of water fell on the river, agitating the waves. The boat rocked, and I tripped and took two steps sideways to steady myself. The watered pummelling the roof and walls was deafening.

But I was used to this, my Grandparents lived in boats all my life. We had no hanging lights to swing and no nicknacks on the shelves to slide off and smash on the floor. My laptop was docked securely on a base screwed to the desk and both my screens were fixed to it too. I stood in the middle of the raging storm, folding my arms on my chest, rolling my eyes at the inconvenience of this bit of British weather, as the window drapes swung all around me.

A ringtone made me jump. I pulled my phone out without looking at the screen, certain Ami must be calling- who else would phone me after midnight?

"Hello?"

"I'm coming over with Woofles! Perfect weather for comfort food."

That voice always made me smile. Even when life was as *shit,* as it was right then. I was even able to forget the radio and the figure outside for a moment.

"Who's Woofles?" I said.

"Waffles that you wolf down! It's the name of the 24-hour Belgian Cafe near the student union. Can't cram a proper revision without them."

"Good for you."

"So, see you in a bit?"

"No."

"Jade! Why not? Now you're back home, we get to have rainy night movies again! I've missed it!"

"Not in the middle of the night."

"When did *that* ever stop us before?"

It never did. But I just couldn't face answering questions right now.

"You're not in the next room now, you're an hour away. I don't want you driving here in this weather."

The enthusiasm melted away, and Leela put on her serious voice. The same voice as when she turned nine years old and insisted we spend two hours taking some sort of test, while Dad and her mum were away, to find out if we were in the same magic house of some kind. That was ten years ago. She still utterly failed to sound grown up to me.

"Jade, I haven't seen you since you came home! You keep saying you're busy looking for a job and I get that, but it's been almost three weeks! I'm not waiting any longer."

"Can you wait until maybe, I don't know, *daylight*?"

"Tomorrow evening?"

"I don't know, Leela. I might have appointments if someone calls me to look at a computer. I'll text you."

"You've said this five times already and you never did text!"

"Surely not five times..."

"I've got all your texts, want me to screenshot you?"

You know how Leela can be, Mum, you dodge her for a while but can't do it forever. And it's not that I *want* to.

"I promise. I will text you on a free evening. Need to go now, I'm waiting to hear from Ami, ok? We'll talk soon."

"Does she have a date yet?"

"No."

"But are they allowed to extend someone's deployment for six weeks like this?"

"They can do whatever they want, Leela, it's the military, not some retail company."

"Surely they must tell her a rough date she's coming home, though?"

"It's an evacuation in progress. Pretty much a permanent state of emergency. The personnel they need, have to stay, and Ami is a translator. They definitely need her."

"The news says it's getting more and more dangerous over there as the final withdrawal date approaches."

A pause. I didn't say anything. I knew how dangerous it was getting, more than anything my sister could ever imagine.

"Surely they won't keep her till like, the last day?"

"I hope not. Listen, I have to go now." I couldn't handle this conversation anymore.

"Ok, I guess I'll go back to studying. Hope Ami gets home soon."

"Thanks, Leela." I was about to say 'goodbye', but she spoke over me.

"Guess what's the best hangover cure."

"Leela why are you hungover at night?"

"It's not hangover, it's wine flu," she said and laughed at her own joke.

I rolled my eyes.

"It's wine flu so it lasts a few days," she added when she was done giggling.

"Then clearly your hangover cure is not a very good one, whatever it is," I said. "You might want to try hydrating with a fresh green smoothie, getting a warm shower and a good night's sleep. That's the only hangover cure."

"Ginger flavoured energy drink with a double-scoop chocolate-chip ice-cream floater."

"I'm nauseous just picturing that."

"Why! It's delicious! Instant headache fix. I'm already feeling better."

"You're drinking that right now?"

Instead of a reply I heard a loud slurp and several stomach churning, frothy gulping sounds.

"Eww stop that Leela! Seriously if that garbage makes you feel better, then I think we can safely conclude that the only cure to a hangover is being under twenty-one years old. If I ate anything like that, I'd be sick for days."

"I can't be sick for days. I've got to make ornamental rapier handles for my two BBQ skewers and then stain the white Regency dress I got at the charity shop with blood paint."

"What kind of fancy-dress party are you going to this time?"

"Jane Austin Zombies."

"Of course you are."

"Isn't it so cool?"

"Leela if I knew you when I was in college, I'd pretend I didn't."

"What!"

"Yup."

"Why?"

"Because when I went to a party I aimed to be wearing as little as possible in the start of the night and nothing at all by the end of it. It's called clubbing. You should try it."

"No thanks, I prefer to look more interesting with my clothes on, and that's why I put an effort, and it pays off."

"You've hooked up with someone at last?"

"No! But I win most of the fancy dress competitions."

"Dork."

"Slut."

We both burst out laughing. I'd forgotten how much I'd missed my sister. I wished I could see her, but I wasn't ready. I didn't know when I'd be ready to be normal again.

"I've got to go, have fun making your stabby sticks and talk later," I said.

"Wait Jade! Can you at least tell me what happened? Like, very quickly?"

I bit my lip. This was it. The conversation I've been running away from.

"Why did you decide to leave the RAF?" she pressed. "You said you'd be a lifer!"

I was trying to come up with something vague to say when a noise made me look up.

"Goodnight, sis," I said and hung up.

Music. In the kitchen.

The radio was on.

The radio was *on*?

How was that possible? I had pulled the plug. I looked across the lounge and spotted the cable coiled before the radio on the counter. Precisely where I'd left it.

It must have a battery compartment I missed. There was no other explanation. I dashed to the kitchen and the static seared my eardrums. A few million hair follicles across my body all at once turned into bumps, my skin crawling with the same odd, icy tingling as before.

As I stood there trying to collect myself, I saw that I had never closed the kitchen blinds.

He was still there. Not even moved, not at all.

Didn't he get soaked? Who stands among wet brambles for hours and hours in the dead of night? In a rainstorm? How did he not have anything better to do with his life? And what did he want from *me*?

Somehow this didn't feel like just a prank. But what else could it be?

I turned the radio over, looking for the battery compartment.

There wasn't one.

Of course, there *must* be batteries in this thing, somewhere.

But the strange dread was rising again, and I couldn't stand it. I had this urge to punch through the thin kitchen wall, but I'd be the one paying for the new plaster job. I turned around facing the lounge, and the tall back of Grandad 's chair was the first thing I saw. I unloaded two sets of uppercuts into the soft upholstery, until I heard a soft warning crack from somewhere in the depths of the chair. I stopped, panting, hoping I hadn't damaged the frame.

I glanced around at the radio.

I'm fucking done. Not even going to try finding out how exactly they are doing it. I've spent enough time on this stupid prank. I'm done.

As I opened the window, rain sprayed my face. A gust of wind blew my hair back.

I pitched the radio our into the storm.

I waited a heartbeat for the loud splash, as it hit the water.

Then I closed the window and took a breath of relief.

It was gone.

Jade downed the rest of her ginger beer. She seemed surprised to see that darkness had fallen and the skies were black. She slid the empty bottle in her backpack, checking the time on her phone.

"It all so weird, Mum. I wish you could tell me what you make of it." The words died on her lips. Her eyes widened, fixed at a spot in the gloom behind the church.

A solitary figure came walking back towards the path. Something about his long coat and soundless footfalls, his figure shrouded in shadows, was mysterious; but at the same time familiar.

How odd. He is coming from the depths of the churchyard out towards the gates. I've been here for hours and never saw him come in. I never saw him anywhere around here this entire time.

Jade's brow furrowed as she watched him walk away. A peculiar white stream of vapours trailed behind him. Her gaze followed it to a thick pool of pearly mist that swum above the grass in the ancient burial ground. She couldn't understand how this mist was so localised, not extending to the rest of the cemetery. And the way the white smoke clung to his coat, stretching thin behind him as he reached the end of the cemetery path— It reminded Jade of Cannelloni biting playfully at her trouser legs, when she had to leave, and he didn't want her walking out of the door without him.

And that was not even the weirdest thing.

"How—...?" Jade stared, unable to continue. His dark coat shone white on the shoulders. White powder streaked his sleeves and white glimmers caked the hem of his coat. White also sparkled on a tall top hat he was now wearing. He pulled the hat off, as he walked briskly, and brushed it with his sleeve.

Jade ducked behind her mother's grave as the stranger passed along the path nearest to her.

He didn't see her. He was busy putting the tall hat away in his carrier case without slowing down. The case was also powdered with white.

"Wait... what?" Jade muttered, gaze fixed on the man's back as he continued, oblivious, towards the cemetery gates.

"Ok, three things," Jade said to the tombstone. "Why does this feel like deja vu, when I've never seen this man before? I would definitely remember a weirdo in the cemetery. Two, how did he get in here without me seeing him? Was he there the whole time? And for fuck's sake..." She stood up and walked to the path herself, craning her neck to see beyond the gates, making sure he had disappeared down the village road.

Yes, she was alone. She knelt down on the path and poked at the little shimmering white pile on the ground where the stranger had brushed his hat.

"...how was he, in the start of the summer, covered in snow?"

Chapter Three

The Watcher In The Dark

OK Mum, I hope you're not getting tired of me since I was only here last night. I need to talk to someone. Today was quiet, and then at night fall, the shit hit the fan.

With the radio in the river, I did not expect to hear from the stalker again.

The nightmares kept me up all night, but I managed to get some rack time on the roof of the barge, in the sunshine. It was only for a few hours, but it made such a difference. I might do it again tomorrow. I dread to think what morning walkers make of me. Crazy boat lady stays up till morning, then carries her pillow on the roof among the potted dahlias, slams on an old pair of her gran's oversized black shades, pulls one of her grandad's fisherman caps over her face and sleeps in the sun.

But, whatever works, I'll take anything at this point.

Feeling much better by noon, I was finally ready to start the day. *Goal for the day, 1. Stay Alive,* I wrote on my little black notebook. *Challenge for the Day: Try a new food*. I mean, I agreed to write in the stupid journal, the therapist doesn't need to know it's only two sentences.

I spent the day cycling the Thames country paths, with Cannelloni running beside me when he liked, or riding along behind me in his doggy bike trailer, when he needed a rest. I spent my first week's pay check on the doggy trailer, don't judge me. I cycle for up to five hours at a time, can't have the poor animal running after the bike all day. He's worth it, though.

We had lunch at his favourite spot, because somehow my rescue dog turned out to be a posh little bugger. He wants this traditional country pub, an old-fashioned cottage conversion, low ceilings, vintage photos of the local village framed on the walls, the works. I never used to go there, because their menu only has one vegan option and it's a plant-based burger. Highly processed trash. But I don't really have much say on the matter. When I try to take him to the vegan bistro, with a huge menu of wholesome plant produce and a new built, wood and glass terrace that actually hangs over the water, for him to sunbathe, he runs off.

Like, gone. Won't come back.

I have to track him with his GPS collar. That was the second thing I bought with my first' week's pay check, and the last, the check ran out. But what am I going to do, lose the dog? He runs straight to that overpriced, leather armchair lounge where all the dogs have grooming appointments and show dates and three-word names (I swear I saw a tag on a tiny yorkie: Goliath Moon Voyager), and there sits my scruffy mutt, with his big doggy smile, tail thumping happily, under the complimentary K9 Cookie Jar station at the bar, fully expecting a treat without having performed any tricks. What can you do?

So, I took one of their doggy water bowls in the beer garden and filled it with fresh water from the cooler, and he chomped on his favourite pub biscuits while I crunched on that stupid burger, lost in thought about the stalker.

Surely, whoever they were, they would have to find someone else to play that pirate frequency prank. No more radio on *my* boat. In the evening, I planned on working late and wouldn't bother to draw the blinds. I refused to live my life in hiding.

As I chewed on the last bits of the soft bread bun, Leela texted.

"Free tonight?"

"Not really." I hated that I had to avoid her but couldn't bring myself to see her.

"Come for cocktails, I'll take you to my fav cocktail bar!" came the second message. I grinned. She has a favourite cocktail bar now? Sometimes I forget it wasn't a week ago I took her trick or treating in a SpongeBob costume.

"Where, the Ricochet Café at the trampoline park?" I wrote.

Her reply started with a puke emoji: "Haven't been there in six years!"

"Too bad, I quite liked the strawberry and cashew cream smoothies."

A yellow emoji rolling its giant eyes was what I got.

I put a laugh emoji under it and hoped the conversation would end there.

A video arrived. I recognised Leela's hand from the faded parchment-coloured nails, complete with tiny cursive manuscript. Lately my sister has turned into your basic, art-school uni chick —she hates it when I tell her— and each finger featured a different Victoriana sticker: a vintage birdcage, a purple feathered quill, the framed silhouette of a lady's profile, a corked bottle of herbal poison. The hand was holding a couple of Leela's favourite cheesy crisps, and dipping them into something that looked like brown slime. I flinched away from the screen. The message that followed it said: 'Best hangover cure. Cheese and onion Pringles in warm chocolate custard!'

"That's vile."

"So tasty! And I'm so much better already!"

"How do you have a hangover again? Don't you have to study?" I didn't want to sound like the Stepmonster, so I didn't add, don't you have exams in just over a month?

"I cram between parties."

"Did you seriously go out last night?"

"Yeah. We had an emergency meeting at the pub to discuss next week's fancy dress party. The theme dropped in the group chat late last night! Guess what it is."

"Pass."

"It's Which Sherlock? You get it?"

"Nope."

"It's any character from any Sherlock Holmes movie or series! Or straight from the books, for the hard core. I need to seriously think on this one. How am I supposed to choose between Enola and Dr. Joan Watson?"

"That's like a full-time project for every time you are going out! I don't get it. All I wanted from nights out as a student was to wear a nice enough top to hook up with someone cute and wear a nice enough bra to make sure we went home together. Oh, and have enough money to buy her a Starbucks the next morning: you know, in case I didn't remember her name. Job done."

"Jeez, Jade, you're such a... guy."

"No, I'm not. No woman fakes an orgasm with me."

"Oversharing!"

"Prude."

"Shall I pick you up at the train station around 7? You can come over first and I'll show you my room."

"Sorry, I got to work."

"Again? Where do you find so many clients?"

"No, I got a freelance job, so that's the project for tonight," I typed, and told myself it was not a lie.

Of course, I *could* have spared a couple of hours to see Leela. Normally I see her every week when I'm here on holiday.

But I couldn't.

Explaining to Dad about the nightmares that got me kicked out was bad enough. And he doesn't want to hear problems, only solutions, so it wasn't a very long conversation. He said to tell him about it again when I was done with the therapy package he bought.

But Leela would want the details. She'd keep asking what *caused* the nightmares. And I'm never going *there*.

I thought of Ami non-stop on the cycle back. I switched my helmet camera on and captured the river and meadows along the path. She loves the Thames valley countryside. I'd make a short clip for her from today's footage. I was in such a good mood that I didn't even shout my usual 'fuck you' to the bunch of guys under the bridge crossing that called out 'Give us a smile, bike boobs!'

I did give them the finger though.

But I made sure it was out of camera view. Ami would have laughed to see it, but she liked to share videos I sent her with her mother and sisters, and I couldn't risk something like that staying in shot.

The world begun to seem beautiful for a little while, a feeling I haven't had in a long time. Pairs of olive trees in terracotta pots on either side of garden gates along the path, seemed to be a new trend. The bitter, smoky scent of their grey-green leaves reminded me of my time with Ami. Most of the time I've spent with her in real life, we were under a huge, magnificent, ancient olive tree. On the rest of the ride home I could not stop thinking of how we first met.

The first time I laid eyes on her, Ami bothered me.

I was sweating away boxing, under this gorgeous olive tree in the desert, with a bark so twisty it was fascinating. Its leaves were most aromatic in the twilight before dawn, and that was also the only time of day I could get some cardio in, without literally passing out from the desert heat. And this tree had a branch that was somehow the right height and strength to hang my punch bag.

Up to my tree swaggered this bod, to muscle in on my workout spot in the shade. She was clearly with the new arrivals that had landed the week before. Clueless. I could tell, just by looking at her, it was her first time on deployment. I was already two months there, this being my third tour.

"You packed a yoga mat?" I said, 'cause I couldn't help a smirk. What a thing to take up bag space on active duty.

Spunky little vamp, she didn't miss a beat.

"You packed boxing gloves and a punching bag?"

That took me a second. My punch-bag? Of course I'd bring it, it was inflatable. I filled it with sand when I got to base, but it packs flat for the road.

But I had to hand it to her: the punch-bag deflated, together with my gloves, was about the same size as her stupid yoga mat rolled up to a tube.

I narrowed my eyes at her. She wiggled her eyebrow at me playfully.

"You're talking to a Flight Lieutenant, Sergeant," I said, holding her gaze. We were both dressed down to workout in our dark olive, uniform t-shirts. My shoulder badge was not visible the way I'd hung my shirt on a taller tree branch, although I could see Ami's rank, shirt tucked under her arm.

"Ma'am." Her gaze shot straight ahead obediently, but not without a twinkle of laughter in her eye.

I didn't look away.

She didn't flinch.

I kept her to attention for a few moments, by saying nothing, before turning to my punchbag.

She unrolled her mat on the other side of my tree where there was still some shade. Perky and bright, she dropped to a Downward Facing Dog, in one fluid motion, and stayed there perfectly still, bottom up, face down.

I started a hundred-uppercuts set, square stance, to keep an eye on the foot traffic. It was a remote spot, but close to the showers, so not entirely out of view.

"This isn't Shoreditch," I said, talking loud over the thump of my gloves hitting the sandbag.

"Ma'am?" she said, without getting out of the yoga pose.

"Need a real work out here," I said, now in the sixties with my uppercuts and going faster, "not that hipster shite."

She dropped to her elbows and lifted a leg in the air and then the other. She was doing a fucking headstand.

I got to one hundred and pulled off one glove to free my hand, then I clicked the rest timer to thirty seconds, grabbed my water bottle and drank, pretending I wasn't looking at her. She was still on headstand when I started my next set, jab-cross-jab-sidekick. So, thirty seconds standing on her head, and counting.

I set my timer to three minutes and focused on my combination-cardio round, trying hard not to glance over at her.

She stayed up till it beeped.

That's a total of three and a half minutes, upside down. It's fucking impressive. I always thought chicks are into yoga as an excuse, to flock to those incense burning studios, carrying oversized cups of extortionate lattes and flashing their emaciated butts in exorbitant designer leggings. I didn't realise there was actual exercising involved in yoga classes.

Ami had some serious core muscle mass under those baggy combats.

"Still hipster shite?" she asked, when she was finally standing on her feet again, wiping her face in her towel, and panting like she'd run a mile. But her smile was beautiful, eyes sparkling like brown topaz gems under her long, curly lashes.

I drank my water and didn't acknowledge.

She waited for an answer. As she slowly realised that she wasn't getting one, she smiled. "It's ok, many people are lost for words watching my yoga practice," she said, with an infuriatingly cute tilt of the head.

"I'm not spending my thirty-seconds rest, chatting."

She flinched and seemed hurt for a moment, but I must have I imagined it, as she instantly started another slow flow. She lunged low into Warrior, arms extended forward, then back, then above, then bending the pose fluidly into one-leg balances.

I monitored the road and said nothing till the end of my training.

"You need to be careful out here," I said, once I had finished my last eight sets. "We're not at home."

When she saw me unhooking my bag, she instantly got up from the ground where she had been tying herself into knots for the last twenty minutes.

"Careful of what, Ma'am?"

"Privacy is not something you get on deployment. Clocking in some exercise without the facilities you're used to, is crucial. But you don't want eyeballs on you, not *ever*. No matter what."

That was the first time Ami noticed the group of five or six, who had come one by one out of the showers and steadily propagated, laughing loudly, openly staring in our direction. I'd been monitoring *that* gradually escalating situation for the last twenty minutes.

She rolled up her mat and quickly followed after me, trotting closer behind me as we passed by them. I recognised a couple of Flight Sergeants among them, and one officer, two ranks my junior. They didn't dare speak so close to *me*, but their eyes travelled up and down her figure, then met each other's stares with a glint and sniggers that made me nauseous. She jutted her chin up and didn't seem to even see them there.

But I was close enough to see the beads of sweat that sparkled along her hairline.

Ami and I parted without a word, once we had left them behind. I didn't see her for a couple of days, which I spent wondering about her.

Why had she shown up at my spot? Was it a coincidence, or had she come to work out together? I was always at the same place, but I couldn't manage same time each day. Missions popped up at all hours on deployment. Sometimes I could do well before dawn, other times an hour after sunrise, just as the heat was turning from grin-and-bear-it, to *nope*. Sometimes I even had to do it, exhausted, after nightfall, if the morning schedule went tits up. Had she watched and waited for me to show whenever?

Before the end of the week, there she was again. Sauntering up to my tree, just as I was wrapping to get my gloves on.

"No," I said.

"Ma'am?"

"Get out of here."

"Why?"

"I'm not running a personal bodyguard service. If you're going to be twisting and stretching and sticking your arse to the sky, in a profession that's twelve to eighty-eight percent women-to-men-ratio— well that's *your* choice. Go do it somewhere else."

I'd expected her to be offended and pout, or to look at me with puppy eyes and protest.

Ami raised an eyebrow sarcastically and flashed me her gorgeous grin.

"I thought this was the martial arts tree," she said.

I stared at her.

"I'm learning how to throw some punches," she said, holding up her tablet. She had downloaded a shadow boxing class.

I side-eyed the yoga mat.

"There's a ten-minute post-class stretching, but it's done by a testosterone packed boxing instructor," she said. "No girly flexibility practice. Ma'am."

I considered her for a few moments.

She squared her shoulders and looked straight ahead, waiting seamlessly for my decision.

"You better have earphones for that. I'm not listening to your boxercise for beginners bollocks during my session."

"Got them right here!" She held up her ear-buds.

I turned my back to her and pulled on my gloves, pressing my timer for the first set.

And so it began. The first few weeks of us working out together. In complete silence. I started looking forward to seeing her there. I was surprised to feel the disappointment on the days she didn't show.

I smiled to think of those first weeks we spent together, not talking at all, just being in each other's company, each doing her own thing.

Cannelloni was barking, and I dropped spin cadence. He galloped ahead of my bike, to fall in Alan's open arms. I didn't realise we had reached the boat already! Grandpa knelt on a cushion on the little garden deck, scooping fresh compost from a sack, into Granny's flowerpots. He rubbed my dog's ears, as I pulled up the bike and dismounted.

"We going to give this mutt a shower?" Alan said playfully. I loved how he looked at Cannelloni, like he was a favourite grand kid. Grandad washed Cannelloni by the barge, using Grandma Tamsin's old pink flower watering can, and I took some really good shots, to add to my stash for Ami. My dog makes the goofiest faces when we squirt shampoo all over his belly and paws for a rub. And as Alan rinsed him off, on the grass banks beside our mooring, he first turned into a cloud of suds and then he emerged, soaked and grinning. Ami will love those clips. But I can't send it to her till she's back. They will never load over there.

My phone buzzed with a mob of tearful emojis—Leela had read my reply—then a picture of a cartoon Mojito with a disappointed pout, sad eyes and a pineapple slice on the rim of its glass like a fascinator. A row of other emojis followed it but I had no idea what they meant.

I ignored, and rubbed Cannelloni dry with his fluffy towel hopping she would drop it.

"Missing you J, hope you're doing ok. If you have any trouble sleeping and want to talk tonight, I'll be up. I'm pulling an all-nighter looking for reference articles. I'm here for ya!" Red heart.

Trouble sleeping? So, Dad *did* tell her about the nightmares. Fucking brilliant. That means her mother knows too. As if she didn't make enough snide comments about me already.

Thumbs up on Leela's message and I put the phone away.

Just after nightfall, freshly showered and cheerfully wrapped in my favourite summer cardi, I sat at my desk listening to Cannelloni's gentle snoring from the window seat.

I sipped in bliss at my banana protein shake and opened a funny little bag claiming to contain popped beet root crisps. The snack looked like thick red potato crisps. It was delicious. I'd missed out on a whole world of new foods all these years away. I crunched away in contentment, elbow deep pen testing this company's website.

Working from home was a new and wonderful thing.

I had never been white hatting while not wearing a uniform before. Or while resting on a cushion with the words "Home is Where The Dog Is". I got it on ebay. Which is what happens, when I spend every night wide awake. Those nightmares are getting expensive now that I have a private home address for online deliveries.

Thoroughly immersed in my work, remediating thousands of minor vulnerabilities per hour, I felt content for the first time in a long time. I was going to head to bed soon, with a feeling I'd quite forgotten: A sense of achievement in a day's work well done. I quickly pulled out the little black notebook and wrote under this morning's entry:

Still Alive, Daily Goal Achieved. And, *Beetroot crisps: New food tried and liked.*

That's when my screens all started flickering.

I sat up and watched them, lapsing into a hypnotic stupor. My daze was dispelled suddenly by the jarring sensation of a strange, odious chill. It made my shoulders twitch, as if icy fingers were crawling up and down my spine.

The screens continued flashing. I checked the battery: all plugged in. The Wi-Fi: full bars. This was no connection issue.

Had to be viral interference. I was about to go offline, to block whatever was trying to get through, when images started pouring in. At first, they changed so fast across all monitors that I couldn't tell what it was.

But the flashing colours, I would know them anywhere.

The browns and greys and sun-bleached stone of the desert.

My heart rate accelerated. I leaned away from the desk, as if that would protect me from what I was looking at.

Because it started to look horribly familiar.

Reds flew past, blood on the ground. That same dirt road, turning crimson and black with bone marrow, like a slaughterhouse kill floor.

Those same images used to wake me up in the middle of the night. Screaming.

They got me kicked out of the base.

And they come back every night, still, even here at home.

The lamenting shrieks of grieving women accompanied those scenes, even though no women were visible in the pictures we captured. They were watching as it happened, just like us, and their dismal chorus resounded inside my mind. I would give anything to unhear them.

The shapes in the scarlet splashes were corpses.

The ones from my nightmares.

Arms and legs sprawled in a tangled heap; the way bodies fall when shot from all angles.

I remember the first time I saw this on the dusty monitors, propped up on rocks, kneeling in the desert sand. I kept glancing sideways at the row of drone pilots beside me. Their fingers moving on the controls, their eyes fixed on their screens, terror screaming mutely from every darkened gaze. I could smell the fear. It grew thick in that deafening silence. Such absolute stillness while unbearable tension pushed down their shoulders; their necks stiff with clenched jaws, veins pulsing under skin that glistened with cold sweat.

On my little desk on Grandpa's boat, half a world away from that place, I watched the same jumbled images come and go. This time I didn't touch the keyboard. There was no one else here, no one piloting a remote camera through which I could witness the grim aftermath of unbridled carnage.

The pictures came on their own.

I was pressed to the back of my chair, paralysed, heart pounding.

One picture returned more often. The face of a young man, beaten so badly it would no longer resemble a face if it weren't for his eyes—his hazel eyes, sparkling with the tiniest speckles of emerald-green around the iris. I knew those eyes. The contrast they made against the grotesque red mask that was his bloodied face; unmistakable.

Those eyes were permanently scorched into my brain. The way he had collapsed on the sands turned dark with blood. You can't look away when you have to spy on a mass execution.

The image became still, and I knew what was going to come next.

Those hazel eyes blinked.

He was still alive, even though the other faces around him were stiff and unseeing.

His head twitched as he bled out. But he didn't move, didn't thrash or writhe.

His body was all wrong. Gaps were there shouldn't haven't been. Stumps at his shoulders, red mud trailing to where his upper arms lay inches away.

The hazel eyes blinked again as combat boots paced around his face, squelching in the slippery mud and gore.

He was quite conscious of them. Stepping carelessly around his head.

My screen didn't show it now, but I remembered how we zoomed out to capture their faces. That was why we flew the drones in: to identify those militants. And I remember the glint of laughter in their eyes. They drank in his last moments, those bastards, amused with his suffering. I had wondered, then: what could have been his crime? What warranted such punishment? The way they smirked, their violence seemed to be driven more by their need to quench their own bloodthirst than to abide by any religious or moral imperative.

But my monitors that night didn't show any of the murderers.

Only the unbearable images of that one man nearing death.

His gaze rose up to the sky.

His torso convulsed, but his arms did not follow the movement. They stayed on either side of him, separated from his body by shredded sinew and shattered bone.

Then his eyes glazed over.

And his final breath left him.

What had haunted me ever since, was how long it took him to bleed out. The top of our monitors said it was less than three minutes, but it seemed like hours that I stood there, watching with hardly a breath. Hardly a blink. My lungs burning, my eyes drying out, my ears ringing.

Why? Why did they do that?

I needed to return to the present. I had to function again.

Pulling out the small, brown bottle from the pouch of my laptop charger, its tiny label print 'Take As Needed' beneath my name, I dropped two pills in my hand. I looked at them. The therapist was adamant I could get through this without a prescription if, how'd she put it? 'Utilised the strategies we discussed', that's it. She'd only prescribed a small bottle as a backup. I had never taken one yet. Was today the day I'd start the pills?

There has to be a logical explanation, don't give in to this damn panic. Breathe. I made a fist over the two pills and took deep breaths, waiting for the choking knot of utter sorrow and despair to subside. The memory played on a loop in my mind.

Just wait it out.

After a while, the soft sound of the river against the barge returned. The sweet scent of the potted jasmine and lavender at the front of the Lady Thomasine was there again.

I was home.

When I was finally able to put the pills back in the bottle, I looked at the time on my screen.

I'd been reliving it for ten minutes.

On my monitors, the image didn't change. The dead man laying still on the red sand. His eyes unseeing.

Where did the clip come from? It's one thing to see him in my nightmares, but how did this enter my computer?

I sat bold upright, realising what had just happened. Confidential material had been accessed and sent to me. I needed to find out what was going on.

I couldn't look at the murdered man anymore and reached out to turn off the screens. My hand stretched halfway to the button under the first screen.

Then he moved.

He turned and looked straight at me. I know it's hard to believe but he was looking at *me*, through the monitor, where I sat on my chair. I don't know how to explain it, he wasn't looking at a camera, he was looking at *me*.

I jumped up, the desk chair crashing onto the floor behind me.

My work project returned on all the desktops, windows of charts and stats and endlessly changing numbers. He was gone, like he was never there.

I switched off the router and Wi-Fi, cutting myself off from the outside world, and put my laptop on aeroplane mode. That would stop them from airdropping any more videos. Then I scanned my systems for viruses and my mind wandered.

Grandad's friends?

I could understand why Alan's mates would find this funny: this was the incident that cost me my career. This was the scene that gave me the nightmares. Those brutal sleep disturbances that got me reported, diagnosed with PTSD, and sent home. Those righteous bastards would think it hilarious to send me this.

But they didn't know.

I never told anyone why I left. Not even everybody in the RAF knew why.

But gaining access to the actual material is impossible. Those boomer arseholes, habitually in various stages of inebriation, are altogether unable to tell a pop-up advert apart from a trojan. They did not have the capacity to obtain this footage, let alone send it to me.

Much less alter the footage to make him look right at me.

But then, who?

Anyone accessing classified information without authorisation would be committing a crime.

Hardly worth it. Just to scare *me?* I mean, I already have the nightmares. I've already lost the job I loved. Watching this doesn't make anything worse for me. Pretty horrific but doesn't do any physical damage. Who would go into the trouble of sending me this?

The scan results interrupted my thoughts, with a notification popping up that they came back clear. So, someone *had* airdropped the video. He would have to be nearby to find my signal.

I sat back and my gaze went to the window.

There he is.

The dark figure, like before. Staring at my boat across the river.

He must have been there all along. The thought of him watching me while the images came through, infuriated me.

This was not a random prank. This person targeted me. Did he want to terrorize me or hurt me? What was the purpose of this?

My first impulse was to go kick his face in but reaching him was impossible. He stood on the opposite bank. Even though we were very close, the river ran between us.

I would either have to hop on my bike, ride three miles to the nearest bridge and across, risking that he may not even be there by the time I got to his position; or I could take the barge off the mooring and steer the fifteen metres across to him, risking that he would have plenty of time to see the boat approach and simply run off. And Alan would wake up if the engine came on. Hell no.

Instead, I went out on the front garden and shouted into the night.

"What the fuck you want? Come and show your face! Come over on this side!"

He didn't move. I couldn't see his face, but I could feel him staring at me.

Here's another question: How did he even know who I was? We were stationed several miles away from the desert village during that operation. How would *anyone* know I had seen any of this?

And you know what? Even though I couldn't see a single feature in that darkness... I swear the bastard was smiling.

Chapter Four

A Ghostly Song

J ade bit her lip, nonplussed by her own story. In the early hours of the morning, the elusive shapes in the scraggly foliage made her weary. The willows swayed in the river breeze like cascading dark drapes, hiding unfathomable secrets beyond. Ambiguous whispers reached her as the leaves shivered in the rising mist, and the sound made Jade glance around suspiciously.

No need to freak out. It's midnight. In a cemetery. Of course it feels spooky.

Her phone rang.

"Ami!" she cried, pulling it out of her pocket, but it was a UK number; although not in her contacts. *Him? Is the stalker calling me now?* Her finger hovered over the 'answer' button, which was a camera: a video call?

Has he decided to show his face? Curious, she switched off her camera but accepted the video call.

The screen lit up with a grand reception room. An antique set of chairs was occupied by a couple dressed in fine Hindu embroidery, smiling down at the screen. The woman had Ami's high cheek bones and arched brows. Jade blinked, confused. The lady wore her hair in a graceful braid, which was draped over her shoulder and studded with butterfly crystals.

I know those crystals. Ami had a single one of those butterflies in her hair every day.

She rubbed her eyes to give her a second to think.

Ami had said her butterfly was one of a set that belonged to her mother, and she wore this hairpin abroad for good luck. Her mother! Can this be for real?

The couple were smiling and patiently waiting for Jade's video to come on. With a trembling finger she switched on her camera, and they instantly greeted her by name.

Jade nodded, unable to utter a word.

The man had Ami's strong chin and captivating tone of voice when he spoke. He said they were her parents, and how glad they were to finally meet her. The image froze for just a second and Jade jumped to her feet. Signal was never good in the heart of the little countryside graveyard, but she couldn't risk dropping *this* call. There was only one place that had good reception. Jade sprinted up the path to the rectory.

They thanked her for being Ami's best friend, and Jade bit her lip.

She still hasn't told them. I've now met them, and they don't know.

That was ok, though, Ami would tell them once she was back. That's the most important thing right now, get her safely home.

Ami's mother thanked Jade for being kind and supportive though Ami's first deployment and this awful extended stay. Jade smiled politely, wishing she had brushed her hair before picking up. The image flickered more, and she sped up across the lawns, while also trying not to look on screen like she was running. Ami's mother sat gracefully in a classy green sari dress draped over one shoulder, leaving her midriff bare on one side. She looked at Jade quizzically, probably wondering why she was barely visible walking in the dark and not home in a well-lit room at this time of night.

Am I making a terrible first impression? Why have they called me? It seems to be good news, but they haven't explained yet! Is it rude to ask?

Jade hadn't realised how close she'd come to the rectory's fence, as she stepped on the gravel surrounding it, without looking— she jumped back, the gravel noise was monstrous in the dead of night. But the little cottage remained dark and silent, wrapped tight in its blanket of lush ivy and purple wisteria along the walls. No one seemed to have heard Jade lurking outside.

But she had gained two bars already. All she needed was a place to hide from view of the windows. One of the fluffy potted conifers on either side of the garden gate would do; it cast an oval shadow into the churchyard, as it was illuminated from the glow of hidden spotlights in the garden shrubs. Jade crouched in that shadow uncomfortably, eyes on her signal bar.

Ami's father was talking about some colleague of his; Jade had no idea why.

That's great, but why have you called me? Is it a universal Dad thing, taking three hours to get to the point? 'Cause mine does it too.

She listened, nervously monitoring the cottage for any signs of life. Thankfully, it was still some distance away, beyond the long garden, vibrant with towering purple foxgloves, glowing pink clouds of hyacinths and a bluish, starshaped Easter flower, which Jade remembered growing in their own garden when her Mum was still alive. She sighed. Her knees hurt, from crouching down under the tree.

Then one sentence made her forget about everything else.

"Amira is coming home in five days."

Jade brought her hand to her mouth to stop from screaming.

Her father was explaining the details of her return. Jade's hands began to shake.

How much excitement is reasonable for a 'best friend'? Don't cry in front of them.

Ami's father continued; he was a Company Law solicitor in London and his contacts at the embassy and the Foreign Office had never officially confirmed it; but they had a date. Exactly five days from now all remaining translators would board the plane.

And not a moment too soon, her mother added, as there were seven days left for the final withdrawal. Her husband took her hand and squeezed, and she wiped away tears.

It was fine, he told her, Ami wouldn't be there for the madness of the last two days. She'd be out, over forty-eight hours before the deadline. It was all good.

Jade felt her face burning, she wanted to laugh and cry at the same time but just kept pressing her hands to her mouth instead.

She asked if they'd managed to get through to Ami; where was she now?

Her mother said they couldn't talk to her, but they would be waiting for her at the airport, even if they couldn't see her right away.

Jade had to wipe her eyes hastily with the back of her hand, to hide her own tears.

She thanked them for calling. They said Ami had demanded they did so, and they were glad to do it. And then, as they said their polite goodbyes, her mother invited Jade to dinner sometime.

Jade had to wait until the call was over and then, she exploded. Brandishing her phone in the air, she jumped to the lawn and silently danced in circles like a stag-headed druid at Beltane. The sense of relief was exhilarating.

A moment later she realised what she'd look like if anyone was looking out of the vicarage windows. She glanced quickly at the cottage. No lights or voices behind the curtains.

They were all asleep. It was fine.

I need to tell Mum. I'm meeting Ami's parents! This is huge!

Making her way back to the graveyard, she tried not to run but couldn't help nervously twisting the edge of her sleeve with her fingers.

Suddenly, the urge to speak to Ami was overwhelming.

She stopped. Pulling out her phone again, she hurriedly pressed the call button. Ami's face beamed in frozen laughter on her screen. Her silky black hair was always pulled back in an elegant bun at the nape of her neck, half hidden under the lopsided beret. An almost imperceptible white dot was all that could be seen of the butterfly pin Ami hid in the neat fold of her bun. Yet on days off, when her hair was down and the glossy black ringlets bounced over her shoulders, the butterfly was proudly displayed above her ear.

Jade wanted to see her so bad. They hadn't had a video or voice call in a month and a half. It was almost physically painful, missing someone so much.

A notification flashed— the call had failed at this time.

Jade pressed the green button again. And again. 'Could not place call', said her screen every time. And yet her own signal had full bars, which meant there was nothing Jade could fix. The problem was once again on Ami's end, and once again Jade had to sit and wait, her hands tied.

She kicked a stone and trudged towards the path that led around the side of the church. Ami would be here soon, and Jade needed to focus on the good stuff. Dinner with her parents... that was great but also so stressful.

What did they think of me?

Suddenly she wasn't rushing anymore. Folding her arms, she dragged her feet along the path, lost in thought. Back in the desert Ami was just a linguist, and Jade cyber security. Ami was a Sergeant, and Jade an officer, Flight Lieutenant. She'd often worried the power gap was too big, that people would think she was taking advantage, if they'd known. Now, Jade was an unemployed woman on the wrong side of thirty-five, living with her Grandfather. Ami turned out to be the daughter of a company law barrister whose house had a reception room bigger than Alan's entire Dutch barge. What if— when!— Ami's family eventually asked to meet Jade's folks? How would that go? Ami's family adored her, while Jade's family, well. Apart from Leela, they didn't really like her much. What would Ami's parents and sisters think of that? Jade had no idea how to tackle this- she'd never done this before. Serious relationships, unchartered territory. Jade's lips pressed together in a flat thin line.

She trudged past the roses climbing between the gothic tracery windows, shaking her head.

And how had she not seen the financial difference? Ami never mentioned her family was loaded... Jade narrowed her eyes, trying to remember. But Ami had only said her Mum taught Middle Eastern archaeology and that's why Ami loved discovering all those temple ruins. She'd show Jade her pics she'd taken driving past them in the desert. And the fashion statement chinchillas, with their constant stream of crochet and knitted and felt hats. Jade had noted that; a bougie kind of quirky, but very cute. And that was all; Jade never realised they were upper fucking crust.

They'll never think I'm good enough for her. I don't even think I'm good enough for her.

Jade pushed her hair back, flattening the few locks escaped from her ponytail, as if trying to clear the bad thoughts away.

A sound in the distance.

Movement.

Her head snapped up. Something wasn't right with the trees in the graveyard.

The shadows of the branches danced in the darkness, and yet the trees stood still as ever.

A strange urge came out of nowhere, that she should stay hidden.

The silhouettes of the trees twisted and swelled, and the tombstones cast wild, swinging flickers on the lawn. Jade crept to the church wall, ducking under the climber roses as she inched closer. This was giving her a headache, and she had to pause. Refracted figures, in constant motion all around her, looked like ghosts of gnarled fingers grasping at the graves.

Bomb training kicked in: When everything is drowned in smoke and fire, quiet the overstimulation, block out the information overload. Find the source, the threat. She blinked a few times, instinctively covering her mouth and nose with her sleeve, even though the air here was not contaminated; she deepened her breath and blinked slower. Her mind cleared.

Many little lights flickered erratically in the heart of the cemetery. This was what caused the alarming dance of shadows to flow like tentacles of solid darkness among the graves. Candles...

Still not sure what she was looking at. How did those candles make the cemetery seem alive in a rupture of mystical illusions? Was it normal for candleflame smoke to swirl and glide in the air?

She stood still like a dream, mesmerised by the scene.

The candles burned, in a circle of five, around an actual grave. Elaborately marbled, knee high pillars of twisted wax, the silver grey of murky winter lakes streaked with the deep greens of moss on ancient stone. A vivid glow illuminated whirling carvings and dark gems along the body of the candles, forming incomprehensible symbols.

There were skull shaped charms tied with knotted string on each candle.

Jade froze. Between the thorny canes of rosebushes on either side of her, she peered at the centre of the circle.

The haze thickened. The movement of the shadows became lethargic, more like the graves were in a cauldron and a thick potion was slowly stirred around the tombs. And there was something abhorrent, repulsive, but she couldn't see what. No idea why she had this strange feeling. Just a sensation she was witnessing something awful, even though she could barely see anything in that freaky fog.

She cast around the scene for a moment. A chill crept up the back of her neck.

The candle flames were purple. Was that what felt so unnatural?

She watched those dark flames, that alien violet hue. Ringlets of mauve smoke drifted into the haze.

Could this be some fancy LED candle that looked obscenely real? No. The flame was actual fire. Surely there was a way to use chemicals and make purple flames. Jade made a mental note to run an online search when she got home: What is the purpose of purple fire? What does it do?

There was a figure standing on the grave, almost completely obscured in the vapours.

He hadn't seen her. He had his back to her.

The outline of a tall hat and long coat trailing to the ground gave Jade pause. It was hard to be alarmed by someone apparently dressed to go to... she wanted to say the Glyndebourne Opera House, but not even there would anyone wear a tall hat. More like a Victorian masquerade ball.

And at the same time, Jade's trained eye spotted the unmistakable signs of concealed weapons. There was a certain manner— something about his stature— that was familiar to her from the many times she saw people strapping on tactical shoulder holsters. And the slight, almost imperceptible bulge between his shoulder blades, confirmed her suspicion. Under his coat, he was carrying a weapon.

He still hadn't noticed her. Jade had to think fast.

Is he the stalker from the river?

Her fists clenched as she fought back the urge to punch first, ask questions later.

This figure was very different from the shadow watcher on the riverbanks. He was fidgety, shifting his weight from one foot to the other. He had a dancer's elegance, a gentleness to his wrists as his fingers fleetingly brushed the dials and toggles of a peculiar device that bleeped and whirred in his hands. His shoulders shrugged and swayed with the effort of adjusting the settings on his gadget. So this wasn't a phone, then. Digital devices have buttons you press with just your thumb. Jade watched him, puzzled.

She was almost certain he was not the shadow stalking the houseboat, although there had to be some connection. But that figure had been utterly still. Impossibly unmoving. One with the trees, for hours on end. This man, on the contrary, looked like a trapped bird, unable to stop twisting and turning for one moment.

But Jade couldn't help but consider him a threat none the less. Was the concealed weapon part of a costume, or was it real? She couldn't see it. And the device? It wasn't fake. No gadget of such elaborate mechanisms would ever be purely decorative. But what did it do?

The device was like nothing she had ever seen before. A complicated little machine, that was analogue, but mysteriously intricate. The cogs ticked away on their own, with dials and clockwork components turning rhythmically.

He moved it like someone trying to get signal on their phone, but instead of holding it up to find a mast, he was waving it low, into the fog that pooled thick above the ground.

"Got it!" he murmured. His hands stopped turning the cogs, and he froze, holding the device low before his right knee.

Jade strained to see. In the silence, the river whispered ominously as it swept along, behind the churchyard walls. In the small hours of the morning, her fingers were turning numb from the cold.

"Well, that's a new one," he muttered. His voice was young, early twenties maybe, but Jade still could not see his face. He brought his hand to his ear and adjusted something.

An earpiece. So, he's hooked to coms with someone.

No that wasn't it. The way he held the device in one hand and the earpiece with the other, he was almost...

He is listening into something!

The stalker used pirated radio frequencies, causing spooky static and playing video recordings from her operation in the desert. There had to be some connection.

Suddenly he leaned back, as if he was done. He stood upright and toggled the parts of the device, in a way Jade was certain he was re-playing what he had recorded.

She expected some ominous music or portentous words to spew out from it. What can anyone expect to record in a graveyard?

But nothing happened.

The man just listened to his recording in his earpiece. Red curls escaped from behind his ear and tumbled gracefully over his shoulder.

Were he and his friends just pranking someone else now? What should she do? Let it go, or confront him? She really wanted to face him and tell him what a twat he was being, but some unusual reservation made her hesitate. A sense of unease and some deeper instinct whispered she shouldn't let him know she was here. Jade folded her arms on her chest and watched.

What's on his recording?

Now the man whipped out a silver candle snuffer, sophisticated carvings running along it from handle to wick-cone and began putting out the candles one by one.

And that's when it happened.

With the vapours subsiding and the dark purple fog dying away fast, Jade suddenly recognised the spot.

This was her mother's grave.

Her breath caught. Her head pounded.

The air cleared more, as the fog was no longer fed by the strange candles. But instead of evaporating like normal mist, it drained down to the ground, sluggish streaks swirling heavily over the grass. The tombstone with the violin engraving emerged in the fading mist.

She couldn't hold back anymore.

"What the hell are you doing?" she shouted, striding up to him, entering the pool of fog he stood in.

He stumbled backwards in shock.

Staring at her was a young man with a polite, startled expression, red curls tucked in his black hood, and from the unbuttoned coat flashed vivid greens, purples, and blues of his outfit underneath. The coal black coat trailed to the ground, and as he buttoned it hastily, Jade got a glimpse of combat grade knee high boots and a belt with sheaths that could only carry knives. But he blended into the darkness once the coat was buttoned up, and the mist was rising thick around them both.

His wide black eyes were staring apprehensively at her. He was barely an adult. *He is armed.*

"Give me that!" Jade demanded, but to her surprise, her lunge at him was much slower than she wanted. She sort of swayed in his direction, instead of grabbing the device out of his hand. Weird.

"I thought you had left for the night," he muttered, far too calm for Jade's liking.

Jade felt a migraine descending fast between her eyes.

"You thought I left? Have you been following me?"

"No. I am the night guard here. I have seen you leave at nightfall when my shift begins."

The tiredness of the long day hit her. She hadn't slept for over twenty-four hours now. What was she doing out here? She really needed her bed.

"Since when is there a night guard?"

"Since always."

She leaned a little where she stood and held on to a nearby tombstone. What was happening? She hadn't drunk any wine tonight, had she?

"I've never seen you before!"

"I'm new, just started on the job recently." His voice had the soothing tone of a parent putting a toddler to sleep. She felt her aggravation melt away as he continued. "We are supposed to be discreet. I need to do better. Apologies for disturbing your visit," he said, and only then, Jade realised, in the haze congealing around him, that he had been packing the candles into his shoulder bag, ready to leave. "You should be heading home soon, it's getting late."

"No, wait a minute!" Jade took a few faltering steps after him. Her legs felt like lead. Why was she feeling hungover?

"What were you doing with that recorder?" she pointed at his hands, but there was no device there anymore.

"Have a good night." He retreated towards the old cemetery, his figure becoming hazy in the thick mist.

"Was it you? Have you been coming to my boat? Fucking with my radio?"

Silence. Not because he didn't reply. But because—Jade realised slowly with intense confusion— because she hadn't spoken at all. She'd only thought it. What was wrong with her? And now he was almost gone.

"No!" Jade'd had enough. He was not going to get away before she found out what he'd been recording.

She ploughed forward, her movements so stiff and clumsy, as if she were wading through mud; but she focused on the figure, trying to see where the device might be hidden. His coat showed no pockets, but a hint of a strap led her gaze to the shadow of a shoulder bag.

She made a quick calculation to decide where, along the middle of his black coat, his hip bone would be. She didn't want to strike soft tissue and cause him undue pain or injury. But she needed to give him a good shove, to pull his bag off.

The sleepiness was so intense, Jade felt like she was about to pass out. She worried it would happen without her even noticing. She did have a bad habit after a late-night movie of lying on her couch, knowing she ought to go upstairs to bed, before giving into a surge of sleep so powerful the next thing she sees is the morning light. Every fibre of her being was calling out for her to lie down and have a quick nap on the soft grass before riding her bike home.

Don't lose him in the mist. Keep going. But why am I so tired? Got to keep going. Like on duty.

Jade's well-honed training kicked in. Sleeping during a workout? Yes, many times. Even while jogging, when necessary. Easily. Extreme fatigue was nothing new.

She let parts of her brain go offline, but put her legs on autopilot, and kept walking after the hazy silhouette. She let her eyes close for just a few seconds, as entire sections of her brain checked out. No decisions to make, no tasks to complete, nothing to say or hear. Just keep walking.

The wave of sleep wouldn't get a full grip if she didn't allow it. During midnight drills and 48-hour hazmat suit training Jade knew how to keep pushing past the limits of exhaustion. She had no thoughts, her mind was blank, a sleepwalker among the graves.

And then it was over.

The river gates of the cemetery loomed over her, and there was her bike, chained on the rails. She could see around her again. Clean out of the mist.

The night was crisp, her mind sharp. The river breeze flowed in playful gusts through the gates, scented sweet with wild buddleia blossoms and Thames waterlilies. Jade took a deep breath. The ancient stone wall on either side of the gates seemed to hold the mists in, but the open, wrought iron railings of the Victorian Gothic revival entrance had never looked so mysterious, or loomed so high, as it breathed fresh air from the river.

Jade stood in the little clear patch before the gates and wondered, bewildered, at how the mist didn't seem to be able to take hold outside the cemetery. Like the gates were portals to the real world outside. Why did it feel so different in here? As if time had stopped and she was standing at the threshold of a shifting black void?

Far to her right, where she'd come from, the block of fog around her mother's grave had expanded along the entire side of the old church, covering most of the main cemetery. How very odd.

Did I lose him, though?

No, he hadn't left through the gates, because the river-path outside stretched away deserted.

Jade turned back.

He was hastily crossing the clear patch, heading to the mists in the willows among the century old graves. The old burial ground to her left was blurry with fog; and he would reach it in only a few steps.

He hadn't seen her. He was craning his head around to check over his shoulder into the main cemetery behind him, where they'd both come from. He appeared to think Jade was still lost in there, shuffling around that bizarre wall of mist by her mother's grave.

Jade leapt forward, closing the distance between them in three strides.

The man heard her footsteps and spun around, caught by surprise. A little yelp escaped his throat, his eyes growing round in bewilderment.

She homed in on the strap.

Two strides to position.

A push-kick.

Landed square on target.

As the ball of her left foot collided in perfect precision with his right hip bone, her right-hand fingers closed around the strap. He hunched down with a cry of shock, and Jade pulled the bag strap over his head and shoulder.

He tripped and fell flat on the ground, looking up at her wide eyed. She turned and ran.

I won't feel sorry for him. He's got to have something to do with the radio static pranks. I need to find that device he used.

She knew it wasn't the same guy stalking her at the river. But the situation was far too similar. Had to be connected somehow.

And for lighting up his weirdo purple candles around Mum's grave? He fully *deserved that kick.*

Aiming for the safety of the only CCTV camera on the church grounds, Jade ran along the church wall. The creepy river gates were far behind her. At the front, someone would hear her if she screamed.

Her path veered around in the mist, which still hovered thick where the candles had been, a dome of haze wide as a chamber. But scraping her elbow against the rosebushes along the church wall, she navigated a route in the clear. The fastest way was *through* it, so she had no idea why she was going *around* but didn't have time to think about this. She kept glancing behind her. The man was getting up to his feet and looking around for his tall hat.

Jade saw manicured hedges ahead as the path approached the church, spotlights illuminating the neat lines of uniform conifers. She tightened her grip on the bag as she accelerated. That recording device had better be in there.

She came to a halt as she ran out of church wall, almost crashing into the wooden pillars of the lychgate attached to the church building. The ancient wood creaked, all the way up to the pointy roof of the Norman canopy. She turned to lean her back to it, as if ready to face an attack. He hadn't followed her.

No, wait. With a jolt of dread, she saw the outline of the tall hat and long coat. In the centre of the hovering dome of mist, still swirling ominously along the side of the church... *there* he was.

She wasn't afraid of him, but somehow the idea of anyone breathing in that spooky mist with purple vapours— it was stubbornly refusing to dissolve— was terrifying.

Jade glanced up to the camera hooked on the corner of the oak church doors. The camera's little light was on. At any point Jade could step into the radius of the CCTV and the vicar would get a motion detect notification. Or at least she hoped so.

He'd charge at her any moment now, probably holding one of the many knives sheathed under his coat. He was standing very still, like the calm before the storm.

Bracing himself to charge. I've only got moments till he comes at me, blade in hand.

She burst into action, to get what she needed before he got to her. The peculiar bag was some shiny fabric Jade could not identify; it made her nauseous to look at. There were far too many decorations on it, which was strange because from a distance it had seemed just black and almost blended into the darkness. But now she was trying to decide which of the numerous pockets was big enough for that gadget to fit in, suddenly there were glowing etchings of cursive writing. They twirled along the creases and made her head swim.

Jade quickly looked up at the man, wondering what kind of technology this was.

The mist was much thicker than before, nothing was visible in it anymore.

And now she wasn't even sure *who* she was thinking about in the first place...

No, there was a man there. He lit candles around Mum's grave. He recorded something. It's in this bag.

The thing in her hands gave her a headache as soon as she lowered her gaze to it. It didn't make any sense why it would.

This thing isn't letting me look at it. Is it one of those 3D puzzles that blurs your vision? It forces you to look away...

She closed her eyes and tried to bring up the memory of the gadget she was looking for. She remembered it, slightly larger than a smart phone, much thicker and heavier looking.

Keeping her eyes shut, Jade felt the bag with her hands. A lot of pockets, all kinds of bumps and cold metallic filigree covering each one. But all of them too small to fit the gadget, apart from one. Jade lifted its little lid and pulled out the thing inside, peering through her eyelids.

Got it!

"Put that back in my purse, leave the purse on the ground and walk away from it," called the man from the distance.

Jade snorted. Keeping the device she wanted, she threw the bag as far as she could back towards the cemetery.

Just like she hoped, with a last glance at the gadget now in her hands, he turned and vanished into the mist.

Good luck trying to find it!

That gave her a few moments to try to figure out how this thing worked. Because Jade wasn't going to run off with it—that'd be stealing— and she wasn't going to trust any explanation that weirdo gave. No, she had to figure it out herself, quick; but it was not like anything she had seen before.

The earpiece was a tiny dragon, that mounded the ridge of her ear. The tip of its tail coiled around the actual earbud and fitted snug.

The little recording device didn't have any ornamental design, and she was able to look at it closely. It was analogue with an exposed mechanism of curious cogs turning like clockwork. Veins of copper ran through it, and steam gently evaporated from it even though it didn't feel particularly warm to the touch.

What the hell is this? What did he do with it over Mum's grave?

Movement caught her eye- he was back. A lot sooner than she'd hoped; how did he manage to see in this gloom and find his bag so quickly? His figure loomed larger in the fog, which brooded around him, coiling ceaselessly under the layers of white smoke spilling towards her.

Jade glanced at the CCTV camera behind her, then back to the device.

She wasn't going to steal; and she wasn't going to fight this person either. She'd have to give it up in mere moments now— but she'd expected it to have been a phone or something with a screen she could read information on. But now that she had it in her hands, the device created more questions than answers. She somehow had to operate it, to figure out what he was doing with it. Before he got to her and demanded it back.

Which, he wasn't. For some reason he stayed in the fog. There was some surreptitious movement in there, but she could barely see him. Was he assembling some weapon? Texting for backup?

I need to figure this thing out right now; I've run out of time!

She pushed the buttons, turned the dials. The red light came on; it was recording again. She stopped it. She pressed another toggle, and a blue light came on.

Music. Graceful but scared, like a captive butterfly.

"Mum?" Jade's hands shook, but the odd gadget in her palms continued to play the melancholy, somewhat agitated violin melody.

Jade looked up at the man, furious.

"This is my Mum practicing *improv*! Where did you get this? What are you trying to do?"

The figure in the mist was only ten paces away now.

What the... that fog's spreading like mad!

She looked at his figure outlined in the depths of the haze. What was he waiting for? He motioned with his right hand. If Jade didn't know better, she would say he was signalling a squad forward. Or commanding a dog to charge.

But there was no one else there.

And the violin kept playing, making Jade's eyes well up. Memories of sunlight afternoons, curtains flowing to the river breeze, Mum practicing the violin, Jade doing cartwheels around the little garden's only tree, or hanging upside down from the old swing ropes on its branches...

"This is definitely Mum, she loved making up this sort of wacky dark melodies..." she whispered, a knot chocking at her throat. It was a bit Vivaldi's Summer, a bit Flight of the Bumblebee, a bit La Danse Macabre. Jade would know it anywhere. "How did you get this? The date on the screen indicates you just recorded it a few minutes ago. How is this possible?"

He remained silent.

"I know it's her, but I've got all the recordings from her improv's and this is *not* one of them. Did you have some old practice recording, did you know my mum?..." Jade swallowed. She checked the screen again, it definitely said the recording was created a few moments ago. Her vision blurred and she blinked. She felt slightly tipsy, lightheaded. Had she been drinking?

Something changed. He was different. Motionless in the mist, a lofty certainty in his bearing, as if he'd won. She didn't like the way he just waited, like surveying a victory already playing out before his eyes. For a moment she thought he'd shot her, and she was bleeding without noticing; but no, she wasn't... injured...

And somehow the silence was too heavy, as Jade tried to make sense of this ghostly song one last time, with everything she had left, her voice hoarse, slow, sleepy. "And how did you record it... if I didn't hear anything? I was... right... there! I should... should have heard..." She felt tears run down her cheeks. How embarrassing. She tried to wipe her face with her hand, and found it was shaking.

"I am so sorry, please, let go. It's easier just to give in," came an unexpected reply from the mists.

Jade had almost forgotten he was there, but his voice had sounded genuine. Compassionate.

That jolted her back into anger. Who the hell was he, to feel sorry for her?

"How the hell did you get this?" She took a few steps closer and swayed. Flailing her arms to keep her balance, she planted both feet firmly on the ground but felt like she was standing on a swing. She blinked. Looked around. No, she wasn't moving. Standing still. Weird. Her head was heavy, nodding. Her energy spent.

Who was she talking to?

She felt so tired. Her eyes were closing.

Where was she? There was nothing but smoky mist around her.

Birdsong. The scent of morning dew on grass. Golden sunshine came through her closed eyelids.

Jade blinked and opened her eyes to the glorious summer morning in the church's immaculate gardens.

"Jade Palmer?" A kindly, middle-aged man was kneeling beside her. No, he was young, in his thirties. Nope, he was over fifty. She *remembered* him young. She'd known his face without the crow feet lines framing his pale eyes, the hair brown instead of silver. "You are Jade Palmer, right? Evelyn's daughter?" Oh yes, that was two decades ago, when he held her mother's funeral. He had been relocated soon after. She hadn't seen him for a long time. He was back, recently. Just like Jade.

Damn, I woke the vicar after all. No wait, I didn't. It's morning already?

"Are you all right, Jade? Can you sit up?"

"Yes, I'm fine." She sat up and leaned her back against the pillar.

The vicar looked at her with concern.

"Were you visiting Evelyn's grave again? Did you stay all night?"

"I didn't mean to... I don't remember..."

"Jade you can't keep coming here."

"Excuse me?"

"This is a place for the dead to rest. You need to do your grieving elsewhere."

"I'm sure I can come see my Mum whenever I like," said Jade, trying to stand up. "You said at the funeral I am welcome here whenever I need to visit."

"That was over two decades ago. Don't come here again."

Jade thrust herself away from him so fast her head thumped against the pillar behind her.

His face. The eyes were hollowing out, turning. Like cogs. With spikes around the rim.

His nose spilled like a ridged tentacle below his chin and looped around his neck.

"Libations to the dead are a component of spirit summoning. You are disturbing your mother's slumber!"

Jade had no idea how he was speaking, because his mouth had become a patch stitched with ragged seams and black thread.

"Fuck off!" was all she could say, although she couldn't help thinking, 'And what the hell is a libation?'

The voice came again, croaky and hollow, like it was coming from the depths of a cave. The patch stretched at the seams as his mouth formed the words underneath. Jade shivered.

"Stop making offerings of wine to the souls below. Those you invoke might not be the ones that answer."

"Back off!" Jade pushed the hideous visage away, and at her touch it broke into a thousand jagged splinters. She stood up, somehow fearing she would end up with a thousand little stab wounds.

Nothing had cut her. But she was so cold, she was shaking.

Fog. Everywhere. Still and silent.

And there was no one else there.

"Where did you go?" Jade shouted.

The voice that replied to her was so loud, she was sure her ears bled.

"Begone!"

She screamed so hard she woke herself up.

Birdsong. The scent of morning dew on grass. Golden sunshine came through her closed eyelids.

Jade blinked and opened her eyes to the glorious summer morning in the church's immaculate gardens.

"Jade Palmer?" A kindly, middle-aged man was kneeling beside her. No, he was young, in his thirties! Nope, he was over fifty. She *remembered* him young. *Déjà vu...* She'd known his face without the crow feet lines framing his pale eyes, the hair brown instead of silver. "You are Jade Palmer, right? Evelyn's daughter?" *What's happening?* Yes, that was two decades ago, when he held her mother's funeral. He had been relocated soon after. She hadn't seen him for a long time. He was back, recently. Just like Jade.

Something's off.

"Are you all right, Jade? Can you sit up?"

"Yes, I'm fine." She sat up and leaned her back against the pillar.

The vicar was looking at her with concern.

"Were you visiting Evelyn's grave? Did you stay all night?"

"I didn't mean to... I don't remember..."

"Jade you can't do this to yourself."

"Excuse me?" Jade said and then realised this man hadn't said anything un-kind— why did she think he was chastising her?

"Look I am terribly sorry for what you are going through, you must be thinking about your Mum a lot," said the vicar, as Jade pulled back, trying to stand up.

"You told me at the funeral..." Jade paused.

I've said this before!

"At the funeral? That was such a long time ago..." said the vicar. "Tell me, Jade. You can't have been doing this all these years?"

"I... No. I couldn't come see Mum very often. Only when I was here on holidays."

"That must have been hard," he said with little nod. Even though he wasn't cross as she'd first imagined, still, his eyes were not as compassionate as the soft timbre of his voice suggested. As if 'that must have been hard' was something he said often, and out of habit rather than heartfelt empathy. Jade pushed herself to her feet, trying to get her bearings. Why was she shivering as if she'd been sitting on a block of ice? He reached out and held her by the elbow. "Being away and not able to come to your mother's grave very often, I mean. I understand why you might have wanted to stay a bit longer. When you've missed visiting for such a long time... And you know you won't be coming again for a while... I understand. But maybe try not to stay so late that you fall asleep here?"

"It won't happen again," Jade said hastily. She pulled herself away. The world was swimming. She stood very still, or she might collapse again.

"How long are you staying this time, Jade?"

"I'm back home actually," she said stiffly. She was grateful when he didn't ask why.

"That's great news! Now you can come and visit Evelyn whenever you like! Problem solved."

Jade was confused; hadn't he just told her never to come back? No, that was a dream, right? But just then, he turned around to smile at someone else. Jade hadn't realised they weren't alone.

Behind him, a plump faced lady in a summer dress was unlocking the church doors and setting up welcome boards at the doorstep. She beamed.

"Hi, Jade! It's so good to see you after such a long time!"

Do I know her? Wait I think I do...

"Come in for a cup of tea and a bit of breakfast, let's have a catch up," said the lady, hooking the ancient wooden gate to the latch on the stone wall, propping it wide open.

Jade looked around. At the end of the path, people were sauntering into the churchyard from the village road. Jade quickly brushed bits of grass off her trousers, hoping they were still too far away to see she'd been asleep on the stone slabs of the church steps.

"I'm sure you can do with some breakfast," the vicar smiled, "I'll join you after the morning sermon."

"No, I'm fine..."

"I think we should talk a little about how hard grief can be to live with. We can't have you wasting your life away sitting by that grave."

She was in for a talking to and was about to refuse, when his wife took her gently by the arm, giving him a reproachful look.

"Let her have a bite to eat first. Jade, you don't have to talk about anything if you don't want to. But I can't let you head home without a cup of coffee at least, love. I've already got the kettle on."

Sarah. The vicar's wife. That's her.

She had been a skinny young woman, newly a bride, when Jade had last seen her. She'd grown into a warm and kindly figure, and Jade noticed that even though Sarah offered no words of sympathy, like her husband had, her eyes glowed with genuine concern.

"I guess I can use some coffee," Jade agreed reluctantly. Saying no to coffee was not really her thing.

Sarah beamed and hooked her arm to Jade's elbow, leading her away from the church. Which was a relief, because the first of the congregation were al-ready-sound polluting the picturesque lawns with their Sunday morning chatter, and Jade avoided social pleasantries, like she avoided a camp loo stewing in the midday desert heat.

But walking away with Sarah was nice. What was it about seeing someone from a very long time ago, who'd left a good impression, but you'd completely forgotten about ever since? It just felt right. Or maybe it was that Jade always loved being in the presence of people who had known and liked her Mum. It didn't happen often. First thing Stepmonster had done, was make sure Jade and her Dad fell out of touch with all the old family friends. Replaced them with Stepmonster's friends. So, Dad would be surrounded by people who didn't know Mum.

Jade sighed. She didn't want to think about all that now.

But this was nice. Being with Sarah again, it felt good.

As the two women retreated together down the side path towards the little door in the wall, Jade caught a glimpse of the vicar's cottage nestled in a lively little garden, and she was instantly glad she'd agreed to this. Besides, every muscle in her body ached, and even in the early summer morning, there was a deep cold that had set into her bones. As if her very marrow had frozen stiff overnight and was only now starting to thaw. She could do with sitting down in a comfy spot with a hot mug of coffee before attempting to ride her bike home. The vicar wouldn't bother them for a while: he was busy greeting the first of his congregation by the church doors. She fully intended to be gone before he came home.

Some of her favourite morning scents filled the air as she strolled through the rose arched gate into the cottage garden: sourdough bread hot from the oven, and grilled wild mushrooms, maple syrup on warm hazelnut milk porridge—the fruity sweetness of fresh blueberries— and coffee beans freshly-ground. Jade smiled as a single white petal from the lush arch of roses fell on her shoulder. She took it in her fingers, because she'd never seen anything like that before.

It was the shape of a perfect heart.

She inhaled the sweet scent of the velvety white petal, and let it fly in the breeze as she walked on beside Sarah.

The petal fluttered into the wind, travelling low over the gravel paths of the churchyard.

It tumbled along the sparkling green lawns of the cemetery, until it got caught in the silky threads of a spider web.

The web stretched delicately across a tombstone, like a sheer veil. Gentle waves rippled across the silvery threads in the breeze, making the heart shaped petal, trapped there, shiver. An embossed violin sat under the web, and the petal sat right on the headstone name: Evelyn Palmer.

Jade reached out a trembling hand and touched the petal with the tip of her finger. She gasped, unable to believe it was really there. The petal was paper thin and dry. No longer white after two days in the mid-May sun, it'd turned grey and shrunk;

like a little dead heart that wouldn't give up even though it had long stopped beating.

Jade's eyes widened.

"Can't be the same one!" she muttered. She shook her head, trying to pull herself together.

Jade had been battered.

She looked half dead.

Her legs were covered in bruises under the loose-fitting cargo trousers, and she winced as she shifted on her little picnic blanket, trying to find a comfortable angle. Red stains blossomed at the knee of each trouser leg.

"Sorry, Mum. Bled right through on the bike ride here. Let me change the dressings. One second." She stretched her legs in front of her, resting them on the grass. Her hand was bandaged in gauze with a large, bright red stain across it. A deep cut ran from her opposite elbow down her forearm, irregularly zigzagging under a line of what looked like dried glue. The scabby wound was a mix of dry blood and yellowish skin adhesive; the flesh around it red and inflamed.

Her ponytail hung lopsided over one shoulder, strands of blonde hair loose over her face. She bit her lip, trying to endure the pain that had become her constant companion, as she finished wiping blood off her knees and positioned new dressings over the cuts.

"I've not been doing too well, as you can probably tell." She raised a sarcastic eyebrow and rolled down her trouser legs. "I'm not sure what's happening, but it's not good." She sighed.

"I'm afraid." She wrapped the cardigan tighter around her, but the shivering wouldn't stop.

"I don't know if I'll make it through this alive."

Chapter Five

Things Best Forgotten

"**B**ut I didn't come empty handed to our picnic," she tried to smile, but she was too sore and gave up. Opening her backpack, Jade took out a knife, a large jar of hazelnut butter spread, and a round loaf of thick crusted bread.

"Comfort food. You'd approve, Mum," she said, propping the bread on her knees to cut into it. "Yes, it's *that* bad. I don't even care about the carbs anymore. I figured, I'm probably going to die so I might as well have the whole damn jar."

The cemetery looked like a garden in the dazzling sunlight of the early summer evening. White dandelion fluff rose up in bobbing little clouds every time the river breeze rustled the taller grasses of the ancient part of the cemetery. The tiny white parachutes spun among the leaning, cracked tombstones, like impish fairies chasing invisible spirits through the willows.

"I love the long days this time of year," said Jade. "Three months ago, it would have been pitch black this time of night. And I don't want to be here after sunset ever again. Sorry, Mum. I'm not afraid of the dark or anything... I just... I don't know why. I came nice and early tonight, it's just five now and it won't be dark until after nine thirty. We've got time to chat. But I'm leaving at dusk." A shadow of a frown passed her face, as she glanced at the distant willows where the ancient part of the cemetery began. Then she looked away and forced herself to smile. "Anyway, no worrying right now. I've got so much to tell you, Mum!"

Jade took a deep breath and begun.

You won't believe this, but I had breakfast with vicar Dawson's wife on Sunday morning. Do you remember Sarah? I think... you two, weren't you friends? I'm not sure.

And the reason for the breakfast at the vicarage is, apparently, I fell asleep at the steps of the church the night before.

Don't ask me how.

I don't remember anything after talking to you the other night. And that's a bit blurry too.

I was so embarrassed when he and Sarah found me. But thankfully they were ok about it, although they did insist, I sit and eat something before I went home. I think they wanted time to observe me: Determine if I had been drunk, ill or just absurdly exhausted for some reason.

I'm exhausted, sure, but that's not it. That bloody radio with the fucked up static really got to me.

The way the radio played music completely normal all day long, then at night-time I couldn't get anywhere near it without it screeching static. What was all that about? I did get rid of it in the water, but I can't stop thinking about it.

If it'd been an equipment malfunction, it would have been static around the clock—but no, only after dark.

So, it was *someone* doing this. I mean yes, I know I've already seen the guy, the figure standing across the water. I know. As much as I'd want this to be a random occurrence, it's not. It's deliberate. The watcher showed up when the static happened, so yeah, it was him. Right? He had to stay close to hijack the frequency.

But that voice... Whispering in the depths of that appalling sound. And I heard my name. What the hell was it telling me? 'Are they close?' What does that mean? Close to where? Near the boat? The watcher doesn't stand that near—always across the river, so even though he seems to be right there, he can't actually get to me. No bridge within several miles from our mooring.

But it's really fucking creepy how still he is. Just facing the boat. He's like a sniper in position, yet he doesn't hide. Sticks out like a sore thumb once you know where to look.

And the damn video— yeah, it's not a prank. It's military intel.

Am I being blackmailed? What for? I didn't do anything wrong. There's nothing I'm trying to hide here. Why send the clip to me like it's some kind of incriminating evidence?

But I'm scared. Is that the goal? Terrorism? Bullying? Hazing? Some asshole trying to punish me for getting discharged?

No...there's no one I've worked with who'd be dickhead enough to hold PTSD against me. Some pieces of work on the base, sure, but no one who thinks PTSD is some kind of joke. All I have to do is not let it get to me. So that's good. I can handle that.

Ok. Right. I've got this. Sorry, I'm rambling.

Anyway, breakfast started a bit awkward, even after I convinced Sarah I had just been very tired, that's all it was. Turns out she's one of those people who feel they have to prove that they're Ok With The Gay. There was me, sitting quietly eating my portobello mushroom with extra sesame seed oil, and somehow, Sarah managed to bring up her new rainbow bumper sticker, the last time she was in London during Pride and how great the atmosphere was, and how Thomas is already going to seminars discussing the possibility of same sex couples' affirmation blessing. I don't know why she thought I'd be impressed. For a moment I thought of stating the obvious: even if this Blessing does happen, it is just an excuse for their Church to look inclusive while still refusing to perform actual gay marriages. But I didn't say it. I looked into her hopeful smiling face and asked her to pass me the jar of hazelnut butter, slathered my slice of sourdough with a huge dollop of nutty, crunchy goodness, and said my dog and I can finish a jar like that in one sitting. Sarah told me to please take it home, which was nice; then thankfully she moved on to talking about her own dogs, and how hard it is to find dog sitters you can trust when you have to be away a lot, and hell yes, lately dogs is a subject I can talk about forever. She's all right when she's not trying too hard.

I ran away before her husband came home to give me whatever grief counselling pep talk he had in mind. Sarah didn't try to stop me.

So that was a morning of free food, good company and a big jar of homemade hazel spread. I rode my bike home through the narrow country roads, savouring the peaceful landscapes. Sometimes under the leafy canopy of oaks and birches, sometimes drenched in sunshine. The fields stretched on either side, hedge lines tattered and patchy in the early summer sun; horses flicked their ears as I cycled by. White clusters of sheep shrank quickly, as the whisper of my tires made them scamper in together. The cows chewed on and completely ignored me. The familiar summer scents of hay and wild roses blended with the cosy smells of late breakfast frying on the hob, every time I passed a cottage or a country pub garden. Memories of childhood flooded my mind, the summer days we cycled these roads together, you and me. First, I was on a kiddie extension attached to your bike, and as the years passed, I got to proudly ride my own bike behind you. I had no idea how good life was then. It's a short ride to the boat, but I felt happy and carefree the whole way.

Which was odd, for me.

I was in not a terrible mood when I wrote Today's Goal in my little black notebook.

New Food. I'd finished this part already: *Homemade hazelnut butter*. Yum! I wrote it down with a tingling sense of pride to have completed at least one journaling target before lunch.

Then, the hard part. I sighed and wrote it down.

Today's Goal: Stay Alive.

I looked at it and shrugged. When the therapist first made me start a Daily Goal journal, it felt this was the only goal I could successfully achieve by the end of each day. Anything more than that would have a large probability of failure, and I didn't need any more failure in my life right now. So I kept writing these two words every morning. Stay Alive. Maybe tomorrow I would think of a different goal. Maybe it was time to level up.

I blinked, instantly feeling exhausted at the thought. Nope. Not ready for bigger goals yet.

Suddenly I needed a nap. Opened my curtains to let in the sunshine, and my eyes watered at the bright shimmer of the glorious blue skies reflected on the wide expanse of water below. I dropped on my bed, fully clothed, and slept for three hours straight.

I know, right? Makes *no* sense. I lost my job exactly because I can't stay asleep. But in the daytime? I pass out like a brick. I didn't even wake up screaming once.

I don't know.

I didn't even get the groggy, drowsy spell from waking up after a midday nap— but I did get a massive headache soon after: That was only my sister, calling during my big Sunday workout.

'Pick up!'

Leela being Leela, she messaged me on the phone app just as she was ringing me on the laptop.

'Pick UP!'

"I can't pick up I've got boxing gloves on!" I didn't care that she couldn't hear me, I just said it to my phone where it vibrated on the floor. "And I don't want to talk to anyone," I added as I jab-jab-uppercut-hook-cross-crossed at an imaginary foe.

My laptop screen, where I was following the workout video, kept flashing with Leela's call, so I used the pad of my glove to snap it down. Without a video, I just dropped to the floor for some push-ups.

My gloves clapped together with a soft rhythmic thump after each push up and tapped with each landing on the floor, as I balanced on my fists for the press. But I still heard the incessant buzzing from my phone. It shivered petulantly on the carpet beside me, the screen crowding with new messages in quick succession.

The first one was a picture of Leela and her friends in outfits so absurd they defied description.

The next message said: "Alice-Minion fusion. You go as a minion, but the minion is dressed as a character in Alice in Wonderland or Through the Looking Glass."

I tapped the voice record message and spoke clearly at the screen: "Leela, I don't know how to put this politely, but you really need to get laid."

Her next text said: "Sex-obsessed much? Aww is it because you're missing Ami?"

I ignored her. But the messages kept coming.

"I know you're not working today!" "Grandpa is over here for Sunday lunch..." "And he said you are taking the day off and having a pyjama day!" "I can hitch a ride with him on the way back and we go for drinkies!"

I felt my stomach clench. A visit from Leela had to be prevented at all costs. The Talk, about why I left the Royal Air Force, was not going to happen right now.

I pulled off the wrist strap with my teeth, loosening my right glove; I tucked it under my other elbow, slid my hand out, and switched on the laptop.

"I can't do drinks," I said as soon as she answered my return video call. "But we can talk on here for a bit."

My sister beamed at me, her round face and half ponytail looking as disgustingly cute as when she was five. She has her mum's baby blue eyes, neither of us got Dad's moody brown ones.

"Hey Jade! Working out?" she said.

"Why do you sound so surprised?"

"I thought you were having a pyjama day! Because you were tired?"

"I am."

"Clearly not! Were you just trying to get out of coming for Sunday lunch? Mum is saying you're avoiding her, you know."

Of course, I was avoiding the Stepmonster. How can someone act all judgmental with backhanded advice and disapproving looks every single moment they spend with you, and then wonder why you don't visit more often?

"Please tell your mum this is a *me* day and it's not about her." I adjusted the weights on either side of my barbell to start a set of shoulder presses.

"Ok, I will. But Jade?"

"Yes?" I said halfway into a dead lift.

"Pyjama day is when people sit in their pjs and stay mostly, you know, in the reclining position."

"Need to take advantage of Grandad being out on Sundays. Can't lay out my mat and weights in the lounge and get a proper workout when he's here all week!"

"I'm exhausted just watching you," said my sister, popping one of Stepmonster's signature after-dinner mint-choc-chip biscuits in her mouth. "Don't you like, jog every day down the river? Isn't that how you get all the photos of Cannelloni making friends with ducks that you send me on a daily basis? Shouldn't you take Sundays off?"

"Running's cardio. I need resistance training as well. I really can't wait till I can afford a gym membership again."

"*There's* a sentence I would *never* say. Although I just got a cupcake box subscription. That's almost a gym membership, right?"

"Do I even want to know what a cupcake box subscription is?"

"Look I'll show you!" Leela trotted out of her pink childhood room— used to be our music room with all the violins, the bedroom adjacent to mine, although that's not mine anymore. In the background, I briefly saw the large window doors of the dining room with the late afternoon sunlight filtering through the frilly French voile curtains. Our handmade drapes are long gone—Charleen doesn't like macrame, she calls it hippie trash. I got a brief glimpse of Dad's broad shoulders and Stepmonster's skinny ones sitting at the dinner table across from Grandad, with his trademark sullen hunch. "It came this morning," Leela was saying, as I peered to look for Cannelloni in the garden. Couldn't see him, she zoomed into the kitchen too quickly. "It's a box with everything you need to bake cupcakes! Even the fresh fruit! And a pretty recipe card for each batch! Two recipes a month, isn't it great?"

"I don't have nearly enough friends to share that amount of sugar with. Is Cannelloni with the smoosh-heads?"

"Umm... I'm not sharing with anyone," said Leela, clearly offended at the very idea. 'They're *my* cupcakes!"

"You just showed me two recipe cards, and each says on it 'fills a 12-cupcake tray'?"

Leela narrowed her eyes.

"Exactly! So why would I need friends?"

"I don't know, it just seems that 24 cupcakes a month is a bit excessive? Can I see my dog? Is he with Lardo and Patsy?"

"That's less than a cupcake per day!" she said indignantly. "If anything, I'd hope my friends would bring me cupcakes on the other six days."

There was a pause because I didn't know how to respond to that statement.

"Don't look so horrified!" said Leela. "And yes, Cannelloni is with Leonardo and Patricia, they are napping by the fireplace."

"I just woke up and didn't find him here, which Grandad knows I hate."

"He just brought Cannelloni here to let you sleep in peace! Apparently, you were out all night and passed out on your bed and were dead to the world?"

I took a sip from my water bottle and switched to the kettlebell.

"At least he left me a note," I said, starting the eight repetitions. Leela watched me swing it over my head with a look akin to horror. "But Cannelloni is new to the family, you know. I wanted to be there when he met everyone. Those Frugs better not be bitchy to him for being a rescue."

I didn't mean the Frenchie pugs. I meant the Stepmonster. Leela knew it. I dropped to the floor for crunchies.

"So long as he," she said pointedly, "is not bitching at them for being chubby and loving... cupcakes!"

She looked at me sharply. She didn't mean my dog either.

"Fair enough." I called truce from the floor, counting the set in my head. There was a silence while I reached fifteen. Then I sat up to get a sip from my water bottle.

"Don't worry, this is not his first time, Grandpa brought him along a couple of times before you moved in. We think he is adorable! And Cannelloni loves it here," said Leela taking her nose out of that box when she saw me on the screen again. "Look at this stuff," she held up a box of ingredients, "there's a cute baggie of chocolate chips, and a pouch of fresh berries, I need to put this in the fridge. And there's a tub of flour and sugar, exactly the amount required for the recipe so there is no waste!"

"I would take the raspberries out of that box," I said, "bin everything else and eat them raw. Cooking fruit ruins it. And there is certainly no need to douse it in icing..."

"Can I see Ami?" Leela interrupted. "Have you got photos?"

"You've seen her before."

"Just the one picture, I want to see more! Tell me everything about her!"

I could see in my own face in the top left corner of the video call. I looked apprehensive and a bit frustrated, so I quickly forced a smile. Leela didn't need to know how much I didn't like where this conversation was going.

"Amira is great," I said, and that part was true. I felt my smile widen. "She's amazing. One of a kind."

Leela beamed back at me.

"I'm so happy for you! Can I see?"

"I don't have time to go through photos right now Leela..." I jumped up, gloves on, and started punching the inflatable bag.

"You never have time to show me photos of Ami! I'm starting to think you're avoiding it!"

Oh no. Don't go there.

"You know what I haven't done in a while? Changed your caller ID photo and ringtone on my phone," I said.

"Oh, come on!" moaned my sister.

"It's been a minute since you showed up with a purple ponytail and one eye when you called."

"I was *not* named after a cartoon..."

"Dad says you were."

"...Mum named me after the Arabic word for Playful Goddess. And you can't bully me like this every time I do something you don't like, Jade, I'm an adult now!"

"No, *Dad* named you. After his favourite mutant."

"Arabic Playful Goddess!"

"Your Mum is so French vanilla, that you both got natural vanilla blonde hair," I said, punching harder. "Charleen has as much of a link to Arabic culture as those fake Japanese culture connoisseurs, getting Japanese tattoos that end up meaning 'pork fried rice'."

"Actually, Arab is the second largest ethnicity in France and Mum had lots of friends growing up who…"

"I saw a good picture of you the other day, one where you're holding your three-eyed pet in a red cape and diaper."

"Can you *not*."

"And for your ringtone I'll go with your very apt quote: 'I usually keep my sadness pent up inside where it can fester quietly as a mental illness'."

"Projecting much?" she snapped. "I'm not the one who does that."

"What are you, a therapist now?" I said, boxing faster.

"Actually, I asked Dad for therapy too, since you're getting it."

"You volunteered for therapy?"

"Yup. He only got me a five-session package, so I'm spreading it out to last me longer."

"What do you need therapy for? Being spoiled rotten 24/7?"

Her face turned serious, and a little hurt, as if I was being insensitive.

"I'm getting help because my one and only sibling came home from a warzone with PTSD."

It hit me out of nowhere, like a gut punch knocking the wind out of me. Great. Now I wasn't only ruining my own life with those nightmares; I was hurting my sister as well. Brilliant.

"Copying everything I do was cute when you were a kid; now it's creepy," I said, sounding way more defensive than I intended.

"Seriously Jade, I'm not falling for your diversion tactics anymore. You're home nearly a month, you haven't agreed to go out with me yet. What's going on? All the other times we saw each other as much as possible on your two-week holidays."

"It's different now, Leela, I needed to find a job!"

"And now you *have* a job and still can't see me, and why only send me *one* picture of Ami? With your exe's, I used to get two dozen albums for each one…"

Albums! That's it. Ami has an album she links to her family members. I could give that to Leela without having to go through my photos.

"Fine! Here's the link to an album, hold on," I said. With two loud screeches of Velcro my hands were free, and I tossed my sweaty gloves on the carpet. Grabbing my towel, I dried my hands and picked up my phone.

"Yay!" said Leela a moment later, and I sat down for a set of side planks, glad this was over. For a while she clicked through pictures on her screen, big smile on her face, making 'aww' noises.

But then, the worst happened.

Ami's face appeared on my screen, laughing beside a man, his back turned to the camera, facing her. I knew him from the tray of miniature cakes he was holding up between them. I'd recognise them anywhere, those thumb sized cubes dressed in pastel coloured, velvet smooth sugar-paste, and topped with tiny flowers or nuts shaped like love hearts. They were the most adorable food I've ever seen. I felt faint.

"Leela, have you shared your screen with me? Why?"

Propping up on my elbow, I wiped my face and neck with my towel, no longer caring that my anger was showing in my darkened gaze on the screen. "Can you look at these photos another time please?"

"Why don't you want us to look at them together? Jade, she is so pretty! Super cute smile! I like her. Oh wow, look at those cakes! They fed you well in the RAF!"

"No, fondant-fancies was not on the menu. They were brought for Ami." I turned my back to the screen, not wanting to see anymore. I sat straight with my feet stretched out before me, hooked my rower to my shoes and started pulling at the straps. A cheap alternative to the row machine I would get at the gym if I could afford a subscription.

"Fondant-fancies, huh? I call that petit four, but they look different than anything I've seen before..."

"They're Indian, I think."

"What are they called in Hindi?"

"I have no freakin idea, they have like twelve different names, but what's with the linguistic interrogation? They're just fondant-fancies."

"Yes, that's what I said, petit four!" she chimed. "I love how tiny they are and each a different shape! Are all the colours different flavours? How come Ami got such a treat?"

I ignored the question hoping it would stop. I breathed loudly with every exhale, pulling the handles to my chest, rowing hard.

"Does that guy fancy Ami, just a little bit? I can see why; those legs are super-model long. She makes those dusty old camos look like a fashion statement. Like your other girlfriend, what was it, Hayley? The makeup tutorial influencer, she had legs for weeks."

"She was hardly my girlfriend, and Ami is nothing like her."

"Yes, you're right. Ami looks more like that other one, Emma, was it? The one with the perkiest tits in the history of women without a boob job?"

"I've no idea what you're talking about..."

"You know, the swimmer who did miles and miles of breaststroke a day because she was breastfeeding 3 kids for 6 years straight and didn't want saggy tits?"

"You know far too much about my private life," I said irritated.

"No really, she was Goals. For *my* snuggle pups to sit up like that I'd have to hide a push up bra under my swimsuit. And I've had zero kids, so what's *my* excuse?" she added ruefully.

"You shouldn't compare yourself to other people like that," I said, "healthy comes in all shapes and sizes."

"You say that, and then look at your girlfriend in this photo..."

"Can we not talk about Ami's looks anymore."

"Ok then. Petit four guy is in so many photos with Ami! Was he a bit of a competition? Did you have bake offs with petit four guy for her favour?"

"No competition, he's happily married, with two little girls he adores. Ami is a total foodie, and she likes to get authentic recipes and spice secrets from the Locally Employed Staff in the kitchens. That's how she made friends with him. Sometimes his wife sent samples of the recipes he had given Ami, if she'd cooked it at home, usually the desserts. That's all."

"I love that she collects recipes from around the world. She seems to be perfect: cultured, gorgeous, and of course super fit. Or she wouldn't be your type!"

"I don't have a type!" I said and stopped the rowing to look around at Leela on the screen.

Big mistake.

Ami was trying a tiny filo parcel sticky with syrup, from a napkin he was holding before her, and they were both laughing. I just snapped the screen shut. It ended the call. I didn't care. I couldn't focus on my workout anymore and started to do some quick stretches before hitting the shower.

My phone buzzed.

'Hey, did you lose signal?'

I picked the phone off the floor without interrupting my hamstring stretch.

'Yeah sorry,' I typed, 'Wi-Fi here sucks.' Which was of course a lie. 'I've got to hit the shower.'

Instead of answering, Leela video-called me. She just would not quit.

I'd pick up for a couple of minutes and tell her I'm busy and need to go.

"Hey," I said, putting her on speaker and lifting my foot to my butt for a thigh stretch.

"Look at her waist, how does she have such a tiny waist and be a foodie at the same time?"

"Can you stop it? That's not at all why I like her."

"Oh please."

"What's that supposed to mean?"

"Your dating history belies you."

"Stop speaking Oxford uni and speak *English*!"

"Have you seen your exes?"

"They weren't my exes. I haven't *dated* anyone, before Amira, in a very long time."

"Ok then, have you seen your friends with benefits?"

"They weren't even that. For them I didn't count, and for me it didn't matter."

"Ok, whatever you want to call them, have you noticed all those cardio bunnies in your old photos of entirely random acquaintances?"

"Oh, come on! I didn't have an option. Military wives on tour are often into fitness. Whether curvy or lean, they keep in shape, and why is that bad?"

"Sure, but no one forced you to take the RAF accommodation," said my sister with a cheeky little giggle. "You could have got a flat *outside*, and you might have met regular women then. You know, out in the wild, where people eat cupcakes and are afraid of the gym."

"Do you know what? I *did* like my options better in the service families housing, and I won't apologise for it," I chuckled with a shrug.

She burst out laughing.

I had finished my stretching and felt like a snack. I picked up the phone and took it to the kitchen counter.

"Well Ami is different," I said, raiding the fridge for strawberries, blueberries, raspberries and two bananas. "She's not some yummy mummy who thinks snogging another woman doesn't count. Those people didn't even think they were cheating on their husbands. What we had was not even an affair to them. I was completely invisible."

"I'm so sorry, I didn't know you felt that way? You never seemed to care!"

"I *don't* care. My life changed when I met Ami. She is in the service herself, and she wants to *be* with me."

"Ok, teasing aside, I knew she was different the moment you said you met someone in deployment. That never happens. I'm so excited to meet her!"

"Me too. And you will see. She is brave and bold and so clever." I emptied my fruit loot in my trusty old blender and went back to the fridge to contemplate the yogurts. "Do I want coconut, soya or oat based?"

"Ooh, you want coconut for sure!" said my sister and continued without missing a beat: "I get the clever part, Ami's an English major like me, we are notoriously smart," she said smugly, "but what makes her bold and brave?"

"Everything about her," I said, pausing to think about the first few times I had seen Ami. My hand travelled to my pocket and I felt the reassuring round shape of the little compact mirror, a piece of Ami always with me. "She arrived at the base with a don't fuck with me attitude and she wanted to have female interpreters and there weren't any, because our local contacts are mostly male."

"Wait I thought Ami was an interpreter herself? Why do your interpreters need interpreters?"

"The local dialects are unknown outside the region. Even to master's degree linguists like Ami. So native speakers are always useful," I said, and scooped a heap of chocolate protein powder into the mixer. I inhaled the rich coco scent and felt ravenous.

"Did you say she didn't like the men interpreters? Why not?" asked Leela.

"It's not that she didn't like them, she just wanted equal opportunities for women. There were hundreds of women living in the nearest city, who would make excellent interpreters. But Ami was told no. Women who were educated and willing to work for us, and whose families would *allow* them to do so, are not easy to find."

"Why not?"

"Women tend to hide the fact they get degrees and run small businesses, to avoid upsetting religious fanatics. Sometimes they even have to hide it from neighbours or their own family members."

"And how did Ami find them?"

"Should I indulge?"

"Huh?" she squinted at the screen to see what I was holding.

"Add some chocolate chips? What do you think?" I hesitated, checking the calories on the label of the delicious Raw Chocolate Chunks pouch, a treat to myself from my most recent trip to the village.

"You absolutely must go for chocolate chips!" she enthused. "And stop looking at the calories! Your skinny butt is already two sizes smaller than mine. It should be the other way around."

"Why should it be the other way around? Good butts come in all kinds of shapes and sizes."

"Because you're the older sister."

"Oh, so that was a bit of a back handed complement," I chuckled. "Watch out, you're turning into your mum," I flashed her a peevish grin.

"Shut up and eat some chocolate. And tell me more about Ami's secret agent mission impossible."

"Ami is brilliant, she utilised her situational advantage," I said, sprinkling quarter of a handful of chunks in my smoothie mix.

"What's that?"

"Her Hindu heritage meant she blended in better, people trusted her more," I said, licking chocolate off my fingers. "She went into the city all on her own. She's so ballsy."

"Wow! Go Ami! That's a generous amount of ice you're shovelling in there!"

I shrugged, adding a final scoop of ice. "I love it when my smoothie is almost an ice-cream. Anyway. She discovered a coffee shop downtown, owned by a woman, with a secret tearoom attached to it for ladies only. Curtains drawn on the windows and a side entrance that doesn't open into the main street. The landlady has lots of students and small business owners coming to her tearoom to read and work on their laptops in a safe environment. They come for the community and for the secure Wi-Fi as well. So, Ami went there a few times and within days she had formed her own little team."

"Ami really does sound awesome, don't get me wrong, but... Isn't it dangerous for these women?"

I rolled my eyes.

"Local interpreters are valuable, their identity is always protected," I said, trying hard not to add 'don't be stupid Leela!'

I switched on the mixer and bolted for the door. Leela burst out laughing.

"Shut up," I said. "One day I'll buy one of those new hi-tech blenders that don't make the eardrums bleed."

"Yeah, that was loud," said Leela, shaking her head. "Anyway, what was I saying?"

I didn't reply. I stood in Gran's little front garden, holding the screen up, and my sister's thoughtful face told me she really did want to be stupid about politics.

"I've heard on the news that those local translators are risking their lives," she said.

"Not at all. There is no danger, we are very careful," I said sharply.

"Were," I thought to myself. "I'm not there anymore."

"I'm sure I've heard they receive death threats and get persecuted," Leela pushed.

I tried not to snap at my sister. She's always acting like I should be apologising for my work. Risking my life to help out where my country sends me, I owe no one an apology. But I took a moment before I replied, trying not to take her comments personally.

"They volunteered, Leela. These women really wanted to work with us. They wouldn't do it if we didn't make sure to hide their identity."

A strange alarm had gone off in the back of my mind. A sense of warning. Instinctively I looked around to scan for danger. The stunning green of the willows reflected silvery emerald on the tranquil expanse of the waters. There was something I couldn't define, something that made me anxious. A shadow in the water?

Such a curious thing: the river swept by in its slow, early summer flow, an invisible movement, almost mystical. The water surface was perfect stillness, a crystal mirror, blue like the sky above. The sun played coy behind a cluster of greying clouds above the western horizon. Another storm gathering? A lot of rainy nights lately. And there was an odd, muted thickness in the air. The endless chirp and natter of the feathered population of the Thames had gone silent, like an invisible predator was prowling nearby.

I looked, bewildered, at the eerily motionless countryside. The leaves lifeless, no wind in the willows.

Was this, quite literally, the proverbial calm before a storm? I'd never experienced this before. Like an invisible hand had hit pause on the whole world.

The Thames was glass. Not a ripple. I felt my brow furrow as I tried to see the movement because, of course, it *must* still be heading to the English Channel; it can't have just paused. But nope. Not the slightest hint of the underlying, unstoppable movement, concealed in the river's forever flowing depths. How does that work, I wondered. How does the same body of water stay motionless on top, hiding the current underneath?

"What about now that we're pulling out of that country?" My sister drew me abruptly back to reality. "I read that…"

"Leela, I have no interest in debating politics right now, okey? The media can say whatever they like, but I can tell you for a fact that all those women who worked for Ami are now getting the chance to relocate over here."

"They will come to live in the UK?"

"Yes." So stop trying to make me out to be the big baddie. I did the things we have to do, to make the world a better place, and will not apologize for it.

I bit my lip to stop myself from saying this, and silently glared daggers at her.

"Are you sure?" Leela did not reflect my irritation. She always defaults to a sparkle-eyed, puppy look when she knows she's pissing me off. "Is it really that easy, Jade?"

"Yes, it is!"

She sounded like she was about to argue, and I spoke over her, because that was a conversation I was not going into. Especially not with a clueless civilian knowing only what the newspapers told her. "I'm going back in, it will be loud for a second." I opened the boat door, and the screeching of the old appliance tore at both our ear drums; we both made the same squinty grimace. I ran across the room and paused the blender. We caught each other's eyes and laughed.

"Is your blender possessed? You know what, can you record that noise and send it to me? I can use it for a prop. I can make a haunted treasure box that screeches when someone opens it!"

"I'm not recording it. But you can have the blender, whenever I can afford to get a new one."

"Ha! Then I'm getting you a new one for your birthday."

"Deal." I was glad she'd forgotten the politics and moved on.

"Looks delish!" Leela beamed as I held up the chocolate shake, so icy that it made the glass opaque around my fingers. "I want a smoothie as well now! And also, a cupcake," she gave me a toothy grin.

"Just what I needed," I said, relishing the cool fruity taste of the first sip.

"That's funny, because after I've had a workout what I need, is pizza," said Leela. "And by workout, I mean re-arranging my bookshelves."

"I actually had pizza the other night!" I said with a nod.

She raised an eyebrow.

"Did you make it yourself with like, a paper-thin flatbread and your... I don't know, cashew-based cheese or something?"

"Whole-meal flatbread with extra garlic and paprika tomato sauce. Loaded with four toppings: pickled artichoke hearts, olives, roast falafel balls and red onions. Covered the whole thing in soy mozzarella that melted in the grill till golden. It was delicious."

"Never mind, you've now put me off pizza for a week," she said with an eyeroll.

"Maybe that was my plan all along." I sipped on my smoothie with an evil grin as she made a funny mortified grimace. "Well anyway, that's what I like about Ami. Not just her looks."

"She sounds amazing! But you're brave too! Ami says here on this video that you risked your life to get her this beautiful sunrise. Is that true?"

"What." My good mood came crushing down. A notification flashed that Leela had sent a video.

The thumbnail showed the fiery red hues of the desert.

My gaze was glued to the image. Wanted to look away with every fibre of my being. Couldn't.

Strange chills shocked me out of nowhere. Stabbing, coursing through my flesh, unendurable. Then they were gone, like a warning fading ominously into silence.

Ever since I came home, I've been having these visceral, physical reactions to images from the tour. It's odd, but I don't think about it too much. Just avoid the pictures and it doesn't happen. Sorted.

But now I'd been taken by surprise. The giant golden disc of the flaming sun blazed behind a cluster of colonnade ruins. Desert sands sparkled, as if strewn with tiny rubies, and the white marble of the temple remains glowed.

I'd forgotten that Ami would have uploaded that video for her family to see. I was frozen on the spot. There it was again, different this time. A terrible crawling sensation running up and down my spine. But why?

Voices. Did someone speak? I snapped around, scanning the empty lounge. Outside the window, a young couple walked along the river path, disappearing at the turn of the river bend.

Just people walking by, no big deal. I'd overheard a snippet of conversation, that was all.

Someone spoke again, agitated. It was an angry retort, but I didn't catch the words. Where did it come from?

A jogger zoomed past, headphones on, her gaze vague, lost in thought. A last swish of her ponytail and the path was empty.

I tried to calm my racing heart with slow, deep breaths. The voices were gone, except for my sister's as she continued to prattle on.

"Wow the sun is bigger than the temple! What a romantic thing to do!"

"We... weren't together when I got this for her." My voice was a croaky whisper, my throat constricted so tight I could hardly breathe. The muscles in my wrist twitched—an involuntary urge to throw the phone away. Instead, I tightened my grip.

Another voice snapped a short, angry sentence, too distant to hear clearly. A short glimpse at the path outside revealed it was empty. Where was the sound coming from?

Nowhere, that's where. The only logical explanation was that it was all in my head.

I ran into my bedroom. Now, where was it? Grandma's letter-writing desk. I pulled out all three of the dainty apothecary-style drawers and brutally wrecked my meticulous paperwork system by rummaging through bills and RAF discharge correspondence until I found it.

The therapist's handout: Panic Attacks.

I held it with both hands, the paper trembling as I read. It felt like a bomb defusing manual, and I stood there, trying to drown out the loud ticking inside my own head. Some sentences jumped out from the text. You're safe... Your fears are valid but not real.

Whatever the fuck that means.

Skipped another bit of annoying stuff about grounding techniques. "Find what reminded you of your last tour and remove it from your environment or remove yourself from it." Ok, this I could do.

I sent the video icon away with two quick swipes of my thumb, deleting Leela's message.

There. Gone. As I waited for the unreasonable fear to subside. Leela's voice continued to drift from the phone's tiny speakers, droning on and on in the background. And underneath it...

Someone said something.

Just like before, it was brief, angry, and gone before I even had time to hear. More like a snarl or a growl than discernible human language. Then it was just Leela talking again.

I stepped back into the corridor, placing my hand against the wall to steady myself as I headed back to the lounge, and focused on the sound of my sister's voice.

"Oh look, Ami captioned this!" Leela chirped. "It says 'My friend Jade took this stunning sunrise, and at great personal risk, for mum's Lost Temples album!' And her mum and sisters have 'hearted' it, aww…. You're in with the fam!" Leela giggled. "Although why does she call you 'my friend Jade'? Hasn't she told them? Jade?"

I stumbled back to the kitchen and had a sudden urge for sunlight. But the Thames was glum, forbidding. I scrutinized the sullen grey clouds that made the hour feel much later than it was. The sunless sky darkened the broody river and deepened the shadows of the trees flanking the shores. Great. It would definitely rain again tonight.

The voice spoke again, and this time… I almost, *almost* discerned the words.

It was becoming clearer. Was that a good or a bad thing?

It went silent right away.

But it would return.

My throat felt swollen. Blocked. I raised a hand to my neck and massaged its soft front, secretly checking its size. Normal. No actual, physical obstruction. Difficulty breathing was part of the panic attack, wasn't it? The leaflet had said so. But seriously, shouldn't this go away already? How long would it last?

"Oh, you said you weren't dating yet…" Leela gleefully continued. "But it's still so romantic! I bet you already fancied her then! Did you? Did you fancy her then?"

Downing the rest of the smoothie helped. My throat loosened. For a moment I could talk again.

"I have to go, Leela."

"Why? What happened? Why do you sound like you swallowed a frog?"

I sat on the couch, head in my hands. I hated being rude to Leela. But I needed a moment to rest.

"Jade! Answer me please!"

"Hmm?"

"I said, why is it so hard for you to talk about Ami?"

"It's not about Ami! I just don't like to see photos and videos from my last tour, ok?"

The voice spoke again, and it was clear. I understood every word.

And now, I knew. I knew who it was.

"Wait..." Leela continued, "why did she say you took 'personal risks' to get her this video? What risks did you take?"

The voices were shouting. Drowning out my sister's words.

"Bye Leela."

"Oh my god, is this video the reason why you left the RAF? Did you do something...?"

"No, I told you already! I left because I was ready to move on. Can you back the hell off?"

If she said anything else, I wouldn't have heard it. I hung up and switched the phone off.

My head felt like it was about to crack open, my face burning like I had a high fever.

And I could barely hear myself think. My mind was no longer my own.

All I heard were those words...

That disembodied voice.

"Are they close? Are they coming?"

Chapter Six

Shadow In The Deep

"I can't stop here, Ma'am, shall I go?"

I shut my eyes and pressed my fingers against them so hard I felt my eyeballs squeeze. Until it started to hurt. He'd been sitting in the driver's seat when he said this, gripping the wheel 'til his knuckles were white. The blazing dawn bathed everything in a crimson tone, like a thin film of blood on his hands and confused face.

"Permission to move the vehicle, Ma'am!"

"Stay put!"

I opened my eyes again; better seeing the room than seeing the desert in my memory. Because that's what this was. A memory. Yet it felt it was happening all around me.

"Ma'am!"

"No, I need three minutes. The road is empty."

Adrenaline made me move at lightning speed. I downed my drink, then rinsed my glass and packed away the blender so fast I was breaking a sweat. It poured off my forehead as I carried my weights to my kit closet.

"Ma'am, the road is not empty. There's a civilian heading our way."

I clanged my rower gear and stepper extra hard on their shelves, hoping the noise would drown out the voices.

"It's ok. I know this man; he works in the kitchen."

I stuffed my boxing gloves into the closet.

"Ma'am, he is agitated."

"He is not agitated. He always gestures like that when he talks. He's enthusiastic."

I put music on my phone and connected to my stereo, cranking it up to full.

"We should move on. Can I drive? Ma'am?"

I smashed my mat on top of my boxing gloves as loud as I could.

The therapist had said something at some point. Something I hadn't understood—there were a lot of things she said I didn't understand—but now I got what she meant. She'd said the words *intrusive thoughts.* That must be what this was. This memory had a mind of its own. It was doing its thing, and I had no power to stop it. At least it was good to know this shit had a name. It meant other people had to deal with this, too.

"This is not safe!" my driver had said, facing forward, as if talking to the steering wheel.

"He's perfectly harmless," I'd told him. "Locally Employed Staff. I know him."

She said to let it play out and not engage with it. Not react to it. So, all I had to do was not get riled up. All I had to do was not freak out.

"We are out in the desert, Ma'am! Outside the base he can be anything, Ma'am!"

It would stop by itself, right?

"Stand by. I need 90 seconds for the sun to fully rise, to end the clip."

I slammed the doors of my little gear closet so hard it almost fell apart.

"Permission to drive!"

Splashing cold water from the kitchen sink tap on to my face and neck didn't do anything.

"I said stand by. Sixty seconds."

I wondered if I should run an ice-cold shower.

"The hostile is five paces from the vehicle, Ma'am!"

"I can see that for myself, airman. And he's a civilian, not a hostile."

"Ma'am, he is coming to your window!"

I couldn't take this any longer. Fuck waiting it out. I *make* it stop.

"Jade!"

I switched off the music. A shower won't stop this.

"Jade!"

There's something better than a stupid shower: A dive in the river.

"Jade!"

I stormed to the door of my cabin. My little black notebook went flying past me, landing on the floor at my feet. It was open at today's page.

Stay Alive.

For a moment I froze. How did this happen? Then a telling pain blossomed at my elbow, and I knew I'd knocked the notebook off my desk as I dashed past. This was no dark omen, just me being a klutz.

"Are they close? Are they coming?"

I ran out to the back of the boat and jumped. Right into the Thames.

My body shuddered as the darkness surrounded me. I pushed to get to the surface, my legs twitching as every muscle spasmed with the shock of the cold.

Silence. My mind had gone blank.

I let myself sink through the dark water, watching the blue of the sky shimmer overhead like at the end of a tunnel. This silence was blissful.

But then, my diaphragm began to spasm, desperate to draw a breath through my sealed lips. I had to go back up.

I splashed to the surface with a few kicks and drew a lungful of air.

For a moment, I bobbed on the spot, gasping, not realising how long I'd deprived myself of oxygen.

Looming over me, like a tall wooden wall, was the side of the boat. I'd never seen it from below like this. It smelled of mildew and rotting weeds.

"Am I supposed to be cleaning that? I should probably look it up online." I chuckled and stopped muttering to myself because I was getting out of breath.

I needed to swim around to the end of the boat, reach the little mooring stairs. Then I could climb out of this grey, cloudy water.

The side of the boat was slipping away.

No, I was. The current carried me down river.

But my mind was still blank. A strange void was taking up the space of the voices, which I'd silenced by jumping in the water. Yes, I could feel it: something else taking over, something worse.

It circled in a loop inside my head, wordless emotions getting louder. The sadness that my Mum was dead. The pain that she was *twenty years* dead. The hopelessness that it never got any better and never would. The despair that time was not a healer; missing her only got worse. The misery that the things I didn't get to do with her only multiplied with each passing day. The anger that Dad married a woman who couldn't stand me. The devastation that by now, they'd been together longer than he ever was with Mum. The sense of disappearing in the realisation that we weren't his real family. The maddening invisibility in being just a parenthesis, a prequel to his real life. The utter rejection in always being an outsider with them; his wife would have it no other way. The loneliness in how Dad never bothered to object to her or defend me. The final failure: My decision *not* to stay where I wasn't welcome, but leave, and go live my own life; it led to nothing. I was back, jobless, where I started.

I had no career, no rank and *no identity*. After twenty years, back to *zero*.

I'm no one.

I went limp.

Floating away, face down in the open river. My arms bobbed, palms down, on either side of me in a T pose, like a corpse regurgitated from brackish waters. Forgotten. Lost. I kept my eyes open, watching the black depths of the muddy riverbed. Sheets of weeds travelled past me in the darkness below. I needed to lift my head and breathe. But what was even the point?

It bothered me that my body took over.

My legs kicked spasmodically, pushing me into a vertical position, forcing my face into the air. My lungs sucked in the oxygen before I could stop them.

Turns out it's impossible to drown yourself, when you know how to swim.

How fucking inconvenient.

I wiped wet strands of my muddy hair away from my eyes, bringing the world around me into focus.

"What the...?"

I spun around in frantic circles, arms paddling manically to lift me as high up out of the water as possible, to optimise visibility. I looked in every direction, trying to recognise the countryside on either shore.

I was no longer at the mooring, nor anywhere down that familiar stretch of river. The boat was nowhere to be seen. I'd drifted to a completely different part of the Thames. But where?

The ominous whispering of waterfalls tickled the edge of my hearing.

No way.

There it was, in the distance:

The red-shingled, Tudor style roof, dwarfed among the oaks and birches lining the river shore. The lock keeper's operating hut.

"The next lock?" My voice came out hoarse, broken. That was three fucking miles away.

Nope. It was right here.

How would I get back? With no phone, no money? I'd have to walk home along the river path. Dressed in wet lycra workout shorts and bra? Yup. And with no shoes.

And that was the least of my problems; right now I had to swim to the opposite side of the river to reach the Lock's gate and moorings. On my side, were the metal rods of the weir and a gruesome death.

I was heading to the Lock's barrier, the spiky structure stretching across the waterway. It blocked boats from shipwreck down the Thames' waterfalls. Sign posts popped out of the water near me, directing boats to the Lock side for safe passage. I had to do the same. Avoiding the waterfall wasn't even the issue, the weir structure would shred me to ribbons first. I started swimming half against the current, to get across to the safe side river at the Lock.

That was exactly the moment when, slicing through the air like bullets, the first raindrops of the brewing storm splattered in the water all around my head. I instinctively looked up, and heavy pellets of water slapped my cheeks and forehead. I bent my head and blinked through the rain.

Just when I thought this couldn't get any worse...

Fighting the current was hard, my chin sank below the surface. I breathed in a gulp of musty river. Coughing, I spat it out, kicking and paddling again to keep my head afloat. I was so, so tired. Swimming after a full workout session was not my brightest idea.

The coughing wouldn't stop, even though I was keeping my mouth above water. There was something stuck in my throat. Deep in my pharynx. I coughed hard and it came up and lodged itself on the back of my tongue. A foul taste in my mouth, bitter and mouldy. Did I swallow a bug? I released a series of dry hacks trying to force the thing out.

It was still there; I could feel it. Making me sick. Panic began to set in.

I reached into my waterlogged pocket and retrieved Ami's mirror. Snapping it open, I positioned it in front of my mouth and cried out in horror. A long black slimy weed had curled at the back of my tongue like a flat slug. Bile rose in my throat, and I puked a splodge of reddish purple, and then another, and then more.

Pieces of blueberry from my smoothie floated in the water before me. I wanted to swim away from the vomit but instead my chest convulsed, and I was sick once again. This time the new splat of blueberry smoothie on the water before me had a long, black, glistening membrane in it: the weed had come out.

I swam away from it, rain streaking down my cheeks. Or it could be tears.

I tightened my fist around the little mirror, and carefully returned it to my pocket, as I paddled to keep afloat. A piercing ache started in my chest. My heart slammed painfully against my ribcage with every beat. Not good. I really, really needed to rest. I needed out of the water. Right now.

Was I almost there?

Fear drained through me when I saw I'd made no progress to the Lock. I was still very much on the weir side. And the waterfalls roared much louder. There was no time to cross. I'd end up skewered on the metal rods in a few moments. I turned around and made a desperate bid for the shore.

The grassy slope came closer and closer... yet higher and higher the closer I was getting.

Oh no. This was not a spot I could climb out of the river. It was too steep and slippery here. I needed to keep going, there *had* to be flatter riverbank somewhere.

When I walk my dog those easy water access sections are bloody everywhere, and he ends up in the Thames every five minutes; where the fuck are they now?

The river threw me in a wall of reeds; no, it was curtains of willows. I fought them as they dragged, slimy on my face and shoulders. I waved like a lunatic, batting them away.

It rained on.

Like a stranded leaf, the current was carrying me faster and faster towards the metal and cement structure of the weir. The growl of the waterfalls was now deafening. I could see the barrier spikes poking out of the water.

I had to get out of the river right away. Like, right now.

Blinking through soaking hair, I scanned the overgrown side of the Thames path as it rolled past. No opening. Zero access to dry land. Nothing but a steep climb and a fortress of foliage. Just my luck, this time of year the water levels are low; in the winter, when the river swells, the steep section disappears underwater. If it were December I could probably swim right out onto the path. But now all I could do was watch the reeds go by as I was carried to my death.

Panic well and truly took over.

A willow branch slapped me in the face as I bobbed past it. I batted away the next one just in time, and swung sideways to avoid another. The weeping willows draped like green curtains over the water, forming imposing arches over the shores, their roots coiling through the shrubs.

The next time a ropey branch of willow hit my shoulder, I grabbed it.

The sudden halt made my neck snap as my head rolled forward. I hugged the branch with both arms, pressing it tight against my shoulder. I felt it scrape the side of my neck as it stretched with my weight. The branch creaked, strained as the river pulled me. But the willow held.

I was no longer floating away.

The weir was perilously near. Thirty more seconds of drifting away and I'd have crashed. This fucking tree saved my life.

But I was now trapped here with no way to reach dry land.

I was still quite far into the open, the shore a good five metres away from me. The willow was tall and its branches thin and slippery. I tried pulling myself up to climb across, and I slid back down, earning myself a few cuts and scrapes on the soft tissue between thumb and index fingers.

Great. Holding on to this end of the tree was completely pointless. Just another moronic decision to notch on my belt.

So then. I would have to ask for help. At this point, I'd have to wave to the next person passing by and ask them to call the Water Rescue. A new low. Not just a civvy; no. I'm now a civvy who needs to be hauled out of the river by the Thames Valley Fire Brigade. Excellent. Fantastic.

A chilling touch of sticky sludge brushed at my feet. The violent revulsion it evoked, shocked me to the core. My whole body cringed, like some deep, primordial instinct had been awakened, buried in the darkest caverns of my mind. Screaming danger.

I looked down—

There was someone hovering down there, in the depths of the riverbed.

I held on to the willow curtain with both hands now and pulled my knees to my chest, tucking my feet under me— get as far away from it as possible... But I was still chest deep in the water; curling into a little ball didn't make much difference.

Down below, where the green murky water turned black in the darkness, the unmistakable shape of shoulders and a head. The dark outline of a torso. No details visible but the shape was clear: a body, slowly emerging from the abyss.

I clung to the branches, resisting the river's flow. My fingers hurt so much I had to alternate hands to give them a brief rest. So how come the figure below me wasn't moving with the current?

Probably some giant garbage bag stuck on a tree root. But I hated how it was directly beneath me.

Then the head—or what I assumed was a head—tilted, as if craning to listen.

My breath hitched; lungs paralysed with fear.

The thing began to rise up. The body was floating to the surface.

I freaked out. Because it wasn't propelling itself using arms or legs. The figure stayed motionless and solid, but now, through some invisible force, it was coming straight at me.

I tried to climb up out of the water, getting a grip higher up the branches, desperate for a foothold on the foliage; there was none. I was hanging by my arms, a bit higher than before, water up to my waist, but my legs had no purchase, and my hands slid slowly down with my weight.

The shadow below kept coming. I tucked my legs tight under me, trying to lift them out of the water- impossible.

Kicking at the water below with all my might to thrust myself up, I let go with one hand and grabbed another handful of a rope branch nearby, swinging my weight from one branch to the other, hoping that somehow the motion would let me grip higher. My heart raced and my chest was about to explode with the effort, but I was getting hold of a bit further up with each swing. This could work—

A crashing sound overhead, and I was freefalling. A loud splashing and the water closed over my head.

Sinking.

My lungs scorched, and before I could stop the next intake of breath, my nostrils filled with water that poured down the back of my nose and into my throat, burning, foul. Grabbing at the first thing I felt before me, pushing my head out of the river, a breath of air. Coughing out murky grey mouthfuls of the Thames, my lungs went into convulsions, cloudy river water squeezed out of my chest and poured from my gaping mouth down my front. I blinked through the water streaming down my face. It stung in my eyes as I tried to see.

Hard tree bark jabbed under my hands. I pushed myself upright, hooking my elbows on to the wood, sharp edges cutting into my flesh. But there was a foothold suddenly available, and I fitted my foot on it and heaved myself further up. Skin gushing open at the knee and the ankle against braking branches and both my elbows erupted in pain, but I didn't stop even when I smelled blood.

Air all around me. The breeze icy against my skin, my shoulders, my legs. Water poured off my body like a waterfall. Dazed, I looked around.

I was kneeling on a branch. The leafy rope I'd been dangling from was gone, and a large bough wide enough to lie on, stretched horizontal like a platform. Something shimmered at arm's length below. It was the river. I was out of the water.

I blinked around, confused, wiping away the locks of hair sticking to my face. The bough stretched ahead of me to the willow, where it had snapped half off.

I broke the tree. I couldn't believe my luck. It hadn't snapped clean off, to float away. No, it was still attached to the tree.

A bridge to dry land.

I crawled forwards, snapping twigs and smashing leaves to make way. It was so hard to balance on such a thin surface. I held on with both hands for dear life, and I could only fit one knee at a time on the branch, letting my other leg hover. And it inclined steeply towards the tree, making me pull almost my whole weight with each step.

I couldn't slip and fall back in the water.

The shadow was still down there.

Floating just beneath the surface, it was still directly under me. Even though I'd moved so much closer to the shore.

Like it's following me.

My heartbeat so fast I had to stop and take a deep breath. I took a good look at it. The shape of a human body. Waiting.

Was it a corpse or a diver? It was far too still. It had to be a bin bag, trapped in the reeds at the riverbed. Had to. My heart thumped loud against my temples. From up here on the branch it was at a different angle than when I'd been in the river. But still the same form of shoulders and a head, with the rest of the body vanishing in the depths below. A cadaver.

I had to get out of here. I crawled on up the branch, ignoring the stabbing pain every time the tiny branches broke under my knees and elbows. Higher and higher I went, red streaking my forearms; I didn't care. Pulse rushing to my ears, I clenched my teeth against the agony of my weight pressing my open wounds and followed the bough's steep incline to the end.

I threw myself and hugged the tree trunk with both arms. I'd made it. I looked down. No more bloody river. Just reeds. Thank fuck for that.

I barely remember getting down from there. Next thing I know, I landed on the grassy path with a painful thud and roll. I lay for a moment spread out on the soft bed of dandelions. I was covered in twigs and leaves and unidentifiable brown slime from the branches. Mixed with blood. But I was on dry land.

What was that thing?

And was it still there?

I stood up on shaking knees, feeling so incredibly weak, and looked over the reeds to the water. My shoulders stiffened.

Still there. The dark shape skulking down those inky black depths.

It had gravitated towards me once again, now floating inches over the riverbed, like something that had crawled out of the mud to watch me from its watery grave.

I could see no face, but the silhouette head was turned up peering at me. Hostility emanated from it; I could feel its predatory intent from where I stood. A tingle at the root of my neck, the disturbing sensation of spider legs weaving icy threads onto the bones of my spine.

I had to fight against the urge to turn and run. I stuck my chin up and clenched my fists. This irrational fear, I had to get the fuck over it. It must be my dehydrated brain, starved of oxygen from all the exertion, making things up. I was safe on dry land. It was time to see. No more guessing and speculation. See what it was once and for all.

The gathering darkness wasn't helping. There was precious little light left.

Well, I'm not leaving without knowing. Is this a corpse? Should I be calling the police? I need to find out. I need more light.

I reached and unzipped my pocket, pulling out Ami's mirror. Flipping it open, I raised it above my head and watched my hand turn rosy gold, catching the last rays of the setting sun. But from the wrist down I was in the shadow. The last warmth of the dying sunlight in my hand was like a healing balm.

I looked away from the mirror and straight in the river. A blob of light danced on the water. As I tilted the mirror in my hand, the light glided up and down, turning the water bright green and leaving it grey when gone.

I cast the reflection on the figure in the depths, and narrowed my eyes to see what the light would reveal. Rotten clothes? Swollen, bluish flesh? Or a diver's black mask with camera attached, zooming in on me?

Nothing.

"Where is it?" I said, my eyes widening, trying to find the dark shape once again. It had been right there, right in front of me!

But now, the water was clear.

As my hand shook, the light reflection danced along the surface, like a laser pointer. But the rest of the river was uniform, uninterrupted grey.

The figure was gone.

"Was that me? Did I do that? Did I blind him or something?" I looked at the mirror, ignited with the reflection of the setting sun, like holding a star in my hand.

No way. It had to be trash, right? Debris that slipped away with the current just now. But why did I feel so relieved?

A sense of peace was loosening the tension in my neck and shoulders. The chilling sensation of foreboding subsided with inexplicable ease. I started to breathe deeper, calm. Like a danger had passed, a threat lifted.

And birdsong returned... Birdsong blossomed for the first time since back when I'd been making smoothies on the boat, with my sister on the phone... Can that be right?

What was this odd feeling, like someone hit un-pause? Like suddenly the world had sprang to life again? Was I loosing my mind?

Quite the opposite, I was suddenly fine. Normal. No longer felt watched. And now, other things became important: Like the pain on my elbows and knees.

Scrapes like small red lines on both my knees, they were shallow flesh wounds and nothing to worry about. But my left forearm had a sleeve of glistening crimson. So. Much. Blood. Turning my arm outwards, I found the reason why. A gush so deep I could see the raw underlayers of flesh, and stretched quite long, from just below my elbow to halfway down my forearm.

"Oh, for crying out loud!" I had to get my ass to the boat and grab some antiseptic wipes or soon I'd be adding bacterial infection to the rapidly growing list of my latest injuries.

As the thickening darkness chased away the frail crimson rays of the sunset, I started walking home, barefoot on the river path. The twigs and leaves that crunched pleasantly underfoot when I went out on my morning runs, now felt like glass. But I was heading home.

"Spearmint-tea, super-hot-shower, clean-pj's," I said in my head, one word per step, like a marching call. "Spearmint-tea, super-hot-shower, clean-pj's." It was my mantra for the next sixty minutes.

Grandad's head appeared at the window, when I finally reached the boat an hour later. Before I could step on the deck, he had come out and blocked my way.

"You're not coming on the boat. You're soaked!"

Confused, I just looked at him. He was angry about something, what had I done now? Cannelloni barked excitedly from behind the closed door, but Alan stood on the deck and wasn't moving out of the way.

I had no strength to argue. I just took a deep breath. The lavender scent of the soft couch throws reached me in the gentle breeze, hints of warm ginger and coconut cream from the kitchen. He must be microwaving my leftover lentil soup I'd boxed for him in the fridge, I thought and blinked, coming back to reality. I was safe. No matter what had happened, I was safe now.

"Not going to ask what you were doing." Alan gave me a head to toe look of utter disapproval. He didn't see the blood, because I'd folded my arm and pressed it against me, which had stopped the bleeding. He saw what looked like mostly me covered in mud, and that's as it should be; the last thing I needed was my family finding out my latest panic attack almost killed me. I was fine. I could handle this.

"I've been out all Sunday to come back and find my laundry basket still full," Alan was saying, "and I'm running out of shirts for my tours again this week!" he added, looking so hard done by, I almost felt a twinge of guilt.

"Grandad," I said as nicely as I could, "you've got to learn to use the washing machine! I've printed out step-by-step instructions and taped them on the side of the machine for you! It's not that hard!"

"That's not how it works under my roof! While you live on the boat, you *will* respect me!"

He glared daggers at me, and suddenly the words poured out of my mouth, before I even had time to think or stop them.

"I've done nothing but respect you! It might have been disrespectful if I'd said that I can't take your new, widowed phase of petulant man-child any longer. But I've never said that have I? I've spent years hearing the same old jokes, that I never wear skirts, jokes that my hands look manly, jokes at my boulder-climbing callouses and boxing-hardened fists, which, is quite disrespectful to *me*, by the way. And I've never said anything back. I never told you to stop throwing tantrums, when you find no clean cups and storm off to your bed without tea, acting like you've been thrust in a dystopian universe where your dishes don't magically appear clean in the cupboard each week. But do you know what, Alan, here's me being disrespectful: This boat is not a time capsule to the Golden Era; I know you like to keep it looking full-on vintage-chic, the way granny left it, but The Lady Thomasine does not have the power to turn every woman living in it, into a 1950's housewife. There. How's that for disrespectful."

"Are you done?" was all he said.

I'd expected anger and yelling, and to be told to pack my bags and leave. But he just looked miserable and, somehow, small.

"I have almost no trousers left either," he announced, sounding completely confused.

For a moment I felt a twinge of guilt, and I made a mental calculation whether I could fit in some time tonight, after I cleaned myself up, to run a round of laundry after all.

But then I noticed I was swaying, as I stood there, from the blood loss and exhaustion. What the fuck was I thinking? I didn't owe anyone laundry tonight. I shook my head.

"It's not happening," I said.

His eyes widened in surprise. He said nothing, he just stood there, like a child. I'd no idea where he summoned all this spectacularly convincing victim energy, and once again I double guessed myself, wondering if I was being too harsh.

"Listen, I know it sucks," I said quietly, "but we all run out of clothes sometimes. And then we go and do our laundry."

The meekness vanished as anger flashed dark in his gaze.

"Put the kettle on, will you!" he said, finally turning to go inside, leaving me space to step on the deck.

And just like that, I knew I'd been right to stick to my guns and not fall for his weaponized helplessness. I grabbed the banister to leap on the deck thinking I was finally allowed to come inside, when a large flapping object flew out of the open door and landed on one of Grandma Tamsin's boat garden chairs. It was green with blue paw prints, fluffy, and covered in dog hair.

"You're giving me the dog's towel?" I shouted, hopping over the gap onto the boat and picking it up. "Can I have one of my own towels, from my room, please?"

Another item, even smaller, flew out of the door and landed at my feet.

"A dish cloth? Alan, how am I supposed to dry myself with this? It's tiny!"

"That's not for drying yourself. That's for drying the dishes. After YOU WASH THEM!"

"I've washed all of *my* dishes Alan! I don't leave stuff in the sink, I'm a use-it-and-wash-it girl."

His bedroom door slammed, somewhere in the depths of the barge.

I gave Cannelloni a scratch under the ears and headed for my shower, squelching a trail, from the door to my cabin, of footprints stained in mud and blood.

Chapter Seven

Missing Ami

"We're running a little low on provisions, Mum." The hazelnut butter jar was halfway empty in Jade's hand. The knife was sticking out of it, covered in hazelnut crumbs up to the hilt. One half of the loaf of bread was gone. The other half of the sourdough sat in a nest of ruffled cloth napkins, in a bread basket lined with a hand embroidered, scalloped tea towel of faded aquamarine and white stripes. It screamed rockabilly glam picnic, and looked genuinely seventy years old, which meant Jade was using her Grandmother's things again.

"That nut butter's smashing. I love it when meat eaters make great vegan food without even realising." Jade chewed and swallowed, dusting crumbs off the corner of her lips with her thumb. "I'll have to run for an extra two hours tomorrow but totally worth it."

Jade yawned, then sighed.

"Sorry, lack of sleep. It's been a rough few nights. And that body in the river... I mean, was it even a body? Should I be reporting it to the police? I just thought I'd end up looking like a fool. They'd drag the river and find nothing. Some trash.

Just like with the video: I saw it, but turns out, it wasn't there. Couldn't find it no matter how much I scanned my drive. Same exact thing.

So, I reported nothing, once again. I'd end up being told I made it all up and wasted police time.

But God, I'm *certain* there was something there, and it looked *human*. And yet, the way it disappeared when I cast the light on it? Fuck. Just gone. Like it had never been there.

So, what do you think? Am I seeing things? Is that normal for PTSD? Voices in your damn head, no stop button, just pushing, pushing, pushing until you'll do anything you can to shut them up? If I told my therapist I jumped in the river to stop that flashback, she'd probably have me committed.

That's not me. I don't want to die; I never have. Not even when the worst things happened. I'm a fighter. I can take it, whatever it is. I'm tough and I get tougher when I need to. What's another mindfuck in a life full of them, huh?

It's so hard having no one to talk about these things with. I wish you were here, Mum. And Ami too. Ami would be the right person to tell! She always got me. I don't think I've ever had a friend like her. We *connected*; you know? Ami would be able to make sense of all this. I have no idea what the fuck is going on." Jade rubbed the back of her neck with both hands. "God, I wish I could talk to her. I miss her so much. I've not told you very much about her at all! With everything that's happened, I've not had the chance. Seriously. I miss her so much!"

Jade pulled out her phone and looked at it hopefully. But there were no messages.

"I got so used to having her there, ever since the beginning, when we weren't even talking. Just boxing away in silence. On either side of the olive tree. For an hour at a time, most days a week. We didn't *need* to talk. It was perfect. She would try something new, something the instructor on her screen demonstrated, and she'd get it wrong; so, I'd tap my glove to her elbow to lift up, or her shoulder to lean back, or her ankle to twist, when she got the kick turned out incorrect. And she'd fix it just like that. And her whole shadowboxing sequence would click together. Flow flawlessly. And she would nod, 'thanks!' with that stunning smile. My whole world lit up. Although I pretended it was nothing and went on with my sets."

Jade's face brightened up with a wide beaming smile, eyes downcast at her hands. She fidgeted restlessly with the band of her fitness-tracker watch on her wrist.

"And I would catch her, sometimes, with the corner of my eye. Watching me. You know, if I was doing something intense. On the longer end of my pyramid rounds, when the punches came fast, and the bag groaned at the seams. And she had that shimmer of shocked admiration in her eyes. Those gorgeous eyes! And her lips parted a little, like she was speechless, even though we weren't talking at all. It filled me with this warm, swell in my chest, when generally I don't give a flying fuck what other people think. But with her, it was so good. To know she looked up to me. And still, we hadn't talked, for weeks. Not so much as hi or bye. Nothing. Just a 'Ma'am' from her when she arrived and when we parted. I just- I just nodded."

Jade hid her face in her hands.

"I was too awkward! I thought, better keep my mouth shut or I'd make a twit of myself! Make some lame joke or grin like a dickwad just because she showed up. Deadpan, show nothing. I'd have loved to smile and chat, you know? Tell her she was doing great with her boxing; how clever she must have been to learn *so quick*! But. We were on duty, not at station back home. And Ami was RAF personnel, not some military wife on her gym-bunny treadmill sesh, before a hot-tub and steam spa with her yummy-mummy group. So, I never said a word. Barely acknowledged her. I was far too distant most of the time, I was sure she'd think I didn't want her there and stop showing up! But I had no choice. And thank fuck, she kept coming back."

Jade chuckled, taking a sip from her water bottle.

"To Ami, the legend," she toasted.

"I think I'm on a sugar high. Haven't had that many carbs in the whole of the last two months combined. I bought your favourite sourdough from the Danish bakery down the road, for this, Mum. I hope you approve. Epic crust, and super chewy loaf inside, so fragrant, and still a bit warm, that's why I'm keeping it wrapped up. Gosh, feels like I'm tipsy. Feels like when I was little, and you were still here, and we sat together for hours and hours in the garden, I was up on the apple tree and you were preparing your cream cheese icing to decorate the banana mug cakes we had left cooling on the garden table... You baked the batter directly in our mugs! One in my: Less Talk More Chalk mug I'd won at the climbing gym, one in your: This Is A Sharp, Not A Hashtag mug with the pink musical notes along the rim, and one for Dad in the mug with the old English fire engine: It's Not Road Rage If You Have Sirens. Because we were waiting for Dad to come home to watch a movie on the couch... all three of us under one blanket..." Jade shook her head with a sudden frown, like she was angry at her own thoughts. "It's fun to be eleven years old and think life is awesome. Doesn't last long."

Jade turned away, a steely look in her eyes. She glanced at her phone again. Still no new messages.

"Then one day, if you can believe it," Jade said to the tombstone, "Ami shows up with boxing pads." Jade laughed and tucked an escaped strand of blond hair behind her ear. "I think she wanted to force conversation between us. Well, I know it. She told me later, it was her strategy," Jade chortled. "At the time, I totally fell for it. Spoke to her for the first time in nearly a month of silent workouts. I was like, 'Where did you get those?' She had made them! Scraps of paper, plastic and burlap bags from the kitchen storage, and lots of string and tape. She had made a decent pair of pads. Showed me the photos she had found online to model from. Her hands fit in just right, and the pad was big enough to take a hit and light enough to hold up. I was so fucking impressed. Then she was like, 'I'll pad for you!' I was in shock. She what, now? 'Yeah, I'll pad for you.' I'm like, 'I don't think so.' Ami had reasons: 'Look, I'm getting all the cardio and technical workout from the videos, but there's no resistance training! Not if I'm not hitting something! And I don't know what it really feels like to take a punch, when I'm shadow boxing! Let's spar!' It wasn't sparring exactly, but close enough. And I really, really wanted to say yes. But was it a good idea? Full contact training with this bird who's a pure hottie and also a sergeant?"

Jade shook her head, smiling in disbelief.

"I did it."

She stared at the tombstone, as if waiting for a comment. Then shrugged.

"Only for ten minutes at the end of each session, those were my terms. Non-ne-gotiable. The rest of the hour we were doing our separate thing. Like normal. But the last ten minutes, that became the best part of my day. My life, even. She is brilliant, Mum.

I'd call out the combination, like 'Cross-duck-cross, upper-upper-slip-hook!' to let her know what's coming at her as she pads for me. And she'd not only get it first time. She also kept a steady stream of conversation without missing a bit of the cardio round. She swerved the pads over my head to prompt my every duck and jabbed the pads at my face for my every slip, met all the punches as I threw them, and still told me all about her plans to make Flight Sergeant, the initiatives she took at her work, finding women translators to liaise with, trying to make a difference in these people's lives while excelling at her job. Her sparring was strong, her stance steady, and she kept up with my pace as I led the set around the olive tree, covering at least a mile in circles in the shade, on our ten minutes training together. Made the sessions so much fun. When we grabbed our towels and water at the end of each training, panting hard, I'd check my watch to find the best heart rates than I'd ever had achieved on my own. She fell back into silence. We headed off together and split up with our usual "ma'am" from her, nod from me. No more needed. It was amazing."

Jade tipped her water bottle and finished it, then put it in her bag.

"Best time of my life. Not kidding. She even brought me sweets that a local friend of hers made, and as I chewed on the tiny fondant fancy she'd flash me a picture of her chinchilla on her phone, with the newest woolly hat her mum had knitted. Or a picture of her kitchen friend holding up little baskets of desserts he'd sneaked into the base for her. Or her sisters, and their newest shenanigans back home. She never said anything, I really liked that. I would just flash her a grin, and she'd put the photos away, and we'd walk back in silence, shoulder to shoulder. If I happened to see her around the base, I put on my sunglasses to be able to watch her from a distance, without everyone knowing I couldn't take my eyes off her. I'd love to go say hello, but not at work. And in the desert, you're at work 24/7. I couldn't be seen chatting away with her. Boxing training was fine, workout buds are normal. I didn't find a reason to hide, everyone could see we were professional and kept every distance. No other contact whatsoever. It wasn't right. But it was so hard.

I wanted to kiss her so bad.

But even if I had somehow been allowed to, I had no way of knowing if she wanted it too.

Back home, I had a way to suss it out: Back home, I'd have suggested salsa class by now."

Jade's face brightened peevishly as she glanced at the tombstone.

"Have I told you how well that works? It never fails," she chortled, looking a little embarrassed at the grave.

"You wouldn't know, because you left so early, Mum, and I don't tell you these things normally. But it's like this: In place of the clubbing we did in our teens and twenties, now it's salsa. Ladies in their late twenties, and thirties, love a salsa class. They never say no. It's the most efficient system to find out where I stand with a new bird. It is usually at a tapas bar with dinner and cocktails before, so they seem ready to agree to it as a 'girls night out'. For crying out loud."

Jade rolled her eyes, amused.

"Then during the class they are happy for me to do the chap's routine, and they do the lady's part, as the teachers' couple demonstrates. Which means that once the class is over and the Latin clubbing beat comes on, they are already comfortable to let me lead, having fun with all our new salsa steps. They have such a good time, it's only a couple of hours of dancing before I get the kiss."

Jade shrugged.

"You'd be surprised how many straight married babes kiss me before midnight on salsa class night. Only like, two in ten don't. And that's fine, I've still had a fun night with a pretty girl. But the ones that do? I don't kiss *them*, they kiss *me*! They think it's funny at first, because we are dancing a couple's dance, they think it's hilarious. Well guess what. When I suggest we pop by my flat before I drop them off back home at midnight to their husband and kids, about five out of ten of the ones that kissed me, say yes. And more giggles, as if that's even funnier. It's like, they are thrilled to try out the gay thing for an hour. I'm game, and I won't go into detail with you Mum," Jade looked a little red around the ears. "I mean, I'm clearly giddy with all that sugar but I think I'm actually starting to come down from that wild sugar high, so let's skip some parts, yeah?"

Jade took a deep breath and continued.

"But once at my flat, their answer is mostly 'yes' to any question of mine, that begins with 'Is it ok if I...'

And they stay longer than an hour.

And on average they come back for more, at least a dozen times over the following months.

Although it never lasts."

Jade paused for a moment before continuing.

"Soon they get the guilt and quit. Whatever. I'm used to it. It's dead easy to initiate, but it never sticks. I've learned not to get attached like I used to. But with Ami? I was dying to know how that would pan out. Would she come to salsa class? Would she kiss me while we danced? Would she say yes to coming to mine? Would she have fun, spend the night? And, after? Seeing as she is single, would she actually want to date me? Did I dare hope?"

Jade stood up and stretched her legs.

"Then I remembered none of this could happen because we are posted miles apart back home. The chance we would serve, even for a few years, at the same station is slim to none. And that's assuming she would even care to see me after this tour, when we are back to reality. I'd be home in just under two months. Two months after me, Ami would be home too. So four months to wait and even then, it would only be a weekend visit at the most."

Jade sat down again and hugged her knees.

"Ugh! Mum! I liked her so much. I was unwrapping my boxing straps at the end of each session, fantasizing about weekends at mine with movies and tapas. And video calls. Wondering what a long-distance relationship might be like." She sighed. "Then I told myself not to get attached. That shit never sticks for me. And then, one more month into our friendship, Ami said it. The thing that changed my life. 'When you come over to visit, I'll show you my collection.' She was talking about running medals, she'd been telling me she's a 5k obstacle-course fun-race addict. I tried not to gawk! She'd done it. She'd invited me to her flat. We were friends, Mum. I'd see her back home!"

Jade gestured with both hands to emphasise the last sentence.

"I made sure my face was completely blank when I turned around and said, very flatly, 'maybe.' Ami went quiet. I pulled the boxing bag over my shoulder, she tucked her mat and screen under her arm, and we walked in silence past the showers, to part as always on our separate ways.

She goes, 'Ma'am.'

I go, nod.

And *wink*."

Jade burst out laughing.

"I winked at her, Mum! I couldn't help it. Ami's face lit up, but I turned my back to her and walked off. That night, for the first time in my career, I started counting the days my deployment would end! While we served together in the desert, I couldn't do anything. Once we were back home, who cared if I drove up to her station to visit her? Sure she'd be hours away, but I'd be glad to do it. I was making plans in my head and looking forward for the tour of duty to be over. And you know what they say, Mum.

Careful what you wish for.

Before I had a chance to see her again, we went on that mission. We recorded that god-awful execution." Jade shifted her weight, unable to find a comfortable spot where she sat.

"And the nightmares began."

She ran her hand over her forehead. Her fingertips shivered.

"Yup. Just my luck. It all went downhill from there. The less I slept, the less I felt like exercising. I only went back to the tree a couple more times. Then stopped. And within a few weeks, they had sent me home early. One month early. I'd only served five of my six months this time. I thought I'd never see her again. Not only was I watching my career get destroyed, without being able to stop it, but I also lost the one good thing that had ever happened to me.

Ami.

I should have been happy to be working in an air-conditioned office again, with water coolers, and a coffee shop downstairs. And normally I'd be over the moon. Back at my weights machines at the gym, and at boxing club twice a week. But nothing has ever been the same.

Nightmares every night.

Trying to function on forty minutes sleep each day.

I was turning into a zombie.

So, I was at the station back home for less than a week, thinking of Ami every waking moment, unable to believe how shitty my life had become…" Jade looked up at the tombstone. "When I got a friend request!"

She chuckled.

"A picture of Ami, the smouldering red-brown hills of the desert in the background, the dazzling blue skies above. She was standing next to our tree, with my bag ready to go, and wearing my boxing gloves! The caption under the photograph said, 'Ma'am, I don't know if you left your stuff for me or not. But I found it hanging from the usual spot and I decided to look after it for you! I hope you don't mind!'

It felt like I was coming back from the brink, that message.

I accepted the friend request, and since we weren't serving together anymore, I replied with the three words I'd wanted to say for months.

'You look gorgeous.'

And then I added: 'Enjoy boxing!'

Wait, what…"

Jade looked around, as if she'd heard something. Her eyes darkened to a frown, her gaze searching the willows, now a darker green than before. As if she suddenly remembered where she was, she wrapped the cardigan around her tighter.

"Nine o'clock. Sun's gone behind the trees but it won't set for a little while longer. Anyway, no idea why I'm talking about Ami. I can't text her any of what's happening to me now. Not where she is, not with what she's dealing with. I need to wait till she's home. Then I'll tell her everything. All of this- this insanity! Mum, you won't believe what I saw yesterday. I have no words… I just can't."

With tremulous hands, Jade pulled an old cable knit jumper out of her bag. It might once have been black. It was now grey and worn out to a soft, slightly open weave. She slid both arms through the oversized sleeves and sighed like she'd been enveloped in a hug. As her head poked out of the jumper's neck, her messy ponytail fluttered in the chilly breeze that carried dead leaves and cryptic whispers from the old cemetery. Jade scanned the thickening shadows, as if expecting to see someone there. But no, she was alone.

Then she picked up the jar of hazelnut butter and pulled the other half of the bread closer.

"Yup, time for round two," she said, smacking her lips.

"So now you're caught up till Sunday night, Mum, and as for what happened yesterday... Last night really... I don't know where to begin." She gave a little sardonic shake of the head and slathered a generous amount of nut spread on the first slice of bread. "I don't think you'd believe me if you heard it for real. Who would? Who the fuck would actually believe this shit?" She took a deep breath. "Sorry, Mum. But the next night I... I..." She shook her head.

"I saw a ghost."

Chapter Eight
Midnight Encounter

You know those days that come out of nowhere and change your whole life? They destroy the future you'd planned. Decimate your entire world. Forever ruin the person you were going to be.

For me, this Monday was that day.

It was meant to be simple and boring, and just as pointless as Mondays always are. It started like that for sure: I was exhausted from my stint in the Thames the day before, and I was so banged up I used up most of my first aid kit patching myself up once I showered the river stench off me.

Then I hardly slept. Nightmares non-stop. The execution. Whenever I dozed off, even for a few seconds, there it was. Playing in a loop. I woke up sweating, shaking all over. Tried to sleep again, because being fired from *one* job, over this, is enough. I have no recollection of actually falling asleep. Next thing I know, I'm sitting up in my bed suffocating, gasping for breath. I'd watched him bleed out in the mud all over again. Weather beaten leather boots thronged around his head, rendering his last moments even more cruel, more unspeakably sad, as he flinched every time their arrogant stomping sprayed red mud into his swollen eyes.

What else is new?

In the small hours of the morning, my eyes burning, bloodshot, and my head pounding from exhaustion, I'd had enough. The sheets were damp, the cabin musty, the whole boat stifling. Grabbing my pillow and towel, I climbed on the roof of the barge.

The earthy, soothing scent of petrichor greeted me like a good old friend, and I took a deep breath of relief. All night the summer rains kept circling around the boat, but the dawn brought with it clear skies. The first sunrays had just found Grandma's dahlias and made them sparkle with diamante dew. I'd managed to emerge at that rare, brief time in a summer sunrise, when the whole world glistens, like glitter has been sprinkled on every leaf.

It doesn't last.

Only takes a few minutes for the summer dew to evaporate in eerie whisps of dancing mist, and then the magic is gone. I stood there captivated for a moment, looking around me like I was being touched by a benevolent, invisible hand. It was over almost instantly.

The sun grew brighter, washing away the soft, crimson glow of dawn. The day had begun. I lay down on the roof, used gran Tamsin's vintage oversized sunglasses to block the sunlight from my face, and pulled Alan's heavy cap down to my nose. A gorgeous calm spread through me. I sank into the deepest sleep, and the warming touch of the gentle morning sun upon my skin felt like a childhood safety blankie.

That's how I managed a whole five hours shut eye, which is shocking really. At midday the path got busy, and I woke up, gradually coming back to consciousness in an easy, pleasant way from the sounds of the river walkway. I'd forgotten what it's like to wake up normally. I even felt rested for a change. Which was good, because today, I wrote a new Goal.

Stay Alive. And Get A New Radio.

I finally felt strong enough to go out and pick up the replacement radio I'd ordered for Grandad. Throwing his in the river was not my finest moment. A single thought played over and over in my mind: But what if the new radio does the same thing again? It was that unspeakable fear that had delayed me from replacing it immediately. Without it on the counter I was safe. No speakers to whisper my name in the dead of night. No haunting static, whenever I approached.

But Grandad had gone pure apoplectic when he found his beloved old radio missing; the only way I could even begin to ask for forgiveness was to bribe him with a new one. An upgrade. This thing did everything, even displayed the weather forecast. It took all morning to make the return train trip to town—because I have to walk from the river to the village to reach the train station—but it was worth it.

I had it connected by late afternoon. When he walked through the door it was already playing in the kitchen, like nothing had changed.

"What's this? I don't want this!"

"Look, it shows the news headlines—"

"I don't want this garbage!" he said, and dragged it along the counter, letting it fall in the trash.

"Alan come on," I said, but he was already heading to his cabin.

I spent the next ten minutes wiping old tomato sauce and apple peels off the new radio. Plugged it back in, switched it on, and sat down to catch up with some work.

Two hours later, I was wiping gravy from it.

Alan had come in to get his frozen dinner microwaved, and on his way out, I heard another clang of metal against metal. He made sure to drop it in the bin first so the bangers and mash container would land on top of it.

"Alan! It's expensive, can you please not do that?"

"Mine was a gift from your Grandmother!" He took his hot plate of food out of the microwave and didn't sit at the table to eat it.

"I said I'm sorry, I really am! I do feel terrible. Look this is the best radio there is! For every song it has photos of the artist, the song lyrics..."

His cabin door slammed shut.

Dammit.

Predictably at 8pm I was wiping chocolate pudding from the radio. He'd come in very quietly. I hadn't noticed him until it was too late.

But even with hands sticky from the mess, I was so relieved.

It still hadn't happened.

For the first time I was standing right next to the radio in this kitchen, and it was nighttime, and no howling static! Nothing but normal music came from the speakers.

I beat it. I won.

The drama with the old radio had probably been some prick coming in here and tampering with it. Grandad leaves the windows open all day now in the hot weather. Dead easy for someone to pop in and out unseen while he is in his cabin or out in the front garden. I'd been such an idiot, getting so scared over nothing.

Only one mystery remained: The video of the execution that had played on my screen the other night. I hunted for it once again. I spent all day trying. I couldn't find it. No video file saved anywhere in my drives. I guess it was streamed, but then there was no link saved either. By now, I had searched absolutely everywhere in my drives.

It pissed me off. How was this possible? Data doesn't just vanish, so how was there no trace of it?

The only explanation was that someone had gone back into my laptop and deleted it. No chance, though. I'm security. I know how to protect myself.

So, it was final: I couldn't report this. Not without any proof. Of course, the RAF needed to know; but if they scanned my laptop and found no file? Not even a dead link? They wouldn't believe me.

This was so, *so* frustrating.

I poured all that nervous energy into my work, and one good thing came out of it: I got more work done in the next few hours than I had in several weeks. Every now and then I glanced up at the radio and smiled, relishing the fact that nothing was happening.

Although, at 11pm it was a close call.

I saw Grandad from the window, as I had just walked out the door with Cannelloni for his evening walk. Incoming: Soggy tea bag and dregs of congealed milk. Alan had waited to hear the door close behind me to shuffle into the kitchen, holding his mug.

I flew back inside like the wind.

By the time I was through the door and ran up to him, the radio was already in the bin. I slammed Grandad's tea mug from his hand before he tipped it over. It smashed against the wall.

"Now you broke my mug too!"

"I'll get you a new one!" I said, pulling the radio out of the bin and shoving it in a backpack.

"You going to walk the radio too?" he smirked.

"Yup." I headed for the door, where Cannelloni stood watching us curiously. "If you keep this up, I'm just going to return it for full refund. That'll be you, without music. Your choice, Grandad!"

"You won't get a refund," he shouted from the window as I paced down the path. "Not for broken stuff!"

"It works perfectly fine!"

He stuck his head out of the window. "I get up first! That should do it!"

Took me a second to work out what he meant. He bins his breakfast milk and cereal leftovers.

"You can try!" I called over my shoulder.

I wasn't going to tell him about the cameras. But I would get a very loud notification if anyone went near that radio while I slept. I'd installed three hidden micro cams around the kitchen. Not for Alan. They were meant for whoever had been hijacking the frequency and making the old analogue device switch itself back on after I'd turned it off. And then again, somehow, after I'd unplugged it... Whatever they'd been up to, they'd have to get their hands on the new radio to do the same – and I'd see them when they did.

Less than an hour later, with Cannelloni tired out from his walk and curled up at the foot of my bed, I checked the cams' feed on my laptop.

All in order.

Putting notifications on loud, so any movement would wake me, I turned around and switched off the bedside lights.

It was quarter past midnight when Cannelloni woke me up with a low growl. The fur standing on his neck, teeth bared, his ears flat on his head; he stared at my closed door as the angry rumble in his throat built up to a warning howl.

"What is it, boy?"

I had a strange feeling someone was here.

Inside the boat?

Surely not.

I glanced at the glowing screen propped up on a chair beside my bed, showing the three cameras' feed all through the night.

The radio quietly played Grandad's sixties rock station, same as always.

I checked the notification history: nothing had disturbed the radio since I went to bed.

Cannelloni stood on his back legs and tapped the door handle with his paw.

"Shh, quiet now," I whispered, flapping my hand in Cannelloni's direction. "You'll wake up Grandad." It must have been a deer. It'd have to be big, to rile him up like this.

He didn't stop, and soon Alan would be out here giving us a piece of his mind. I could hear his TV in the next room and hoped he had already dozed off, as he often did, with his shows still on.

My cabin door handle creaked.

My eyes widened.

Who's there? How the hell did he get inside?

My door was still closed. Was someone really trying to open it? What stopped them? It wasn't locked.

A piercing pain in my stomach, anxiety burning my insides. For a moment I lay there, frozen.

Then I kicked off the covers and jumped up, scanning the room for anything I could use as a weapon.

The sound of the door bursting open made me swerve around. Just in time to see a white fluff whooshing out of view.

"Cannelloni!"

It was the dog, he'd opened the door. I heard him scurry away into the kitchen and let out a deep huff. "When did he learn how to do that?" I whispered, as I pulled on my grey cargos and black hoodie. Because facing a potential burglar in my pyjamas was not an option. I followed the hound out of my room. Switching on the lights, I saw no one in the lounge. Cannelloni, however, was running from window to window, sniffing in the air, eyes wide.

I was relieved all was normal in the quiet lounge, but there was definitely someone out there. Unusual for this time of night. But I refused to let myself freak out.

"Cannelloni, we don't mind people walking past! It's a public path, you know that!" I tried to give him a big hug, but he wriggled himself free from my arms. He made a dash for the door, barking low.

My dog had never registered the figure on the opposite shores; only the radio static ever bothered Cannelloni. Which made sense: he couldn't possibly smell anyone across the river, right? But all I could think of was, it's that fucker again. Even though the radio is gone, the watcher must be back.

I ran to the window. The blinds were down, so I parted one with my fingers to peer, unseen, across the water. Nope. He wasn't there, and no figures lurked among the trees on the opposite banks. Cannelloni tried his new trick, standing up to tap the handle with his paw.

"That won't work, boy, front door's locked!"

He threw himself at the wooden panel, scratching as if he could dig a hole through the front door of the barge. Every few moments he looked up to growl at the windows. That's when I realised. I'd been focused on the wrong side of the river.

The hound's not looking across the water; he's worried about something here on the path.

I stiffened at the thought. That meant *he* could be standing right by the boat. I could go out there and meet him face to face.

A knot tightened my throat. Why would he come here? Shivers raked my spine, and a vague urge to put the heating on came out of nowhere. But I couldn't even walk to the thermostat: I was paralysed with fear. Did he want to do something to me? Or else why the hell had he come?

Last night I shouted across the water and dared him to come over. To show me his face.

What a stupid, stupid thing to do.

A loud bang.

One of the windows had been pushed open. Cannelloni's body slid through. He was gone.

Fuck! Thanks for leaving it unlatched, Alan.

I grabbed the dog cookie pouch and scrambled outside, slamming the barge door behind me. I jumped over the gap to the grassy side of the path, my gaze drifting in search of the bit of white fluff that could be his tail.

A sharp chill blasted through me. Strange to be so cold this time of year.

The fields to the right stretched pitch black, dead silent, and tiny lights twinkled where the land met the night sky; farmhouses or country pubs, miles away from here.

"Cannelloni!"

He stood quite far down the path, looking ahead in the darkness.

I shook the cookie bag, which is usually a sound that causes instant reaction: he comes running.

He swatted his tail right and left, sign that he heard me. Then shot off into the night.

"Oh, come *on*!"

I followed, as fast as I could go without running. I needed to get my dog back into safety; anything could happen to him if he went near the watcher.

As I left the boat behind a growing worry gnawed at me, a hardening tension on my shoulders. I shouldn't be out on the path right now.

What choice do I have? I'm sure as fuck not leaving my dog alone out there!

Pulled out my phone to switch on the torch. Phone was dead. The device unresponsive, as if it'd run out of battery. Which made no sense, I was sure I'd plenty juice earlier—I keep it charged in case Ami calls...

Must've been mistaken. Not much that could be done about it now. I shoved it in my pocket and tried to make peace with the fact I'd be doing this in the pitch fucking black.

I tried to remind myself that I knew this path well. We've moored here a whole lot over the years. This is a safe part of old English countryside, with picturesque villages and sleepy hamlets up and down the river. I have always felt at ease on the familiar Thames footpaths near Grandad's home moorings.

Not tonight.

I glanced one last time at the Lady Thomasine over my shoulder, its reflection on the waters shimmering softly in the distance; then I pressed on down the path, the night thickening all around me. The fields to my right emitted sounds of nightmare quality, sudden atrocious shrieks that faded into unworldly lamentation, or repulsive guttural squawks in frenzied, chaotic repetition. But I knew it was only the call of the foxes scuttling across the fields and the frogs ensconced in the watery undergrowth. Gooseflesh raised on my forearms and my pulse quickened as I stepped further into the dark. Even the stillness of the inky, languid waters of the river sweeping by, seemed ominous, unnatural. I wrapped my open knit cardi tighter around me, because leaves and soft branch tips I couldn't see, brushed against my arms and shoulders.

They smelled like fetid, terrible fingers of invisible spectral things; but of course, they were just the overgrowth of the path. I had zero visibility in the dark to duck and swerve away from them, as I normally would in my day walks. Feeling them suddenly run cold along my skin, it was not just icky; it was almost maddening. They left wet lines I had to rub away. I'd been out here this late a few times, now that I was a new dog owner. Sure, it's deserted after midnight; but it never felt like I was the only one left in the world.

No... not the only one. Instinct told me there was someone else. Someone lurking in the shadows, unseen.

"Cannelloni come on!" I shook his cookies again. "We need to get back inside!" He stopped to look at me for one second, then his head flicked around, ears standing sharp. His teeth were bared.

A funny shaped tree stump stood where the dog's line of sight guided my gaze. Backlit from the silvery shimmer of the inky river flowing beyond, it was silhouetted clearly from the tall birches on either side of it, and it had a hint of a human figure. But it couldn't be. The obscured outline was deathly still. Could those be shoulders? Very hunched, strangely shrivelling. Revealing a torso so tall and narrow, it appeared inhuman. There was something asymmetrical about the body, as if something was missing. It stirred a dormant horror deep within me. Or maybe it was the way the neck arched grotesquely, the head thrown back, like a wolf sniffing the night for prey.

I peeled my gaze away from it, scanning the tree lines and watery expanse whispering below.

When I glanced back at the tree stump, just to make sure, I couldn't find it.

He's moved.

But it was me who was moving, ever walking onwards after my dog, and the scenery changed around me as different shrubs appeared or hid behind the trees at various angles.

My poor dog's throat swelled with rumbling growls. I have never seen him do that with things he likes to chase after, like squirrels and deer. He wasn't play-chasing this person. He was terrified.

I still couldn't see anyone. I had managed to sneak quite close to my dog and decided to run the last few steps. The clip of his lead in my hand, I aimed straight for the ring on his collar.

He leapt forth with a yelp and galloped away.

"No, no don't!" I called pointlessly as a strange foreboding tightened my chest. I ran after him. I had to stop him before he caught up with whoever watched us from the shadows. Sprinting after an escaped dog is not the best strategy, but I didn't care.

I peered into the trees, scanning for movement in the distance.

A disconcerting shape sat still among the trees separating the path from the fields to my right. Quite far ahead still. But undoubtable.

Well, that's a bit distressing.

Between the straight narrow outlines of the tree barks, a wider frame of shoulders, a round black shape of a head, a figure of human height. It *was* him I'd seen before, from further away. And now a little closer, I knew the figure from all the previous nights. Only this time, he was on *my* side of the river.

"Cannelloni stay away! No! Don't go there! Cannelloni? Where are you?"

My dog had disappeared into the reeds.

I walked as fast as I could, peering among the trees.

The stranger didn't make a move. He couldn't have grabbed him. He was just standing there.

Maybe I was panicking for no reason? I tried to think rationally as I slowed to a walk, panting hard, unable to keep running. Ok there's someone on the path, but maybe there's a legit reason for it. Fishing? Too late. Maintenance work? No high vis jacket or torchlight. Dog walking? Too still. And not homeless either.

Destitute people stay in urban areas, not this empty countryside in the middle of nowhere.

He was looking in my direction. And he still hadn't moved.

He's here for me.

"Come here boy!" I called as casually as I could, aware the stranger could hear, but not wanting him to know I was scared out of my wits.

Ok even if he was here for me, was it for me specifically? Or was it a random creep waiting for any woman passing by? No facial features or any other details were visible. Just like every other night, he was only a dark figure in the distance. Although his outline was now so familiar, I just knew it was him.

He's here for me.

I frisked myself for my keys and I felt my fingers lacing the whole set from my keyring between my knuckles, before I realised I was doing it; pure muscle memory. At this point I normally set my intention to key a fucker in the gut, sure to leave a good bruise and have him doubled over in pain, but *this* arsehole had really pissed me off. If he made the mistake to come at me now, he'd taste a key through the eyeball.

That thought did not make me feel any safer. I had a vague sense this was not among my best laid plans... So, what was I supposed to do? Let him get away with it?

But with what, exactly? What did he want? That's what I needed to know.

I couldn't figure it out. My mind went blank. All I could feel was dread for the moment I would walk past him. He would then be *behind* me. I wouldn't be able to see his next move.

He was still quite far ahead, which gave me some time.

Good.

No.

Wait... How was this possible?

He's not getting any closer.

I was still walking and the distance between us should have gotten smaller. It didn't. The figure appeared a little further down the road every time I blinked. Felt like a video-game glitch.

He never walked while I kept my eyes on him.

No one can move so fast and stand so still.

Was I asleep? Was I having a nightmare?

No, I'm awake. My nightmares are spilling in my waking life.

Still the same distance away, with every step I took toward him. I fixed my gaze on the figure and willed myself not to blink. Three steps, six steps, my eyes were dry, ten steps, eyes now burning. Fifteen steps.

It turns out eyes blink of their own accord even when you tell them not to.

And he's moved.

No longer between the pair of narrow trees, he was now further down the path, his shoulders visible over some shrubs. I missed his transition in a single blink.

How is he moving away like a flicker on a screen?

That feeling of unreality. The creeping dread I'd been living with the last few months. Ever since the nightmares started and I was sent home.

I've lost my mind.

A great big growl alerted me to a short, four-legged shadow among the trees, its scruff standing on end.

"*There* you are!" I gasped, relief washing over me. "And you see him too, boy." But of course! Cannelloni escaped tonight because of this man, whoever he is. That's what he's been going after.

It was a real person. I wasn't imagining it. I was glad; the supernatural doesn't compute... but this? I got this. Arseholes trying to intimidate me, they get what's coming.

"Cannelloni I'm not playing anymore. Come here!"

He didn't.

I'd had enough. I broke into a run.

Big mistake.

I hadn't noticed I'd veered into the slimy reeds lining the edge of the water just off the path, and my foot slipped, my leg flying sideways.

The world twirled as I tumbled. Pain erupted in my left knee and then my thigh crashed into a rock. As I bounced towards the water, I swerved and grabbed that rock with both hands, stopping my descent.

Agony blazed at the tip of a finger where I held on. One of my nails had broken right in half. It was sticking up like a sharp piece of plastic. The exposed flesh glistened red— not too much blood, but enough layers of skin removed that the end of my finger resembled a raw steak. Within moments, it felt like my entire hand was on fire.

At least I had stopped the fall. And I was mostly dry. Just inches away from the water, which was lucky. But that nail felt like my finger was dunked in a frying pan full of sizzling oil.

"Fucking brilliant!" I said, feeling wet patches of mud all along my trousers and sleeves.

And a wet nose on my cheek.

"Hey boy, I'm ok," I muttered. He licked my ear. I steadied my feet on the slippery reeds and let go of the rock with one hand, clipping his lead on his collar. "Gotcha!"

I had my dog back. Nothing would happen to him now.

Take him back to the boat, lock all the doors and windows, shower, and bed. I'll figure out a plan to deal with this prick tomorrow.

I'd be ready the next night he showed up.

But when I glanced around at the boat, I couldn't see it past the river bend.

How did we get this far out? I checked my watch. We'd been doing this for twenty minutes! That meant I was twenty minutes away from the boat.

For fuck's sake.

The ominous outline of head and shoulders stood still, same distance from me as always, glaring in my direction.

Well, at least the fucker hadn't hurt my dog, and we were going straight home. I blinked in relief.

Gone.

He'd vanished in that one split second. Accustomed to this by now, I scanned for him further away. He was nowhere to be seen.

Puzzled, this time I let my gaze drift back, to the trees near us.

There he was. The figure stood, stock still, beneath the arched bark of a willow that bent out over the water.

He'd moved *closer*.

Chapter Nine

Apparition

R *ight. Get to the bloody boat. Alive.*

Might help to get up, for a start.

I was still kneeling by the rock. My whole body ached from the tumble. But I'm no stranger to pain. Cannelloni sniffed my injured finger and nudged my legs, as I stood and scrambled up from the slippery riverbank and onto the main path.

I started for home at a brisk pace, Cannelloni on short lead at my heels.

I need to look behind. I need to see what he's doing.

My finger looked repulsive. Several cracks had separated the other half of the nail that hadn't been removed. Part of the soft nailbed underneath must have been sliced along the angry red cracks, because the nail was now black with blood.

The other half of the nail, that angling piece that looked like plastic, shot a new blast across my nerves every time it moved. I pinched carefully with two fingers and pulled very gently, to see if it could come off.

The pain was unfathomable.

I let it go, but I couldn't have it stick out like that either. I had to immobilise it.

Without slowing down, I used a tissue to gently press the nail back down on the skin.

It hurt much less than I expected, as if it was mere contact with oxygen that made the wound feel like being dragged on broken glass this whole time. The tissue turned red but wasn't soaked wet.

"I only have the doggy pouch attached to your lead, Cannelloni, with your pooper scooper bags. So that will be fun."

I used a new plastic baggie, wrapped tight around my finger, to keep the tissues in place. The knot I tied at the side of my finger looked ridiculous.

At least the pain was now reduced to a mild burning sensation, which I quickly put in the back of my mind. I walked faster.

The river bend was not far ahead. I'd be able to at least see the boat once we'd taken that turn.

I need to look behind.

My trousers seemed torn in several places. A quick inspection revealed that at least I wasn't bleeding anywhere. Though some angry red patches on my legs were throbbing. They'd be purple and blue tomorrow.

"Just a scrape, huh, boy?" Cannelloni regarded me with raised eyebrows as he trotted along.

I need to see what he's doing.

I couldn't do it. If he came after me, I'd hear his footsteps. The silence behind me meant no one was following me. I was at the river bend now; as soon as I cleared it, the barge would be within seeing distance.

No idea why I thought that would help; I'd still be ten minutes away. If I shouted loud enough, could Alan see me from the window?

The familiar meadows didn't give me comfort. The path was not peacefully meandering along the water like usual but seemed to coil through skeletal un-derbrush of crumbling vegetation. It had transformed into a desolate passage, crowded with lurking dangers and some lingering, unknowable threat.

I needed to stop being dramatic. There was no vague danger here. What had been happening was quite specific. The figure had to be connected to the static from the radio, but there was no clue as to what he wanted. The video of the execution, *that* had to be a hint. But I couldn't make sense of it. Those images were the reason I had been deemed unfit for service. The only issue here was who was sending those and why; whether it was the same person lurking on the path; and what the hell did they want from me.

I blinked in surprise. Ahead of me, the barge swayed gently in the distance, casting rippling strings of light on the black waters. We were in the home stretch.

A noise came from behind me.

Footsteps.

He was coming after me. An impulsive urge to face him once and for all surfaced its ugly head; can't let anger take over. I didn't come out prepared for a possible physical altercation. And Cannelloni was an uncontrolled variable— if I engaged, he'd try to help, and that shithead might kick him, or worse. No, right now objective was: *Bring team safe to base*— get my dog to the boat. I was almost there now. I walked faster.

Cannelloni suddenly resisted. He pulled and stood on his back legs, aiming for him.

"Ignore him, boy!" I whispered. The hound didn't appear to know the meaning of that word. I wrapped the lead around my good hand to keep the dog's head at the level of my knees, forcing him to look ahead and walk on. We needed to get inside.

The relentless pounding of hurried feet behind me, brought a grim sensation of imminent danger. I was so cold. My mind grew foggy. I focused on keeping my pace faster than his.

"Cannelloni you're not helping by trying to get him!" I said under my teeth. "I'll deal with him, later! Right now we need to get inside!" The hound finally obeyed. I felt terrible, on top of everything, putting the poor dog in this situation. He could have been adopted by a normal person in a nice and safe home... Instead, here he was, trying to protect me from stalkers, living in a house watched every night. I'd think of a way to make it up to him tomorrow.

The black web of boughs overhead loomed strangely quiet. I used to welcome the tunnel of foliage that shaded the path from the weather when I went for a jog in the daytime. Now it felt suffocating under those trees. Not a cricket, nor the hooting of a night bird broke the heavy silence.

That echoing sound of footsteps hounded me.

I monitored the noise, to know the gap between us did not become any smaller.

He picked up speed, slightly faster than me now.

I accelerated as much as I could without breaking into a run. Cannelloni whined loudly beside me. Then cried out in frustration, a long pitched call that rose to a howl. I've never heard the dog make that noise before. The pacing behind me caused my teeth to grind together.

The footfalls hammered louder and louder and became a swift beat.

He was running.

I spun around, standing tall, fists balled and seeking a target. The path was empty. Silent.

If he was agile enough to jump out of sight so fast, I couldn't afford to turn my back on him again. I started walking backwards.

I found it easy, and the dog leading the way made it even easier. Cannelloni led me down the familiar path towards our mooring, he wanted to go back home too. I kept my steady pace backwards, facing away from the boat, scanning the footpath I came from.

For a while nothing moved around me, the shadows of the trees were unchanged. Wherever he was hiding, he stayed put.

And finally, there was no more river to my left. Through the narrow glass door on top of a tiny staircase, I caught a glimpse of Grandpa's pilot hat, carelessly thrown on his ancient captain's high stool before the steering wheel. This was the little tower wheelhouse of the Lady Thomasine. We'd made it.

The sleepy vessel swayed on the quiet current, and whispering echoes of splashing waters, perpetually licking at the dark woodwork, rose from beneath it. A soft glow came from above, where Grandma had threaded strings of fairy lights along her handsewn bunting over the roof. The night was warm and brighter here. We were home.

Still retreating backwards, making sure he had not come down the path after me, I went past Grandad's window and mine, almost reaching the ramp to the deck.

Footsteps pounded behind me.

Behind me?

How was that possible? When did he get to the opposite end of the pathway? The clatter had a chilling quality, an echo welling up from fathomless depths.

I stopped moving, confused. Cannelloni went very quiet. A baffled look on his face, his head swerved back and forth, eyes narrowed, ears pricked.

I still hadn't turned around. I listened to the approaching footfalls.

Yes, from the direction beyond the barge, as if somehow the invisible stalker had run ahead of me. I took a deep breath.

I swerved around, landing boxing stance, fist up. I balanced for an uppercut to fracture a jawbone or pulverize a taller target's solar plexus.

The path beyond the boat was empty.

What?

The inexplicable silence mocked me. Not only he stopped walking when I did, but he also vanished when I turned to look.

My heart rate accelerated again, breaths rapid and shallow. My fist still raised; I stood powerless in the night.

Just get inside!

I lowered my fist and pulled the dog close. I stretched my leg over the narrow gap to my right, shaking. Caught a brief glimpse of the black waters flowing beneath me, and then I was on the barge.

The hound and I sprinted across the deck as I made a bee line for the door, key in hand. I fumbled to get it in the lock. Somehow it wouldn't go in.

Panic overran my thoughts, making them roll rapid and chaotic. I couldn't peel my gaze from the path, trying to see where he was, because he had to be here, hiding. And which side? The side we came from or the other side? The footsteps had come from everywhere. Fidgeting blindly, one handed, holding the dog lead and looking at the path the whole time, was not getting the damn key in the damn lock. I had to keep my eyes on the bloody door.

Did he run past me behind the trees? So cold! No, not possible. I would have heard him. Where is he? Why am I so fucking cold? Did he really come from the other side of the path? Maybe there's two of them. But where are they? I'm fucking freezing. Well maybe there's ten of them, how does that help when I can't see them?

"Shut up and focus!" I said out loud. This chattering in my head was totally foreign to my usual processing of any tactical threat, whether cyber or combat.

This isn't me. Focus.

I wrapped the dog's lead around my wrist and let go of the handle, freeing my hand. I kneeled. I brought the lock level to my eyes. I held up my phone, and just the screen light was enough to see what I was doing.

I slid the key in.

The door opened.

We ran inside and closed it behind us. I double locked it and stood there, panting hard. One hand still on the door, the other holding the lead.

We were safe. We'd made it. It was over now, I could relax. Have a shower, get back to bed... My heart was still racing. Cannelloni stood tense at my feet.

"He's still out there, isn't he, boy? Nothing he can do now. He'll get bored and leave."

A beeping sound made me jump.

My phone was ringing.

I pulled it out reluctantly, expecting to see some unknown number. Expecting it to be him.

It wasn't. I smiled and answered right away.

"Leela what are you doing up?" But of course, she'd be pulling an all nighter again. I kept forgetting she was a uni student now.

The two heads blinking at me from the screen were not human.

The deformed flatness of the snouts, the sunken noses, the painful piled up wrinkles, the asymmetrical eye sockets too far apart, the eyeballs bulging, squinting cross eyed and almost popping out of the skulls.

"Leela, why are the pugs looking at me."

The image zoomed out a bit to reveal the dogs were sitting with a sign propped up against them.

'Smoosh-heads want to say 'Sorry!' They didn't mean to bring up things you're not ready to talk about!"

I bit my lip to hide a smile and kicked off my muddy shoes. I headed to the couch feeling the soft carpet under my tired feet. I collapsed into the couch with relief, keeping the hound with me. He was looking anxious at the windows. And the window he'd escaped from was still open. I had no energy right now to get back up and shut it, so the dog was staying on the lead.

"Jade?"

"Ok, you're forgiven Leela," I said.

"Yay, thanks!" Leela's beaming face appeared on the screen, but I could still see the pugs in the background, as she gave them a handful of treats for good performance.

"But from now on," I said, stretching out my aching legs on the cushions, "can you not make a big deal of it? I needed a change of career. I wanted to be home. That's all."

It's so hard, to lie. I *hate* doing it.

"Kay, I guess," she said looking unconvinced but clearly wanting to move on. "Whatcha doin?"

My breath had slowed down to normal and I was starting to feel the tiredness the adrenaline had masked. I leaned back on the cushion with a sigh.

"Just back from walking the dog."

"Shall I come pick you up for a movie night sleep over?"

"That's a hard no."

"Why?"

"Well, Dad and your Mum didn't want me staying there, did they. So I'd rather not be an imposition."

"What are you talking about?"

I rubbed my aching eyes, wondering if the stalker was still out there, thinking I should go and close the window. It wasn't big enough for a grown man to get through, but still. I shouldn't take any chances. I pushed myself up again.

"I'm talking about your Mum turning my bedroom into a bloody craft studio. I asked to stay there when I came home, just while I was sorting my shit out, but no. They sent me packing to Grandad. So no, I won't be having sleep overs at the house ever again. Sorry." I snapped the window shut and locked the handle.

I still didn't free the dog. He was now low-growling again.

"Gosh I'm sorry Jade. I didn't know you felt this way. But sure, let's do movie night at my dorms. We shouldn't give up on sisterhood traditions just because of all that stuff with you and the parental units!"

"I keep forgetting you have a room at college now. You still look like the squeaky five-year-old who threw a tantrum when I brought you an RAF air cadets' outfit, instead of a prom dress, for your barbie doll."

I fell into the couch again and pulled the dog in, rubbing his ear to calm him down. He was watching the windows. But there was nothing outside as far as I could see.

Leela beamed.

"Trust me, I'm over it. And we are doing movie night at mine this week, I won't stop calling you until you say yes."

That's when the world disappeared.

It re-appeared right away. I blinked. It took me a second to catch up. The lights on the boat had flickered. It had felt a lot darker than just the lights going out. It had felt like a veil parted, disintegrating all material existence into a black void, an undecipherable nothingness, where inexplicable horrors were about to spawn. But no, the lights were back up, the lounge was still here, and so was I.

And Leela was still talking.

"I had no time to ask yesterday, have – any news – Ami? When – home?" Her voice was cutting out. "Jade? You th..."

My phone died.

The boat went dark.

I jumped to my feet. It took a moment for my eyes to adjust to the pitch black. My mind raced while I stood there, blind.

The TV's background noise is gone from Alan's berth. And the hordes of Tiffany lamps in here, littered round Grandma 's legion of coffee tables. All gone at once.

Is it right to be so cold in the summer?

Why is Grandad not putting the TV back on? Probably asleep.

As my eyes accustomed to the darkness, shapes begun to appear. The couches, the love seat, black outlines against the gloom.

Cannelloni's growl was a deep, hostile rumble, like a wild animal.

The panic returned. A tornado of thoughts in my mind.

And the fairy lights in the garden. Gone. The watcher... he could have turned those off if he came on the deck very quietly. My fingers are numb, turning blue.

I looked out of the window. There was no one on the deck. I walked along all the windows, making sure. The hound didn't object this little patrol around the lounge, even though I kept his lead short.

Nothing outside.

Maybe it was only a generator failure? But no. Grandma 's winged fairies and painted-glass butterflies outside had all gone out too; and those were all solar powered lamps she had stabbed in each and every one of her flower-pots. The generator didn't power them. They would have to be switched off manually, one by one. How did they all go out at once?

This is more like a graphite bomb taking out all electrical grids on the houseboat ... My phone was dead in my hand too. But who would do this? Why put so much effort to get to me? What did they want?

"Just shut up for a second," I murmured to myself, hoping the sound of my own voice would stop my thoughts unravelling. The radio had lost signal when I came near it. Could the barge be losing power in much the same way? And then, when I got closer to the radio, it started talking to me in strange tongues.

I waited, half expecting a creaky, malevolent whisper to groan my name from the woodwork.

Cannelloni didn't wait. He pulled at the lead towards the centre of the room, his teeth bared.

Someone's here. Right in here with us.

I scanned the familiar outlines of the couches, window seat and my desk monitors, determined to detect the slightest movement.

No one here.

But something was different. Something was happening. I didn't know how I knew, but I was sure.

I tried to reason with my rising anxiety: No one could get inside. The house-boat was locked from every side. There was no way. It was simply impossible.

He's right there.

The unmistakable outline of shoulders and a head, a person standing in the centre of the room.

My breathing faltered. I wanted to take in a breath, but it turned into a feeble cough. My lungs had shrivelled from the shock. That figure had not been there before.

And I never saw him rising from behind anything. He just appeared in the blink of an eye.

For once, the hound was frozen in complete surprise, like me. A stillness swept the main cabin.

Like time had ceased.

It wasn't a person. Even the dog was just as stunned as I was. We were looking at a shadow. A shadow that was somehow not cast on a floor or wall, but just on thin air. Vertical in the middle of the room.

I blinked again, trying to make sense of what my eyes saw.

A shadow in the air. A shadow in a lightless room.

I know this figure. It's him!

The watcher. The outline broader at the shoulders, ending with the oval head, without any features. The impossibly tall and narrow figure, not quite a human shape. Made of darkness.

No, he couldn't be a shadow, it must be someone dressed in complete black that blended flawlessly into the gloom.

But there was smoke around the edges.

His limps dissolved to nothing. Where on the floor... where was he standing? He wasn't touching the floor at all.

"Who are you?" I kept my voice even. "What do you want?"

My right-hand muscles tensed, as I resisted the firm pull on the dog's lead. He tried to pounce at the intruder in the dark, but the lead stretched and bounced his slender body back, so the dog crashed against my legs.

The man lurched forward.

His face gained shape out of the darkness.

I was queasy by how unnatural it appeared. I thought some moonbeam must have illuminated his features, but that wasn't it.

The contorted contours of the face somehow glowed. Like a hideous light-up mask, the visage emerged out of the darkness, pressing through it, as if it were a barrier. Like a deathly face struggling viciously against a black sheet. The staggering apparition writhed and twisted, then its bizarre countenance leaned in towards me, the skull lines protruding unnaturally out of pitch black, and I had to swallow a scream.

It was trying to take form behind the veil, and the dark sheet of smoke prevented it. The face pressed against it, closer and closer to me.

Then the head stopped moving, an inch from my nose. The ethereal smoke that surrounded it, swirled with my every breath.

The hair stood on the back of my neck.

I expected hands to grow out of the smoke and grab my throat, but the face was attached to a contorted shape without discernible human parts. The gruesome spectre was still rooted where it had first appeared, yet diagonally stretched across the room, so the head was next to my face.

And then the eyes opened. A chilling menace dripped into my very soul.

The eyes glowed like burning headlights in a dark tunnel. I stared, mesmerized. The whites were ghastly yellow and the irises vivid hazel. Emerald drops sparkled around the iris.

His eyes.

I lost all control of my limbs. I heard a crash and realised it was my knees hitting the floor.

I braced myself against the door frame, my legs refusing to bend to my will, as every sense dulled beneath a cold blanket of dread. The skull shape from which the eyes blazed, had the features of a familiar face.

Not him. It can't be him.

The ghastly entity pushing against the mysterious, shifting veil, pressed furiously once again, trying to close the distance to my face, where I'd crumpled to the ground; then closer. Its long narrow body stretched now across the floor, a repulsive anomaly, so much like a giant serpent with its tail caught in a profound struggle to break free. It was still trapped in the rippling sheets of black smoke stemming from the other end of the room, where it had first appeared; but its gaze was fixated, monstrous and immovable, on me.

Closer.

I wanted to lift my arms to cover my face, shield my head behind my elbows, but I was left to stare into its frightful eyes.

Closer still. That mystifying veil, stretching at the open pit of its gaping jaws, was about to touch my forehead.

I tried again. I couldn't. My arms, like my legs, were not functional.

And Cannelloni was free.

He lunged, dragging his long lead behind him.

"No, don't go near that!" I shouted, but it only came out as a croaking whisper.

I tried to scramble to my feet, but my limbs were numb, frozen stiff in the gloom. I watched helplessly as the grim outline rose to tower over my dog— and then, the impossible happened.

He pulled away from my dog.

Cannelloni had gone for the root of the spectre across the room, ignoring the fearful face hovering above me. Nearing the smoke that pooled there, he crouched, ready to pounce.

The shadow shot back, shrinking away with an urgency I could not explain.

It didn't walk. It imploded, dissolving backwards with the same unnatural, oblique trajectory from which it had extended.

And then it was no longer there.

Cannelloni sprang and reached high into the air after it, his jaws snapping into nothing but smoke.

Not even smoke. There was nothing left of the figure by the time the dog landed on his feet again.

The lights came back on.

It happened all at once, from the garden and the kitchen and all around the main cabin. Blinded by the sudden glare, I wondered if the generator had come back on by itself.

I didn't allow myself to blink. Gradually, my sight adjusted to the colourful brightness of the multiple Tiffany lamps, the glow of the fairy lights from the garden and the soft overnight light in the kitchen. There was nothing in Grandma 's vintage sitting room except the dog.

And the dog was no longer on edge. No growls, no baring his teeth. He looked at me. Smugly? Self-satisfied. Then, his tail wagging with glee, he trotted off to his water bowl to lap with loud splashing, as he always does after a walk. Like nothing had happened.

My mind was reeling. What had I just seen?

I used the back of my sleeve to wipe drops of cold sweat rolling down my temples to my cheeks. My wrist was shaking. I felt fluid, like all my muscles had turned to goo.

What was that? Was it an intruder? No. It was something else.

The image of him leaning away into the darkness and shrinking into nothing kept replaying in my mind. The ice-cold dread dripped acid in my stomach.

Was it really gone? I needed it to be gone. I couldn't take anymore of this.

Cannelloni returned from his bowl with a contented look and jumped on the window seat, spinning around in circles before plopping down on the cushions for a nap. So yeah, the dog agreed: the man was no longer on the boat. I stood gingerly and my feet erupted with pins and needles under my weight, as if the carpet was made of tiny razors.

It blinked into fucking existence and out again. It was someone's shadow, a shadow that moved by itself. It was smoke, with a man's face behind it.

I staggered across the room and collapsed onto the couch. I reached out and touched the side arm as if to check the love seat was real. Grandma 's crocheted rose throw and pink cushions, slightly tattered and faintly smelling of lavender, were innocuous as ever.

Those eyes. They were burned into my mind. This stalker—

It was *him*.

So, what'd been happening wasn't *about* the man they executed. It *was* the man they executed.

But how was it possible?

The dead don't stalk the living.

Chapter Ten

The Man In The Mist

"He's dead, Mum. The shadow in the lounge had that poor guy's eyes." Jade had her face half buried in her hands, her voice muffled, as she hunched where she sat by the tombstone. "What is going on?"

It was a warm night. A waning crescent moon was rising. Tomorrow would be a moonless night.

The soft rush of the Thames was soothing, drifting behind the churchyard walls. Jade lifted her face to look around. Green reflections glittered on the cobalt blue of her eyes, as she watched the perpetual rippling of the weeping willows. The foliage had an eerie quality as its tendril tips tickled the tombstones from above. There was always an enigmatic feeling here in this cemetery. A silent echo of something stirring behind an invisible veil.

"It's ten thirty. So much for not staying past sunset, huh?" Jade rolled her eyes and shook her head at the tombstone, as if it was going to nod and grin back. "Anyway, I'm not sure why I was dreading being here after dusk. It's fine," she shrugged. "On a more important note... I've run out of hazelnut butter," she said, holding up the empty spread jar, where the knife rattled uselessly. She brushed at her lap with her hands. Where the loaf of bread had been sitting a while ago, only crumbs remained; she flicked them away. Licking her lips, she shook her head. "Can't believe I finished all that in one go. What the hell is wrong with me? Think your friend Sarah will give me another jar?" She tried to smile but failed.

Her face grew still, her eyes glazing over.

Ghosts? Are we talking ghosts?

Jade shook her head. She inspected the sticky white bandage that was neatly wrapped at the edge of her finger. She nodded, pleased it had no red marks blossoming from underneath. The bleeding had stopped.

"I'm such a mess, Mum! This morning I woke up with a doggy poopy bag still tied into a knot on my fingertip. Woke up is a figure of speech, though, for someone who barely shut their eyes for an hour. The whole night was me dozing off and waking up screaming with nightmares. Same old, same old. I'd had to climb on the barge roof in the morning and get some rack time in the sun for an hour or two. As you do. Stumbled back into my cabin when the footpath got too busy, to try and start the day, at least, before noon.

When I removed the doggy bag, to wash my face in the bathroom, the nail was stuck back on the nailbed that was completely black with dried blood. It would probably fall off when the wound healed underneath. But I bandaged it tight, and now it only hurt if it touched anything.

I couldn't jog or cycle today. I'm covered in gashes and bruises that would tear open or sear in agony at the slightest exertion. So I spent the day working on my laptop, trying not to get annoyed at having to type without my index finger. I refused to think about the thing.

The shadow in the lounge.

I promised myself I would only think about it tonight, when I came to see you. Otherwise, I would get nothing done. So, at nightfall, I closed down the laptop and hopped on the bike, for the slowest, most painful ride in the history of cycling; and here I am.

One more night at the cemetery.

Good thing was, they know me at the Danish bakery down the road; Peter's Mum still remembers you. When I told them I'm home for good and I'm visiting you, Peter told me to pop by after they closed, for a freshly baked loaf for my evening picnic. Got to give it to the Danes, they don't sweat a bit of morbid melancholia," Jade said with a glint in her eye. "Nighttime picnic at the graveyard? Sure, come get bread fresh from the oven, and say hi to Evelyn from my ma."

Jade shrugged, briefly amused. Then the silence wrapped heavy around her, and her eyes were downcast.

"I wish you were here, Mum. I need someone I can talk to. Someone who will believe me and help me make sense of it. Of what's happening! And who won't tell anyone else. I can't have Dad finding out." She sighed. "He already thinks I've lost it, ever since I told him about the nightmares." She shook her head, trying and failing to shake the dark images from her mind.

Ghosts. Fucking ghosts.

"You know what?" Jade said as she pulled out her phone. "Time to get some answers." She spoke the question aloud as she typed it in: "Are ghosts real?"

"Right. 'Not scientifically proven.' Yeah, tell me about it! Okay... I wasn't asleep, so not a dream. Hmm, mould? What the fuck? No. I don't keep the boat Charleen-clean but I know we don't have mould either. Hallucinations... ok, sure, that fits. I guess the next question is—"

Jade shivered as she tapped the words into the search bar: "Am I going insane?" She scrolled through the results. "Lack of sleep will cause psychosis. Right. That fits too. Lack of sleep is my middle name." With a sigh, she slipped the phone back into her trouser pocket.

"But I don't think it was a hallucination, Mum. You know why? Cannelloni saw it too." Jade turned around and leaned against the tombstone, resting the back of her head on the cold stone. "And if the victim of that execution really showed up last night, then... shit. What if he really *did* turn around in that video? What if he really *did* look at me from the screen?" She shuddered violently as her shivers intensified.

"How could a ghost send someone a video? Of course, that would explain why I never found a trace of a file with my scans. And the creepy static from the radio. A dead man calling my name." Jade chuckled at the incredulity of it all. "Ah, bollocks. It wasn't a ghost for fuck's sake. That guy last night was human. He ran off while the dog was loose, and came after us when Cannelloni was on the lead. A flesh-and-blood, scared-he-might-get-bitten, garden variety shithead. But then, he wasn't exactly *running* away, was he? More like he was flickering. Reappearing further down the path, like a live feed stuttering through weak WIFI. Not like a human being at all."

Phone back in hand, Jade began typing again.

"Can dogs see ghosts?" She scrolled down a bit. "Okay, ignoring the 'not scientifically proven' part, *again*—which I can't believe I'm doing, by the way, but hey—looks like hundreds of pages of articles on how dogs in mythology and folklore are said to see the spirit world and guard against it. Brilliant. Cannelloni the bodyguard. The protector. Against ghosts."

Jade sighed, deep and loud.

"Actual freaking ghosts."

Jade's nose wrinkled and her eyes squinted in a worried grimace. Then her head snapped up, eyes searching. She quickly sat up and knelt forward to a tense crouch, without taking her gaze from the trees.

There was no one there.

A sense of warning kept her searching the area for movement.

The fog. It was gathering again in the old cemetery. It looked like movement because it wasn't thickening into existence out of early morning humidity. Instead, it spilled out from behind the tombstones in the ancient burial ground.

Jade frowned, watching the grey vapours surge.

This is unnatural...

It must be coming from the river, for sure. The water was just behind the wall on that side of the cemetery. Condensation from the Thames had to be causing it.

This is dangerous...

It pooled like an odd grey lake. Jade felt a twinge in her stomach. Her logical brain struggled against the primal fear these thoughts awakened.

"Okay, it's just mist, why am I so worried about it? Time for an emergency appointment," she muttered.

It's not just mist.

She pulled out her phone and put a reminder for tomorrow morning: 'Get emergency booking with PTSD counsellor'. She scowled, returning her phone to her pocket.

Therapist's going to say I dreamed the shadow in the boat. But who cares. Let it be someone else's problem. It's her job to make it stop, right?

Ghosts... I'm someone who believes in ghosts now.

"Shut up!" she muttered aloud.

Was the mist getting closer? She rubbed her eyes and looked again.

The grey haze spilled out over the lawn. It had swallowed the path dividing the old part of the cemetery from this side, where the graves had fresh flowers, and inscriptions dated in the last 80 years.

How bizarre. She'd never seen mist approach so fast.

It's unsafe, need to get away from it... Go-go-go!

Standing up, Jade backed up a few steps.

"I'm gonna have to call it here. I need to get away from this freaky mist, Mum. I can't explain... I don't... I just really don't want it touching me. I guess I'm truly getting paranoid." She rubbed her forehead with shaking fingers. "Bye, see you again soon." Kissing her fingers, she touched them to the tombstone and shrugged her backpack on.

The grey smoke oozed up over the path, her only way to the exit quickly vanishing under the milky vapours. Now the only way out was to the right, from the front of the church.

Nope, that was too close to the vicar's cottage. What if they were up late? Should she risk it? Couldn't handle another attempt to explain why she was here in the middle of the night.

Just walk through the damn mist, for fuck's sake. Fastest way to the bike!

She could see her bike, tied to the railings at the side of the cemetery gates, just across the spreading lake of fog. A few minutes fast walk.

Not going through the mist! Look at it, it's revolting! No idea how fog can look gooey like that.

But if she tried to go around the church and leave via the front of the church grounds, she'd end up in the village main street, a total of over half an hour to return to the river path and the cemetery gates. What a pointless, irrational thing to do.

Just walk through it.

She headed for the mist.

A few paces away, she shuddered and stopped. Couldn't do it. Her gut twisted in knots at the very thought of it. The fog was forcing her towards the church.

I'm so exhausted. Why is it so hard to make a simple decision? What's the matter with me?

She looked around for somewhere to sit for a second. An angel stood weeping on a tall pedestal five paces away.

Jade hopped and plonked uncomfortably on the edge of the square plinth, right beside the angel's bare feet. The stone toes were covered in moss, as they peeked under the granite gown, while the angel knelt in eternal prayer over the name of the deceased.

Movement in the darkness made her look up.

A man marching among the graves. Seemingly borne out of the darkest depths of the night, he had embarked on some graveside expedition of utmost importance, judging by the tempestuous urgency of his stride. There was an unusual gravitas in his slender bearing, although any respectability it might render was mitigated by his bouncy curls and slightly odd manner.

Jade ducked. Hidden behind the flowing granite skirts of the weeping angel, she peered to see.

Was this the stalker?

He didn't appear to have seen her, as he almost ran down the cemetery path.

Is he looking for me?

The peculiar vapours coiled around the bottom of his coat that trailed to the ground. Jade cringed at the thought of someone letting the mist touch them like that.

Where did he come from?

The ancient burial ground? Surely that was impossible. No entrance that way.

This has happened before.

The strong feeling of deja-vu made her apprehensive, because at the same time, she had no recollection of this man.

At least there was one reassuring thing about him: he didn't resemble the sombre figure of the stalker. He had a goofy, uncertain gait, graceful slender shoulders, and an elegant stature. And the stalker was always menacingly still, a dark outline with its attention fixed on Jade.

This bloke sprinted down the cemetery path, towards the exit, heading away from Jade's hiding spot in the heart of the churchyard. His coat billowed behind him, and he had an air of panic about him.

Why do I feel like I know him?

He bounced the last few paces to the gates, behaving weirder and weirder. He came to an abrupt halt at the wrought iron arch of the gates, his arms flailing as if to stop his body from crossing an invisible line. He stood there looking at the sleepy village road outside.

But there was nothing there.

He jumped backwards away from it, panting hard.

What the...? What does he see that I don't?

Jade narrowed her eyes, trying to find something in the empty country road. Nothing at all.

As if too scared to stay there long, the man retreated from the gates. Walking backwards, never losing sight of them, he wiped his brow; his face darted left and right, as if checking the perimeter.

Is he looking for me?

He was a lot closer to Jade now, still with his back to her as he retreated facing the gates. Treading the swamp of swirling mists. Not seeing where he was going, he bumped into one of the lampposts lighting the path.

Startled, he recoiled sharply. As if the metal of the lamppost had zapped him with an electric surge.

Then, even weirder: instead of turning around, seeing it was just a lamppost and relaxing a bit, he turned around, saw it was a lamppost and his gaze shot up it. As if expecting to see someone hanging from the lantern top.

The man squared his stance and Jade recognised, from the way his legs were wide apart making his long coat into a triangle, that he was about to pull out a gun.

He slipped his hand behind his neck and grasped it from between his shoulder blades.

Jade's whole body stiffened.

She didn't have an issue with the presence of the firearm. She'd be glad for it if the situation warranted it. But this was a sleepy riverside cemetery in the heart of the Home Counties, and that was not a hunting rifle. Jade frowned. It had the general short and thick shape of a double barrel handgun or revolver, but it looked somehow unfamiliar.

He wasn't aiming yet so she couldn't see it well.

He pointed it to the ground, half concealed behind the folds of his trailing coat, his stare fixed on the light.

Jade stared.

There was absolutely nothing there.

He pulled up the tip of his sleeve and tapped on the wristband there. Jade nodded: she knew it. He *did* have coms gear on.

"I need help. Can you come here?" he said to his wrist.

"When?" replied a woman's voice.

"Just now, please."

Jade slammed her back against the granite skirt of the angel. He was getting backup.

He's not after me, he doesn't seem to know I'm here. Let's keep it that way. Get the hell out.

"What is it?" The woman on the other end of the call was not impressed.

"There's something out there..." his voice was shaky. He must have been a lot more nervous than he looked. "I don't know what it is, but it's big." His gaze was fixed away to the cemetery gates.

"What do you see?" the woman asked from the other end of the call.

"I'm not sure..."

"Can you be more specific please?" She sounded posh; her politeness had a thinly veiled impatience.

Jade leapt off the ledge and landed softly on the grass.

He never noticed. He chewed on his lip, scanning the darkness in the distance.

Her escape plan was simple: duck from tombstone to tombstone in the opposite direction from the gun man, and get out via the front of the church, even if it *was* the long way around.

A slight chill. A hint of a frosty whisper crawled along her spine. The tiniest memory of the way she felt when the stalker was around.

Her feet twitched like she had jumped in an icy puddle. She looked down. White swirled around her ankles.

The mist had reached her.

She'd forgotten about the encroaching fog, but it was now stretching as far as the eye could see. And with a yawn, Jade was suddenly sleepy.

"I cannot see it enough to identify. It's lurking behind the wall," the man was explaining. "The circle is buzzing. I've got several breach warnings. It's trying to get in."

What... circle... What buzzing? What is he talking about...

Jade would have rolled her eyes if her lids weren't so heavy. For a moment she contemplated resting her head on the stone angel and dozing off for a few moments. What harm would it do?

Sleep... Is this how I ended up asleep... at the steps of the church the other morning?
She forced her eyes open.

When that didn't work, she tried to concentrate.

Get moving... Stay awake...

But her feet were heavy like lead. In this blinding stupor, each step was a struggle.

The angel loomed over her head. Why was she trying to get away from it? Without thinking about it, she climbed up the pedestal where she'd been sitting, and didn't stop there. Dizzy and with eyes half shut, Jade climbed all the way up the angel statue.

Once nestled securely between her wings at the nape of her neck, Jade took a deep, refreshing breath. The river breeze was crisp and rose scented. What was she doing up here? She looked down the sheer drop from her perch, like waking from a dream.

Oh, I was running away from the vapours.

Acutely aware of that menacing mist below, Jade observed it closely. The texture, thick and unnatural, its opaqueness vanishing into a solid pearly grey. In a peculiar way, it seemed heavy: it stayed under knee level and sloshed like cream cooking into custard. Never before had she seen a gas agent behaving this way.

It's the mist that made me lethargic.

Jade looked at the only other person in the churchyard. She'd missed some of his animated conversation but now the voices came loud and clear once again.

"Maybe you've just got a runner?" said the woman's voice, sounding almost amused.

"No," he grunted. "It's not one of mine!" His chin jutted up, offended. "I keep my place tidy! Everyone is asleep..." He glanced around mid-sentence, his shoulders hunching guiltily. Jade had this strange certainty he was looking directly at the violin on her Mum's grave. Then he corrected himself: "Well *almost* everyone."

"What does *that* mean?"

"Trust me, no one is trying to get out," he insisted, looking away into the cemetery gates and squaring his shoulders. "It's the opposite. Something trying to get *in*."

I'm trapped. I need to get away from here.

Jade frowned at the grey smog that licked the coat of the man, coiling up to his knees.

How is he standing right in it without falling asleep?

He'd been walking around this whole time, the pearly tendrils swirling around him. It didn't seem to affect him one bit.

Biological warfare? Who's doing this? Is it him? And am I the target?

"Fine, I'll come check it out," replied the posh lady with a sigh.

"Thank you, Theo!" He sounded relieved, his eyes never leaving the gates in the distance, gun still in one hand.

"You owe me, newb. I'm pausing my Wick solo practice to get there. It's not often an alto gets cast for the gardener's part in the Secret Garden. I can't afford mistakes."

"Sorry, I don't speak Musical Theatre, you might want to tell me that again in English," he replied, as he sprinted to the nearest tombstone.

"Less snark, more gratitude, newb, or I'm not coming."

"No sorry, no snark, I'm eternally grateful!" He propped his shoulder bag on it with urgency, plucking out a small chest box and setting it carefully on the stone. "Where are you?" The lid popped open and his hand hovered over a multitude of linen pouches, waiting for her reply.

"Home." There was so much of the Queen's English breathed into that one syllable, that Jade instantly pictured some manor on a hilltop. She covered her mouth to hide a chuckle, surprised she'd find anything funny in this predicament.

Great. Even being close to this gas makes me tipsy. This is serious, focus!

What did he have that she didn't, rendering him immune?

The man had lost no time. His fingers dived for a specific pouch and freed it from the others, tossing it in the air with flair and catching it energetically.

"On my way," he said, as another hidden compartment slid open as if of its own accord. From it he claimed a series of fanciful, clockwork objects. Jade couldn't decide if they were mechanical devices or just a bunch of jars that some unoriginal wedding planner had stuffed with fairy lights to make into bridal lanterns.

She chortled again.

You're being an idiot. Need to get the fuck out of here.

The man slid his gun between his shoulder blades with a weary sidelong glance towards the cemetery gates. He snapped the side compartment closed, and trotted off hurriedly, jars tucked under one arm, the pouch heavy in his other hand.

He forgot the main lid is open. And left it unattended. If I had a safe way to cross the mist to that box, I could nick all his stuff.

Jade looked at his outfit, trying to understand what protected him from the gas that perpetually licked the bottom of his coat. The fabric was thick and shiny, and seemed to have a black-on-black pattern woven in with metallic thread that faintly glimmered when he moved. She caught a glimpse of combat grade boots underneath.

So then, several layers of protection.

Jade looked at her own light cargos and trainers. She searched her pockets for old hairbands and found two. Hastily, she used the elastic bands to tuck the end of her trousers tight around her ankles, limiting the amount of exposed skin between her trousers and shoes.

She hoped this would work. The gas must have attacked the nervous system through the skin earlier. It was the only explanation: the lethargy hit her when she stood in the mist ankle deep. She hoped the elastic keeping her trousers tucked in would not let the gas up her trouser legs. At least now she thought she had a much better chance. All she needed was the right moment to run away.

He had retreated a good distance away into the wall of fog, in the taunting depths of the ancient section of the cemetery. His figure was only a dark shadow against a strange purple glow. It took a moment for Jade to realise from the way he kept bending to the ground and causing the glow to get brighter, that he was leaving the lanterns on the ground and igniting them.

It's now or never.

Jade held on to the wings of the angel as she climbed down her back. Then she slid carefully to the pedestal and sat on it, dangling her feet over the mysterious vapours. Holding her breath, she jumped in.

Didn't sit around to examine the chilly tingling sensation at her feet.

She ran.

Eyes fixed on the tiny shape of her bike tied on the railings by the cemetery gates, she sprinted towards the cemetery path. The pooling vapours sloshed angrily at her knees as she disturbed the lake of mists.

She was walking.

Her head pounded with a migraine.

She was standing still.

Chin bounced off her collarbone...

No! Climb on something, anything!

With the last of her resolve, she hauled her body on top of the nearest tomb; then heaved her feet up and curled herself into a ball, hugging her knees. Mists dripped down from her trouser legs and shoes, like thick tears weeping down the headstone. Then her feet felt warmer once again. The tiredness was dissipating.

Where am I?

I'm running away from this biohazardous fume. I've come a good distance.

She had managed to stay in the mist much longer than before. This could work. She could take breaks and keep going till the end of the cemetery. Judging by the distance she had covered and the distance remaining, she could get out with only three more stops. There were plenty of headstones along the way to sit on and wake herself up as needed.

This is good.

No. This is bad.

On the tombstone right beside her, was the box. She had somehow come and sat right next to the gun man's stuff. She glanced up to the ancient cemetery, scanning the fog for his figure.

The purple glow was now strong. A circle.

He stood in the middle of the circle of lanterns and was pouring some dark substance from the fat pouch in his hand.

Then, he wasn't there anymore.

She rubbed her eyes. Nope. Gone. The glowing circle still shimmered in the grey fog, but his silhouette was not there.

Where does he go and where does he come from?

I've asked this question before. And I've seen this damn box before! Just can't remember it. But I know the feeling.

It made her nauseous to look at. She felt she was eavesdropping on secretive whispers behind forbidden doors. Was it made of metal or black wood? One moment she thought she saw serpentine carvings along the sides and the next, the box almost completely blended into the darkness.

Jade rubbed her eyes again. The bag beside the chest was a whole other headache. Every now and then symbols shot through it, glowing etchings of cursive writing. They twirled along the creases, shimmered, and fizzled out. Made her head swim. Then the whole bag vanished, its shape barely distinguishable in the darkness.

Ok, so this is some type of stealth tech.

Military vehicles could be made less observable in any number of ways. This had to be something similar. Although it meant that the contents of the box were weapons grade material.

Jade pulled out her phone and aimed the camera at the box, but her screen was blank.

The phone was dead.

No matter how long she tried, the phone didn't respond.

I'm sure it was at more than 50% when I left the boat...

No time to wonder at phone battery life right now. Jade wanted evidence of this weird box. If she couldn't take a photo of the chest, she had to commit its contents to memory as best she could.

Narrowing her eyes, she registered something surprising: It wasn't hard at all to look at the contents of the box, but only if she wasn't looking at the sides. So, the outside was protected, but the stuff inside was not? If so, he had been a complete twat leaving his box open.

Testing this theory, Jade brought her fingers up and hid the sides of the box from her view. She formed a small square hole between her hands, and aimed it at the pouches inside the box, screening the sides of the container: protecting her eyes from the stealth tech, while looking inside the box.

Her vision instantly cleared.

Fascinated, she spied on a tray of pouches, that looked far too ordinary to warrant that level of security. And rather dirty, too. She wondered what was in them.

They were labelled in all kinds of languages. Jade skipped those with Chinese and Japanese and similar, squiggly characters, and focused on the letters she could read:

'Highgate, Recoleta, The Old Jewish Prague, San Andrés Mixquic, Necropolis, Pere-Lachaise, Kensal Green, Fiumei, St Cuthbert's...'

Locations? Then she noticed among the few Arabic labels, a sign she had often seen in the desert: The name of a cemetery only a couple of miles away from the base.

That's near where Ami is right now.

No, this was no time to think about Ami.

But this reminded Jade of something else: Leela had raved about one of these places, she wanted to go all the way to Mexico because of it. Apparently, some hugely popular, animated movie with a kid, who got somehow sucked into the Day of the Dead, was based on this cemetery called San Andres Mixquic.

And come to think of it, Highgate, Kensal Green, the Glasgow Necropolis...

Could it be that these labels were not just names of places, but specifically names of cemeteries?

What the hell is *in these pouches?*

The sound of approaching footsteps and of a woman's sharp shout froze Jade in place. She looked up from behind her hands.

Shit.

Chapter Eleven

The Crystal Blade

T he grey depths of the ancient burial ground were stirring. At first only outlined in the mist, two figures swiftly emerged. They stood in the circle of purple glow, waiting there as if expecting veiled curtains to pull aside and clear their way.

Jade scanned her surroundings for anywhere she could take cover, and let her feet dangle over the mist.

What the hell was I thinking? Hide!

The nearest funeral monument big enough to hide behind while staying out of the grey vapours, was the angel she had come from.

FUCK! I was halfway to my bike! But they are blocking the exit. The only way is back.

Jade landed in the mist.

She threw one last glance at the gate, where her bike was tied to the railings. But voices were approaching. She turned her back to it. She ran.

"There is a binding here that leads to Hades." It was that woman's voice again.

"Do you mean besides the graves?" came the man's voice from the distance.

"Not that! One of the living is tethered to the underworld."

Jade never took her eyes off the angel even when her legs slowed down. Even when her eyes had begun to shut, and she could only see through a narrow sliver between her eyelashes.

Sleep. Yes. I'll go to sleep. Once I'm on *the fucking statue.*

"Tethered to the underworld? Does that mean bound for death?"

"Exactly."

"Who? Who is going to die?"

Jade tripped the last few steps and fell on the pedestal, hugging the legs of the kneeling angel. She pulled with all the strength she had left. She didn't know if she'd gotten her legs fully on the plinth. She'd run out of strength completely. She took a few breaths, waiting to see if she'd pass out.

"Theodora, I don't know what you mean?"

"You've got someone else here," the woman snapped.

"No! Wait, what?"

"Jeronymo, who else is here right now?"

"No one!"

"Did you check before commencing tonight?"

"Er..."

"So you *didn't* check."

Jade could see them coming into focus. The man with the long coat had left the glowing circle behind and was reaching the end of the ancient burial ground. With him was a woman that made Jade stare.

"Well, I looked," he said in a strangled croak. "And I saw no visitors."

The silhouettes approached quickly, the newcomer pacing slightly ahead with an air of expert authority that Jade found captivating. The young man trotted beside her obediently, as she scanned the area, eyes gleaming from beneath the round rim of her hat. She scrutinized each grave she walked past, with a sweeping gaze, reminding Jade of a wing commander conducting inspections.

"I didn't ask if you looked. I asked if you ran your initial checks."

They wore gas masks. Jade was dying to identify what kind of equipment that was, but she barely had time to see it. Their technology was basic analogue but also highly automated. They both pulled the masks off, in motion as accurately synchronised as their step. Instead of removing them, they just tipped up their hats, and some invisible mechanism hidden there sucked the masks out of view and into the hollow of their hats.

Everything about them said squadron training.

But their outfits screamed vintage circus troop.

"I couldn't check, I've not been assigned my Kappa Beta yet. But they said I'll have one in a few days!"

"Tell them to hurry up and match you a dog, because you're knocking people out as you're coming through!"

"I really didn't!"

"Yes, you did. There is someone lying unconscious somewhere in the mist right now. Careful where you step."

Ha. No I'm not. I'm still awake, bitch.

But curled up in a little ball on the plinth, Jade was far too exposed. Head spinning, she crawled up the statue again, taking cover between her wings.

This fog knocks people out and these arseholes know it. And they have gear to walk in it.

Their masks had covered their nose and mouth with corrugated metal pipes, filter cannisters on the sides and speech modules, before they vanished, within the blink of an eye, slipping up into the hats as if they'd never existed.

So then, the fog. It had to be lethal. Some biohazardous fume came from the ancient part of the cemetery, where the mist was as tall as the churchyard walls.

How was this area not closed off to the public? Why hadn't Vicar Dawson said anything? Jade shook her head, receding behind the stone wings.

"Aren't you coming?" the woman called over her shoulder.

"The circle," he grumbled, "it's still flashing red."

"Yes, it is very peculiar." She sounded concerned.

Jade glanced at the purple circle of lanterns he had placed in the depth of the mists. It wasn't flashing. It wasn't red. And neither of them looked at those lanterns as they spoke. They were both facing out of the mist, scanning the walls of the cemetery. As if the circle they were concerned with, was the graveyard periphery.

There's nothing there.

"Not only peculiar but way above my rank! This is a tiny post in a quiet village, I'm not supposed to be getting a breach like this!" The man hesitated, hunching miserably, still not coming out of the ancient part of the cemetery.

"Pull yourself together, please." The woman moved on, leaving him behind, and Jade did a double take.

Is she in fancy-dress costume?

Nothing felt real. Or rather, she had lost all sense of what was real and what wasn't.

The newcomer was now drenched in starlight, crossing the lake of grey, ankle-deep mists, towards the tombstone where the box lay. She was a tall, black woman in an intense, ice white gothic outfit. She wore an Edwardian skirt with far too many layers, frilly bits, lacy trims, gleaming pearl strings, and all kinds of fluff that Jade didn't know the names of. Leela would have probably enthused and pinned it on her online wish boards under a stupid album title like 'crinolines' or something to that effect.

"Can you get out here please." Her tone was much less polite than the actual words.

"You know what it is?" he said, finally coming towards her.

"No but I'll have a look."

Jade felt her jaw drop. The gleam under the woman's hat was not her eyes. She and the man had both come out of the fog wearing shiny big goggles. Not cycling or swimming goggles but thick, metallic binocular lenses with dials and settings around the rim. They now stood side by side, and seemed to be adjusting the lenses experimentally, as if trying to see which setting was the right one.

"They are inside the cemetery."

"Who? Where?"

"I don't know what they are yet, Jeronymo, give me a second."

"Which lens?" he asked.

"I'm trying microwave altimetry and I'm going to frame it with dark gamma."

Microwave altimetry? Dark gamma?

Jade decided that it was too far away to know exactly what they said, since what she heard made zero sense.

"Yes, that's the best visibility you can get." The woman had stopped touching her goggles and stared in the distance for a long moment.

The man not so much. Both his hands fidgeted with the dial lenses on his goggles, never settling. He stomped a foot and sighed, his fingers changing settings, growing impatient.

The woman unfastened the buckles around her neck and on her chest, parting the pale velvet of her ice blue shoulder shrug top, overlaying a corset underneath. Jade's breath stopped as the woman slid it right off, baring her arms and shoulders.

Those biceps are the right amount of defined and elegant.

When she proceeded to open the double rows of medallion buttons, Jade had to cough into her hands and hope they hadn't heard her.

"What *is* that!" Jeronymo almost screamed.

"Took you long enough," the woman said.

He was done calibrating his goggles. He appeared to be shaking with fear.

Jade frowned. There was nothing on the path.

"It's not here for us! Calm down."

"Get it out of here!" He rushed to her side, standing just behind her. "You can get rid of it, right?"

"Not necessarily. Certainly not until I know why it's here."

They are role playing.

Jade couldn't believe she hadn't realised it sooner. They were doing some live action role playing game. They just had some exorbitant props for it; that gas thing was over the top for sure. That total pillock over there had brought the mist with him when he first showed up, so it must be some second rate, or even makeshift fog machine, which would never pass a safety check: it was clearly toxic. Fucking nitwit.

But she was certain now that it was make-believe. There was nothing where he aimed his gun.

Pop-pop-pop went the buttons, up and down the satin corset. 'Damask-in-white-and-silver', the step-monster would probably call it; not that Leela's boring mum ever commented on titillating lingerie (she'd skipped all the fun parts of being French, but she had wall-papered one side of the dining-room like it and called it a 'feature wall').

Jade couldn't take her eyes off that corset.

A gleam of metal flashed in Jeronymo's hand. His gun.

His prop, rather. He probably made it out of tuna tins and hot glue.

"Jeronymo do not shoot at it!"

"I need it out of here. It can go sit outside the wall."

"It's not just the one. Look further down the path. Look at your gates."

Jeronymo's shoulders went rigid. For a moment he froze, staring at the three lampposts along the cemetery path and the gates at the end.

"What *are* they?" he said in a wretched cry. "Why are they *here*?"

"I'm trying to get a better look; will you give me a moment?" With the buttons all opened, the stiff garment had loosened around the woman's slender middle.

Jade, who hadn't breathed in several heartbeats, now forced a deep inhale, as her eyes never left the woman in the distance.

"Can you please put the gun away. And pack your things." The woman's voice trailed away darkly. "It might be us who have to leave. Not them."

"I'm not leaving with these things within my gates!"

"You will if I tell you to."

He pressed his lips together in a sour grimace.

The woman pulled the heavy corset right off, revealing a full set of abs and a well-rounded, tight chest in a yoga bralette wrap. Jade's heart was thumping against her ribcage.

Is she going to stop undressing at some point?

In fact, it seemed the stranger was done stripping. Jade's fingers went weak where she held on to the stone. If the stranger had gotten rid of the crinoline skirt, Jade would have ended up flat on the ground like a sack of potatoes.

Maybe Leela is right. Maybe my type really is people who work out. Maybe I really am that superficial.

No, she refused to accept that she was so easy to impress. She loved Ami like she had never known love before. This woman was just... nice to look at. That was all.

But Jade was distracted again, as the woman pulled a hairpin needle from under her hat and an enormous braid of black curls tumbled down her almost naked back. Jade swallowed as her heart jumped to her throat.

"I've never seen anything like it, Theodora..."

The woman's chin shot up, her head sliding sideways reproachfully, and he quickly corrected himself.

"Not outside a manual's appendix pictures." He was holding his gun with both hands but still aiming it down.

"Stop looking at it, it's riling you up. Pack your things! You're done here." Theodora pulled the goggles up to the band of her hat, where they clicked into position. Taking the hat off, she dropped it carelessly on top of the pile of garments she had already discarded.

That's when Jade saw it. She wasn't naked. Her body was covered in a web of fine silver chains, strewn with crystal gems. It hadn't been noticeable up till now because the whole net of jewellery had been translucent against her skin. But then, she ignited a mysterious light current with a sudden movement of her hands, and the whole lattice lit up.

It reminded Jade of Ami's Tai chi classes, the videos she'd seen on Ami's social media. They all pretended to balance a flaming ball of energy in the palms of their hands and shift it around their body. This woman made it seem even more convincing as she channelled luminescence through the veins of silver along her muscles.

Jade was momentarily sure that she yielded an invisible flame in her hands. Arms spread wide, legs grounded on the earth like a yogi warrior, she controlled the luminous flow with smooth motions of her arms, as if writing curly symbols in the air. It gave the impression she was manipulating a kind of living energy inside the crystals.

Super fancy gamer gear. She sure is invested in her roleplaying.

"Their anchor is somewhere over there," her hand drifted vaguely, "at that weeping angel statue."

"What do you mean?"

Jade ducked a little and peered out from the curve of the stone wing to see if the woman's eyes had found her.

A little cry left her throat, this was horrendous. Cracked, burnt holes where the woman's eyes should be...

No. Copper coins.

Jade sighed with relief. Two metal coins on a thread thin chain. Some kind of blindfold jewellery kept the woman's eyes closed. A gem between her brows glowed blue. It was radiant with layered crystal circles in the shape of an eye, shining in the middle.

She continued the slow flow of drawing invisible shapes in the air with graceful dancer gestures. The lines of light pulsated along her skin, and Jade couldn't decide whether her body's warmth was somehow powering the luminescence of the gems or whether the glowing gems were feeding some cryptic energy into her body to generate those fluid movements. But there was an obvious connection between the dance and the shimmer travelling from stone to stone along her skin.

Don't forget it's a costume. Fiber optic fountain threads with LED diamonds probably.

"An anchor? I don't see anything!" Jeronymo was still looking through his goggles.

"It's your visitor, Jeronymo."

"What, where?" his tone was hopeful. "Did you find them?"

"I can't see your visitor, but I can see the links. They are all bound to the direction of that weeping angel. So many of them. Threads everywhere!"

"These things are after someone visiting one of *my* graves?"

"We need to leave." Theodora's voice was harsh.

"I can't leave one of *my* visitors, asleep, at their mercy!" He thrust his arms wide, palms up, in protest. "It's my job to protect the living!" He stabbed a finger to his chest. "Or what am I even doing here?"

"No, Jeronymo, this has nothing to do with your section. It's not your duty to..."

But he wasn't listening to her. He ran to the lamppost, aimed, and shot.

Jade chuckled.

Laser gun.

And it was some higher-frequency beam that was visible. Very impressive. At laser tag the guns never fired visible rounds. This one, though, glowed white red. She could see the light shoot to the top of the lamppost.

Then Jade's grin instantly dissolved. He had hit something in the air. The light spread and vanished against a black shape.

"Get out of here!" he shouted.

Jade blinked. Did a shadow fly against the night sky, between the lampposts?

Bat, maybe? Was he firing at the wildlife now? What a complete lunatic.

It wasn't a bat...

He'd cleared the first lamppost and charged at the second, aiming one handed as he marched.

She had to give it to him, he must have had shooting training to play this game, because he looked quite striking. His coat billowed around his long legs with every stride, taming the tentacles of mist that fumed from below.

Jade caught sight of thigh high boots of thick black material, and a bad-ass amount of buckles. A heavy belt sat around his hips with several short sheaths.

Knives?

Jade wasn't sure, she only got a brief glimpse as his coat parted up to his slender waist for a few moments, when he stopped under the second lamppost, arms raised to aim above his head.

He shot at the lantern top.

"Get out!" he yelled. The muzzle of his gun tracked a path towards the gates, as if following a flight out of the cemetery. He shot a third time, the light missile covering the distance to the third lamppost and exploding against a shadow above it.

Leave the bats alone!

"Don't come back in here!" he bellowed, his posture emanating defiance.

He turned to walk back, a big grin under his binocular goggles, arm bending behind his head as he sheathed his gun between his shoulder blades. "I guess I didn't need your help after all, I did it all on my own," he called out to the woman.

"We need to leave." Theodora watched the sky. The eye gem between her brows burned brilliantly blue. The coins on either side still weighed her eyelids shut. Currents of shimmering energy ebbed and flowed between the palms of her hands, on winding paths along her wrist, arm, shoulder and chest. They streamed to the opposite shoulder and through the gems dotting her other arm to the palm of her hand, then they returned, washing over her in tidal waves of sheer luminosity. The cluster of stones on her finger rings sparkled, as her open palm aimed at the night sky, like a radar reading invisible signals in the dark.

"You made them angry."

Jeronymo paused, perturbed. He shuffled backwards, turning his face to the sky.

His mouth fell open, his hands balled into fists. An anguished scream rose from his throat, which turned into a deep howl as he crouched sideways, both arms wrapped protectively over his head, as if to avoid something flying at him.

Jade stiffened, for the first time since she had thought he had a real gun. Nothing had flown past him, but a gush of wind brushed his red curls away from his ears, and his coat waved violently behind his legs.

He's pretending, right? That's what live action role paying gamers do. They go to parks in big groups all dressed up and act like they are fighting an imaginary monster. Act like they are taking damage and dying.

Jeronymo started running while still hunched over, practically bent double, elbows over his head. He tripped and fell sideways, smashing ribs first into the ground.

Pushed.

No, there's nothing there. He tripped.

The wail escaping his lungs was soul crushing. Jade realised she had leaned too far out, trying to see. She shrank back between the angel's wings, peering carefully behind the stone head.

He's playacting. Right? He's just very convincing.

He hadn't gotten up to his feet, just knelt there, one arm protectively against his sore side, the other arm scrambling for his gun, his panting breaths hoarse, broken with vicious coughing.

Why is he not managing to draw his gun?

He was feeling at his neck, yet somehow failing to find the collar of his coat in order to slide his hand to the concealed holster.

He's too distracted.

His head snapped right and left, little cries of terror gushing out of his throat, his whole upper body jerking back in surprise every time. As if something was scaring him. As if something was hitting him?

"Help!" He bellowed, then gave up and fled, first crawling on all fours and then scurrying to his feet, running as fast as he could for the ancient part of the cemetery.

"No!" he wailed, coming to a halt as if a door had been slammed closed in front of him. He lost his balance and crashed headfirst against the back of a tombstone.

This time he sprang up to his feet, hands out before him, shaking.

"Stay back! Stay back!" he barked, spinning around, as if addressing a crowd closing in.

He's bleeding.

Blood poured from a cut along his left temple. Half his face glistened crimson, and red streaks oozed from his chin, dripping onto his black coat.

Jade slid down the back of the angel and stood on the plinth.

He needs help. He's hurt.

The man wasn't pretending. He really *believed* something was after him. And he got himself injured in his panic. A puddle gleamed dark on the grass before him.

Blood?

The grey lake sloshed down below her, halfway up the stone pedestal. Jade would pass out one quarter of the way to him.

Is there another way to reach him?

"Let me through! Let me pass!" he shouted, but he was panting too hard to continue.

Still acting as if something is blocking his way.

He raised a quivering hand to reach for the gun again, and swayed, as if he was intoxicated, and lost his balance completely.

He's losing too much blood.

A tombstone broke his fall, and he grabbed it with both hands, holding onto it to stand back up.

Stay there, dammit!

Jade wanted to shout at him, tell him not to try to run again. He was in no condition. He'd crack his skull open next. He needed to lie down and wait for help.

But, shuddering with visible convulsions of visceral horror, he let go of the stone holding him up and toppled sideways. Within three steps, he was flat on the ground. Face buried in the grass.

He didn't move again.

Chapter Twelve

Arcane Powers

The woman crept up behind Jeronymo.

Her skirts flowed wide around her, as she glided soundlessly across the lake of mists. She moved stealthily, her gems dulled in a pearly light that almost blended with the grey mists. Something eerie about the energy she brought with her, like a ghost floating among the graves.

She didn't go to him.

Instead, she quietly headed to the side, almost obscuring Jade's visual of the fallen man, standing nearly exactly between them. Halfway to Jade, halfway to Jeronymo. The woman glanced over her shoulder, and Jade quickly climbed back up the angel to hide between her wings. For a moment it had felt like the woman looked directly at the statue Jade was hiding on. But her eyes were closed under the coins. Only the glowing eye gem had flashed in her direction.

Jade peeked cautiously over the stone curve of the wing. The woman was trailing an invisible line with her hands, like feeling along a thread that was tied on one side where the man had fallen, and on the other side, to Jade.

A blade shone, bright like a diamond, as the woman raised her arm high above her head. She brought the knife down on thin air. Jade flinched. She could swear she felt a tug.

She brought both hands to her chest, just to make sure there wasn't anything attached to her that was being pulled right out of her flesh.

The woman swirled around, her other arm still flowing in slow motion, keeping her crystals shimmering along her body, and once she'd come full circle, she slashed again at a spot very near the first one. This time she slashed on the way back up too, and Jade gasped in amazement, as she felt two separate tugs.

Is she doing this? Is she somehow causing this sensation?

Then Theodora spoke, and the timbre of her voice had a dark, imposing resonance.

"Do not come back tonight."

With the crystal blade still gleaming in her hand, she looked up into the sky and then down at the ground, as if watching something dive.

While the luminous energy flowed around her body, she gracefully arched her neck and spread her arms. She looked up one last time.

"Follow your sisters. Go. We will not be here tomorrow. Let us go, and we will not get in your way again."

Her face turned down to the earth, as if once again watching something dive deep.

And then the gems went out.

Jade covered her face with both hands. The cemetery was far too dark all of a sudden. The incandescent lattice of chains and jewellery suddenly extinguished, it took several minutes for her eyes to adjust to the darkness of the night. She could hear footsteps and whispered conversation in the distance.

Then she started to discern figures again, Theodora was shrugging into the velvet overlay, fastening the carved silver buckles on her neck and chest. The satin white corset was already fully buttoned underneath.

The complete outfit was, once again, breath-taking. Jade rubbed her brow angrily, as if brushing away her own thoughts.

Jeronymo leaned weakly on the tombstone beside Theodora. He was upright and functional, which made Jade sigh with relief. He wiped his neck with a rather red hanky. There was no blood on his face anymore.

And where the gash had been on his temple, stretched an angry red scar.

Jade frowned.

Surely there must be some kind of sticky stiches holding it together. Maybe a skin-coloured plaster or something. It was just the distance and the darkness that made it seem as if the wound was healed already.

A loud snap made Jade turn. Jeronymo closed the lid of his box and was stashing it in his backpack.

"Why did this happen?" he said. "I've done everything by the book, followed every rule and regulation..."

"It's not you. You didn't cause this. Well, you shouldn't have shot at them. You just incensed them." Theodora said. "But anyway, they followed someone here. Vengeance spirits don't just wander."

"Oh no," he said in astonishment. "Vengeance, really? Which type?"

Theodora grabbed his bag and pulled a booklet out of a side pocket. She flicked through it and when she found the page she wanted, she thrust it at him.

"No way," said Jeronymo, looking up from the page. "Are you certain?"

"Yes." Theodora set her hat on her head.

"So, this one," said Jeronymo, his neck tensing, "is tethered to its prey, that's why you said—"

"The afflicted is in here right now."

"And probably passed out in the plasma." He grimaced, guiltily.

Then he sat up abruptly. He turned around, to look at the grave with the violin.

"I think I know, who it is," he said. He swept across the mists, the few paces to Jade's mum's grave.

Jade's eyes narrowed.

"This one has a bereaved daughter, visits nearly every night," he said, tapping his foot against the headstone. "No matter how much I tell her not to. She keeps coming back. I don't know why the Command is not working with her."

Tell her not to? I've never seen you before in my life, mate.

"Is that why the violin is playing?" asked Theodora, following behind him.

What violin playing?

"Pretty," said Theodora, a hint of sadness in her eyes.

"It gets louder every time she returns. I don't know what else to do."

Me? Every time I come to see my Mum, those weirdos hear a violin song? What the hell?

"Well, she won't be coming here much longer," said Theodora.

"What do you mean by that?"

"You've got a manual for a reason," she gave an exasperated sigh. "Start reading it. She's marked for death."

"Don't say that!"

Theodora listened for a moment, as if lost in a sad song.

Jeronymo skimmed through the pages.

Jade watched them, the words 'Marked For Death' echoing in her ears.

"This is awful," said Jeronymo, looking up from the page. "We should do something."

"What can *we* do?"

"Well, if not you and me, then who should I ask? Who can deal with this?" Jade tried to see what was on the pages. She couldn't.

"No one. This is not a haunting. It's not a building to clear or a forest to cleanse. She brings it wherever she goes."

I do fucking what now?

"So then,'" Jeronymo said hopefully, "there's plenty to do about that! An exorcism?"

"She's not possessed."

Jade shook her head, and looked away, so angry, she could barely restrain herself from jumping out and punching some sense into them both.

"Then what is she, if not haunted or possessed or—"

"She is guilty. A murderer." Theodora tapped the page with her finger.

Jade snapped around and fixed the woman with a piercing gaze across the distance.

You lost the plot, ya daft cow.

"No, I really don't think so! I've seen her, I spoke to her," said Jeronymo. "She couldn't have. I know she is a soldier but I'm pretty sure she only does computer stuff."

That wee ginger cunt though, how does he know all this about me?

"The thing that's after her rose out of the laws of retribution," said Theodora. "A life for a life. There is no stopping that type of vengeance revenant."

He seemed lost for words.

"I need a cup of tea. And to curl up with my cats and go over my scores, I've got choir practice tomorrow. Let's go." Pulling the strap of her slouchy over her head, Theodora turned towards the wall of fog in the ancient graveyard.

He put a hand on her arm.

"Wait! There's got to be something! You made them leave tonight. Can't you stop them from coming back?"

There really was something here tonight.

Jade's temper deflated. Fear dripped like icy water, putting out the fire in her stomach, turning her guts into sludge. Could there have been something here tonight? Was it all for real?

She listened.

"No, Jeronymo. They only let us go because I promised we won't interfere."

"Why would you promise that?"

"Because they were trying to kill you!"

"But those three that you cut with your knife? Clearly, we can help, we just need to make a plan..."

"I didn't kill those three. I just cut their bond to their pray. That's all I can do. Break bindings."

"So what does that do? Without the binding, can they come after her again?"

"No, those three cannot. They are strays now. They have no pack or power over anyone. Which is really bad actually, because they will roam aimlessly, burning with wrath, until they fade away. I took away their purpose and their power. It's not right, what I did. But it was in self-defence. So I won't be in too much trouble. You might, though. You shouldn't have shot at them. You don't want to be involved in this. You really should not have done that."

"Ok so let's cut them all off of her!"

"Have you heard a word I'm saying?"

"But I'm sure that she's not a killer!"

"It's not up to us to stop her from facing judgement!"

"No! She is lying asleep in my cemetery, and I have a duty to protect her."

"She brought it in here herself! You are not responsible for every human that wonders into your cemetery!"

"It feels so wrong!"

"Read your manual. It is what it is. Are you coming? Because I'm heading home with or without you."

"Can we not just—"

"Good night."

"Hold on, there has to be something here..." As Jeronymo lifted the book to read it, Jade held on to the wing and leaned in close to look.

She saw a picture.

A shadow, but it seemed to be standing vertical, not against a floor or wall. Smoky at the edges, the drawing showed black vapours where its hands and feet should be. The eyes were empty, white holes. The hideous being leaned in unnaturally towards the reader, so that its head was grotesquely large, almost jumping out of the page, while its body stretched away behind.

A sheer black veil pressed against it.

Or was the shadow pushing at it, trying to tear through the veil?

In an inexplicable way, the sheer, rippling barrier only existed where the figure was, and then faded into smoke in the air. As if the veil was invisible... but for where it touched the creature it contained.

Jade shuddered.

That's what I saw in the lounge. That's exactly it.

"Theodora?" said Jeronymo, as if waiting for a reply. He looked up, only now realising his companion had walked away. Her silhouette was shrinking in the fog.

"Oh, come on," he said into his wrist, "we can't—"

"For any more questions please call the Countess." Her voice came from his wrist band, sounding exasperated. Then she stopped in the mist. She turned around to face him. "If the afflicted returns here again, leave. It's too dangerous.

Don't stay here and witness her death. And absolutely do *not* try to stop it." She turned away to walk into the depths of mist.

Who she calling afflicted?

Jade was pissed off again. She'd had enough of this. She wanted to know what that book said.

She stepped a little lower, to the base of the angel's wings. If he turned around now, he'd see her. But he had his nose buried in the book.

Jade crouched, calibrated. She could reach him without touching the ground more than three times.

She took a deep breath and leapt as far as she could. She landed halfway to him.

It was a blur.

Instant exhaustion hit her, but she had expected it, and in two strides she fell on him.

He screamed, but in his shock, offered no resistance.

She wrestled the book out of his hands, but she was so drowsy. When he saw who she was, he seemed to recognise her and frowned with anger. Grabbing the book back with ease, he held onto it, and she couldn't wrangle it from his grip, because she was so, so very sleepy.

Leaving without the mysterious image on that page was not an option. Jade grabbed a handful of the pages before and after the image and tore them clean off, then she turned and ran.

She wouldn't make it.

Three steps in and she'd already blacked out for a second, forcing her eyes open again in the next breath.

The angel was right beside her. With the last bit of concentration she had left, Jade held on to the stone gown and heaved herself back up out of the fog. She stood on the pedestal, flat against the angel's skirt, trying to regain her senses.

A couple of heartbeats later, her head had cleared enough. Jade climbed. She crawled up the back of the angel once again, seeking the familiar shelter between her wings.

Jeronymo was staring at her wide eyed. The book still open in his hands, the jagged edges of the torn pages clear evidence of her wrongdoing.

She met his gaze defiantly and folded the pages to push them into her bra.

His brows jumped up to disappear under the rim of his hat in bewilderment.

"Throw me your mask and boots so I can get out of here," Jade called, "And I will give you back two of the pages. She had taken a few extra, so there was room for bargain.

"You will return all of the pages," Theodora's voice came from the mist. That's why he hadn't moved: he'd called for backup. Peering from behind the angel's wing, Jade saw her come to stand beside Jeronymo, who looked grateful she'd returned.

"No," said Jade. "And what exactly is it you're doing here?"

"I wasn't asking," said Theodora. Then, turning to Jeronymo: "What are you waiting for?"

"Er..." He stared at her confused.

"Put the manual away and do your job!"

"Oh yes, of course," he mumbled, tucking the book away into his shoulder bag and rolling up his sleeves.

Jade feared he'd pull out a gun, but instead, he waved something forward, as if signalling a squad to attack Jade's vantage point. But in slow motion, as if taking a Tai chi martial arts tutorial.

Behind him, like cream swelling to boiling point in a saucepan, the mist rose.

Now he looked like a waiter lifting an invisible tray to the sky and his elbow bent close to his body, as if supporting a great weight.

Jade heard something slimy beneath her and looked to see the white lake of vapours clotting in gooey spirals licking the skirt of the angel. Climbing on it.

Somehow climbing *up* the angel.

"What the...!" Jade pulled her legs up and tucked them under her. Was there an animal in the vapours?

No, it was the mist itself. The entire body of this pearly grey gas seemed to be animated, using the stone statue to rise up to her.

Jeronymo in the distance was similarly animated. He was now swaying his arms like a dancer.

He is remote controlling the mist. But how?

The smoky assailant had crawled up the entire skirt of the weeping angel. Jade had to shift her seat to the nape of the angel's neck. She balanced herself, holding on to the intricately braided bun of her hair with one hand, the tip of her wing with the other.

"Why are you doing this?" Jade shouted.

Jeronymo didn't answer. Instead, he thrust forward like throwing a ball, and Jade heard the mist bubble and froth below her.

Both he and Theodora had tipped their hats up, and their goggles and masks were lowered to fit on their faces by some invisible mechanism. Standing knee deep in the white lake of smoke, Theodora crossed her arms over her corset, watching Jade. Jeronymo continued his theatrical arm waving beside her.

"You fucking freaks!" shouted Jade. She'd had enough. She held on to the stone wing and carefully elevated herself to a standing position. She was now quite high up, practically standing on the angel's hair.

The vapours were crawling up the wings. She had no time left.

Crouching carefully, Jade calculated the distance and jumped. She dropped on a tall tombstone in the shape of a massive Celtic cross. This grave was a bit lower than the angel had been, broad enough to give a good landing platform. The two sculptures were fairly close together, but the fog here had not risen. It sloshed away meekly at the root of the cross' headstone below.

"Wow! She's good," Theodora said behind her, as Jade squatted on the stone.

Theodora tilted her head sideways and Jade was pretty sure that under the gas mask, she was hiding a smile.

Jeronymo got to work right away, shifting the bulk of the smoke towards Jade's new anchor. He erupted into exaggerated signalling movements, pointing at Jade dramatically with one outstretched arm, whilst with his other arm he drew sweeping circles in the air.

All around the Celtic cross, the fog started to spin into a swelling vortex.

Jade waited for him to run out of energy, drowning this grave in fog, before she jumped to the next one. Just to wear him out. He was working hard to thicken the smoke where she was now, the rising progress slow. Behind her, the angel she had leapt off from was slowly emerging again, as the mist subsided around it.

How is he doing *that?*

The wrist bands Jade had noticed bulging under his sleeves were luminescent. Not the telecoms devices she had imagined. Their prominent feature was turning cogs and swirling carvings that glowed a greenish grey, like gravestone moss. Pearly threads of radiant silver veined over the top of his hands into rings around his fingers. The rings also glimmered with foggy gems. He wore some of the rings on his smaller knuckles just below his fingernails, which were painted white.

The whole system of intricate jewellery pulsated with light, shooting across like a heartbeat with his every move.

The fog rose higher and higher.

Time to go.

Jade crouched, swung her arms several times and focused. There was nothing around she could leap on to directly. But she had a plan. At High Intensity Interval Training the coach would pile up boulders as high as her chest, so she had practice jumping from ground level and folding herself in a tiny ball in the air, to land on top of the gym obstacle.

I can do this.

Her execution was perfect. The landing was rough, and her shins groaned as they absorbed the impact of her feet with the ground, but that didn't slow her down. Her knees touched the earth for the briefest second as she leaped in the air to broad-bounce towards her target with minimal exposure to the mist below.

Feels like I'm executing the jump with a twenty-kilo backpack on, dammit.

She kept going. The second landing gave her the perfect base to load and explode on to the tombstone she had targeted. She hadn't been sure what this sculpture was when she chose it from a distance, but now she found herself perched on top of a tombstone shaped like an open book, a gargantuan tome, complete with carved writing on the stone pages. She placed one foot on each page; the best space afforded by a gravestone to stand on so far.

"She is brilliant! Is she an athlete?" asked Theodora behind her.

"I told you she is a soldier!" Jeronymo sounded irritated, almost offended. "Do you mind helping me out a bit? She needs to stand still!"

"You are quite slow, aren't you?"

"Well, it's my first time! And we were never taught our visitors would be jumping from sculpture to sculpture! They're supposed to just walk on the ground!"

"She's clever to have figured it out."

"Taught what? By whom?" Jade called to them. They both glanced surprised at her but then looked away. They weren't going to give up information that easy. "I haven't killed anyone," Jade tried another approach. "So, whatever you were saying about me back there, it was all speculation. I'm no murderer."

Theodora was now staring at Jade sceptically. Jeronymo forgot to swirl the mists, his hands falling to his sides, the jewels on his fingers losing their glow. His eyes, dark under the thick lenses, grew very round. He believed her. He wanted to talk to her about this.

"I've seen a shadow follow me and it looks like a man whose death I witnessed," Jade said, speaking fast. "It has his eyes. But I didn't have anything to do with his execution. It was my job to gather intelligence. I supervised my team to record it as it happened. But I didn't know the murderers or the victims, never even been in that village. We work with drones. We were a few miles away."

Theodora's stance had changed. Her shoulders weren't as square, and her gaze focused intently on Jade, burning behind the dark lenses with sincere curiosity. Jeronymo beside her was nodding a lot.

"I knew it," he said. "I knew you were innocent!"

"How did you know?" Jade asked, because that was another big question she'd had for them. "Why do you talk like we've met before?"

It was the wrong thing to say. His face closed off, the warmth in his eyes going out like a light. His body tensed, and he leaned back, in a stance of avoidance.

"How do you know me?" Jade demanded.

"You might believe you're innocent of the killing," Theodora spoke over her. "What matters is what the spirit thinks. If he has been following you... if it's actually manifested before you, that's because he believes you're responsible for his death."

"Responsible for his death? In what possible way?" Jade said, exasperated. "I'm network security for Christ's sake! I'm just the computer guy!"

"It's not us you need to be convincing," Theodora replied. "Jeronymo," she nodded to him meaningfully. She was telling him without words to get the mist going again. The vapours were low like a lake at their feet. But Jade wasn't done with this discussion.

"So what do I do? Do I tell him? Next time the freaky-ass, smoke person poofs into my living room, do I shove my discharge papers in his face? Will that get him to leave me the hell alone?"

Jeronymo had lifted his arms but now dropped them again, looking at her curiously.

"What about your discharge papers? Are they proof of your innocence?"

"Well, they mention the incident!" Jade said, throwing her hands up in exasperation. "It says clearly, we were on an information gathering mission. Only watching. Didn't participate or help either side, that's not my job! It's all in there!"

"No, he will never believe you," said Jeronymo. "The spirit of the dead wants vengeance. He can't change his mind at this point. Although—"

He turned to Theodora and started asking her something, but Jade didn't hear it, because Theodora spoke over him.

"Jeronymo, enough!" Theodora grabbed his wrist and lifted his arm up. "Get a move on!"

"Although what? What can I do to fix this?" Jade shouted.

"I'm sorry," Jeronymo said, and looked away as the jewels ignited along his skin with the flowing movement of his hands.

"You've got to give me something! What did you see on the lampposts? What are those things? Are they also coming for me? Why? Why can't I see them?"

"I'm sorry." This time it was Theodora apologising, and she sounded sincerely gloomy to be refusing.

"*How* can I see them? Do I need gear like yours? Where do I get it?"

She had lost them. They had both taken several steps back and looked like they were regretting the few things they'd said already.

"Look I get it, your job is classified, I respect that. That's fine. Don't tell me any of that, ok? Just tell me how to fight it and I'll do it all myself."

"That won't work," said Theodora. "Even if we tell you, you won't remember it in the morning."

"What? You will make me forget? How?" Jade yelled, truly pissed off now.

"It's already done," said Theodora. "You're only stressing yourself out by prolonging this."

"Tell me how to fight him. Jeronymo! Look at me! Tell me how to fight him!" Jade called as the mist was swelling up the stone and halfway to her feet once again.

He didn't stop the eerie slow dance that controlled the vapours, but even so, he looked straight at her.

"I'm so sorry!" was all he said.

Jade's face darkened, and her gaze turned to steel.

Fuck this, I need to get out of here.

Her aim was the front of the church, with the CCTV at the church doors and the vicar's cottage across the front lawns. She could see it from here, the dwarf conifers lining the gravel front path. She was so close. One more sculpture would be enough to bridge her way out of the mist. But which one?

"Stay back!" Jade shouted to Theodora, who was already walking past the angel.

"No need to fear the plasma. It won't hurt you in any way," said Theodora, her voice mechanical through the mask.

"Then take off your mask if it's so fucking harmless," said Jade.

The woman laughed, and Jade hated that she had a beautiful, warm laughter.

"Stay the hell away from me! I'll kick you," Jade shouted, as Theodora walked past the Celtic cross.

"Don't be afraid, it's all good."

The smoke was twirling in tight coils up the tombstone of the open book, and Jade watched Theodora circle around to approach from behind. Jade stood up on the open book, ready to kick Theodora if she came too close.

"I'm not afraid. But that's your last warning to stay back!"

To her surprise, Theodora raised her hand to her goggles and lifted them off her face, revealing a stunning gaze fixed on Jade.

Instantly lost in those brown eyes.

A glitter of laughter, and the warmth of genuine admiration made Jade swell with pride. She had impressed this gorgeous woman. How awesome. And she wanted to get to know her better.

"What *are* you guys?" Jade said. Her voice came out soft, surprisingly gentle. Slightly embarrassed.

"Just guarding the cemetery. What is your name?" replied Theodora, very pleasantly.

"My name is Jade. What exactly... do... you..."

Jade woke up in the early morning, blinking in the golden sunlight of the fresh summer day.

Her brain pounded against her skull with every beat of her heart. She was propped up against a tombstone with a book on it, which was quite far from her mum's grave. She rubbed her temples with shaking fingers, her mouth dry, her eyes burning. Had she fallen asleep in the cemetery? Again?

I can't be doing this all the time! What is going on?

Getting up was impossible, her whole body was stiff solid. She leaned against the tombstone and started to massage her neck, arms, calves and ankles. Get the blood flowing for a few minutes, so she could stand up and get to her bike.

She'd had the strangest dream.

She had been falling... falling... into the arms of a stunning woman. Ami, at last!

No, Ami smelled like warm cinnamon honey, prince of citrus bergamot; her glossy braids a velvet, musky vanilla. Ami's hug would be like a frothy warm drink on a cold winter's night. This was someone else.

A cooling fragrance of jasmine blossom and crisp green apple emanated from the skin of her neck. Her soft braid, like a puffy cloud of curls, had a coconut cream scent so enticing, Jade felt dizzy. She'd looked up into her face. Who *is* she?

A horrific distorted countenance of twisted metal, protruding tentacles and spikes had made Jade scream.

She struggled free and felt cold, wet ground under her head.

The woman was arguing with someone... about... Jade?

"You have to *get* it!" the man had said, desperately.

"Why should I get it? It's your manual, *you* go get it!"

"But it's in her *bra*!"

"I know!"

"I can't put my hand in there!"

"No, I should think not," she'd said.

"Right, that's what I said! So can *you* please get it?"

"I'm not touching an unconscious person's underwear!"

"Look, you're both ladies. It's fine."

"Ok next time you're asleep I'll send a bloke to put his hand in your underwear."

"Oh, come on! Can't you just get it, *please*?"

"No, it's rapey! Stop being a creep!"

"I'm sorry! I just don't know what to do!" he'd sounded in the verge of tears. "Do you realise how much trouble I'll be in if the Countess finds out there's pages missing from my manual?"

"Well, I won't tell her, so you can try and get it back before she finds out. While Jade is awake and knows what you're doing! And I won't put Jade in my report at all. Just make sure the place is actually empty before commencing next time! I told you there was someone here!"

He'd sighed.

"You're right. I'll be more careful. And thank you for not mentioning her."

"It's fine. You did manage to knock her out, so she *will* forget. Just, avoid it next time. You need to not be seen to begin with."

"Yes. I'm sorry. And I'll figure out another way to get my pages, I guess. I'll tell her to come again tomorrow, and I'll think of something."

In the dream, a face appeared before Jade. Was it a horrendous—

No. It was Mum. It had Jade's thick, arched, dirty blonde eyebrows, dark cobalt blue eyes, and thin line of lips.

Mum said, 'Come visit me again tomorrow, honey.'

"Mum! Is that you?" shouted Jade. She had woken up from the sound of her own voice.

Yes, that had been a very strange dream.

Although, come to think of it, she wasn't sure why it was strange... or what it was about. Did it matter? She didn't remember. After the quick flash of images when she first woke up, everything was now swiftly fading away. It left a sinister residue of piercing dread, ill-disguised as anxiety. Life sucked.

She sprang to her feet, irritated. Every muscle felt like gravel as she headed down the cemetery path to her bike at the entrance.

"Morning Mum," she said, passing the tombstone with the violin. "See you again tonight!"

Jade wasn't sure why she said that. She had no plans to come this evening. She needed a rest, and a full night's sleep.

"Curiouser and curiouser," she muttered, reciting the quote on Leela's Mad Hatter coffee mug as she reached the gates and stepped out of the cemetery.

Chapter Thirteen

Gates of Hades

I opened my eyes and felt so cosy. I never wanted to leave this bed again. The divine comfiness of the pillows. The snug bliss of the cushions against my back. The soothing warmth of the throw over my legs.

The time!

How could it possibly be noon already?

It felt three minutes ago, when I walked in this room at 7am. I thought I'd have a shower before taking Cannelloni for his morning walk. And then suddenly, the day was half gone. I was still in clothes that smelled of graveyard lawn. And my dog was not here.

"Cannelloni?" I called, stumbling out of bed, still groggy. My legs were achy and stiff. Those nasty bruises I got the night before last, when I tripped by the river running after my dog; they wouldn't quit. Although it felt like I'd taken another ten tumbles during the night. Weird. I cracked my door open a tiny sliver. The brightness of the warm daylight in the corridor blinded me.

"What time you call this?"

Grandpa was sitting in his favourite chair in the lounge. A newspaper was open on his lap.

"Sorry I meant to get up earlier," I said, winking at my dog who had lifted his head from his snooze spot at the window seat, to blink happily at me. "I'll come get Cannelloni for his walk in just one second…"

"I've walked your dog, four hours ago. You should know that, since the floor isn't nuked with hot steaming piles of dog shite. And that would have probably been an improvement for the floor anyway. Since it's not been mopped in weeks. Your Grandmother had this parquet floor sparkling every day, good as new after thirty years. It was her pride and joy."

I glanced at the several oily skid-marks on the wooden floor, where Alan had spilled bean sauce as he carried the open tin to the bin, the sticky sweet black tea stains from carrying his cup on the way to his cabin, and several other uniden-tifiable discolorations that certainly didn't come from my smoothies or salads. Because when I spill, I wipe. In the same fucking breath. Military-engrained reflex. So none of that was me. But I didn't say that. I tried so hard to be nice.

"Thank you for walking my dog, Grandad, and I do clean the floor, when I have time. But there's two of us here, so maybe you can do it the rest of the time."

"The nerve," he said to his newspaper, and buried his face behind it.

What do you do when you live with someone who refuses to do their fifty percent of the cleaning? I'd either have to do all of it all the time, or I had to do half of it, and live with the half he didn't do. God, I missed living on my own. Where the things I cleaned, stayed clean.

Alan hadn't emerged from behind his newspaper so that was that.

I closed the door and retreated to the merciful darkness of my cabin. Irritated, I started stripping while switching on my stereo, turning on my morning play list, and running the shower. I tossed everything I'd been wearing in the laundry basket.

Wait, what's this?

A bit of paper fell to the floor at my feet, as I pulled off my bra.

I wrapped my dressing gown tight around me and picked up the neatly folded triangle of papers.

Did I hide it there?

I must have, I guessed. This is how I used to fold money, back in university when I used to hide my cash in my bra, because pockets on women's jeans are useless, and before the military it had not occurred to me I'm allowed to opt for unisex clothing.

But when? I had no recollection of doing this.

And the peculiar feeling of unease returned. The same unease I've had for days now. Weeks.

That I'm forgetting something.

I scanned the pages in my hand, trying to remember how I came to have them. Their ragged edges meant they had been violently torn out of a book. I don't use paper books. I'm an audiobook and podcasts type of gal. Paper books are so last century. My sister and I always clash about that, but I win because when she does 'That book smell tho!' I go 'All those dead trees tho!' and she changes the subject.

How did pages from an actual paper book end up on me? Was it something I was absolutely certain I couldn't find online? I scanned a few paragraphs, to see what it even said.

It seemed handwritten. A journal, maybe?

```
THE ERINYS
Threat: Deadly. The Fury is indestructible. Her
goal is the death of her prey.
Sentience: Articulate. The Fury will taunt and
debate with her prey to worsen their feelings of
guilt.
Offensive: Stalker. The Fury creeps up on her
prey, targeting their emotions until they sink into
despair.
```

The chattering in my head lately, that was so alien to my usual logic assessment of challenges, I'd wondered where it came from. This unravelling of my rational thoughts into raw emotional chaos... Not at all like me. What an uncanny coincidence, to find a game, where the same thing happens to the players. A stab of warning in my gut. Aware this line of thinking steered me straight into the realm of paranoia, I shut it down and read on.

Attack: Necromancy. The Fury is non-tactile, unless provoked by a direct physical assault; nor can
she wield weapons. She obeys only the shadow of the
murdered victim and conjures this spirit to take
form and claim the life of its own murderer.

Approach: Anchored. The Fury is tethered to her
prey. Wherever they try to escape during the day,
she will always find them at night. Invisible at
first, the curse binding gets stronger as the end
draws near; and renders the demon fully perceptible
to her prey on the Night of Judgement. On their
last day, before the night of judgment, some cases
report the afflicted perceiving a mirage of the Fury
daemons sleeping around them, even though the daemon
is not active in the daylight hours.

Not exactly a journal entry, even though it seemed hand-written. It had to be a printed font, right? The best impression of cursive font I'd ever seen. Looked so real. Maybe it was part of the game, to seem like a manuscript, because I was certain now, I was holding some kind of video game manual. It was obviously a chapter about some undead boss, with typical walk-through style info: when the player may expect an attack, what is the most effective way to fight it, what the monster is usually hunting for, that sort of thing.

I scratched the back of my neck, frowning.

"You're wasting the water!" came Alan's voice from behind my closed door.

"Grandad! I'm about to get in the shower!"

"I've told you not to run the water until you're *in* the shower!"

"How do you know I'm not!" I said, exasperated.

"I can hear you strutting around your room! And if the tank runs out, you won't be able to do laundry tonight!"

"I didn't think I was doing laundry tonight," I said, confused.

"I don't have any clean shirts for tomorrow!"

"And?"

"And I have two tours booked in! One from Canada and one from New Zealand!"

"I'm still not doing laundry tonight," I said, "but I'll make sure there's enough water for *you* to do it!"

"I'll have you know I'm giving the tours in the *cathedral* tomorrow!" he said indignantly. "Do you expect me to discuss the historical artefacts of our village's rich heritage in a t-shirt?"

"That sounds like a *you* problem!" I said.

"Preposterous!" His footsteps stomped away from my door.

I headed for the shower, unable to look away from the paper in my hand.

```
A Lesser Earth Daemon:
The Fury is a Chthonic deity and as such, she has
all the attributes of underworld entities. Her bane
is sunlight and her catalyst is living blood.
Sunlight: The Fury cannot tolerate the light of
day and will withdraw even as twilight progresses.
Every effect the Fury has on her prey clears
in the sunlight: symptoms of her affliction like
headaches, recurring memories of the murder, panic
and paranoia will be alleviated upon direct contact
with uninterrupted sunlight. This is not permanent,
and symptoms return.
```

I paused. If I got to play that game, I'd have my character stand in the sun as often as possible. It would refill the energy, or power, or magic, whatever this game has; that little crucial bar would max out. I'd even have them sleep in the daytime outdoors.

Ha! Like me on the barge every morning lately.

Funny.

Several ancient sources maintain that the sun's
power to remove the Fury' curse is so potent, that
it can even undo death itself. This claim has not
been verified in historical record. There is no case
evidence of sunlight restoring life into a dead body.
Death cannot be undone: as with everything else,
once the soul has departed for the underworld, death
is final.

Did that mean you can't revert to your previously saved progress? Play again from an earlier spot in the game? 'Death is final' seemed kind of strange wording for a video game, where you're supposed to get as many tries as you need to finish. Which game was it? I am up to date with all the new releases, and I didn't recognise this boss from anywhere. I'd check online later. The cabin was filling up with steam. I tossed the pages on my bed and ran under the shower.

Quick and extra hot, the water cleared away the stickiness of those cold sweats clinging to my skin from last night. I sighed. Fallen asleep in the cemetery, again. What the hell was wrong with me? Exhaustion? Was somebody doing this to me? But why would anyone want me to keep passing out in the graveyard? No fucking sense whatsoever.

Love hot water. So soothing. But today, it burned on my hands, on my legs. Of course, my feet were in medical waterproof bags, from my much depleted first aid kit; had to keep the bandages dry underneath. The barefoot walk back to the boat the other night had gotten my toes and heels mangled. But this pain was not it. Weird.

Blue and purple marks ran all along my thigh and calf muscles. What the hell? How did I get *those*? Maybe the tumble by the river two nights ago, but wouldn't old bruises be darker? More blue than red by now?

So two things I couldn't explain. Those bits of paper. And a truckload of bruises and scrapes on my legs. Brilliant.

Even as I stood under the hot shower, a feeling of foreboding crept up. It stayed heavy in my throat, like a bad memory refusing to surface. It was a warning that

I should be wary of something. That I was in danger. But what from? I just couldn't freakin remember.

I tried again. It was me who folded the papers and put them in my bra, because that's how I fold things for safe keeping; things I want to make sure I don't lose. I tried to imagine myself doing it. Where was I? What time? With whom?

Nothing.

So, I was missing a chunk of time from late last night. I didn't remember much after I'd eaten about half the jar of hazelnut butter. The more I thought, the more hazy my recollection became. And I woke up quite far in the opposite direction from where I left the bike. Like I collapsed halfway, but going- where?

This was so annoying. How much time was I missing? Minutes or hours? What happened to me before dawn?

I rinsed shampoo off my hair. The peculiar sensation that I was exposed, vulnerable; it intensified. Maybe because the plaster slipped off my finger and the raw nailbed seared with pain in the hot water.

This shower was a disaster. It made everything hurt. I sped up the rest- squirted my coconut conditioner on my hair quickly, and tried not to hyperventilate as a sudden sense of being stalked brought up this urge to start running... but from what? Rinsing the coconut balm from my hair made my hands really sore. I looked at my palms and fingers: scrapes? Lesions and bumps, as if I'd been climbing, or hanging off from sharp stones? What the fuck was going on?

Why? Why was I missing time?

I just wanted out of the shower. And to be dry. And with clothes on.

Wrapping a bath sheet around me, I switched the plastic waterproof bags on my feet for flipflops, because of course, I was a walking encyclopaedia of injuries at this point. I checked the big cut at the back of my arm. The other night, I had to glue that one to stop the bleeding. Glue was still there.

I re-applied every bandage, plaster and gauze like I was back from a mission. Turned out civvy life was not as different from service as you'd think. Look at me, barely home for a month and I needed refills for everything, even surgical antiseptic, sticky stitches, and skin adhesive. I opened the bathroom door and emerged in my bedroom in a cloud of hot steam, hobbling stiffly like a ghoul.

The video game pages stared at me from my bed. I froze.

The way the papers had landed, a drawing was now on top that I had not seen before. The tough looking boss glared at me from a full-page picture. Its body a shadow, its arms and legs ending in smoke as it loomed towards the reader. Something about the way it leaned in, as if stretching out grotesquely from across a great distance... The way it seemed to come out of the ground, or dissolving into it, while at the same time pressing its face close to mine?

I've seen this before.

The memory hit me full force.

The shadow in the lounge.

The eyes.

The dead man.

Ghosts.

My knees gave in, and I sat on the bed, beside the strange pages.

Two nights ago, the stalker had shown his sickening face. The loathsome presence had appeared inside the houseboat. Terror coursed through me as the heinous memory blinded me. I shut my eyes, hating this reality-adjustment that dropped every single morning. I'd woken up like life was normal, and then boom. Ghosts. Remember?

I believe in the freaking supernatural now. I don't remember details, I was so tired. But I've thought it through, I know I did. I found no other explanation. I've seen a ghost. I really did.

The world is a whole other place now.

The ghastly image burned behind my eyelids, and when I opened my eyes, the same spectre stared at me from the damn page. I flipped the picture on its back, couldn't look at it.

What *were* these pages? How is the ghost that I saw, drawn by someone else on this bit of paper? Where did it come from, how did I get it? I looked for answers in the text.

```
A Daemon of Blood Origin:
Essence of the murder victim: the Fury rises from
the drops of dying blood that hits the ground. The
amount of blood spilled is proportionate to the
```

number of Furies awakened during the murder. This
is a rare phenomenon and a Fury curse will only
manifest if the circumstances meet a set of complex
criteria, for a full list see appendix.

Essence of the murderer: The Fury will seek to
spill the blood of her prey. She draws power
from the guilty blood to solidify the spirit of
the murder victim, whose death was the source of
her manifestation. To achieve this, the Fury will
confuse and terrify her prey until by accident
or self-harm they are injured and their blood is
spilled.

Once summoned to materialise, the shadow of the
murder victim becomes a tangible entity. It will
hunt down and kill its murderer, thus classifying
the Fury as:

Haunting Level: Lethal.

This videogame, I needed to learn more about it. Those demons it talked
about, should I start looking them up? Initiate an online research day?

I got dressed at warp speed. Which gave me a brief break, enough for logic to
prevail, at last. Seriously, what was I on about. Raving like a lunatic. When had I
lost the ability to tell reality from fiction anymore?

Looking up demons for God's sake? What a fucked up notion.

I needed to see the therapist. This PTSD shit was getting too real. She needed
to sort it out. I was going straight to town to tell her everything.

Scary coincidence to top it all off- when I grabbed my phone to check the time,
a notification flashed at me. I had an entry in my calendar for today, which incidentally I did not remember putting there. It said: 'Book emergency appointment
with the therapist. You're seeing ghosts for fuck's sake.'

Excellent. Even memory lapse me seems to know I need help.

It's confirmed, I've lost the fucking plot. I jumped to my feet and before knew it, I'd folded the pages again and tucked them into the side pocket of my olive chinos. Why was I taking them with me? Who knows.

I looked through my smart summer blouses and chose the beige one. A bit dressy for me but didn't want the therapist to think I'm just a gym rat, always in cycling leggings and Lycra hoodies over a workout bra. So, I ended up going out looking as if I was heading to a lunch date.

Fucking ghosts?

Nope. No time. Just keep going.

I opened the door of my bedroom to find the boat very still and devoid of the usual judgmental comments and scowling glares.

"Grandad?"

His chair was empty. Cannelloni's cushion too. Where did they go? They were here minutes ago.

The familiar scent of Grandma Tamsin's geranium blossoms filled the boat. The kitchen was drenched in warm sunshine. The river path was full of cheerful, daytime sounds. Alan probably went for a walk, which he did when he was annoyed with me.

I shrugged.

When is he ever not annoyed with me?

Grabbing a vanilla protein shake packet, I ripped it open and emptied it in my blender with oat milk, inhaling the sweet scent. I like my morning ritual and doing it in the barge is infinitely better than any crammed little flat I ever had on base. Sealing the blender and switching it on, I felt my tumultuous thoughts quiet for a moment. Outside the window, dog walkers strolled past, smiling in the sunshine, with music escaping from their headphones; ramblers chatted in their steady paced groups, and couples strolled hand in hand, their heads close together in intimate conversations.

I brought the soy Greek yogurt and a cup of ice, to pour in my shake and thicken it perfectly into an icecream. And I wondered if there would be a time when Ami and I would walk this river path together. One more day. She'd be home tomorrow.

I miss her so much it physically hurts.

Someone pointed at Gran's colourful garden on the front terrace of our barge and made an appreciative comment. Not unusual. Strangers often pulled out their phones and took pictures of it. Made Alan proud.

The ice in my blender crushed the shake beautifully into the ultimate vanilla ice-cream breakfast; it only needed a few more seconds. It's fun people-watching from the boat without anyone knowing I'm here. In the light of day and with Grandma's doily lace curtains, the windows become mirrors, reflecting the trees and water, and I'm invisible.

Of course, the evening always comes and flips this around. When the country-side disappears in the black of night, then our rooms, even in the dimmest bedside lamplight, become illuminated beacons across the river...

And the anxiety was back. The feeling I was being hunted. Like I know some-thing, something crucial— But what? That sense of impending doom pounded my heartbeat in my ears, reverberating in my mind like an invisible march of funeral drums. The moments of quiet bliss were over. Now I wanted to move, get out of here, do something.

I put the glass I'd laid out for my smoothie back in the cupboard and grabbed my travel cup instead. I'd have it on the go.

Just keep moving.

The stuff on those pages were completely irrelevant to what I'd been seeing. Apart from the image of the shadow person, nothing else matched. I hadn't seen female demons of any kind. All I'd had actually seen was a stalker, when I walked my dog, right?

I slipped my feet in my comfy Barefoot shoes.

No female legion like the text described. I remembered it clearly, the outline of a man watching among trees in the night. My dog and I trying to run away from him. The sound echoed in my mind. Footsteps. Those ominous footfalls hounding me. Something wrong about them. What was it? They'd come from behind me when I walked to the boat, and they had come from behind me again... when I turned around. That's it. That incongruent noise from all directions, rapping at my every nerve, and no one there wherever I looked on the darkened path. I had felt like I'd been surrounded by an invisible horde.

I pulled my ponytail through my sports sun visor hat and plonked my big sunglasses on. I needed to stop this. That's why I was seeing the therapist today. So this didn't take over.

Stop thinking about it. Keep going.

I opened the front door and grabbed a note in Alan's handwriting, from the key table, without stopping. I slid my keys and phone in my pocket and took a cooling iced sip, standing at the open doorway.

'Had to take my shirts to the ladies at the laundry service,' said Alan's note.

I scowled. 'Brought the dog with me,' the note continued. 'You can't look after a pet if you are passing out every day. And if you're going to be staying out all night and lying unconscious, in your clothes, on your Grandmother's bed all day, I'll have to tell your father. It's not even the weekend for crying out loud.' Then at the bottom, where Gran would normally have written 'Love, your Grandma Tamsin', it said 'Sort yourself out.'

I crumpled it to a ball and shot it to the bin as I walked out on the deck.

The fresh air and sunshine made me smile, as I locked the boat door and leapt over the gap to dry land.

I gasped.

Once again, that strange feeling of something appearing out of thin air.

A woman was sleeping on the old bench down the river path.

She hadn't been there while I was gazing out of my window. I'd have seen her.

And yet, she seemed fast asleep, as if she'd been there for hours.

on their last day, before the night of judgement...

What was it the game had said? My hand reached for the crumpled pages, but reason prevailed. I had to stop this. Right now.

She was just a person asleep on a riverside bench.

But the feeling that something was wrong wouldn't go away. Her matted, sticky hair clinging to her sinewy neck, the mud stains on her face and hands. The tears on her blouse, the tattered skirt covering her legs like a rag.

A demon, that looks like a sleeping woman.

I had to check. I pulled out the pages from my pocket and flicked through them quickly. There it was.

They appear like sleeping women... The day before the night you die.

Without daring to look at her again, I searched for everyone else's reactions.

A couple walked past me and smiled, two golden retrievers galloping beside them. On the opposite direction a woman came jogging past, checking her heart rate on her wristwatch every few seconds.

No one was noticing the strange woman on the bench.

I was imagining it. It was just a person, nothing more.

Pull it together, Jade.

My gaze returned to her, to look at her again, to make sure there was nothing sinister about her.

She was staring at me. Straight at me.

I ran.

Turned on my heels and flew down the path as fast as I could.

It wasn't until after the turn of the river bend, when the Lady Thomasine was no longer visible behind me, that I slowed down. My heart rate subsided, and I gradually caught my breath.

What was wrong with me? Why was I imagining things? Maybe this was a panic attack. What had the therapist said I should do, count colours and smells or something?

Resting my gaze on the deep cyan expanse of the Thames, I breathed in the musky scents of midsummer oak bark, fir cones, and birch leaves. The verdant strips of the rolling riverbanks and the cerulean skies beckoned beyond.

Ghosts. I'm now one of those people who believe in ghosts.

I couldn't stand the idea. But they say seeing is believing, and I had *seen* the dead man.

I walked faster. I pulled out my phone to call the therapist.

It buzzed in my hand.

I was startled, but the face on the screen made me smile.

"Hey Leela!"

"I'm declaring a Woofles emergency."

"Please don't."

"I'm coming over right now. I need a break from my essay, I'm bringing a mahoosive Woofles haul. We doing a quick pit stop to catch up. I'll be there in an hour."

"I can't eat waffles so early in the day."

"It's one in the afternoon! Proper lunch time!"

"Too early for dessert though."

"You make it sound like alcohol."

"What?"

"Mum says it's too early to drink mimosas when she goes with her friends for brunch, you are treating sugar like people do alcohol. Do you have an only after 5pm rule for waffles or something?"

For a moment I had the urge to hung up on my sister and get back to my brooding of gloom and doom. But Leela is like a balm for the soul. Always has been. My little ray of sunshine, even though she is also a big pain in the ass. I was actually grateful she called; my thoughts had been spiralling so bad I believed I was seeing demons, for crying out loud. That notion sounded bat shit now that Leela was on the other end of the line. That stupid kid, she grounds me. Gets me out of my head. I could chat with her for a while, why not? I was heading to the therapist anyway, and nothing could be done until I got there.

"Well yes," I said. "Your body needs clean protein, fibre and vitamins to get through the day, sugar this early would be poison."

"I'll have my cupcake while I'm thinking about your advice. I made my first batch just this morning. Turns out three cupcakes for breakfast are a great hangover cure."

"Leela how could you possibly have—"

"I'm kidding! I wouldn't drink the night before cupcake day. I'd never be able to bake with a hangover."

"Glad to hear it. I was the same. On nights out at uni, I had fun but stopped drinking before I felt I I'd have to skip gym in the morning."

"We're so NOT the same," Leela chuckled. "My mission in life is to never know what the inside of a gym looks like."

"Why not? Working out is healthy."

"Unbearable."

"Really?"

"Quite vile."

"It actually releases happy juice in your brain. It's called endorphins and dopamine. People get addicted to exercise, it feels *that* good."

"Eww, getting sweaty and sore on purpose? Why? Life is hard enough as it is thank you. Can you imagine? Looking at my calendar and going, oh good, I have a two-hour gap between classes, let me quickly hop on a machine especially designed to cause muscle fatigue."

"Muscle fatigue? Please," I chortled. "A bit of a gym workout is not tiring, it's invigorating."

"Can you *not*," said Leela.

"What's tiring, is an air force muscular endurance drill."

"Are we really doing this again," Leela moaned, like she was being tortured.

I sipped my gorgeous icy drink and swallowed the urge to say anything else. It really did bother me, though. My sister finding it 'unbearable' to do things that were nothing, compared to the shit I've had to survive in two decades of service. Princess Leela can't even begin to imagine what 'unbearable' really means.

I sighed. I tried to think of something less divisive to say. Leela hates it when I bring up how different our lives have been, even though we have the same Dad.

"How did the baking go?" I said, walking faster.

"Awful. I opened my cupboard to find my new baking tray black. Covered in cake batter burnt solid. And none of my flatmates admitted to knowing anything about it. It's like, come on bitches, one of you used my new tray, ruined it and put it back in my cupboard? Really? Couldn't you at least replace it? I don't need to know who it was, but I'd like a new tray please. But they all pretended total ignorance. I had to go out and buy a new tray myself!"

I rubbed my forehead. I too had my stuff taken away and no one claiming responsibility or replacing them. One time I came back from leave and all my tampon boxes were empty, and I didn't notice until my next period started. Too late to get new ones in time. I had to make pads out of loo roll paper and hope it didn't seep through the uniform. Never knew if it was someone's idea of a joke or another female officer in an emergency— although I'm sure any woman would leave me a note for heads up. Another time, just as I'd newly been made officer, I went for a shower and came back to find both my uniform issued bras replaced, but the new ones were three times bigger than my cup size. Someone thought it was funny to leave a note, 'Stuff some socks in there. Flat chest bitch'. And I don't think that would have been a woman either.

"Jade?"

"Yeah. Er... Yes, housemates are hard work," I said with as much empathy as I could muster. Then I looked for an example my sister could relate to, so she wouldn't say I'm belittling her problems again. "Grandad," I said. "Grandad scolded me the other day that the floors weren't clean, he said: "The Cleaning Fairy must have skedaddled off on a holiday!" I said "Alan, the dust bunnies have proliferated so much in this barge, they killed the Cleaning Fairy and ate it. If you'd like to do something about it, there's a thingamajig, right over there, called a hoover." And he turns to me and says, "Nah, I don't have to hoover the floors, I don't use them." What am I supposed to answer to that?"

"Poppycock!" Leela said in Grandad's deep voice.

"Bosh!" I answered in Grandad's voice too.

"Poor Grandpa, he's so discombobulated without Granny," Leela continued. "When his bin gets full, he puts a little protest note on the top: 'The bin is full up.' Like how dare we, who *don't* live there, let that happen."

"Yes, the bin note! Wait, he's done that to you too? How? You've never lived with Alan, have you?"

"No. Since Gran died, Dad said I had to earn my pocket money cleaning the boat every Saturday, while my mum did his laundry and prepped his mid-week meals for the fridge. We used to come in and find The Fourteen Mugs." She burst out laughing.

"You know the fourteen mugs?" I said, infuriated.

"Yup, in the sink. Little neat towers. Each mug with a tea bag rotting inside," said Leela, still laughing.

"Drives me up the wall! He drinks his tea. Twice a day. Leaves the empties in the sink! Then once a week he comes knocking on *my* door to tell *me* there's no clean mugs for tea!"

Leela was snorting with laughter. "Ah, Grandpa," she said amiably.

"It's not funny Leela, if he wants a maid, he can hire one."

"It didn't bother me, why do you flat out refuse to do it?"

"First of all, they paid *you*, whereas they expect *me* to do it for free."

"Sure, but you live there."

"I've lived with flatmates long enough to know everyone should clean up after themselves. Chores should be split equally around the house."

"But he's not a flatmate, he's our grandad!"

"Yeah, but did you know that women are emotionally blackmailed to doing 75% of the housework globally?"

"Emotionally blackmailed?" Leela sounded mortified.

"Yes, exactly that little bit of guilt tripping you just did. I do feel terrible for him that Gran's gone and his life has changed completely. Watching him try to understand why his shirts aren't clean and hanging in his closet ready when he needs them. It *does* make me sad. But that was Grandma Tamsin's life, not mine. It would take several hours daily to do the level of housework she did. That's either a chunk off my work, or a chunk of my workout, or a chunk of my down time. And none of these are negotiable. So no, I'm not cleaning what's not mine."

"I wish I had the guts to be more like you, but Mum would kill me."

"You're an adult now, sis. You can be whatever you like."

"When I'm home from uni, I'd feel terrible leaving everything to Mum; not helping her out."

"Of course, you should help out- but have you noticed that Dad does nothing?" I said.

She let out a baffled squeak. She had never considered this.

"You were a kid when I was having those fights with your Mum," I continued, "and I left before you can remember it. But we argued about it all the time, because I was used to the way my Mum did it. My Mum worked full time, and made Dad do as much housework as *she* did."

"Wow!"

"Yup."

"And he did it?"

"Of course! Dad did the dishes and changed the beds and hoovered, and all sorts, back then. Until Charleen, the part time French wedding planner extraordinaire, came along and appointed herself the resident domestic Goddess."

Leela chuckled.

"But I'd feel so guilty telling Dad to, what? Like, load the dishwasher? He comes home from work so tired every day."

I shrugged.

"You wanna override that hard gender programming, sis."

"Maybe it's written straight in my chromosomes, feels so normal to me; I can't even open the glue gun case if I've not helped Mum chop the dinner veg."

"You don't have to 'buy' your art and crafts time with chores time, you're not eight years old; and Dad should help Charleen with dinner half the times, not just you. Just remember, unpaid housework doesn't only diminish women's ability to get degrees and paid jobs. It takes away the chance to mind their own wellbeing; have you ever wondered why Dads are always the calm, cool parents and Mums are always one tick away from a breakdown? Push back now or you're building a very bad habit and setting yourself up to fail in the long run. If *my* wellbeing says to slap my headset on and play my videogames till my brain melts, that's what I will be doing, not scrubbing limescale off Alan's en-suite sink or getting him fresh towels, no matter how many times Charleen calls to check."

"I need time to process this... Anyway, when's good to come by with waffles tonight?"

"Did I agree to waffles?"

"They have a whole page of plant-based options on their menu."

My objections wavered. Leela took advantage of the momentary hesitation, to press on.

"I'm getting you the protein packed one," she said.

"Vegan protein?"

"Of course! It even has pumpkin seeds."

I bit my lip. "Oh, go on then."

"YEAS!" I had to hold the mobile away from my ear, to prevent hearing damage, while that gleeful scream went on.

"But it's got to be late tonight, I'll be out all day and want to get some work done in the evening."

"You got it."

"Great, see you then!"

"Jade?"

"Yes," I said, trying not to sound irritated.

"You won't text me two hours before and cancel it? You promise?"

"I promise. It will be good to see you."

She thought about it for a moment.

"Absolutely one hundred percent waffles tonight?"

"Absolutely one hundred percent," I said.

"You know what's funny?" she said. "In horror movies, when two people are absolutely certain they will be meeting up, that's when one of them dies."

Normally, I would have laughed, which was what she was doing, giggling on the other end of the phone as she hung up.

But I just stood there, staring at my phone long after the call had ended, and all I could think of was my daily journal goals:

Stay Alive.

I'd forgotten to write it down today.

Somehow, with every passing day, this felt harder and harder to achieve.

Somehow, I had this irrational fear today would be the day I failed.

That today would be my last day...

Chapter Fourteen

Erinys

Of course that's the kind of thinking that got me on the way to see the therapist, so I immediately called her.

She answered on the first ring.

She instantly said no.

I could not come for an emergency visit.

Why am I not surprised. She's got to listen to this, I don't know what else to do.

I spoke non-stop. I had to see her right away. I walked on even faster, closely observed by three palomino horses grazing on the other side of the wooden beams that lined the path. They chimed in with loud exhales from their giant, quivering nostrils.

The therapist politely declined to listen to my story about a dead man in the living room.

"Jade, I don't have any openings today. How about Thursday?"

That was two days away.

"I need to tell you today!"

"Ok. I can refer you to a crisis counsellor if you need to talk to someone today. But frankly, Jade, unless you start actively working on your mental wellbeing, all the sessions we are having will come to nothing."

"Work how?"

"Like we have discussed. What is it you did today, or this week even, for your mental health?"

"Didn't you say it's good that I go for a run down the river every day?" I had reached the first cottages, and my audience switched from horses to cats. They each peered at me with eyes half-closed, as they stretched in the sunshine from their dazzling-white pebble driveways.

"And exercise is brilliant, but not enough on its own. Tell me one thing that made you happy since I saw you last week."

I wanted to say, 'Are you kidding me? Nothing made me happy, my life sucks!' But this seemed like a test. I tried to think of something.

"The only good thing about my life right now is that Ami is flying home tonight. I'll finally get to video call her tomorrow."

"That is fantastic, Jade! I'm so happy for you. So, there you have it. Instead of seeing me today, I want you to book a self-care appointment of your choice."

"I don't do spa, you know that."

A sigh came from the other end of the phone.

I was still headed for the train station, despite her objections. I was going to see her. She would *have* to let me in if I kept buzzing her doorbell, right?

"I need some advice here, I really got to tell you what happened the other night..."

"It doesn't have to be a spa," she interrupted me. "Of course, a massage is highly recommended to release anxiety..." I stopped listening. I'd be at the train station in five minutes and outside her office in half an hour. This was an emergency. I was almost at the end of the cottage lane and the cats had now lost interest and were all dozing off. They even ignored the feathered splashing from the birdbaths in each of their garden lawns. Cannelloni is not compatible with a birdbath, I thought vaguely, he'd see it as a snack buffet.

There was a pause from the phone. She was done talking about spas.

"Sorry, no one rubs my back unless it's a chiropractor for a sports injury or my girlfriend on date night," I said. "If I can just talk to you for only ten minutes in person..."

"How about you go and get your hair done?"

"I don't get my hair *done*."

"I'm sure you get haircuts," she insisted. "Your hair doesn't trail to the floor, so you get it done somewhere!"

"I've been going to the same barber all my life, whenever needed. And it's not currently needed. Listen, I think I'm getting worse, what happened was..."

"What is it you would normally do ahead of a big day?"

"What big day? My life is a train wreck." I turned the last corner and left behind the cottage road with the loud buzz in the rosebushes lining every garden. The fuzzy bumblebees swirling around the vibrant bee-friendly shrubs was the opposite of idyllic- loud bugs made me tense. Glad to get rid of that as I entered the main street of the little village.

"Jade what have we said about using negative words to describe yourself?"

"*Not* to?"

"Very good. Isn't your new job a great thing? And don't you have a reason to celebrate?"

"It's just damage control, hardly a reason to celebrate."

She wasn't letting me tell her what I had seen, and I was failing to find the words to convey it. I felt crowded. I was now in the heart of the village, where the narrow main street, built several centuries ago for horse drawn carriages, had pavements so narrow they were nearly non-existent.

"Jade, you *do* have a big day coming up. You just told me Ami is due home soon."

"Oh yeah, but—"

"Are you allowing yourself time to enjoy and prepare for seeing her again?"

"Err..."

"Well then. I think what you need right now is to give yourself permission to be happy. Get ready. Savour the anticipation." In the distance, a squad of yummy mummies in designer sunglasses and uniformly pastel summer dresses rolled out of the Indian restaurant's walled garden, pushing their prams single file straight at me. Had to step into the road to avoid them and a car careened out of nowhere and almost ran me over. How do I explain that I'm seeing ghosts in the middle of all this?

"So 'happy thoughts', that's what you're giving me? Maybe if I can get a few minutes to tell you what happened you might want to prescribe something stronger..."

"Write it all down and we will discuss it next time."

A gaggle of Grannies bobbed out of the designer bakery, babbling about a party. At first, I thought they were laughing at a toddler, who was standing up on an old-fashioned, perambulator style stroller that two of them were pushing together. The rest had formed a circle protectively around it.

But it wasn't a toddler.

It was a five-decker cake, with the words 'Happy' and 'Retirement' glittering from the second and third tier.

It wobbled precariously inside its plastic tower container and as they brushed past me, the robust human chain around the cake did not give an inch. It was me who had to get flattened against a short, crooked cottage door, to avoid 'veteran involved in pedestrian collision with senior citizens' being part of tomorrow's headlines in the local newspapers. The Grannies didn't break formation even to glance back and say thanks.

"You need to train your brain out of the dark feelings, Jade. You work out daily, right?"

"Work out? Of course. I run and I'm in boxing club in town twice a week."

"Think of your brain as another muscle, which you are letting go weak. You have to practice mental health like any other skill."

"What do you mean, weak?" A lycra-clad swarm of cyclists rolled their bikes across the road to my side of the street, elbowing past me on their way to the café. I was pinned on the lopsided Tudor beamed window of the next cottage. And even so, one of them ran over my toes with the rear wheel of his bike, as they filed past.

"Ouch!" I yelped.

He didn't even look back.

"I'm pretty good at my job so I'd say I have a strong brain."

"There's intellectual intelligence and emotional intelligence, we've talked about it."

"Oh, that."

"Yes Jade. Working under stress is a good skill to have on your active-duty tours, but now you need to practice feeling happy and feeling safe. For the next few hours, I want you to empty your mind of any thoughts of danger and threat. Set your intent to have an enjoyable day."

I didn't reply.

Was I really interpreting everything as a life-threatening situation? Even when it wasn't...

I pulled out the bits of paper and looked at the picture. This was clearly a videogame monster. Even though I was sure I've never played it, could I have seen a trailer somewhere? And could it not have possibly given me a bad dream? Could it be I dozed off on the couch on the lounge after walking the dog and dreamed the shadow?

I didn't know what was real anymore.

"So go get some pampering, it is your homework until our meeting. I hope you have a *very nice* day."

"Oh, ok then."

"Goodbye Jade!"

"Bye."

I stood beside the red brickwork arch of our pocket-sized Victorian train station, irritated. While talking on the phone, I had tapped my card to the machine and a ticket had been printed out. Now I didn't need it. I had nowhere to go. No therapist appointment for me today. I came all the way out here for nothing.

Only thing to do was head back to the boat.

Did I really dream the ghost? And what about those pages? Those pages with a sketch looking so much like that thing...

I pushed the phone in my pocket but held on to the crumbled papers, my eyes fixed on the drawing of the monster staring at me. This couldn't be a coincidence. The smoky edges of the figure, the inky black form, the way it dissolved into the ground like the shadow had melted into the furniture.

The holes for eyes, as if the artist simply left the eyes blank to be filled as applied to each case?

"This is no fucking dream," I said out loud and was aware of a few people glancing at me as they walked past. I didn't care. I looked through the pages for a clue I might have missed.

There was a new chapter starting on the last page, when the one about the demon finished. It said something about gates of hell.

```
THE ALPHA DELTA SIGMA GATES
A Gate of Hades is a significant area on the Earth's
energy grid, where a naturally occurring path to
the underworld has been sealed with a piezoelectric
crystal portal, to regulate and monitor its activi-
ty. An A.Δ.S. Gate is a dangerous zone and must be
guarded at all times.
An ALPHA DELTA SIGMA Guard's Primary Duty:
When Closed: if a death occurs within the crystal
portal's radius, the soul of the deceased will not be
able to cross over and will be trapped to linger in
between. The A.Δ.S. Guard will then need to urgently
arrange for the appropriate cleansing ritual and
ensure the crystal portal is open for it to succeed.
When Open: energies and entities of the shadow
realm will be attracted to the pathway, since
the crystal portal has amplified it, removing its
natural concealment and normal barriers. The A.Δ.S.
Guard must never leave an open Gate unattended and
must immediately report any activity…
```

That's where the page ended, and I didn't have the next one. Where could I find it?

Where did I fuckedy fuck fucking get this?

A violin started playing, making me jump. I scanned the busy train station for the busker, when—

"Jade!" Sarah the vicar's wife waved at me from the ticket machine.

"Oh, hi," I waved back with a quick smile, hoping there would not be any need for a conversation. Looking back down at the writing, I tried to seem busy.

Footsteps approached.

Great. That was the last thing I needed.

"The Furies, huh? Are you watching a play tonight? That is a very cool theatre program!"

I glanced up at her, surprised. She was appraising the pages in my hand with curiosity.

"There is a play about this? I thought it might be a videogame walkthrough."

"Oh, did they make it into a game? I know nothing about videogames, but our daughter plays on the computer for hours. Is it any good? The Furies can be pretty scary on stage."

No way. Information. Mum's old friend could actually help me here. I needed to keep the conversation going, but I felt completely lost for words. Mr Dawson had approached us, holding up two train tickets, and Sarah took one.

"Hello Jade!" he said politely.

"Hi Mr Dawson."

"Heading to town or coming back?" They had already turned to head to the stairs for the platform. This was going to be goodbye if I didn't pretend I was also catching the next train.

So, I did.

"I'm told I must go to town and have some sort of pampering day. Apparently, self-care is the new prescription for PTSD. Though I have no idea what it actually is," I blurted without thinking, and without even hiding my irritation. I bit my lip when Sarah gave me a sympathetic look.

"I've got an appointment for a pedicure, bit of pampering for me too," she smiled, as we climbed up the stairs.

I nodded, embarrassed. Talking about my PTSD was not why I was following them. I thought about ways to ask her what she meant about the Furies being scary without sounding like a total weirdo.

"So have you got something planned?" she asked.

"Oh no, I was just going to get to town and figure it out there," I said as we reached the platform.

They glanced at each other in a knowing way that made me self-conscious. As if they had spoken about me recently and what they had discussed was relevant to what I just said.

"I'm buying you a pedi," Sarah said, "and you can tell me all about your game!"

"Thank you, that's so kind," I said, fully intending to ditch her in town. I'd make a run for it at the end of the short train journey. I don't do pedis. I'd say I forgot to feed my dog.

But the quarter of an hour it would take to get there was enough time to find out what she knew. I could not believe my luck. Someone was going to shed some light on this whole ghost thing, finally.

That's how I ended up, five minutes later, sipping a double shot iced americano. The vicar handed one to me and one to his wife, at the cool shade of the platform kiosk. The summer sun scorched the stone slabs around us, but the icy drink made the heat bearable. A punch of wind blew my hair back; an express train flew past. This village is too small for the fast trains to stop here. Two minutes to our train.

"Jade is playing a video game about the Furies," Sarah said to her husband.

Finally, I thought; tell me more.

"Oh, they are dreadful, it must be one of these scary games," he said to me, and without waiting for a reply, he turned to Sarah. "Remember that time, in Berlin, the chorus of Furies came out covered in strips of flesh. Actual bloody meat. It was absurd. The smell! Quite unhygienic if you ask me. I suppose they were meant to look as if they had torn apart some poor person and wore the rotting remains. Rather unnecessary, to take it that far."

I stared at him.

I couldn't make sense of what he had just said.

"Costume designers these days," he said with contempt. "They do everything for shock value. Where is the art in it?"

I blinked.

"Costume designers? Are you talking about a theatre play again?"

"Of course, dear," Sarah said. "We've seen many adaptations, but the German was by far the most intense." She gave a nervous laugh, looking at her husband who shook his head in disapproval. "There was this other one in Italy, beautiful adaptation, and for me the most frightening of all the Furies I have ever seen. Not so much gory, that one, as psychological. Whenever they were due to come on stage, the lights went out! Pitch black. Hundreds of people in that theatre and everyone held their breath. Then Furies would walk right past us. Right where we sat at our seats. Breathing heavily, brushing against us in the dark, with their ragged sleeves, it gave me such a fright! And we couldn't see anything. And then..."

"They screamed," Mr Dawson concluded, because Sarah had been so overtaken with the memory, that she brought her hand to her throat, blinked, swallowed and shook her head, unable to convey anything further. "Screeching, like animals put to the slaughter. Right next to us, but we couldn't see them in the dark."

Ok, this is bad.

"Once again, shock value," continued the vicar. "Such a pity it has come to this. It used to be the Furies came on with some bold, feral choreography and dark costumes. Using art to convey the fear. But no. These modern adaptations are not even worth seeing if you ask me."

His wife was giggling again, in the nervous way people do when frightened. She didn't seem to disapprove of the horror element in those shows the way her husband did.

"I like horror," I said. "Games, movies, and books; and by books, I mean audiobooks, so I can hike or cycle at the same time. Currently listening to my favourite Lovecraft Anthology. Well, I'm actually saying goodbye to it. You know the drill, recently read a few articles about how problematic the author was, and I had no idea when I devoured his stories as a teen, but now it doesn't feel the same, knowing what kind of guy he actually was... So got to let go. It's my farewell to Lovecraft. But I'll keep my Great Cthulhu statue on my desk and the baby Devourer pyjamas my sister got me, he's got a vegan smoothie in every tentacle. I can live without Lovecraft but I won't live without Cthulhu."

Sarah was nodding uncomfortably but the vicar pierced me with his gaze.

"I don't believe in this separating the art from the artist nonsense. Yet another example of people taking things too far, these days. However, American horror writers are not for me."

An awkward silence followed, and I inwardly hated myself for talking without a filter. I'm not good at this social thing. Chitchat is not my strong suit. For a moment I thought I should just go; but I had so many unanswered questions. How much of the plays and videogame was made up? Which part was real; and by real I meant something like the spectre I saw. But how would I ask them this question without sounding two sandwiches short of a picnic?

Just then, our train came in, and we shuffled on. I thought I should give them a moment to recover, as they chose a four-seater section before I asked them to tell me everything about that play.

I pulled out the pages to look at them again, trying to find a clue. How come the sketch was so similar to the ghost I'd seen? And how come the text said nothing that sounded familiar to me? Well, the whole 'feeling better in the sunlight' *was* a bit familiar. I've been up every night with nightmares and only been able to sleep after dawn. And I have been having strange thoughts... But to a hammer everything looks like a nail. Or like the PTSD therapist said, confirmation bias. But she'd refused to see me, so I had to make sense of this myself, and I'd start by making notes of what fit my experience.

Gates of Hades. Sure, I'd heard that before: King of the Dead, classical mythology and all that. Absently, I noticed an inconsistency in the text and felt the urge to underline it, to look over it later.

Gosh, how cringe. I haven't actually underlined anything since I was at university. I just save online addresses, screenshots, and bookmarks when I need to. This felt so nineties.

"Are you ok?" said Sarah. "You just made a funny grimace."

"Yeah, I was wondering if you might have a pen?" I asked.

"Yes, here," Sarah handed me a pen with a smile.

Journal Goals aside, the last time I held a pen was to sign my medical discharge documents at the military tribunal. And yet underlining this dorky text felt just as monumental for some reason. Maybe it's the power of a pen and paper, makes things feel important. The section read:

When Closed: If a death occurs within the crystal
portal's radius, the soul of the deceased will not
be able to cross over and will be trapped to linger
in between.

But a little earlier in the text, it said:

Several ancient sources maintain that the sun's
power to remove the Fury' curse is so potent, that
it can even undo death itself. This claim has not
been verified in historical record. There is no case
evidence of sunlight restoring life into a dead body.
Death by a Fury cannot be undone: as with everything
else, once the soul has departed for the underworld,
death is final.

If I were solving puzzles in a role-playing video game, this might be a useful
hint, so I wrote down the inconsistency in the margins, my handwriting looking
extra untidy next to the artistic penmanship of the text:

'But what if the gates are closed? What happens if the sun comes out just then?'

Before I could write down anymore, my phone buzzed in my pocket.

Withheld number.

I answered instantly, it had to be Ami.

"Hello?"

"Jade, I don't mean to sound cross, okay sweetheart, but why did your Grandpapa just call me from the dry cleaners, where he is having to *pay* for his shirts to
be laundered?"

Stepmonster.

"How should I know, Charleen? You should really ask *him*. No one is stopping
him from washing them himself."

"Darling, have you lost your senses completely?"

"Did I say something unreasonable?"

"How do you expect a nearly eighty-year-old man to learn something like that, Jade?"

"Apart from the fact that I showed him? How about, Granny figured out how to use every new digital appliance Dad ever bought them all by herself."

"You're being impossible again, and I say this for your own good, okay my darling? You know it's not the same."

"How not?"

"He has never done it before in his whole life! Men his age need help with that. This is no time for your silly feminist hero games, sweetie, this is real life."

"I can't talk right now," I said. This was a very big conversation to have over the phone. Meanwhile, Sarah was trying hard to make polite chit-chat with her husband to give me privacy. I was not going to argue with Stepmonster in front of her.

"Well good, because there *is* nothing to talk about really. Next time, you make sure your Grandpapa's clothes are ready for him to get to his appointments please, thank you."

"No."

"Whatever do you mean, Jade?"

"Granny's been gone nearly six years now. I only moved in a few weeks ago. How'd you let him go for such a long time without figuring out how to live alone?"

"Me and Leela made sure to helped him with everything he needed, of course!"

"Then you're going to have to keep doing it," I said.

"But you *live* there!"

"Yes, I do, and I pay half of all the bills and boat expenses."

"So?"

"So, my job title is IT security, not maid service."

"Oh. Oh, you want to take it *there*, do you?"

"What?"

"What about your role in this family? Do you even know what *that* is?"

"I don't need you to tell me my role in this family, I was born into it; and however hard you spin it, nothing will ever change that fact," I thought, but bit my lip. I'd sworn long ago I wouldn't get into that fight with my stepmother ever again.

"Goodbye Charleen." I ended the call and muted my phone, in case she called back.

My role in the family, really? I grew up loving my Grandparents for sixteen years before she turned up in our lives. How dare she try to imply she cares more than I do?

But then, why was I now feeling guilty? Was Grandad really too old to learn to look after himself? Am I failing to help someone who needs it?

And yet, Alan is perfectly capable of doing very difficult things.

When he *wants* to.

Alan enrolled himself in history courses and art in architecture courses and public speaking courses when he was retired from the Coastguard a decade ago. He even went to Madrid on a summer course to learn Conversational Spanish. And in Italy, although that was to learn about churches again. He has joined History of Art clubs up and down the country, visiting cathedrals from Edinburgh to Penzance to learn more about his hobby, and that involves following complex travel itineraries, catching trains and planes and boats on time. Not to mention the educational load of everything he's learned to qualify as a tour guide here in the Royal Borough.

No, he is not too old to do his laundry. He just thinks it's beneath him.

I sighed and looked up from my phone.

"Everything ok?" Sarah asked, her eyes warm with concern.

"Yeah, all good," I shrugged.

"How are things going with your step-mum?"

No one ever asked me that question- when people brought up Charleen, they were usually just ordering me to be nicer to her. Those people were usually Dad.

I locked eyes with Sarah and there was that surprising feeling again; of finding a friend where you didn't know you had one. Something about the way she had pronounced the word 'step-mum'; something about the tiny sad smile she gave me; it felt like what she'd actually said was 'hang in there. You're not alone.'

"Not great, but I don't care. So, this play, what's it called? Who wrote it? Maybe they made this game too, I could find them online?"

The couple glanced at each other, Sarah's eyes flickering with humour, while a pained frown across the vicar 's brow seemed like he was embarrassed on my behalf.

"I'm sure you can find it online, but the author certainly didn't write your video game," Sarah said, grinning.

"It was written five hundred years before Christ was born," Mr Dawson said firmly.

My brows shot to the roots of my hair.

"What, a two and a half thousand-year-old stage play?"

"Yes."

"It's a classical tragedy, dear," said Sarah kindly. "We love a good classic, especially on holiday: it's great to catch up with international productions."

"Oh," I said, a twinge of fear making me shift in my seat. "So, this is a monster that people have talked about basically forever." I glanced back at the pages in my hand with a sense of unease.

"Monster? There is no monster in that story," said the vicar.

"I mean the Furies."

"The play is not about monsters, it's about moral dilemmas," Mr Dawson corrected me in his sermon voice. "Whether murder can be justified, or even required, what is a fair punishment that corresponds to the crime committed—"

"Interesting," I interrupted him because it wasn't interesting at all. "So, the monst... the Furies, I mean. What are they? Why do they come, what do they want? How do you kill them?"

Mr Dawson looked astounded I had interrupted him. Clearly it doesn't happen to him very often. But I didn't care about his feelings right now, I just had to know more about this ancient myth. Somehow this legend from the dawn of time scared me shitless.

"We're here," Mr Dawson said, standing up. The train was slowing down, as it rolled into the station.

I'd run out of time.

Swallowing my irritation, I followed after them as they led the way down the busy platform escalators to the station exit. I was going to turn around and take the return train right back home. I'd tell them I forgot to feed my dog.

"I got you an appointment along with me," Sarah smiled at me as we walked out in the sunshine.

"What do you mean?"

"I texted my salon, we're getting pedicures together," she said and threaded her arm around my elbow, like we were best friends.

"I'll see you in forty-five minutes," Vicar Dawson said to his wife. "Please don't be late."

"Yes dear, see you then," she called cheerfully after him as she led me down the street. "Thomas is getting a haircut and a shave at the barbers, and we have dinner reservations afterwards," she told me. "I like this thing you youngsters do, a date night! We are having a date night! Isn't it fun!"

I've never done a date night. You need a committed relationship for that.

"Oh, good for you," I said, trying not to sound as awkward as I felt.

"But I'm glad you and I can catch up a bit first. Can I see your game while we're having our nails done? I think my daughter would like it; I should get if for her birthday."

"Sure," I said. It looked like I was about to have my first ever pedicure. But at least I had another forty-five minutes to talk about this Fury boss. I scanned the text as Sarah led me by the arm, through the busy town.

I'd read everything by now, nothing else new. I had to find a way to beat this thing with what I'd already read. But the player's options could only be summed up as Not Good. It said clearly, there was no way to *beat* this Fury creature. It seemed that the only way to survive this side quest...

Was *not* starting it.

You had to pretty much revert to saved game and *not* let the victim die in the first place. So I'd already lost.

Because once the Furies rose, one demon for each drop of blood spilled during the murder, the player was doomed.

Chapter Fifteen

Tragedy In Tickled Pink

ΤΕΙΡΕΣΙΑΣ ΑΘΗΝΗ ΠΥΛΑΔΗΣ ΟΡΕΣΤΗΣ
ΑΙΔΗΣ ΙΦΙΓΕΝΕΙΑ ΗΛΕΚΤΡΑ
ΕΡΙΝΥΣ ΟΡΕΣΤΕΙΑ ΑΓΑΜΕΜΝΩΝ
ΑΡΤΕΜΙΣ
ΚΛΥΤΑΙΜΝΗΣΤΡΑ ΕΛΕΝΗ
ΑΙΓΙΣΘΟΣ ΤΡΟΙΑ ΜΕΝΕΛΑΟΣ

There's pink and then there's pink, and then there's tickled-pink. And I was sitting in a tickled pink waiting room with my arms tightly crossed and my foot tapping, trying hard not to look at the cloying walls. It was soundless, since the rug was fluffier than a long-haired poodle. A cheerful twenty-something boy, in black tights, black mini skirt and black platform stiletto pumps, arrived to hand Sarah and me some flutes of bubbly and blocks of colour samples. I picked out the cream and white range of nail polish to choose from. I don't do colours. Especially pink. Each card had about five identical looking whites, so I just picked one at random. Caleb flashed me a glitter-mahogany smile and took the cards away announcing that I was getting Old Chalk White, with Ivory Tips.

I tried to find the right moment to ask Sarah what exactly it was a Fury did to its opponent in the play. I had to wait a few minutes while Caleb clickety-clacked across the salon, ushering us to a palatial dais, complete with sheer drape canopy, where a pair of fuchsia, silver-studded, high-backed thrones were to be our seats.

"First time at our salon?" he asked, holding out a wicker basket for me to put my shoes and socks in.

"First time at any beauty salon," I admitted, hugely embarrassed to be removing my socks in front of someone whose fingertips, with perfect polish and sparkly silver stars, fluttered like mauve fairies. My feet were all bone, pasty skin beyond the stupid tan line where my ankle socks reach, and my toes suddenly seemed unreasonably long. What was I thinking, coming here?

I put my shoes in the basket, sure he would leave with the usual scowl I got from people back in the nineties, when I was still entering hyper-feminine spaces. Before I realised, I don't belong and stopped trying all together.

"Jade, you will love it," said Caleb, like we were best friends, his voice brimming with excitement. "I'm so glad you decided to come. You will not regret it. Let me know if you need anything, I'll be over there," he pointed at the front desk lounge.

"Let's do this," said Sarah, dipping her feet in her basin.

This was unexpectedly nice. Exactly three minutes later, soaking my toes in a warm footpath of cerise, turquoise and gold swirls of bath salts, with dried lilac flowers bobbing around my ankles, I decided Sarah was relaxed enough. The moment had come.

Sarah saw me looking at her and smiled.

"With these buttons," she bounced excitedly where she sat, in the armchair beside mine, "you choose which massage you want the chair to start next. Isn't it nice?" she added, pressing the button with an icon of a neck and shoulders beside it, and leaning her head back.

I pushed all the buttons on mine at once.

Just to see what happened.

The chair buzzed and whirred frantically as it kneaded at my back, neck, arms, and thighs simultaneously. If I'm doing Mental Health Day, I'm doing it on Difficulty Level: High.

"So, what do the Furies do to the characters in the play?" I asked. "I know you said they are not the enemy but... I mean, does it have a happy ending? Does the main character win? Or do they die?"

"Well they could be the enemy, depends on which play you're watching."

I shot her a confused look, her husband had said otherwise.

"If it's the trilogy, The Furies are not exactly the enemy, more the enemy's weapon," she said. "They are only the chorus, or one of the choruses."

"I don't know what that means. Are they singers?"

She chuckled.

"Yes! It's a classical play. They sing." She finished her glass and picked up the drink menu from the table between us. "The Furies are the atmosphere of threat, the tone of danger. They are not really the adversary." She perused the cocktails.

"Who is?"

"The ghost who invoked them. Shall we do Strawberry Daquiris?"

"Oh, er... I don't order cocktails when I'm out. It gets tricky, I'm vegan and sugar free and I hate to cause a fuss," I said hesitantly.

"Do you like rum and strawberries?"

"I love rum and strawberries."

"Great!" she said. "They have vegan buttons for everything."

"Vegan buttons?"

But I got it right away, as she used the barcode on her seat to open a digital order form on her phone. She was paying a heap of money, and it made me feel a twinge of guilt. I should save in the next few weeks to take her out to lunch or something. But this was useful, it was worth it. And apart from the information I was getting, I was also feeling a little better. It didn't seem like a life and death thing anymore. In the cheerful ambiance of this salon, my earlier panic seemed a bit silly. But of course, I still was far too curious about the whole thing.

As she bought the cocktails, I flicked through my game manual pages. "So, by ghost you mean, the spirit of the murder victim?" I read aloud.

"Exactly! The ghost is the problem, the Furies are just... a side effect."

"So, the ghost is not a Fury?" I asked. "And the Furies are not ghosts?"

"That's right. The ghost is the soul of a human who was murdered. The Furies are a specific band of revenge demons. Demon actually means lesser deity, not creatures from hell or anything like that. At least, originally, back when the play was written. Which was long before Christianity."

Because of course the vicar's wife would find a way to tie this conversation to the church.

"And what is the revenge?" I asked. "What do they do?"

"The murderer loses their mind. They slowly go insane. Oh, can you smell the strawberries? They must be blending them with the ice. Yum," she said, her eyes sparkling.

"How do they make someone lose their sanity?" I asked.

"I'm not sure, but the Furies follow their prey everywhere, and they are hideous."

"So that's it? They just hang around looking scary? I can live with that."

"Well, there is that verse about them being covered in the blood of their previous victims. I expect some gruesome death is in store. But it doesn't happen in the play."

"How come?" I asked, switching off the massage chair. I needed to hear this.

"The Furies are appeased. They become benevolent, protector goddesses."

"A demon that can be turned into an angel? That's a handy loophole."

"Regular for you madam; and vegan, sugar free here," a smiling server placed our vibrant pink drinks between us, the glasses already frosting from the ice. I sipped at the fruity rum blend, the aroma of lime infused strawberry making my tongue prick. But I still didn't know how to beat this thing, and Sarah might.

"Do you know how it's done? How were the demons turned to angels?"

Sarah looked at me quizzically over the two entire strawberries, fragrant with white rum, fixed on the frosty rim of her hurricane glass.

"I mean, do you give them gifts? Or I don't know, sacrifice someone to them?" She laughed.

"Not at all. The Furies were simply convinced. The accused proved his innocence before a jury, like in a court of law." She used the little bamboo cocktail stick to spear one of her strawberries and then dipped the strawberry in the big fluffy dollop of whipped cream perched on her daiquiri. "A jury heard the murderer's case and acquitted him."

"So, he wasn't a murderer? The defendant was wrongly accused?"

"No, he *was* a murderer. The jury decided that the murder was justified. So, the Furies lost their thirst for vengeance." She popped the cream covered strawberry into her mouth whole. "Quite a let-down, if you ask me," she added once she'd swallowed. "I think they should have exacted their revenge and killed him. But don't tell my husband I said that."

"Why do you think the demons should have killed him?"

"I don't know, I don't like him. Orestes killed his own mother. The play is about how the ghost of his mother has summoned the Furies to punish her son and murderer. Why should her death go unpunished?"

"Right. But suppose we don't want the human to, you know, lose to the demon? Turning them to angels means everyone's happy. It's a good move, if I can find out how it's done... Oh, you're right, there is something in here about the Fury letting their prey go free, if they changed their mind." I took an extra big gulp of my drink, excited. Was this the solution? Had I found what I needed? I'd flicked through the pages and there it was. I underlined that full section:

```
A Daemon of Dual Aspect:
The Erinys can be transformed into its own oppo-
site, the Eumenis, the Gracious Ones. There are very
few recorded instances of this phaenomenon.
```

"Is that a scoop of soy frozen yogurt in your cocktail?" Sarah said. I'd been taking a sip of my drink without looking at it and didn't know what to answer. "They probably improvised a dairy free option for you, instead of the whip they put on mine," she shrugged.

"What a great idea," I said absentmindedly. I wanted to tell her to take this more seriously but there was no way to explain that I feared this might be a real-life problem for me. So, I just swallowed my irritation and kept reading.

```
If this occurs, the Fury has been convinced to
spare the life of her prey. The spirit she has
summoned will return to the underworld without
claiming their murderer's soul. See Eumenis chapter
for this transformation as well as the disposition
and attributes of the benevolent daemon in her new
form.
```

I didn't have the rest of the book to look that up, but didn't need to. What I had was good enough. My note in this margin was brief:

'This is how to win. Prove innocence. Doesn't matter that demon is 'indestructible'. Don't need to *destroy* it. Just *convince* it. Truth is on my side.'

I sighed and laid back, relaxing a bit. I could do this.

A fresh tray of cucumbers, swimming in what smelled like iced green tea and decorated with rose petals, arrived on the round table beside me. Sarah and I were no longer alone, two manicurists had joined us on the dais.

"Oh, no thanks, I'm not feeling like salad right now," I said, looking at it gobsmacked. Who, in their right mind, would eat that?

"Please lay back and close your eyes for me," I was told, with a polite smile. Sarah, beside me, had already done so, and looked like she was sleeping. Who ordered the side of cucumbers then?

Oh. The vegetables were placed directly on her eyes.

This was the most ridiculous thing I'd ever seen. But glancing around, everyone here acted as if it were normal. To have on your face what the Stepmonster usually puts on her charcuterie board.

My pedicurist was looking at me, her eyes getting bigger and bigger, like a confused owl in a children's cartoon, as I failed to comply.

In a pleading tone, I was told something about rejuvenating properties. I tried hard not to roll my eyes. This was such a waste of time. I had a major clusterfuck to untangle. I downed the last of my drink, annoyed I couldn't ask Sarah anything more for the time being; she still had cucumbers for eyes, and now her pedicure lady was taking— I swear I'm not making this up— an actual cheese grater to the heels of Sarah's feet. I saw another cheese grater ready and waiting beside my basin too.

So, the flowers floating in the footbath and the loveheart shaped thrones were just bait. Once they'd got you in the chair, the torture instruments came out. I glanced at the rest of the implements on her tray, which were tiny and pink handled so I hadn't paid them much attention. They were a bunch of sharp as fuck pliers, stabby-looking scissors and miniscule scalpels. What exactly was about to happen here?

Meanwhile my pedicure lady was starting to exchange nervous glances with the older lady at the booking desk in the other end of the room, and I wondered if she was calling for reinforcements. Would there be *consequences* if I didn't have cucumber slices on my closed eyelids in T minus one second?

"Is this part obligatory?" I asked.

"Oh, not at all, it's an extra to help you relax during your exfoliation, your friend has already paid for it," the reply was a tiny whisper, so Sarah wouldn't hear. "Shall we process a refund to your friend's card instead?"

"No, I'll do it," I said and lay back. I'm not scared of your tiny pink knives, love, and I'm definitely not scared of your cucumbers.

The sensation on my eyes was quite pleasant and not disgusting as I'd imagined. I felt hands lifting my feet out of the water, one after the other, and all kinds of scraping of dead tissue begun with a vengeance.

It actually felt quite nice.

Cathartic.

Before a minute had passed, I was thinking again about the execution video that had popped up on my computer the other night. Once again, I tried to make sense of this. I hadn't ever killed anyone. Why me? Why was this happening to me?

I didn't like not being able to see. I felt watched.

I ripped the cucumbers off my face and dropped them back on the plate.

The salon had a calming, serene energy as customers quietly chatted with the staff tending to them. Our two pedicurists talked together as they worked, hunched over our basins, where our feet, now baby-soft and moisturised with several lotions, were propped on towel cushions. Their voices were so low I hadn't even heard them until I saw their lips move, but then there was chill lounge music in the background and a lot of conversations around us. Where was this persistent feeling of threat coming from?

Outside the huge front windows, the street of the little town buzzed with shoppers.

A woman lay asleep on the bench across the road.

I narrowed my eyes.

Oh, not this again.

I tried not to pay attention, but it was impossible. I began to examine every detail of the sleeping woman obsessively.

Her face was stained with mud, although now I looked carefully, it seemed more like black dried blood. Was she in need of help? But no one was stopping to see if she was ok. No one noticed her at all.

I tried to see if she was injured. She had no wounds, but the dark streaks around her mouth looked like she had either bled from her mouth or bitten someone so bad the gore ran down her chin.

She must have spilled coffee or something. Get a grip!

I had to snap out of this.

"Such a lovely afternoon," Sarah said, "the weather is beautiful." She was just removing her own cucumber mask and caught me staring out of the window.

Ask her if she sees it.

Great. I now was at the stage where I had to cross reference my own perception with others, like some lunatic.

No. I see her. That's enough. She's there...

She wasn't. Blinking at the empty bench, I felt bile burn up my throat as my stomach clenched. The woman had left. When did that happen? I only looked away for one second when Sarah spoke. One second.

I scanned the pages on my lap again nervously. Even though I had a plan now, I started to actually wonder what was in store. I'd only seen a shadow so far. A ghost. That was bad enough. But demons? Was I about to see a legion of she-monsters tonight? My fingers were trembling as I held the pages. The text said: 'Non tactile'. So why did the play show the creatures covered in blood and gore, as if they had been biting their victims?

"I'm on the side of the Furies, you see," said Sarah beside me, looking at my pages curiously, while the pedicurists began filing our nails into perfectly symmetrical and smooth ovals.

My feet would soon be too posh to be attached to the rest of my body. But it was ok because they would instantly get shoved inside my comfy old trainers so no one would ever know. Meanwhile, I was today days old when I learned that sandpaper, which I buy in hardware stores and keep in my toolbox, comes in the form of pink sticks.

"I hope one day there will be an adaptation where they change the ending, and they win, Sarah continued. "People shouldn't go around killing their mothers and getting away with it! That's just rude."

"No, I suppose they shouldn't," I said, not really paying attention, because my nails were getting scraped almost all off. I was grinding my teeth trying to endure it. Why would you pay someone to torture your feet this way?

"His mother was no saint, I'll grant you that," she chattered on. "Queen K and her lover murdered Orestes' Dad." She sounded thoroughly amused. I looked around at her. "It wouldn't be a true tragedy if it wasn't morally convoluted," she said, delighted.

"Oh. Well, that changes matters a bit," I said.

"Does it, though?"

"Sounds like this man was avenging his father's death," I shrugged. "Why did this woman go that far? Couldn't she just divorce?"

"She killed him because, listen to this," said Sarah. "Her husband, a decade earlier, had murdered their daughter."

"Are you kidding me?"

"No," she said. "Man kills his own daughter, so his wife gets a lover and kills *him*, so her son kills her and her lover, so she rises from the dead to haunt her son. Wouldn't you be on her side?"

"I don't know." I thought about it for a moment. "It sounds less a Not The Asshole and more an Either Is The Asshole."

Sarah looked at me blankly.

"You know, Reddit? Am I The Asshole?"

Her expression never changed.

"Just a website, never mind," I said quickly.

"I'm not saying I condone murder, of course," said Sarah. "But if I were unfortunate enough to marry a man who killed our daughter, I can't guarantee I wouldn't be angry enough to at least think about it."

"I should hope a man who killed his daughter would go to prison," I said. "That means his wife doesn't need to become a murderer herself to see justice done. If the laws of her land failed her then it's complicated."

"Not exactly the laws of her land; more the historical period she lived in, *that's* what failed her," said Sarah.

"Was it ok for men to kill their daughters back then?"

"Not unless a seer demanded it."

"A what?"

"A seer. The man you'd go ask whether the gods are angry with you, which you'd do if your plans weren't working out," Sarah said, a smile twitching on her lips.

"When your plans aren't working out, a troubleshooting template tends to work better than a priest," I said. Then I realised I was talking to a vicar's wife and moved on quickly. "What wasn't working out for him?"

"Queen K's husband was trying to lead his fleet to war," she said, not looking offended, "but there was no wind for the ships to sail."

"So, he didn't need a seer, he needed a carpenter to make him some oars," I shrugged.

"The seer said the god would only bless the king's expedition and let the winds blow, if the king sacrificed his daughter, the princess. It wasn't a crime. His people actually felt sorry for him that he had to sacrifice his daughter to get the fleet to sail. They blamed the god for asking for the girl's death, not the king for killing her."

"Couldn't the queen refuse, tell him to fuck off? Did she first let him sacrifice their daughter and then plotted to murder him? That's a bit passive aggressive," I said.

"No, she didn't know. He deceived her. He told his wife and daughter that the princess was going to be wed. She went to the temple in her wedding dress, then her father pulled out a knife and killed her on the altar."

"For god's sake," I said.

"Quite literally," she nodded.

"I can see why the Queen took a lover and murdered her husband," I couldn't help saying. "Even though she later turned into the ghost captain of the Fury squad. If I were her, I'd have gotten the seer as well. And the damn god who wants girl sacrifices too. All the men involved should die."

"Oh, it was a goddess, not a god!" said Sarah brightly. "And, the goddess actually saved the princess at the last minute, swapped for for a deer that died in her place. Then she flew the princess to her temple in a far away land, to be her high priestess, forever more."

"Wait. What?"

"Yes, the princess didn't actually die at all, just vanished," said Sarah.

"Ah, now it makes sense. It was a goddess-princess love story. Good on them."

"What do you mean?" It was Sarah's turn to look confused.

"You know, clearly the goddess and the princess wanted to run off together, that's the story here. The goddess blocked the naval expedition, asked for the princess' life. They ended up running off to far away land, together forever. The perfect plan. Love won. It's a happy ever after for those two."

Sarah's eyes widened. She clearly had not thought of it that way. I blinked- I probably shouldn't have blurted it out.

"They should have let the mum in on it, though," I added quickly, trying to move on, "letting a mother think her kid was murdered was a bit inconsiderate. Especially since a chain of deaths ensued."

"I like your version of events," Sarah said. "And now I think you will also side with me, when I say the Furies should have won and the son, the murderer, should have died."

I frowned. I'd forgotten about the son and the demons coming after him for matricide.

"Well yeah, I guess the son should have sided with his mother and sister, instead of his lying, murdering father..." I said half-heartedly. I really didn't want to agree to anyone dying in the hands of the revenge demons.

"Not only that, but, remember I said there was another play? A stand alone, not a trilogy?"

I knew I'd forgotten something.

"Yes!" I said. "How do you beat the demons in that one?"

"Oh, a goddess gives you a quest and you go fetch an artefact from a barbarian temple for her."

"Right."

That had absolutely entered videogame territory and didn't sound realistic. Probably not the right way to go.

"In that play, the son, before he killed his mother," she continued, "went to fetch the statue and discovered the temple his sister was in."

"He found his sister?"

"Yes. And then, he took her back home. So, he ruined her happy ending with the goddess," Sarah giggled.

"Bastard," I said.

"Exactly. Men in classical plays tell women's stories the wrong way, to make themselves be the heroes. Orestes was no hero; he was the villain in his mother's story- but no one tells his mother's story. The Furies should win. We need to re-write the whole trilogy."

Normally I would agree, but I was currently experiencing a new level of empathy for people hunted down by supernatural entities, and I bit my lip.

"Men do that in real life too," I said instead. Sarah shrugged. Clearly her feminism did not extend from literary criticism into real life.

For a moment I wondered what the hell I was doing, having pedicures with a vicar's wife.

Awkward.

"Are you ok with this?" the pedicure ladies had brought out a pair of lamps, ready to put our toes under them. I near panicked, having no idea what they meant, but Sarah answered for both of us.

"Yes thank you that's fine," she said, and they placed the warming lights over our feet. It felt kind of nice, I must admit.

"What does that lamp do? Make your feet look ten years younger or something?"

I didn't mean to be sarcastic, but I had heard the word 'rejuvenate' more times in the last forty minutes than in the rest of my life.

"Dries the gel nail polish," Sarah smiled, basking in the pampering comfort of the little gadget.

"When did that happen?" I said looking at my toes. They all had nail polish on, perfectly white and yummy looking. I had no idea my feet could be sexy. I wondered if I should re-evaluate my opinion of beauty salons. And flipflops.

"Yes, we are done," Sarah told me. "As soon as our nails dry, we are good to go! How did you find your pedicure?"

"It's... It's very nice," I admitted.

"We should do this again next month," said Sarah. "I'll be needing a new pedi for my holiday, I'll text you if you'd like to come."

I looked at her in disbelief. No one has ever invited me on a monthly ladies' day out before.

"Ok," I said, thinking that first and foremost, I owe her a lot of money for this, "but next time will be my treat."

"Lovely," she said. "I guess you are looking forward to going home and playing your game?" she said indicating at the pages in my hand.

"Not particularly," I mumbled.

"Pardon?"

"At least I have a plan."

"What's your plan?"

"I hope the way to win this, is for the player to prove they are innocent," I said.

"Just remember one thing," said Sarah. "Tragedies are not usually Who-done-it's. The opposite, actually."

"What's the opposite of a who-done-it?" I asked.

"A tragic irony play: Where the audience knows the killer's identity from the start, and they watch the hero figure it out or die trying."

"That's a bit ominous."

"I mean you as the player," she said, "you'll need to keep your eyes open in that game for very obvious clues you might have missed. Typically the tragic hero's downfall is a truth about himself that he refuses to acknowledge."

Well that didn't apply to me. I was being falsely accused of a murder I didn't commit, that's what was happening here.

"So, enjoy your game!" she smiled.

"Thanks," was all I could say. A knot was tightening my throat out of nowhere.

"Let me know how you get on! I'm sure you'll defeat it in the end, even if it takes a few tries!"

"I have a bad feeling, that I have to get it right the first time," I said.

"Oh, I was sure my daughter gets to start over when she dies in those games."

"Different kind of game, I guess."

"Well, I'm sure you will get it right the first time then!"

"Yeah, I hope so."

After all, I'm not a murderer.

But then, ghosts don't exist.

I couldn't think about this anymore.

What about demons, do they exist?

I looked up and scanned the sunny day outside. A car had stopped at the traffic lights, and I couldn't see the bench with the sleeping woman. I waited.

"How was everything, ladies?" In a stylish swish of shoulder-long earrings, Caleb was back with our shoe baskets.

"Lovely as always, thank you dear," said Sarah, taking hers.

"That's gorgeous, Jade!" Caleb enthused at my pedicure.

"Yeah, I didn't realise my feet could look so good," I said, still embarrassed.

"Now you know, we hope to see you again soon," he said, and popped a pair of bamboo flipflops with the salon's logo in my basket. "Complimentary," he grinned, "for first-time customers!"

"Oh, you don't have to do that—"

"And a tote, to carry your trainers home while you're showing off that stunning pedi," he added, emptying my trainers in a pink burlap bag with the salon's logo on it too. "Wear it loud and proud, girl," he winked at me with extra-long eyelashes, before he turned to go.

Kid, I won't be taking Pride lessons from someone who wasn't alive when Queer As Folk came out.

"Zoomers," I muttered, hiding a smile.

"What?" said Sarah.

"Oh, I was just saying, my sister's generation really is something else."

"Ah yes, we have a phrase for it too, we call it: Kids These Days! We've been saying it since people your age were teens," she winked too. "Is that the time? I have to run!" Sarah slipped into her sandals with a cheerful bounce and gave me an apologetic smile. "Please take your time, sorry I have to rush."

"No worries, thank you for this!"

"It was a pleasure! Pop by the cottage sometime for tea! It would be great to catch up again!" she said, speeding away with a little wave.

"Sure!" I called after her and grabbed the basket with the flip flops. At least they weren't pink, they were white. I could give this a try. As I stood up, my feet feeling like little clouds in the open air, I paused.

The traffic light turned green, and the cars moved on.

The sleeping woman with the bloodstains was not on the bench.

A strong metallic odour permeated the air. I scanned the room. The salon was cheerful, brimming with pleasant conversations.

The smell of blood was still there.

I looked down my front, wondering if it was me? Had I cut myself on something?

"Are you ok? You're good to go, your friend has paid in full online," said a staff member in cleaner scrubs, who had arrived with a caddy of disinfectants, to empty the basins.

I watched him kneel by the water that was no longer foamy, and I gasped.

Reflected on the surface of the opaque water basins, were two women, asleep on the chairs Sarah and I had just vacated.

They were wrapped in leathery black garments like bats cocooned in their own wings.

I looked at the white massage chairs.

They were empty.

I glanced back down at the water. For one more second, I caught their reflection again.

But they weren't there.

Swirls formed as the cleaner pulled a plug lever on the side of the basins, and the water siphoned fast down the drains. There was nothing to reflect the chairs on anymore. I was panting hard, not knowing what to do. Had I caught a glimpse of something no one else could see, or had I imagined those two women sleeping beside me?

With an irritated eyeroll that said, '*Are you going to sit there and watch me?*' the cleaner sprayed the empty basins with antibacterial and started to scrub them.

The chairs were still empty.

I turned and ran out of the salon, fleeing the overpowering scent of blood.

Chapter Sixteen

The Last Night

I walked back on the deck of the Lady Thomasine that evening feeling a hundred times more frightened than when I'd set off.

I sat on Grandma 's bistro chair and took in the glorious early evening skies over the waters, a sense of foreboding rising in my chest. Butterflies danced among the potted begonias and delicate dahlias, and I sank in the murkiest depths of impending doom.

I had failed to come up with anything I could call a logical explanation. I was now convinced not only ghosts, but possibly also demons existed. Cool.

Just fucking brilliant.

I unlocked the door and stepped into the lounge.

Nothing loomed over the couch.

Well not yet anyway.

Grandfather and Cannelloni were still out, which was a good thing. Whatever was coming after me, I wanted my family nowhere near it.

It comes with the darkness. It will start again soon.

Not for the first time, I thought that maybe I should leave home to face it alone. But I was so very tired, and hungry. I checked the time. Just turned six pm. With sunset around nine thirty, I had over three hours still to wait. I'd be ok here for now.

What does a demon look like? What will they do?

I could run an online search... But I stopped myself. I had enough of classical tragedies for one day. And I was not putting the word 'demons' in a search box. Nope. Enough was enough. I had a plan. I would stick to it. And until then, I needed to rest.

I ran to my cabin, straight for the bureau, where my military correspondence filled several drawers. Right under my discharge documents was my PTSD report from that day. Just as I remembered, it described my job: Supervising the drone team. The wording stated clearly that I had not caused the execution; of course, I was never even accused of the killing- I was simply discharged for my post-traumatic stress. But it was evident in this description that I had no part in it.

I snapped a photo of the document and sent it to my printer.

Once the copy was in my hands, the paper still slightly warm on my fingers, I felt a little better. Sarah had said the demons let their victim go when a court of law acquitted him, right? A military tribunal was very much the same thing. This must be the answer. This copy should make those creatures leave me alone. Just like in that play, where their anger was appeased, and they turned into protecting angels.

Of course, facing them wasn't going to be easy. They would probably be terrifying. The women on the bench were deeply unsettling, and they were asleep. I did not want to come face to face with them when they woke up tonight...

I clenched my fists to stop my hands shaking.

I got this. I'm fine, I can do it!

I folded the copy and put it in my backpack. I folded the mysterious pages about the Furies and put them there too. I took a deep breath and exhaled. I'd done all I could to be ready. Now all I really needed was some fuel in me, and some rest.

Quarter past six. Still over three hours to sunset.

I was just finishing the second slice of hummus and avocado toast, when—

A message buzzed.

Ami had texted!

Only one sentence, but it felt like the best message I'd ever read: 'At the airport! Queued up for the next flight out!' This was it. She would fly overnight. She'd be here tomorrow. My heart warmed a little, the knot loosened in my chest. I'd typed the single word 'Amazing!' back with lightening speed but it was, once again, not received. No matter, as of tomorrow she'd be here and we'd text and video call all day long. Till then, I just had to be patient...

I was SO impatient. My thumb scrolled up and up through our old messages. Glimpses of the weeks and months before, the conversations we had and the moments we shared across the miles. I drank in her words from the old messages like a healing elixir. I didn't want to stop. If I had only a few hours left till sunset, all I wanted to do was read Ami's conversations and disappear in our memories together. All the way back to how we... how we first *got* together.

Within a few minutes I had sank among the cushions on the window seat, with a large steaming mug of chai with cinnamon, thinking only of her. My favourite part of our relationship is those first few weeks of video calls, before either of us dared say it. I looked at the two word notification, Voice Call, with the date and time underneath- the day we started dating. I closed my eyes.

"You are so lucky to be back at an indoors gym," Ami had said from my screen that night, about four and a half months ago. "Every time I shower after a workout, I have to pluck leaves and dead bugs from my hair! And the water runs burgundy from the red sands. This sand gets everywhere!"

"Everywhere," I said, smirking. I was lying in my bed, like I did every night, wide awake when she called. I guess it was the only good thing about my night-mares. Ami preferred to call me first thing in the morning before the camp woke up, which was the middle of the night for me back home. But no chance that I'd be asleep anyway, so it worked well for both of us. "But even though it gets everywhere, I'd put up with all the dirt in the desert to have my cute boxing partner back."

Ami blushed.

"Oh, is there a sudden shortage of cute girls at your gym?" she said.

"None like you."

I had never been so open about it with anyone else. Telling a woman I find her attractive *before* I went out with her? Nope. I wait for the night out, and even then, I don't *say* it. Things might or might not happen organically. But having Ami on my screen every week, chatting away for hours, it was all so new. And I really liked her. It would feel dishonest, hiding how much I fancied her. It would be like faking a friendship to be close to her.

But then again, once the word 'cute' had come out of my mouth, I was terrified she'd hung up and ghost me.

She didn't. She flirted back.

"Do you remember the things you said to me about my yoga practice, Ma'am," she said.

"I've asked you not to call me that. We're not serving together anymore. I'm just Jade."

"It really bothered me. You put gender to the exercise. Made out like yoga is feminine, and boxing masculine. Implying somehow that women's workouts aren't good enough. That we must train like men, to train for real."

"That's not at all what I meant," I said.

"But then I saw you boxing. Super-hot stuff!"

I paused, startled.

"So, I changed my plan."

"What plan?"

"At first, I meant to show you that yoga is hard core. To change your mind about it. Actually, I still plan to do that—"

"Never gonna happen," I said.

"We shall see," she said with a sneaky smile. "But the way you were boxing on that bag, I was like, wow!" she continued. "Need to get me some of *that*!"

"Some of... what, my boxing bag or my combat mojo?" I chuckled.

She tilted her head playfully to the side and her gaze dropped to my lips for a moment. Then she slowly looked back up, her long lashes heavy, her eyes sparkling.

"No. *You*, Jade."

That was the first time she had said my name.

"That's why I made the pads," Ami said. "Get you to quit that bag. Have you to myself."

I raised an eyebrow.

"I like having your full attention," she added. She'd been fidgeting with the top three buttons on her khaki uniform shirt and now she let her top part open, just a sliver. She had the black uniform bra on, but below it, her skin was smooth and nicely lined by a solid sixpack. I felt my breath catch. She grinned and quickly buttoned up again, her eyes scanning around her to make sure no one had noticed.

Remembering those moments makes me smile, no matter how shitty my life is. I took a sip of my cinnamon chai, looking out in the quiet waters. It's amazing how close Ami and I are, considering we haven't had the chance to know each other *that* way. I've got a girlfriend I've known for over seven months, whom I've never touched with my bare hands.

Making it official didn't take long. I think it happened when I said, "I wish I'd known you in different circumstances."

"Why?" she replied.

"Because I'd have asked you out weeks ago."

She smiled. "What's stopping you?"

By the end of that call, we were in a serious, committed, long distance relationship.

And the three months that followed, while I waited for my medical tribunal to decide on the future of my career, I had this one bright ray of sunshine: Ami's calls.

Sometimes she told me about her family with such detail, I feel like I've known them for years.

How she is secretly saving money to buy her own place, because she lives in an attic flat by herself, but not *really* alone. Family is constantly crowding her. Her parents didn't want her living in military accommodation and didn't want her renting a place on her own, either. But she had to move near her base, four hours away from her parents' house in London, to work. She has an uncle in that city with a large old town house and he converted his attic to rent out online for extra income. When Ami got a placement in the station nearby, her family sent her to her uncle. Not only that; they also take turns so her Mum, or one of her two sisters, is staying in Ami's spare bedroom as often as possible. Pretending to visit her uncle and his family downstairs. She wouldn't stop saying how much she wants her own place, away from family, completely independent. And how she fears they will freak out when she does.

At other times Ami didn't talk at all- she sneaked her phone in the showers and face-timed me silently.

Letting me watch her.

God, those nights, lying under the covers in the small hours of the morning, waiting for the call. Answering the phone, seeing where she is calling from. And just watching.

I didn't ask her to do that, and I told her afterwards I didn't feel comfortable doing the same, but she smiled and said she didn't mind. Next time she hung her phone higher up on the shower, so I could see all the way down to her waist.

But I've never seen more, and that's ok. I can't wait till she is back home.

I can't wait till I get to kiss her for the first time.

Remembering those moments, standing alone by the boat window, knowing what happened next, brought a bitter taste to my mouth. I finished my chai, trying and failing not to think about it. Things had gotten so bad so fast. Because for some reason, it seems, I can never find happiness.

As my tribunal had approached, the nightmares had wrecked me so bad, I was barely functional at work. I made mistakes, came in late, couldn't do my job. Who can, with less than an hour sleep per night, going on three months? A week before the tribunal I'd been told it didn't look good. They'd decided to let me go. That they would formally dismiss me on that meeting.

When Ami called after that, I didn't pick up. I couldn't face her. Not being a Flight Lieutenant? What even was I? A civvy? Why would she want to be with me?

I avoided her calls for a few days, and her texts came in full of worry. She thought something had happened to me. I took a whole day writing and deleting a breakup text.

No explanations just don't contact me again, I don't want this anymore. I pressed 'send' late one night. It was 'read' right away. She left voicemails, and video messages, and she was crying. And it broke me.

"I'm so sorry! Did I do something? Please tell me what I did? Why are you not talking to me? I'll be home so soon now... Can't you just tell me why? I can't imagine never seeing you again! Why, Jade?"

I didn't answer any of them. After a few days, they stopped coming.

Five days later, at my tribunal, I was told to pack my things and leave military accommodation within four weeks. I was no longer a service woman.

And five days after that, the evening news on television announced the evacuation. We were pulling out. Negotiations had fallen apart. We needed everyone out of the desert within 6 weeks.

I texted her. Just to check.

"When is your date? When are you flying back? Stay safe."

Her answer destroyed me.

"No date for our unit."

"But you've been there six months now, you're due to come home."

"Our stay was extended, till end of evacuation. Translators are last to leave. We have been moved to the embassy."

I knew what that meant. Translators now had one job: listening in on all the security channels. All day every day. Until everyone else had been evacuated safely.

I couldn't believe it. Another 6 weeks for her, on top of the 6 months she'd already been there. Unthinkable. And during an evacuation? This was far too dangerous. Staying last... While the base slowly emptied?

I should have been there with her.

"Call me," I texted her.

"Usual time," she replied.

That was the last time we spoke. After that night, the signal got fucked up. But that night I had the chance to tell her everything.

"Ami, are you ok?" I had picked up and it was a voice call, because video calls were no longer going through.

"Yes. Jade! I didn't think you would pick up!"

"Of course I'd pick up darling. I told you to call me."

"Why did you disappear like that?"

"Because I'm a selfish cow. Something really bad happened and I thought it was the end of the world. But now... Now I realise it was nothing, nothing compared to... I can't believe you're stuck out there."

"I can't talk about that, Jade," she said quietly, and of course she was right. "Please tell me what happened to you? Was it something I did?"

"No. You were the only good thing I had going for me."

I told her everything. Without naming the event that caused the nightmares, as it is classified, I explained I have been diagnosed with PTSD and have been medically discharged. I didn't *want* to break up with her. But I was just such a loser right now, I didn't deserve her. No job, no *home* even! She can do better than me.

Ami listened.

"You should get a dog," she said in the end.

"What?"

"I've heard a dog helps with PTSD. You should go to the rescue and find a big fluffy pupper to adopt."

"That's actually a good idea. I might do that. I love dogs, in Dad's house we always had dogs growing up. And I could use a real friend right now."

"I'm looking forward to meeting your pup!"

"I'll send you photos of the candidates in the next couple of days!"

There was a pause. We were both thinking about *her*, over *there*, and neither of us could talk about it. Then she said the most incredible thing.

"Jade, this is actually a blessing in disguise!"

"How?"

"Now we are no longer posted on separate stations on either side of the country!"

"No, I'm not posted anywhere," I said dryly.

"Exactly! Now you can come to *me*!"

"I will. As soon as you're safely home, I'll come for a whole weekend! We'll celebrate. We can break the rules, and have pizza," I joked.

"No, Jade," Ami said. "Not to visit me. You should come live with me. Let's move in together!"

"What?"

"I'm getting ready to buy a place of my own. Before my super-loving family totally suffocate me. They will take it so much easier if I tell them I have a flatmate! And even better, not some stranger, but someone who served with me! An ex-officer, none the less! Oh my god, this is brilliant! They would accept that, Jade! That's something I can actually tell them and not get disowned for living on my own!"

"Live together?" was all I could say.

"I'm sorry, I guess it does sound like moving too fast... We haven't even really been together... But hear me out. We are not doing it as a couple, I can't tell my parents any of that. We do it as flatmates, right? Separate bedrooms. That's ok, right? It's not too soon to be just flatmates!"

Of all the things I never expected to happen to me, top one is, someone asking me to be a military girlfriend. Me, a civvy, living with a Sargent. If I'm not careful, I'll end up a military wife in the end.

"Why aren't you saying anything?" Ami asked.

"It's just... I'd be renting a room in the flat you will buy?"

"Yes, I guess!"

"And you don't plan to tell your parents about us?"

"Well, they don't know... you know. They don't know."

"You haven't come out?"

"No."

"To your sisters?"

"They'd tell Mum and Dad."

I sighed.

"But from what you've told me about your family, they will come visiting quite often. They will meet me."

"Yes! Its' perfect, isn't it? You're the perfect flatmate. They'll love you!"

"But I'll have to pretend you're not my girlfriend?"

Pause.

"I'm not ready, Jade. Can't we get them to meet you first, so they have time to *like* you, which I know they will! And then when the time is right, I'll tell them, ok?"

"No," I said. "I'm not hiding. I'd love to get a flat with you, Ami. I don't mind the separate bedrooms. I agree we should take it slow for sure. It's a big step."

"Great! That's great, Jade!"

"When I say get a flat with you, I mean, buy it together. Not pay you rent. Split the mortgage. We'll be a couple; it'll be *our* flat."

"Really?"

"It does feel far too soon," I agreed to her unspoken question.

"I think it's perfect!" she squeaked. "Getting a place together! That's so grown up!"

"Welcome to your thirties," I said. She's thirty-one, but I get to be bossy because I'm thirty-eight. "But there is one more thing."

"What is it?"

"I'm not pretending we're friends."

"Oh. Maybe... Just for a little bit?"

"No."

"Why not?"

"This is only going to work if, on their first visit to our flat, I can introduce myself to your family as your partner."

Silence.

"I can sit with you when you tell them, if you like. Whatever you want, any way I can help. I know it's hard. I'm here. But I won't lie to your family."

She still wasn't saying anything.

"Look, it won't be right away. If we are going to start looking for a place, that will take months. Buying? Year and a half most likely. So it gives you some time."

"That's right!" her voice was bright again. "You'll come visit and we'll start by going house hunting! How awesome is that?"

"Pretty awesome," I agreed.

"Oh, Jade I can't wait!"

"I can't wait either." I tried not to think of the four weeks ahead, how much danger she was in.

"You and I and the chinchillas! And the new dog!"

"Sounds amazing," I said.

"It *is* amazing!"

"But once we find our place and move in... we are not hiding."

"Ok!"

"So, you will tell them by then?"

"I'll tell them by then. Let's do this!"

"Yes!" I said. And just like that, I had a girlfriend again.

A girlfriend whose voice I haven't heard since.

With a sigh, I finished my tea and picked up the phone.

"I'll stay up (haha)" I wrote, because I'm always up. "Text whenever you can, call when you land. I'm thinking of you constantly. I'll see you tomorrow!"

Then I sent another quickly: 'Hey, I got a pedicure. My toes have polish on, I think they might fall off from the shock.'

And then a last one: "I love you."

I had to force myself to stop texting or a hundred messages would all download at once when she finally got signal. I threw the phone across the lounge, to the furthest seat away from me. It landed with a little bounce among the cushions on Grandma's love seat. I would try to forget about it for now.

I checked the time. Seven thirty. Still ages to go. I hated this helpless waiting. And at the same time, I wished it would never get dark again. How did this escalate so fast? Only this morning I was trying to wrap my head around the whole 'ghosts are real' thing, and now we're talking about demons?

And here's a question that kept gnawing at me: What does a demon look like? What am I up against exactly?

Those women... the sleeping figures who kept appearing in busy public places... was *that* it? I wanted to say no, they were homeless people. But the third time I saw them, their reflection on the water was clear like a mirror—they were sleeping in the armchairs beside me— while the armchairs were empty. Only the water draining in the basins showed them there.

I now wished I hadn't fled in terror, but stayed and done something, anything! Tapped the seat of the chair. Waved my hand in that space. See if anything swatted at me.

This would be so funny if it wasn't so fucking terrifying.

Seven thirty-five. Officially less than two hours to sunset.

Maybe I should be searching online for tickets to the North Pole? A day that lasts six months, that's what I need right now.

And what then? Keep running from the darkness, forever? I'd have to face this thing sooner or later.

I've got a plan. I know how to beat it. I can do this!

Even if actual demons show up. And even if what I saw on those women was blood, and they are covered in gore... which they probably will be, judging by the stench of rot that chased me out of the salon... still, all I need to do is prove my innocence. And I can do that.

Why me though? Out of everyone that witnessed that execution, am I the only one? Why?

I knew for a fact that none of my team that day had nightmares or any other symptoms like mine. It's not that anyone liked what they saw. Everyone was subdued for days after that mission. But that's normal. That's what happens. I was the only one with a diagnosis. Everyone else was still in service. So yeah, it was just me. Like I was the weakest link or something.

Maybe that was the answer.

Maybe that's exactly why this was happening, because I was the most affected by it. Just plain sadistic, picking on the easiest target. 'Oh, *you're* the one suffering PTSD from my death? Let me come and have some fun with that.'

Maybe all I needed to do for it to leave me alone was not give a flying fuck.

Well, hopefully the therapist would help with that. At some point. Right now, the best I could do was not overthink it.

I sat at my desk to search for a movie to stream. I didn't have the brain capacity to work tonight. I could feel something was coming, something was going to happen.

I gave myself the night off. I opened the supernatural horror section. Not my thing. I'm more of a zombie apocalypse kind of gal. But in light of recent developments, why the hell not? The film began with a family moving into an eerie old house, which was mysteriously much cheaper than it should be. Yawn.

Very soon the teenage daughter, perturbed by all the doors opening and closing of their own accord, decided to take a bath. Because that's what you do. When you feel unsafe. In a creepy old room.

You take your clothes off and keep them off for a very long time.

The scene was mostly close-ups of her terrorised facial expressions. Combined, of course, with the insinuation of nudity under the foam and bubbles.

I caught myself nodding off. Propped my head on my hands to hold it up. I'm all for ladies in the buff, but the male gaze was a major vibe killer.

By the time the mother expressed she had a terrible foreboding about the house, prompting the father to angrily ignore her concerns, my eyes had closed, and I was only listening.

Once the little son started talking to an imaginary friend, I blacked out.

I woke up to the end credits rolling on my screen.

Pitch black outside.

I winced, as a sudden chilling sensation crept down my bones. Plunged me into shivers, once again, as if I were neck-deep in water, with ice cubes bobbing all around me. For a moment I looked around bewildered, not sure why I hurt like this again.

And then, boom! A stream of white noise.

Static.

I jumped and looked to the kitchen; my fingers turned to icicles.

The radio.

No, it's in the river.

I stood from the desk to peer at the counter, too wary to step closer. The new digital device was still playing Alan's rock station in the background, I could see the display on its screen. But something else spewed static. The same obscene noise, moody and changing like a living thing. Its daunting fluctuations surging, like the call of a bottomless pit, paralysing me with fear. Then it lulled to a sinister hum that tricked me into doubting if it was even there. I was back where I'd started. I'd come full circle. After all that had happened, I had changed nothing.

Where is it coming from?

I took a deep breath. The sound was much closer than the kitchen. Almost next to me. I looked around. My phone sat at the other end of the love seat. Exactly where I threw it before the movie.

The screen was lit. A video.

It wasn't the execution; I didn't know *what* it was. But I was shaking. Once again, a video that appeared by itself.

This is it. It's starting. Whatever is coming tonight, it's started talking.

Chapter Seventeen

Leela

I reached out to pick up my phone. A zap sparked with static electricity, its potent sting piercing my fingers.

"What the...?" I said, rubbing my sore digits in the palm of my hand. The phone just sat there, making that sound, like the angry winds of a winter storm. I reached for it again, knowing static electricity rarely shocks twice. Nonetheless. Another spark flew and the unpleasant sensation tingled in my fingers. The phone howled.

"You can fuck right off," I said to it. I left it where it was and perched beside it.

I was frozen, unable to move. I thought I should leave the boat. I couldn't put Grandad and Cannelloni in danger, and they would be home soon. But I couldn't move. My gaze never left the mobile across from me, and somehow it switched itself on, overriding my lock-screen without a password.

I was shaking, trying to suppress a twinge of panic in the back of my mind. Nearly two decades working as tech security and I never thought I'd see the day I'd be scared of an electronic device. My elbow collapsed against the back of the couch, so I leaned over the screen, seeing without coming into physical contact with the phone itself.

A dusty expanse of rolling hills, stone and dry earth as far as the eye could reach.

Spatters of thorn bushes squirming in the winds.

Fast flying clouds of reddish fog.

Sands swept up from the ground and thrust like angry swarms in the gale.

The desert.

This was the scenery surrounding the base. A knot in my chest tightened.

I wanted to find a way to stop the video, but instead, I kept watching.

A gust whistled across the land, loud like the black call of an endless chasm. The succulent arms of the grey-blue stars of aloe, scattered across the dry slopes, shivered and twitched. Red sands rose into fog and swarmed over the hills. Then just as swiftly, the blazing wind subsided to the throaty whisper of an unsettling breeze through dead leaves.

The video reminded me of something, but I could not pinpoint what it was. And a warning echoed in my head: 'Stop it! Stop watching!'

A ruined temple. White pillars and half collapsed chambers of some ancient civilisation.

The friezes were carved with monsters and demon gods.

This video breathed a strange, dangerous familiarity. The warning bells turned into deafening sirens in my mind. A rising migraine slowly melted my brain into soup. Instinct old me to get out of this room. Stop watching. Stop listening.

But I was completely fixated on the screen.

Little human figures of stone fought gallantly against the heinous marble deities. But whatever story might have been told, high up on those tall white walls, now lay fragmented and incoherent. Shattered among the pieces that littered the floor of the ruins.

The wind screeched like steak knives against dinner plates, and then hushed, settling just at the edge of hearing.

And god have I heard this nightmare sound before...

The camera zoomed out to capture the stunning scenery. I hadn't realised how far away the temple had been... but now I saw it from the actual distance, I recognised the location.

The ancient shrine was nestled in a hollow valley of ferocious beauty—just stone and sand, rolling hills; a purple sky, hewn with crimson.

The sun was rising. The solar disc was enormous in the desert, and it framed the entire temple in a fiery semicircle of gold.

I had taken this video myself.

It was the one my sister found in Ami's photo album. Last time I watched it, it sent me into a paroxysm of flashbacks. I had jumped in the fucking river to avoid the memories, the voices in my mind. I had almost drowned.

I hit the pause icon. The screen sparked. A high-pitched "Fuck's sake!" escaped my lips as the shock burned my hand. I lost feeling in my fingers and stared at them. They hung limp for a couple of seconds, before a soft twitch returned and I was able to move them again.

How is that possible? Only my fingertip had come into contact with the damn screen, yet all my fingers were paralysed. More than that, a hot buzz still felt like it was frying my flesh and muscle up to my wrist.

I rubbed it with my other hand, wondering if a mobile phone could even have the voltage to produce such an effect when not plugged in.

No. It couldn't.

Meanwhile, the video played on. The magnificent disc of the sun kept rising slowly in the horizon on the screen.

"Shit!" I said, turning my face away from the screen. Last time I saw that sunrise... The shadow in the deep. The way it followed me from beneath, as if ready to pull me into the cold abyss below...

My chest was heaving, I was panting hard, had the room ran out of oxygen? I turned back to look at my phone and stabbed at the pause icon with two fingers.

This time, the shock was so vicious, it shot up beyond my elbow.

"What the hell?" I rubbed my arm and tried to ball my fist, to make the pain subside. My muscles were seizing. My whole hand and arm went numb. The entire limb fell to my lap like a rope.

What is happening? The phone was refusing to stop, and it was showing me something I didn't want to see.

A distorted voice began to whisper. It came insidiously under the loud sound of the desert gale. An urgent suspicion pierced my gut, that it was not a human voice. An inexplicable, horrific impression that the voice was dead. Whatever the hell that meant.

How do I stop this fucking video?

Slowly, the feeling returned to my arm but brought with it an excruciating attack of pins and needles. It was so painful my eyes teared up. I swallowed hard and glared at the sunrise video once more.

The image jumped, as if the camera shook a little. It momentarily revealed part of the inside of a military vehicle, before focusing back on the temple sunrise out of the window. The vehicle was stopped along a dirt road among the dry hills. The engine hummed in the background.

"Ma'am!"

Please, not again.

"No, I need three minutes. The road is empty," came my own voice from the phone.

"Ma'am, the road is not empty, can't you hear him yelling? He is heading our way," my driver replied.

The voices were not in my head. They were... in the video? But that couldn't be. I had deleted that part.

And yet there it was, on the screen.

Another jump of the image flashed a dirt road, stretching long behind the vehicle, and a donkey in the distance, laden with baskets brimming with flea market goods. The animal stood confused, waiting for the man who had left it behind.

The man was striding to my vehicle, waving both hands over his head. Then the image turned to the temple sunrise again. I had of course re-directed the camera to its intended shot.

'It's ok. I know him; he works in the kitchen,' came my voice again.

"I deleted this part!" I said to the phone. Then I bit my lip. Had I actually got to the point I was talking to an electronic device now?

"Ma'am, he is agitated," came my driver's voice from the background, while the sunrise was still in the shot. I had kept my camera pointing to the temple and I remembered I fully intended to mute the sound, so our strained exchange would not be heard when I sent it to Ami.

So how am I hearing it now?

Because this was clearly the un-edited version. The original.

"He's not agitated; he always gestures like that," I went on trying to get my driver to calm down till I finished the shot. The sun was now almost two-thirds up, but the bottom of the golden disc was still hidden behind the rolling hills. The temple glowed gold, and I remembered how the glossy marble stones reflected the sun rays of the beautiful dawn.

"We should move on. Can I drive. Ma'am?"

I deleted this. I DELETED IT.

"He is getting closer!" My driver was proper freaking out at this point.

"He's harmless. He is Locally Employed Staff! I know him."

"We are out in the desert, Ma'am! Out of the wire he can be anything, Ma'am!"

"Standby. I need 90 seconds for the sun to fully rise."

A third voice, like someone was approaching, but still distant and incomprehensible. A voice carried on the powerful wind, twisted and desperate.

Gooseflesh spread on my arms, making me squirm.

This voice sounded so strange, like something was corrupting the recording. Its rhythm flowed irregularly, the timbre too dark and breathy. One moment it reverberated, unthinkably low with searing rage, and then grew miserably shrill, shifting impossibly fast for human vocal cords.

'Permission to drive!' My driver had started to panic at this point.

'Stand down. Sixty seconds.' The sun was almost completely clear off the horizon, and God help me I was still recording the sunrise. I must have had a steady hand, because now the temple was flawless, never losing focus. Meanwhile, two people were clearly unravelling behind the camera. I felt a twinge of guilt.

"The hostile is ten paces from the vehicle, Ma'am!"

"I can see that for myself, airman. And he's not a hostile, he's a civilian."

The loud desert gales, the man calling as he approached, his words unfathomable. My skin crawled to hear him. As the winds howled the unbearable static; the agonising urgency of the underlying whisper was disturbing.

Static? Did I just call the wind 'static'?

Looking at the phone, the sudden revelation hit me:

This was the noise.

The ghoulish sound from the radio.

The repulsive static, the whispering voice underneath. This sound, which naturally accompanied these images: Strong winds on sandy hills. Not static at all, it never had been. My breath caught with newfound dread.

And why had the gales of the desert played, like some ominous message, out of the old radio night after night?

"Ma'am he is coming to your window!"

"Don't come any closer!" came my own voice. The reply was deafening. A pleading, desperate string of words.

"I don't know what you're saying. Stay there!" came my own voice.

I grabbed a cushion in each hand and sandwiched the phone between them. I squeezed them together and lifted them up. It worked! I was carrying the phone between the cushions.

Now what? I fought the urge to throw that in the river too. I couldn't afford a new mobile.

"Drive, now! Go, go, GO!" came my voice, muffled between the cushions.

But the next words didn't just come from the phone I was trying to drown out.

They were whispered directly in my ear.

"Jade... Jade, Jade! JADE!"

I swerved around, rounding a left hook punch at whoever was standing behind me. There was no one there. The room was empty.

And the phone was now on the floor, buried under its cushion padding, but the gales and the desperate voice cried loud as ever. The engine roared, accelerating. I knew the vehicle was finally moving, even though I couldn't see the screen.

And then the footsteps came. They pounded from the phone. He was running behind us, as if his life depended on it.

And I remembered him. His face was drenched in tears as he ran with all he had.

The footsteps from the phone intensified, mirroring my memory. The clatter had a chilling quality, an echo welling up from fathomless depths. The sound made my teeth grind together. The footfalls hammered louder and louder and became a swift beat. That was when he had managed to lean in and look at me through the window, and my driver floored the accelerator, and I was slammed into my seat as we shot forward, leaving the running man to grow smaller and smaller in the sideview mirror.

It took a moment to get back from my memory and realise the video had ended.

I stood in the silence of the lounge, unable to believe what had just happened.

Those footsteps I had just heard from my phone…

They were identical to the pacing following me the other night, when I walked the dog.

I remembered how odd it had been, coming from both directions: While I faced the boat and while I faced away.

The footsteps always sounded from behind me. No matter which way I had turned, always they followed. But it wasn't a real person stalking me and my dog. It was this memory. The memory of his footsteps running after us.

Logic would dictate I was, officially, losing my damn mind.

But who was I kidding. My logical brain wasn't even trying anymore. We'd entered the realm of the inexplicable. We took shit at face value now: If it looked like a ghost and sounded like a ghost and talked like a ghost, through deleted videos that came out of nowhere, then I should drop the therapist and go see the vicar.

No, dammit. I'd be useless if I didn't check my phone for any files that shouldn't be there. I wasn't expecting the video to show up stored in my media file. I gave up that hope in the endless days I searched my laptop for the execution clip I'd received back then. Now I knew there would be no evidence of the stream. But I can't be in tech security and not run an antivirus after my device streamed something on its own. I just can't.

I reached out to my phone, hand trembling slightly. Ready for the pain. I tapped the mobile lightly, testing.

It didn't spark.

I touched it firmly.

Nothing happened.

"So, you're done zapping me now, are you?" I asked the phone. It didn't answer.

I ran the scans without getting electrocuted. The phone was clean.

I'd expected nothing less.

So... not advanced tech; just another a paranormal event. Fuck my life right now.

I stood and started pacing around the lounge. I tried to shake off the trepidation of that whole *supernatural* thing. Because apart from that, the... enemy, shall we call it, the enemy hadn't done anything *that* bad.

Not to start with, but the night is young.

I went to the sink and splashed cold water on my face to stop the adrenaline rush pounding in my ears.

Come on. It was just a video. A video trying to shake me.

It just throws at me stuff I don't want to remember. That's all.

Uncomfortable memories from the desert, things related to Ami, anything that would set off my condition. And specifically, thoughts that reminded me of her. That wrecked me, when I was so worried about her, whether she'd get home safely. So that's what it goes for. It's just trying to break me.

It's done it before and it's getting old. Fool me once, I'm a dunce, fool me twice, you pay the bloody price.

And it was my fault, really. Shit you hide, it fucks you up. I never told Ami I saw her friend on the road that day. I felt like utter garbage, driving off without a word—not that I *could* talk to him, without a translator!

Not that I was allowed to, either.

I promised myself there and then, I'd tell Ami that I ran into fondant-fancies guy and had to drive off because he was scaring my driver. I'd tell her every detail of that meeting, as soon as I saw her. It makes me feel like shit, but I'd never meant to keep it a secret. Of course, omitting it wasn't right either. Once it was out in the open that bloody ghost wouldn't be able to use it against me and freak me out like that.

Although that couldn't happen until tomorrow. And that *thing*, it was coming right now.

I could feel it.

And if that whole *demon* story was real, well then. Grandpa and Cannelloni didn't deserve whatever was about to happen.

I grabbed my jacket and bike keys. I had to get out of the boat right away.

Because it knew the boat. This is where it came to find me. But there was one place it had never been. One place I might be safe from it.

So here I am, Mum.

The cemetery was dark in the small hours of the morning, the silence heavy. The night frozen, like a black void in time.

"I'm so tired. I really hope it doesn't find me here. It's never found me here. Right? I've had enough. I've just had enough of this. Can't it just *stop* now?" Jade was curled tightly into a ball, smaller even than the tombstone she leaned against. The phone laid on the grass before her. She glanced furtively at it every now and then. As if waiting at any moment for the device to do something.

The crumpled pages hung limply from her fingers, where she'd been fidgeting with them while she spoke. She folded them and pushed them in the pocket of her backpack.

Her hair was dishevelled, half spilling from her ponytail. Her old, hand knitted cardigan askew left one shoulder bare.

A bike had been thrown haphazard on the lawn, caked with mud, half buried in the wet grass.

When the river breeze stirred the leafy drapes of the willow trees across the path, she'd look up hastily, her eyes darting uneasily back and forth. Then she'd slump, her gaze returning to the screen. The phone stayed dark and silent.

"Ami should be almost home." Jade reached out for the mobile.

Then hesitated.

She drew her hand back again.

"She should be texting soon. I expect they will be landing before dawn. Not long now."

This was only a diversion tactic. Trying to keep her thoughts clear of the *other* thing. Biting her nails, she stared fixated at the phone.

It can't find me here. I took all kinds of mad turns and off the road paths along the way. Almost wrecked my bike. I'm safe here, with Mum.

The gravestone she leaned against glowed white and eerie green, streaked with moss. The words 'Beloved Wife and Mother' sat lonely under the name and date. Jade's fingers traced the violin engraving.

Why do I feel like I'll never have another sunrise? Why can't I stop thinking that I'll be dead before the morning?

"Shut up," Jade said out loud.

That must be what they mean by 'Witching Hour'. Felt so strange. Everything still and poised, for the light that was yet to come. A little bit more texture defined the shadows. Hues of indigo rose from the horizon, diluting the pitch-black skies.

Footsteps.

Jade jumped to her feet, fists at the ready.

"Jade! Hey!" said a young woman, with baby blue eyes and the same dirty blonde hair as Jade.

"Leela!" Jade stuffed the pages in the front pocket of her backpack as she sighed with relief.

The two sisters were very different: where Jade was a dirty blonde with sun-bleached ends, Leela was pale-grey blonde with darker tips where she had died her hair black, a long time ago. Where Jade was sinewy muscle, zero curves and all rough edges, the woman before her had the pleasant softness of hours spent in comfy reading chairs. Smokey shadow rendered her almond shaped eyes quite dramatic; and a confident smile played on her lips.

She was dressed girly, in an open weave tunic top and jeans with flowers along the bottom leg. She threw her free arm around Jade in a cute little hug, as she carefully balanced a takeaway paper bag in the other hand.

"What are you doing here?" Jade barely returned the embrace before stepping away.

"What are *you* doing here? Couldn't you wait a couple more hours till daylight?" Then as an afterthought she added, "wow I love your tan!"

"Thanks. How did you find me?"

Leela handed Jade a bit of paper.

"I found this taped on the houseboat door?"

'*Rain check, need to talk to Mum*'. Jade crumbled the note in her fist.

"That means I want time to myself, Leela." She knew she should have texted instead of leaving a note. But at the time she'd been running away and didn't want Leela texting back and arguing about it. The note had seemed the best way to cancel without an argument.

Leela looked pleased with herself.

"That's what sisters are for," she shrugged gleefully. "To bring you waffles when you're lonely."

"I'm not lonely, I want to *be* alone, but someone's getting in the way of that," Jade said.

The scent of sugary dough and melted chocolate mixed with the fragrance of summer berries, as Leela opened her paper bag. Jade was presented with a pizza box, but with pale blue flowers printed on the cardboard.

"The best hangover *prevention*," Leela announced, plopping down on the grass and lifting the lid off her own box on her lap.

Jade observed the triple decker waffle tower inside, each layer dripping out the sides with melted chocolate and whipped cream.

"Banoffee extra-large waffle the night *before* the party. Then I can have a double shot of rum with each strawberry daquiri tomorrow," Leela said, through a mouthful of sliced bananas and toffee syrup.

Jade's stomach growled. She had not been hungry a moment ago.

She was starving now. And the smell of hot dough and melted chocolate was so good, it made everything else seem less dire. Less grave. Maybe it would turn out ok after all. Maybe she had just been lost in her head and this was all her condition, making her freak out. Surely a box of waffles and a quick chat with her baby sister was not something a sane person would turn down. It was fine. It was going to be fine.

Jade was done debating the great To Waffle Or Not To Waffle question.

"Ok, let's eat, but then you have to go."

"Sure," Leela said handing her the other box.

Collapsing on the grass, Jade opened her own box on her lap. This felt like an unexpected blessing. She was ravenous and could sure use the sugar rush right now. The waffles had silken layers of yogurt cream with aromatic coconut, and a generous sprinkle of bitter chocolate shavings. She inhaled deeply.

"It's so good to see you," Leela said, her eyes round and sincere.

"It's good to see you too. Thanks for this."

"You're welcome!" Leela grinned.

"So. Is it some kind of pirate party tomorrow then?" Jade was mersmerised over the contents of her box, unable to decide where to dig in. Fresh cherries glistened like rubies on top, and the whole thing was drizzled in dark, mouth-watering cherry syrup.

"How did you know?" said Leela, handing her wooden utensils in a recycled napkin.

"You said *rum*."

"Ah. Yes. But it's London Underground Pirates!"

It was the toasted pumpkin seeds.

Just like Leela promised, they were dotted everywhere, mixed with crunchy hazelnuts.

What the hell, make it treat day today, right? The left side of her mouth twitched into a lopsided grin.

She unwrapped her fork from her napkin.

"So what, train pirates?" Jade dug her plastic fork into the waffles and scooped out the first bite.

"No, regular pirates. But: Your costume has to include clues to the name of a tube station. Like a pirate with angel wings is...?"

Jade swallowed, savouring the flavour of cherry mixed with dark chocolate.

"Angel station?"

"Exactly! Or a pirate with a queen's crown?"

"I don't know... Victoria?"

"Yes! And a pirate with a Napoleon hat, but! With a cupcake on it?"

"Water— Bakerloo. I get it. What would you wear for Cockfosters then?"

Leela sighed. "There's always one," she said, unimpressed.

"Oh. So people do that station often then?" Jade smirked into her waffle box.

"Same clue, every time. So uninventive."

Jade was laughing too much to reply.

"So, how've you been!"

"You know how I've been, we chat every day."

Leela ignored this.

"I've missed you so much! I'm so glad you're finally back home, Jade!"

"Thanks," said Jade gloomily. She didn't want to say she hated to be back. She was pretending that her career had ended out of choice. She had to sound like this civilian life was what she wanted. And she had no idea how to do that convincingly.

Chewing on a mouthful of waffle, she tried not to think about it.

"You haven't asked what station I'm going as!"

"Pray tell," said Jade.

"No, you figure it out! I found a green corset online second hand, and I cut leaves out of felt and glued them on. Then I..."

"Green Park?"

"No, listen! I dug up an old layer skirt that is super fluffy," she said with a motion of her hands like puffing something up, "I sprayed it with green glitter. Then I also sprayed an old bird cage I found at a charity shop with the same glitter. Now they match..."

"Canary Warf!"

"No, I'm not putting a canary in the cage! I'm putting my *sheep* teddy."

Jade frowned.

"Green and fluffy and a sheep... Oh, Shepherd's Bush."

"Yes! Isn't it awesome?"

"Leela, you really want to know what I think?"

"What do you think?"

"Every evening you plug in that glue gun and sit down to stick leaves to corsets, is an evening you'll stay a virgin. You'll be a nun soon."

"Excuse me," Leela said, flushing red, "how do you know I'm still a virgin!"

"Wild guess," said Jade. "Are you?"

"None of your business!"

"So that's a yes then. What are you waiting for?"

Leela sighed. She loaded the last chunk of choc-chip cookie on her fork and cornered a bit of banana in the toffee sauce before skewering it too.

"I want it to be special. I haven't met the right person yet."

"Oh please. The only thing a first time can be, is sloppy and awkward. The sooner you get it out of the way the better."

"I hope not! If it's someone I'm madly in love with, who loves me back, it will be amazing," Leela said with a dreamy look in her eyes.

"That's a myth," said Jade, happily chewing on the last forkful of crunchy hazelnuts she had chased around the nearly empty box. "Sex gets better with practice."

"Shouldn't you be telling me *not* to rush? To wait for the right time? Some kind of sanctimonious sister *you* ended up being!" said Leela.

"Sure, and I did say that, when you were sixteen! You're past nineteen now. What's taking so long!"

"Jade!" Leela laughed self-consciously. "I'm just scared I'll ruin a big milestone."

"The first time is not about creating memories, what are you, an eighties teen romcom?"

"How can you be so cynical?" Leela was using her last crumbs of waffle to sponge the milk chocolate from the bottom of her box.

Jade stopped and rubbed her arm against a sudden chill. "I'm just saying that you want to know what you're doing, *before* you find the one."

"That's one way to look at it," said Leela. "But it feels wrong to sleep with people when I'm not in a relationship."

"You're the daughter Dad always wanted." Jade shivered again.

Then her eyes darkened, as she realised.

Something is happening.

"You always say I'm his favourite daughter, but if I am, he is not acting like it," Leela continued, as Jade looked around wearily.

The lawns were silent and the graves sinister under the orange lights of the lampposts along the path.

Leela pulled a cardigan out of her backpack and put it on. Jade tucked her hands snug under her arms, to warm up her freezing fingers. At the back of her mind, something was on alert. Waiting for an alarm to go off. But she couldn't see anything wrong in the quiet cemetery.

Leela had been silent for an uncharacteristically long time.

"It's getting a bit cold, isn't it?" she said finally. "I've got picnic blankets in the car; shall I bring them, and we can wrap up?"

"It happens when the mists rise in the old cemetery," Jade said. She didn't remember how she knew that.

Leela looked around at the ancient burial ground.

"Wow, it's like that whole part of the churchyard has vanished! How cool. A bit strange though, how the fog gets so thick over there and yet there is none anywhere else?"

"It's early morning condensation, that side is closer to the river," said Jade. "Is that a man over there?"

For a moment they both stared into the grey haze on the other side of the path.

"Yes, someone is coming out of the mist," said Leela, pulling herself to her feet. The sisters stood side to side, their shoulders almost touching.

"Ok, this is just a person, just a person walking," Jade muttered.

"What? Of course it's just a person walking," Leela whispered. "The question is, what would anyone be doing in a cemetery in the small hours of the morning?"

"Just a person. With a face and hands and feet and everything."

"You ok?"

"I'm fine. Everything is fine."

"Right. Well. We shouldn't stare, let's pretend we've not seen him," Leela whispered awkwardly. She turned her back to the mist, facing Jade.

Jade's gaze stayed fixed, over Leela's shoulder.

"He's coming this way."

"Oh God," said Leela, nervously. "Should we run to the car?"

"Don't be daft," said Jade. "Guy that skinny? I could beat three of him unconscious."

"Yeah ok, but maybe not let it get to that?" Leela glanced over her shoulder. Her eyes widened. "Why is he coming straight at us?" she said in a panicked whisper.

The man had crossed the path in two steps and strode across the lawn in haste.

"Don't worry, I've got this," Jade said under her breath, walking to stand in front of her sister.

"Why would he want to talk to us?"

"Check that coat," said Jade, lightly, to calm Leela's nerves. "He looks like he just walked out of the Royal Ascot. He's harmless."

Leela's head tilted and her eyelashes batted curiously.

"Can we help you," Jade called out firmly. Though logic said there was nothing threatening about this man, something in the back of her mind screamed at her to stay far away.

Too late. He was standing right in front of her.

Chapter Eighteen
The Final Hours

"Can I help you?" Jade repeated in an icy voice.

"I was wondering if I could help *you*, actually," the man answered, his tone disarmingly pleasant.

"We're fine, thanks." She was about to use her on-duty voice and order him not to come any closer. But he was faster.

"Jade, is it? Bit late tonight huh?"

"How do you know my name? Who are you?"

"I am the night guard, on my rounds. I think you were here last night, although you might not remember. You were very tired."

Jade's jaw clenched.

"No, I *don't* remember you," she said, not even trying to hide her hostility. She had fallen asleep here last night. The thought of a stranger seeing her, while she was unconscious on the lawn, was appalling. And there was something odd about him. Despite his goofy face and big, childlike eyes, she was sure he was a threat. She watched his nervous hands fidgeting with the strap of—was there a shoulder bag? She couldn't see for sure— and she had a gut feeling that, somehow, he was armed.

"Nice outfit, I love the hood," Leela popped out from behind Jade and smiled at the young man appreciatively.

"Not right now, Leela," said Jade, but then she realised her sister was no longer twelve, and couldn't just be ordered *not* to talk to strangers. Leela ignored her and took a few steps closer to the man, cooing, impressed.

"What fabric is that, it seems to blend into the shadows, how did you get that effect? And does it have runes on it? I can't tell, it fades away," said Leela, fascinated. "Let me guess. Lord of the Rings? Was it All Elves? A Night In Rivendell, maybe?"

"Excuse me?" said the man, taking a step away from Leela.

"She thinks you're in costume. What's it you want? We're not doing anything wrong and there's no rule against night visits."

"Jade!" said Leela shocked. "Sorry about my sister, it's all that battle fever. She is newly a veteran and isn't used to talking like a normal human being yet." Leela threw Jade a scathing sideways glance, then she fluttered her eyelids at the stranger again.

"I was wondering, Jade, if maybe you found something I lost last night," said the man, ignoring Leela. His eyes darted nervously at the backpacks sitting on the lawn by the bike.

"What did you lose?" said Jade. She didn't like his casual use of her name, too familiar.

His eyes rounded and a smile twitched on his lips. He was looking at Jade's backpack and seemed far too pleased with himself.

"Oh, just a few pages from my book," he finally replied. "There they are!"

Before Jade could stop him, he dove and pulled the crumpled bunch of pages that had been carelessly sticking out, a little, from the front pocket of her bag.

Damn, he moves fast for a civilian.

"Excuse me, that's mine," said Jade, and instantly checked herself.

But it's not mine, is it? I have no idea how I got it.

The man had now retreated several paces away from them and was straightening the pages out, rather irritated.

"What did you do to them? And you *wrote* on them as well? Seriously," he shook his head annoyed.

"How do I know these are yours? You can't just take something out of my backpack," said Jade, equally annoyed.

His brown eyes looked at her and quickly away.

"Thank you for finding them and keeping them safe for me," he said. "Here," he pulled a tome out of his bag and opened it on a place where jagged ends showed pages had been torn out. "You know they are mine because they go back in my book." He fitted the pages flat with his hand.

They *did* match the space perfectly. Jade blinked. He was telling the truth.

"Gorgeous prop, how long did it take you to make it?" said Leela, ogling at the open book.

But he had already turned to leave.

"They are not in the right order," he muttered, and he shifted the papers while walking away, towards the path.

That's all? Jade felt her eyes narrowing. *He grabbed those papers and now he is off? It's almost like he came here for them. But how would he know I had them and how would he know I'd be here?*

"Aha! You were telling the truth!" he said suddenly, and Jade recognised the paper he pulled out, holding it away from his book. It was her copy of her tribunal documents.

"Hey, that *is* mine!" she said.

For a moment he gazed at her as if mentally registering something, and he nodded to himself.

"What do you mean I was telling the truth?" Jade demanded.

"Oh nothing, here, sorry I picked it up with the rest," he replied, leaving it on the tombstone nearest him, with a little nod. He never stopped walking.

She ran and took it back, folding it again and shoving it in her pocket, all the while unable to take her eyes off him. He was so damn strange. She watched him walk away, shoulders hunched as he got his own pages in order, studiously flattening out the creases with his hand.

He stumbled on a tombstone, tripped, hopped sideways to regain his balance, and said the weirdest thing under his breath:

"Oh, sorry Mr Hemsworth, Mrs Hemsworth."

He walked on.

Jade glanced at the names on the tombstone. Then back to his retreating figure.

"They're dead. They can't hear you."

"No way," he said, stopping in his tracks, eyes fixed on the pages. "Jade!" he looked up at her.

"What?" she said, unnerved that he acted so very genuinely like they were on first name terms.

"That's a great idea!" he tapped the page with his finger.

"What is?"

"You wrote it down!"

Jade paused.

For the first time he looked at her straight in the eyes. Jade almost gasped. There was so much compassion in his gaze.

"Do you know each other?" Leela said.

"This is good," he said, snapping the book shut. "I promise I'll give it a try. I hope it works, Jade."

She had stopped breathing. The intensity in his tone. It reminded her of friends back on base, strapping on their helmets, before heading on missions out of the wire.

"You hope *what* works?"

Instantly his face closed off. All emotion washed away from his eyes, and his voice became flat.

"Sorry, I can't stay," he said, walking away again.

Oh no you don't!

Jade ran after him.

"I'll stay with our stuff, then, shall I?" Leela called after her.

"Yes, I'll be one second."

He didn't slow down but she caught up with him, glad to be putting some distance between her and Leela for what she was about to say.

"What is that thing, on that page? The shadow?"

He glanced at her wearily and looked quickly away, accelerating.

Jade walked faster beside him.

"The Erinys, right? What do you know about that fucker?"

No reply.

"I'm not leaving till you talk, mate. They want proof of innocence, right? Then they leave you alone?"

No matter how much faster he walked, she easily matched him.

"Look if you start running I'll just grab you, okey? How about we have a chat and get it over with?"

He was starting to pant and she wasn't even out of breath. He looked undecisive, and begun to slow down to catch his breath.

"Is this paper enough? It says I'm innocent. It will turn them from demons to angels, yes?"

His jaw clenched and he gave a little shake of the head.

She grabbed his arm, forcing him to stop.

"Talk to me!"

"I don't know what you mean," he said defensively, and somehow he sounded genuine.

"Look, it's not just in your book. There's some ancient play, I think," said Jade, hoping now she'd actually asked Sarah for the title of the damned thing. "The demons were appeased when the killer was acquitted in a trial or something like that? Is that what I'm supposed to do?"

"Oh," he said, comprehension dawning in his face. "That's a very difficult thing you are going to attempt."

"So what the fuck should I do?"

He bit his lip, and pulled his arm free.

"I'm sorry. I'm not allowed to stay, and they're near. I've been ordered to be gone before they're here."

"They who? You mean...the demons? The demons are coming here now?" Jade's voice was only a trembling whisper. "My sister..."

He sighed, and spoke quickly, as if against his own better judgment.

"She needs to leave. They don't target random bystanders but if she tries to help you... they don't let anyone get in their way."

"Shit!" said Jade, rubbing her temples with both hands. "Dammit, Leela won't leave without me right now. I can pretend to go home with her and then sneak away..."

"Don't leave the cemetery."

"What?"

"I can only help you while you're in here. Out there, you're on your own."

"Help me?"

"No, stay back! Don't come into the mist, you will pass out."

"Huh?" Jade halted, only now realising he was standing in an eerie pool of mist.

"Go back. I'll close the Gates to protect you, but I must go now. The longer I stay, the bigger the chances you will forget it all. Try and remember what I said. Good luck, Jade."

"What do you mean?"

But he'd turned his back and plunged into the fog. He was waist deep in two strides. Gone in the next heartbeat.

Close the gates to protect me... But what Gates? Those pages said something about... Gates of Hades! Will that keep the demons away? Is he shutting them out somehow? Or shutting them in? But he said they're coming?

"Hey! Will that stop them? If you close the Gates, am I safe from them?"

No reply came from the fog. Jade wanted nothing more than to run after him. But some hidden warning clawed at her, not to go near the curling edges of the mist. She stared, mystified, as it coiled on the grass before her.

"Jade, what's happening?" Leela had headed towards her.

"No, let's go back, and you should leave," said Jade, swerving around to lead her sister away from the mist.

"What did you write in that book? What did he say to you?" asked Leela. She was looking back and forth from Jade to the fog behind them, curious.

Jade cleared her throat.

"I'm honestly not sure."

"Where did he go?" said Leela.

"I have no idea. That's the old section of the graveyard. There's no way out of the cemetery that side," said Jade.

She stopped to look over her shoulder one last time. The fog was solid, no indication anyone had ever been there.

"Ok, Leela, you should..." Jade paused.

A nightmarish creak of hinges and a booming clash reverberated across the tomb strewn lawns. Jade stiffened, glancing around at Leela, whose head was tilting dreamily to one side, a silly smile lingering on her face.

"I should what?"

"Er... Didn't you hear that?" Jade said, looking from her sister to the fog and back again.

"Hm? He was so cute," Leela sighed, and reaching the spot they'd been eating their waffles, she sat again down on the grass, looking tired.

"Leela did you hear that crash?"

"No, was there a car crash? Isn't the road a mile away?" Leela looked surprised.

"Not a *car* crash," Jade said impatiently. "It was more like... a door, I guess," her eyes glazed over as she searched for the sound in her mind. "A giant door creaking and smashing shut against a huge metal frame."

Silence weighed heavy between them, as Jade cocked her head, listening into the night.

A Gate closing... wasn't I just thinking about a Gate closing... What was it though?

"Can you hear it now?" said Leela, frowning.

"No." Jade bit her lip nervously.

"So, someone closed a door, why are you so worried?"

"I don't know. I— I think there's something I need to tell you..."

"Tell me what?"

"I'm not sure."

"Jade, are you ok?"

"Well first of all there is no door in the cemetery. So, what the hell was that sound?" Jade mumbled.

"Maybe there's a, what's it called? The little house graves?"

"A mausoleum," said Jade. "Those would be locked, and I don't even think there are any here," she said, her gaze fleeting towards the ancient part of the cemetery. If there *were* any, she couldn't see them in the mist.

"Maybe the wind blew a door shut over at the vicar's cottage," Leela shrugged.

"No, it was too loud... as if the door weighed tons, you know? Like industrial size... a warehouse gate that's two floors high..."

"How did I miss all that?"

"I don't know."

They stared at each other for a moment.

"I'm sorry, I don't follow. What are we talking about?" Leela spoke slowly, like she'd had several cocktails instead of a waffle. Jade paused as well. For a moment she forgot what she'd been saying.

"That sound... And the creaking before the door shut..." Jade blinked. "It was like something... howling."

"What? I didn't hear anything?"

"I know, you just said you didn't hear anything."

"I did?"

"Yes!"

"Wait, what was it *you* heard?" Leela asked again.

Jade looked thoughtfully at the fog. There was much less of it now.

"Fog is going away."

"Oh good," said Leela, "We'll be able to see what made the sound that spooked you."

They paused again. Their sentences left gaps they didn't seem to be aware of.

"No, it didn't come from *that* direction..."

It had seemed to rise like a hidden echo from under her feet.

"I think there's something underground," said Jade. "But I've never heard of this church having subterranean vaults."

Leela turned to look at her like waking from a dream. She quickly nodded as if to show she'd been following the conversation all along.

"Vaults? Like catacombs? That's not uncommon for churches *that* old," she said conversationally.

"Yeah, I should ask grandad, he might know," said Jade.

They smiled awkwardly at each other, both a little uncertain.

"What were we talking about?" said Jade.

"I don't know," Leela laughed. "Was it about a church door? Or some guy I fancy? But I don't fancy anyone," she chortled. Jade chuckled.

"Oh yes, I was telling you to hurry up and—"

"Shut up, already," Leela laughed, "I'm done talking about my sex life, ok?"

"*What* sex life?" Jade grinned, and Leela playfully hit her on the elbow.

The skin on Jade's arms crawled with goosebumps. She rubbed harder on her sleeve to stop the strange sensation.

"You know what," Leela continued as soon as she had run the tip of her finger inside her empty waffle box and licked a splodge of banoffee. "If there's vaults in this church, we should ask grandad to see if he can give us a tour. I could get photos of stuff down there to make authentic props for Halloween. Jade. Are you even listening?"

Jade couldn't shake the rising dread that burrowed, like wisps of vaporous fingers clawing down her spine. She wriggled at the bizarre feeling. Instinctively, she looked up, in the direction of the old cemetery. But she was surprised.

The fog was completely dissolved.

The ancient tombstones stood cracked and lopsided among the curtains of the riverside willows. Not the slightest bit of haze obscuring visibility. The mist had cleared completely.

So why am I shivering?

This wasn't the cold of the early hours of the morning. This was the foreboding she used to get back at the boat. The chills from the nights she'd heard the vicious static.

Even though she could spot nothing worrying in the quiet churchyard, something had changed in the darkness beyond. If she believed that sort of thing, she would have described it as a shift in energy.

Is it happening here? How did it find me?

Jade scanned around for the figure. Nothing among the boughs of tree barks, nothing among the headstones surrounding them. He was nowhere to be seen.

"What are you looking for?" asked Leela, who had been observing her sister quietly.

"Nothing," said Jade, suddenly aware of Leela's piercing gaze. She snapped the empty waffle box closed on her lap and punched its middle to make a dent and fold it in two.

"You *show* that box!"

"Just packing up so we can go. You done?" Jade took Leela's box without waiting for a reply. She pounded that one even louder.

"Jade! What has come over you!"

"Just packing up!"

"Why do we have to leave right this minute?"

"It's almost dawn. Aren't you tired?"

"No! Let's have a walk down the river and watch the sunrise."

"Sunrise is still well over an hour away," Jade shrugged in exasperation. "I'd rather head home."

"What is it that you're not telling me?" Leela narrowed her eyes. "I can tell it's something."

This was why Jade had tried to avoid meeting her little sister. This thing Leela did. Sensing something was up when she had no business knowing.

"Tell me why we're *really* leaving. What happened?"

Jade coughed, her lungs contracting violently. Like someone had pushed her into an ice-cube plunge-pool, she felt instantly neck deep in frozen water. She had to blink and look around Leela to make sure she was still sitting on the grass with her.

"Jade, are you ok?"

"I'm fine," said Jade, her voice shaky.

I'm supposed to face it. Make my stand. Show it my proof of innocence. But I'm so... so very tired...

Jade wiped her eyes because tears of exhaustion were running down her cheeks. If she could delay this confrontation till tomorrow night, that would give her a full day's sleep in the sunlight. She could deal so much better after a good rest! Leela saw her drying her eyes with her sleeve and gasped.

"Jade, you're really not okay! That's it, I'm not dropping you off at the boat. You are coming with me," said Leela.

"Dad's house? You must be joking."

"No, my dorm room! We'll nap till the afternoon and then we'll have our movie sleepover at last!"

Jade fell silent. She was running out of excuses to refuse.

"So, college rules, I'm allowed two overnight visitors a month and I haven't had any. That means you can stay two nights!"

"Leela those passes aren't for relatives, they're for you to get laid!"

Leela looked mortified for one second.

"Women don't need romantic partners to live full lives."

"I didn't say romantic partners, I said sex."

"You're just changing the subject, Jade. We're not talking about my dating life again! You're coming to mine, that's the end of this conversation." Leela tucked the empty boxes under her arm with an air of finality.

If this shadow is following me wherever I go, I'm not bringing it to her dormitories.

Then again, she remembered taking Leela to one of many open days at the uni. Security at the gates and walls all around. Medieval level fortification. Oxford colleges are literally castles. Maybe it couldn't follow her there.

"You'll love the food at student halls. If we leave now, we'll be on time for breakfast."

Jade was too tired to object. Leela pulled up the bike with her free hand.

"How on earth can you eat breakfast after that triple decker waffle?"

Leela giggled and said something that Jade didn't hear. Because suddenly, facing the distant entrance to the cemetery, Jade noticed something.

Right in the middle of the thicket. Against the black ivy veins of the brick wall. Very still.

The shape of shoulders and a head.

"What? said Leela. What are you staring at?"

"There's someone here."

How did he find me here? I made sure I was not followed. Does he just know where I am at all times?

"Where?" said Leela.

Or maybe he followed Leela?

"Jade there is no one here," said Leela, looking all round.

"He is hiding."

"Why?"

"We should leave." Jade took the bike handles from Leela. She led the way, trying to speed up, her heartbeat racing. But she couldn't go fast. Pushing the bike on the lawn slowed her down, and she had to be careful not to get it scratched as she navigated a route around the tombstones.

"Who is it?" Leela whispered, looking apprehensive now, as she followed beside Jade.

"I don't know."

"Where are they hiding?"

"Right by the big tree."

Leela's eyes darted on all corners of the wall. Her gaze never fixed in any one spot.

"Are you sure? I don't see anything."

Jade sighed.

"I'm looking at him as we speak." She had to keep veering the bike around graves. She wondered if she should leave it here. Just get out.

But the bike was her only way to get anywhere at the moment. She couldn't lose it.

"I don't see anyone! Are you sure?"

Cannelloni spotted him right away.

"Maybe I imagined it, never mind," said Jade sourly. "Maybe just a funny shaped tree. What matters is to get out of here."

Leela frowned.

"You know what, we need more light." Leela switched on the torch on her phone and then, to Jade's utter surprise, she jumped sideways, in the direction of the shadow.

"No stay away from the oak tree!" Jade called.

Leela ignored her.

"Don't worry, I've got the cam on," she called loudly. "This creep is going viral and serve him right."

The figure made no move.

Leela walked among the graves on the opposite side of the cemetery. The shadow waited. Jade paused.

Leela had run off a good distance to the left and stopped close enough for the light from her phone to illuminate the shadows thickening under the trees. In the torch beam, the shapes acquired colour. The tree barks were now warm red-browns and silvery-greys against the dull green veins of ivy sprawling on the stonework. Jade had difficulty breathing.

The torchlight was moving up... up toward that shape of the face and shoulders...

Nothing there.

Red crumbling brickwork lit up on either side of the twisted tree bark, even on the exact spot where he had been. Leela stood dangerously close, shining the torch-beam left and right. Showing empty space. Jade could not believe her eyes.

When did he move?

"Nothing here," called Leela, "hope he's not ran off on us now that we were about to make him famous!" she added with a smugness that Jade found unnecessary.

Then Jade gasped.

He was back.

Leela turned her back to the tree and walked on along the wall, the beam of light sliding away with her, and the oak plunged into darkness. The shoulders and head shape were right there. In the same position as before. As if he never moved.

He is only visible in the dark.

"Good news. He's gone." Leela shouted from the other end of the cemetery. When Jade didn't reply, Leela frowned. "What? I looked everywhere!"

"Leela," Jade called back, "if you *don't* use the torch, and look in the shadows, do you not see the outline of a man? Beside the large oak?"

"*That* tree?"

"Yes?"

"It's only brick wall on either side of that tree, Jade. And too narrow for anyone to be standing behind."

Jade shivered.

Because he was still there, his head facing in their direction.

Peering at the black outline of the shadow, she had the impression it was staring straight into her eyes. But no matter how hard she squinted; no features were visible on its dark face in the distance.

And it never moved.

Leela can't see him. Only I can.

Taking a step back, her heart pounding against her chest, she tried really hard not to think the word—

Ghost.

Seized by a sudden dread, she wavered and almost fell to her knees. The trees seemed to loom giant and close in on her, and she couldn't breathe.

"Jade? Are you still looking for someone? I'm sure there's no one there. Let's get going!"

Leela had dawdled back from her search and stood beside her, holding the smashed waffle boxes in a bundle.

"Yes, let's get out of here," said Jade, rubbing her temples as she began to walk among the graves. Even though she was no longer looking at him, she could now feel the repugnant stare crawling over her; it was a pressure of eerie quality at the back of her mind, the deathly chill of some nameless terror intruding in her every thought.

Furious with frustration, she looked up straight at the figure and muttered under her breath:

"What do you want?"

"How do you mean? I want breakfast, and I'm probably going to need a nap, I guess," said Leela, who had been walking beside her, one hand on the bike handles. "You need to look where you're going, this is the third time I had to steer you away from crashing into a gravestone!"

Jade didn't even turn to look at what Leela meant.

Because when she'd spoken to him, he moved.

The shadow tilted its head in the distance. Like a dog cocking its ear to listen.

Jade stopped walking altogether and held on to the bike handles so hard that her fingers hurt.

Can he hear me?

Her heart was now pounding in her ears.

Does he respond to questions? Wait. I've actually spoken to him before!

She had called out to him in anger the other night. She had stood by the barge and yelled at the figure across the river, still thinking it was some stalker or idiot pulling a prank. She'd told him to come to her side of the shores. To show his face.

And then he did. He fucking did.

The following night, he had showed up for the first time on *her* side of the river, as she walked the dog. And then he appeared in the lounge and leaned in and *showed her his face*.

Jade shuddered. That was two out of two of the things she had challenged him to do. Could it be he'd answered?

Do I dare to do it again?

She took a deep breath to steady herself.

"Jade! Why did you stop? Are you ok?" Leela had walked on, not realising her sister wasn't following. She now trotted back, with a little skip and hop that caused her to almost drop the waffle boxes.

Jade needed to get rid of baby sis for a second.

"I'm fine. I was just thinking, Leela, why carry those empty boxes to your car? The dog-walkers' litter goes over there. I'll wait while you go bin the waffle bag."

"Oh, good point," said Leela heading back the way to the trash can.

Finally, alone for a few moments, Jade took a deep breath and faced the figure. She stared fitfully at him across the lawns.

Stop trembling like a wuss. He's an innocent villager, persecuted and murdered by fanatics, right? He's not actually evil. Ask him.

"Tell me what you want from me," she whispered.

For a couple of heartbeats, she held her breath.

The silence weighed on her shoulders.

The shadow made no move.

Jade's phone blasted with static.

She pulled it out from within her pocket, fingers crawling with revulsion like she touched a spider. A zap stung her hand, sending a shock up her arm. She dropped the device onto the grass.

The screen glowed.

A video was playing on her phone.

Terror washed over her.

He's answered.

The bike slipped from her shaking hands and toppled over.

What does his answer mean?

She didn't need to pick up the phone. She already knew which video it was. Hated everything about it.

Jade turned her back to her phone and paced away from it, pulling her hair off its loose, lop-sided ponytail. Blonde locks tumbled chaotically over her shoulders. She stretched and flattened her hair up on the top of her head, fixing it in her little band so tight that her skin hurt. Pulling her ponytail through the band's last loop, one extra time with strict precision, she made sure not a single strand of hair could escape it. You can't fight with hair in your face. She was ready.

She glanced sideways at the darkness and whispered one single word.

"No."

She was not going to sit there and listen to all those desert gales over again.

Clearly, all the shadow wanted was to torture her. She was done with that phone. Leave it there, and get a new one tomorrow. Done.

"Oh, it's Ami's pretty sunset!" said Leela, emerging casually from the darkness. She picked up the phone. "I don't remember this video having sound before?" When Jade didn't reply, Leela continued: "Is that your voice? Who are you talking to?"

"This is the original. I removed the sound from the one I sent Ami. I'd rather no one watches this."

"Secret, is it?" Leela said playfully, with no intention of turning it off.

Jade pulled her bike back up, trying not to get pissed off at her sister. The only thing she really wanted right now was to get out of there. She began to lead the bike around the tombstones.

"Are you talking with your driver? Why is he so tense?" Leela tagged along in no particular hurry, no longer helping her steer the bike through the cemetery. Curiosity burned in her eyes, as her face glowed from the screen, the rest of her drenched in darkness.

"Can you switch the phone off please."

"Why? This is a longer version. I want to see what you cut out."

Her sister was trying, once again, to nosey about why Jade was discharged from duty. The bike bumped against something, and the back wheel ran over Jade's foot. "Dammit!" she muttered, swerving around a Celtic cross. This walk from her Mum's grave to the path would have been so much faster in daylight, and without dragging the bike along.

"Leela turn the phone off!"

Jade wanted to take the phone from her. But at the same time, she didn't dare to touch it. One more zap from those weird static bursts and her fingers might fall right off.

"No need to get angry!"

"Oh fine, you can watch the whole damn thing," she snapped. "It's not in there."

"What's not in there?"

"What you're looking for. The reason I left. It's not in there. You're just wasting your time."

Leela peered at her with narrowed eyes. She didn't believe her.

"Hey, is that Ami's friend? Fondant-fancies guy? You met him on the road?"

"Yes, that's him."

"Why did you cut him out of the video?"

"Because I was already breaking about a hundred rules to take that temple sunrise clip for Ami, and posting a Locally Employed Staff member's face on Ami's family group chat was a step too far. And you watching it is breaking about a hundred more."

"Oh please, I'm family too. What is he saying? Was he meant to catch a ride with you?"

Jade rolled her eyes.

"Of course not! This was a road not far from the base. Locals use it and we use it too. Just a coincidence he showed up while I was taking this shot."

"Why are you ignoring him like that?" Leela asked.

"Just doing my job," Jade muttered, her eyes returning to the silent watcher in the darkness.

He had vanished.

Jade paused, her gaze searching. Only one thing was worse than seeing the dark figure: *Not* seeing it.

If the light makes him invisible, he could be right here!

And then she knew why he'd disappeared. Jade and Leela were standing just outside the pool of light from the first lamppost on the cemetery path.

Did he stop existing in the light? Or was he still here, completely concealed?

The sisters were about to enter the illuminated path towards the gates. He could very well be standing a few steps away, waiting for them to do it— to step right into him. Jade took a step back.

Lampposts illuminated the path all the way out.

And the gates were blazing in the distance, brighter than any of the lampposts.

How in the ever-loving fuck are we going to get out?

Chapter Nineteen

Trapped In The Cemetery

L *ight hides him. I need it to be dark so I can see where he is.*

"What now?" said Leela, as Jade had fallen very still and quiet.

Jade counted the Georgian lampposts lining the little path. Three. They each stood in a pool of orange light. And at the end of the path, the Victorian Goth revival, wrought iron archway of the cemetery gates. With a lantern on either side, for good measure.

Is this really happening to me right now? Can an invisible spectre really be standing under one of these lights?

She couldn't take the risk.

"Leela let's walk around the path, from the lawn," said Jade, looking longingly at the darkness of the grave strewn lawns that would reveal the shadow right away. On the grass, they'd see him approach.

"No way! I've stumbled three times over funeral wreaths. Almost kicked over a flower vase! Like, eeew. Imagine the bugs that would slither on my shoes out of *that* water? No thanks. I'm staying on the path, that's what it's for!"

Leela scowled, and stepped right into the pool of light.

Jade's breath came ragged. She wanted to scream, 'No! Get out of the light!' But she had no way to explain why. She couldn't think of a good lie.

Meanwhile, Leela made slow progress, her face buried in the screen, no rush to get out to the darkness on the other side.

Jade shivered. This mind-warping cold was *him*. She was sensing his presence. Her sister was in danger.

The invisible figure could be reaching out to touch her right this minute, and Leela was completely unaware.

Jade pushed her bike with all her strength and exposed herself to the bright light patch.

He'll have to get through me if he wants to lay hands on her.

But immersed in the brightness around the lamppost, Jade's resolve shattered. The first few steps were so alarming, they'd been barely endurable. The remaining distance seemed insurmountable.

An icy breath singed the back of her neck.

Her heartbeat frantic.

Her combat instincts sent a shrieking alarm to get out of the light. Mindlessly bursting into a jog, the bike creaking as it rolled beside her, Jade fled. Before she even knew how, she was on the other side and safe in the darkness.

She turned around, grabbed Leela and pulled her out of the pool of light.

"Get a move on, Leela! Look alive!"

Leela's face was glued to the screen, and nothing seemed to trouble her apart from the content of the video.

"He sounds desperately afraid!" was all she said.

"What?" said Jade, briskly turning towards the middle of the dark patch of the path, before the next lamppost. Good, a few moments of dark respite on this feaking path.

"Jade how could you ignore him like that?"

"Oh, come on Leela! You have no idea what standard operating procedures are in a forward area."

Problem was, they were past the middle of the dark patch already. Unavoidably approaching the next lamppost. Couldn't risk crossing the light again. She'd felt him. Had to do something about it.

Smash the lamp.

"Leela, take the bike for a bit?"

"Nice try, did you think I'd stop watching this?" said Leela, taking the handles with one hand and making a point to keep Jade's mobile in the other, her finger hovering over the play button on the paused screen.

No, I thought it would slow you down and it has.

"Careful you don't stumble, Leela. The mobile is blinding you in this dark."

"How do you know?"

"Every time you look at me, your eyes are unfocused; you talk at my general direction, not actually seeing me. So just be careful, ok?"

"I'm fine, the path is pretty straight forward," said Leela stubbornly. Jade shot ahead, searching the ground for stones. She needed to be able to see him again, this blind guessing, is he there? To the right? To the left? Fucking where? It was nerve racking.

"By the way, I'm sure fondant-fancies guy had a reason for being so stressed, looks to me like he was asking for your help." Leela still in her own little world of digital social justice.

"Where'd you get that from? He's not speaking English! We had no interpreter with us, we didn't know *what* he said." At least that kept Leela busy, so Jade could smash the lamp unnoticed.

Spotted a stone. Weighing it in her hand, she walked, cautiously, to the edge of the pool of light, leaving Leela behind her. Leela, predictably, didn't notice; nor did she look up from the screen.

"Can't you tell from the tone of his voice? It's universal for 'scared'."

"He came running and screaming up to my vehicle and ignored verbal warnings. I had no option but to leave."

Leela still wasn't looking. It was now or never.

Jade stepped into the pool of light. Her skin erupted with the stinging of those same prickly goosebumps, impossibly stretching her flesh like gnarly icicles trying to tear out of her.

Yup that's him again. He must be really close, dammit.

But Leela's voice distracted her, made her slow down for a moment, just as a new shiver run through her.

"Fine if you're going to be like this, I can figure it out *myself!*" Leela was having a moment, and she brought the bike to a halt, stopping completely. With a big dramatic huff, she pulled out her own phone too. Her nose inches from the two screens as she played the video from one phone close to the other device for some weird reason.

An icy breeze rippled Jade's right sleeve and she leapt to the left; she'd been stupid standing still in the bright light. She sprinted to the lamppost, aimed and hurled the stone.

Glass rained down before her, making her leap aside.

Darkness spread.

Blinking as her vision adjusted to the gloom, her body found boxing stance without her even noticing.

Nothing.

Where is he?

Jade glanced around at Leela who was still not going anywhere. Only her screens mattered.

"Wanna know what he's telling you?" She hadn't realised what happened, thank god.

"Leela come on, lets walk, we're just standing here," said Jade. The nearest light now was a good thirty paces away.

"It's something about his girls."

"What girls?"

"He is talking about how he has two little daughters." Leela finally plodded on, pushing the bike along while working between the two phones. She had done the same thing Jade had thought about, when she first heard the words in the static on the radio: download a translator app.

Jade tried to get ahead, but the word 'daughters' made her nauseous. Faint memories returned; the way he held up photos of two school aged girls, cute as buttons in their child-sized saris, how Ami smiled brightly as she looked at them. A headache pounded behind her eyes.

"Ok, I got it," said Leela. "He says that he was teaching his girls schoolwork at home. He is telling you that he did it in secret, but some of his neighbours might know."

The world spun.

Ami's friend taught his daughters schoolwork at home? Oh no. Oh no, no, no...

"Yes, that's it. He was worried his neighbours would find out he home-schooled his girls. Why is that a secret, though?" Leela continued. "He says his life is in danger if they find out? Is that true?"

Hell, yes that's true. But surely, he was careful. Surely, he would make sure no one knew.

Just then, the man in the video, shouting to be heard over the desert gales, spoke the only two sentences he ever said in English:

"Are they close? Are they coming?" This time, the phrase was not distant and eerie like when it came out of the old radio. It was just the familiar voice of Ami's friend, his English broken, unsure. The timbre of his tone heavy with despair.

Leela's face turned pale, and she stopped walking. Her hands shook, and the bike zig-zagged uncontrollably.

Jade stormed ahead, fleeing those intolerable words.

Coming up, this was it.

The *last* lamppost.

She was done. She couldn't take this rollercoaster of harrowing emotions one ghastly minute longer. What was normally a two-minute walk had taken what felt like a century to traverse.

Smash the final light. Get to the damned gate.

"Who does he think is coming, Jade?"

"I don't *know* Leela!!! Can't you hear my driver freaking out and wanting to go? I was already breaking every rule in the book not to leave sooner!" Jade halted at the edge of the last pool of light before the exit.

The cold rapped at her every nerve, with a malignant undertone. A hidden threat. She wrapped her cardigan tight around her.

He could be face to face with her right now and she wouldn't see him.

Can I hit the lamp from here? I really don't want to get in the light a third time...

"Let me check if there was anyone else on the road, if he was being chased," said Leela from behind, tapping the screen to rewind.

"For god's sake Leela! Of course he *wasn't* being chased! He didn't mean "Are they coming?" right that moment!"

"What *did* he mean?"

"Just let it go! Ok? Just switch the bloody video off!" Jade yelled.

"If you know what he *didn't* mean, then you're hiding something," Leela called, still at the previous lamppost, leaning against the still bike and scrolling back on the video.

Jade wanted to go back and try to knock the phone off her sister's hand, but the chills were so strong beside the lamppost, she could hardly stand.

It paralysed her. Feeling him so close and not being able to see him.

She aimed and hoped she could reach the glass from here.

The stone flew from her hand.

Glass shattered overhead.

The light went out.

Jade eagerly scanned the darkness.

Nothing. He's not here.

Leela was still ages away, refusing to move again, sleuthing away in her obsessive quest to find why Jade left service. Shitty as that might be, it gave Jade the chance to clear the gate so they could get the fuck out of this place. She quickly picked up another stone. The only light source remaining, was up ahead, shining from the arched cemetery gates. The way out would soon be open, and then she'd drag Leela out by the hair if she had to.

Pain stabbed her hand. Glass in her fingers. She hadn't noticed it in the dark and she'd picked up a shard of the broken lamp together with the stone. Blood streaked her skin. A fat red drop rolled swiftly to her fingernail, about to fall to the ground.

Jade wiped it on her top.

Blood can't fall to the ground...

In shock, she glanced at the stain on her blouse. Why on earth did she wipe the blood with it? Her brows met in a frown of disgust, this would never come off.

Blood can't fall to the ground, make it stop bleeding!

Separating her fingers, she exposed several cuts on the tender flesh in the fold of her knuckles. They were small in length but disquietingly deep. As she straightened her fingers to look for glass still lodged in there, the wounds tore open further. A scream rose to her lips, but she swallowed it down. Real women don't scream.

There was no glass in the raw flesh, but blood was everywhere now. Bunching the end of her sleeve into her fist, she applied gentle pressure to slow the blood flow.

"There was no one around you for miles, the video shows it without doubt," Leela called from where she still stood by the bike. "There is no one coming. Why would he ask, "Are they coming?" What did he mean?"

"Leela I'm ten seconds away from grabbing you and dragging you along. Get your arse moving."

Leela's brows set in a stubborn frown, and she looked down again, making zero effort to move.

"Isn't it mainly the religious extremist militia that people fear in those countries? They would be the only ones who'd care that he was giving his daughters schoolwork, right?"

Jade made a beeline for the last target, putting herself in position to aim. There were two lantern style lamps above the cemetery gates. They cast a much broader illumination. She'd have to enter the pool light with these ones. She tried not to panic.

I'll have to run like the fucking wind, in and out of this. And it'll take two reps, to clear both lamps.

"Jade, I asked you a question! Isn't it mostly religious extremists that people fear?"

"Yes, of course, the outer villages are terrified when they drive through," Jade called back without thinking.

"Oh my god!" said Leela, suddenly looking up.

Jade bit her lip, trying to think of a quick excuse why she'd been bursting lights this whole time.

"You *did* know what he was talking about!" Leela said.

"What?"

"What you just told me! He asked you whether *they* were close to his village! If they were coming to his home! You knew this!"

Well ok, she shouldn't have said that. In retrospect, it would've been better if Leela asked why she was vandalising lampposts.

"What are you staring at me like that for, Jade?"

"What do you want me to do?"

"Tell me what happened to him?"

"Nothing happened to him! He's perfectly fine! He just heard some rumours and got frightened! And we are not supposed to talk about my work, so drop it."

"Sure, but *were* they close? *Were* they coming?"

"Oh yeah, let's sit down and I'll draw you a map and give you all the classified information on the movements of the enemy during my last deployment."

Leela flicked her hair behind her shoulder, annoyed.

Jade calibrated the distance to the glass, steeling her resolve to step in the light.

"Fine don't tell me. But did you tell *him*?"

"Who, me? Leela, there are people whose job it is to liaise with the local communities. People like me are not allowed to say a word to anyone outside the unit. Specialist officers get years of training to do the talking!"

"Who cares? He's not a community! You are not your job title! He's just a person asking another human being if his life is in danger!"

"You know I would be discharged if I told him that, right?"

"You were let go anyway, Jade! Why?"

"That's none of your fucking business!"

Leela stared at her sister straight in the eyes.

"Jade, if you are going to swear at me, then I'm not talking to you."

"I'm *fucking* devastated. My juvenile sister is not *fucking* talking to me."

"Fine," said Leela, and turned her back to Jade.

Perfect opportunity. Bracing herself, she jumped into the pool of light, ignoring the violent shudder. The stone left her hand and flew in a precise trajectory straight for the nearest lamp.

But it never made contact. The stone jerked aside, like something had swept it out of the way. It fell to the left on the lawn.

Jade dashed out of the gates' illumination.

"Fuck!" she yelled when she was safe in the dark patch, doubling over, her chest heaving with laboured breath.

It had seemed as if someone had swatted the stone away from the glass.

Leela's face turned red. "Do *not* swear at me, ok?" she shouted, looking over her shoulder.

Jade said nothing.

He must be standing in the light. Right in front of her. Blocking their way out.

He won't let me brake those and leave.

We are trapped.

"You done shouting at me?" Leela said, grudgingly starting to approach.

Jade looked at her sister mutely.

How do I tell her we are stuck? That we can't walk through the gates?

Leela had sauntered up, to stand beside Jade.

Is this it? Have I reached the point when I tell another person there is a ghost after me?

"What? What's that face for?" Leela asked.

"I'm not making a face, just—" Even the light from the phones in Leela's hands felt too bright. Breaching the safety of the darkness here, away from the bright entrance. "Just can you please turn those phones off now? Aren't you done with *that*?"

Leela seemed to finally accept that they weren't fighting any more, probably because Jade's tone was so, so very quiet.

"Okay. Although this final shot is gorgeous, his eyes are so unusual. I never noticed in the photos," Leela said, holding up the phone. "Hazel with green dots. How very pretty."

"What."

"Hazel eyes with emerald specks! Extraordinary," Leela said.

Chapter Twenty

The Man with the Hazel Eyes

"No," said Jade.

"What do you mean, no?" said Leela.

"Let me see!" Jade grabbed Leela's wrist to bring the device closer to look, avoiding contact with the phone. "It can't be!"

Those eyes.

She blinked several times, hoping she hadn't seen clearly. But the picture never changed. Jade stood there, gripping her sister's wrist, staring at the phone. Finally, Leela pulled her hand away.

"Jade, ouch! What's wrong with you?"

Jade wasn't listening.

They tortured and murdered fondant-fancies guy.

Oh, my fucking god.

Shifting her uninjured hand to her forehead, she rubbed hard with trembling fingers.

Did Ami's friend really have these stunning hazel eyes? Jade tried to remember the few times she'd met him. It wasn't often. It was months ago. Never made a point to check his eye colour.

But there he was in this shot: Close up, looking directly at the camera, Ami's friend with bright hazel eyes speckled with emerald green.

The face of the executed man flashed in her mind, covered in blood and mud caked hair, and bruises. But the eyes...

The eyes were the same. These eyes. It's him they executed.

Jade sucked in a hissing breath.

She hooked her arm around her sister's elbow and led her back the way they'd come.

"Where are we going?" said Leela. Jade dragged her almost at a run, back into the heart of the cemetery.

"Why are we going back? We've left your bike! Aren't we taking it?"

Jade had to think of a lie. Fast. She couldn't tell her there was an invisible ghost that turns your insides into gut popsicles, lurking in the light at the gates.

"I... I want to go back to Mum's grave. I think I dropped my wallet there."

Leela stared, half annoyed, half worried, as they retreated back to the darkness among the graves. Jade avoided her sister's eyes. She kept glancing behind, scanning ahead, checking all around.

No sign of him.

Reaching the only lampost she hadn't smashed, she made a sharp turn into the lawn-without the bike she zigzagged among the tombstones- straight for the grave with the violin.

When she reached her mother's tombstone, Jade held onto it as if she needed help to keep standing. Blood squelched from her fingers on the grey stone. Crimson washed warm over her hand, seeping on the dusty granite.

Can't let it touch the ground, careful!

But why though? Why do I keep thinking that?

Leela was watching her. Jade quickly hid her injured hand behind her back.

"Are we not going to look for your wallet?" Leela asked testily.

"Yes, could you? I'm out of breath," Jade lied. That would keep Leela occupied for a few moments while she tried to figure out what just happened.

The stone was going straight for the lamp, and it jumped aside on its own. It bounced off something. Something completely invisible.

No matter how many times she replayed it in her mind, there was no other explanation: He must be there, under the arch. Waiting for them to walk into him. Jade glanced around to check the shadow hadn't followed them here- still no.

Light blinded her. Jade stiffened. A bright beam shone from Leela's phone.

"No! Turn it off!"

"How are we supposed to look for your wallet without a light?"

The cemetery acquired colour. Green lawn stretched empty. Tombstones stood lonely with veins of luminous green moss crawling over them.

"Just switch it off!"

"Is this better?" Leela cast the torch app beam to the ground.

Jade sighed with relief. The cemetery went dark once again, drenched in shadows. The light was now only a small patch at Leela's feet, and as she trudged about, checking around the grave where they'd sat, Jade's eyes got accustomed to the dark quickly.

Still no sign of the shadow.

"What the fuck do I do now," Jade muttered, wrapping her cardigan around herself as tight as possible against the constant chill.

"For the last time, can you stop swearing?" Leela answered, from where she crouched behind the tombstone. "We will find it, ok?"

"Yeah, sorry," said Jade, her attention drifting to the gates, a small luminescent arch in the distance. There was very little light left in the cemetery. She looked longingly at the other way out: The front church gardens, the lines of manicured conifers along the path glowing with hidden spotlights shining on; the lawns blazing green with concealed floodlights; the flowerbeds lip up with circles of bright beams.

No fucking chance we go that way.

The expanse of darkness she had created back here was reassuring. Their only safety. She could see he wasn't... wait... what's that?

On the lampposts.

Figures crouching over each and every smashed lamp. Two or three heads were crowded together, peeking around each lamp top. Staring straight at her. Jade blinked.

Were there angel statues on the lampposts? No, gargoyles? Since when was such artwork installed on the lights along the path? Jade remembered seeing the lamps only minutes ago. When the lights were still on. There had been nothing on them.

Nothing at all.

Jade felt the pit of her stomach drop to about her knees.

"They're just decorations," Jade told herself through gritted teeth. "This place is full of stone freaking angels. Get a grip." But the one lamppost she hadn't smashed-it seemed to have no such decorations, somehow...

"What? Are you ok? Sounds like you're hyperventilating," said Leela, looking up from behind a nearby tombstone, her torch light aimed to the ground.

"We need to keep moving. We need to get out of here."

"We haven't found your wallet!"

"Vicarage, now," said Jade, grabbing her sister by the elbow again.

"What? Your wallet's at the vicar's house?"

"Shut up Leela, just shut up for one..." her voice trailed away.

Just as her sister switched off her torchlight with a frown, Jade realised:

More of them, all over the church too. Dozens. Hooked all along the towering, gothic edifice.

Angels were perched on top of the steepled windows, crouching on the medieval niches, their black wings spread out to keep their balance.

Did angels have ink black wings?

No, they were gargoyles.

Do gargoyles look like women in fluid, shredded gowns?

They mounted along the wall like human sized spiders. Their skin was dark grey, just like their weeping counterparts, the limestone angels elegantly draped over many of the tombstones. Locks of slimy hair cascaded over their shoulders, flowing gently in the breeze.

Flowing gently in the breeze?

A statue's hair doesn't move in the wind.

Jade's legs gave in.

She collapsed to her knees, hid her face in her hands, and burst into tears.

"Jade? What's wrong?" Leela's face was a mask of dismay. "Jade? Please, what's happening?"

Jade looked up to her sister, and her cobalt eyes burned with anger.

"You're about to get what you wanted, Leela."

"What?"

"I hope you're happy."

"Happy with what?" said Leela, starting to sound angry as well.

"Though I suspect you will be very sorry you asked."

"What did I ask?"

"I'm about to tell you the reason I was discharged."

"You really will?" Leela's eyes widened eagerly, but her gaze darted around with apprehension. "Here? Now?"

"Medical leave. I had a break down. Because Ami's friend was executed."

"He's dead?" said Leela, taking a step back.

"Very dead. Lakes of blood. Butchered. I had to watch it all. Intel gathering. My job. I've seen executions before. Never someone I knew! Apparently, I was so traumatised, I blocked it. I didn't know it was *him*! Didn't even think about it, till tonight. Till you showed me his eyes, right there."

"Oh Jade, I didn't... I didn't mean to... I'm sorry! Did you really have a breakdown?"

"For months now, I thought it was some stranger. Kept having nightmares about it. Little morsel of knowledge trying to come to the surface. Woke up the whole squadron with my screaming. Or didn't sleep at all. For weeks. Deemed fucking unfit for service. Sent back home to the station. I waited bloody *months* for medical tribunal. And when it finally happened? Discharged. They just let me go. Just like that." Jade swallowed a sob. "For doing exactly what they told me to."

"Oh Jade!" Leela leaned in to hug her, but Jade pushed her away.

"And still I had no idea the dead man was *him*. How could I have been so blind? The way I couldn't stand watching those videos, those photos. So fucking obvious. How could I not see it?"

"That's why you wouldn't show me pictures of Ami!"

"Yes."

"I thought it was because you missed her so much!"

"Me too. That's what I thought. That I couldn't stand the videos, 'cause it hurts so much, not being with her. But what if... I was trying to hide the truth from myself? Maybe, on some level... maybe I've known all along that the man they murdered, was Ami's friend."

Leela had both hands on her sister's shoulders, squeezing gently.

"Gosh, I'm so sorry... I shouldn't have played that video from your phone, when you weren't ready to see it! It was very stupid of me. I don't know what I was thinking! Oh Jade, I didn't realise you were so unwell... I'm really sorry, I feel awful!"

Tears glistened in Leela's eyes too. But Jade's tears had dried. Her face had a steely, dark expression.

"Now of course I also see scores of them. Demons. Hovering all around the cemetery. And his ghost. It's been coming after me. I've completely lost it. Go ahead and tell your mum, she'll be delighted to know I've gone stark raving bonkers."

Leela's eyes widened.

"You see demons?"

"Yup."

"Right now?"

Jade nodded.

"You realise there aren't any, though, right?"

"Sure," said Jade. The screech of a razor-sharp nail against metal made her shudder, as the angel on the lamppost closest to them latched her bat wing's hook on a filigree rim.

"Ok, you know they're not real. So... what do you mean, you see them?"

Jade shrugged.

"Jade, you are the most rational person I know. Most of the time your obsession with logic is, quite frankly, irritating. You love video games and horror movies, but you know fantasy creatures are not real life, right?"

"Right, I *do* know that," said Jade. "And I completely agree with everything you just said. The only problem is," she glanced around to the church wall, "they're right *there*."

Leela blinked several times, then cleared a few errant strands of her hair from her eyes and tucked them behind her ears. She nodded, decisively.

"Not a problem. Not a problem at all. It's... shellshock, right? Don't sweat it. We'll get you into bed and make an appointment with your doctor tomorrow, right?"

Jade shrugged.

"Ok, let's head to the car and I'm sure you will feel better once we are out of here," said Leela.

"We can't go anywhere."

"Why?"

"We can't leave this shelter".

"*What* shelter?"

"Mum's grave. I think we are safer here, somehow. And they don't seem to make a move while we're sitting still."

"Jade, we are going to the car, come on."

"There is no way out, Leela! They are all along the lampposts *that* way, and all along the church wall *that* way. We are trapped."

Leela stared at her sister for a moment.

Then she sat down beside her once again, taking her hand.

"Ok Jade. Let's talk. What do they look like? Why can't I see them? What do you think they want to do to us? How do we escape?"

"They look like that." Jade pointed to a weeping angel with her face hidden in the nook of her arms where she kneeled over a tombstone, her lavish feather wings framing her slender shoulders in an imposing manner. "Like her... but their wings, Leela, they're..." Jade's words caught in her throat. She swallowed. "They're not feathers, they're webbed. With hooks at the knuckles. Bat wings! Or if I saw it in a game, I'd say... I'd say... Dragon wings." Jade was panting, as if she'd been running. "And their dresses are not preppy robes like that one. They are filthy. Torn to shreds and stained with old blood!"

"Sounds unsanitary," said Leela. "Maybe we can get them a first aid kit?" She gave a little smile.

"Really, Leela?"

"Sorry. Ok. Where does the blood come from, are they injured?"

Jade looked at the church wall. A moment passed. Leela watched her wearily.

"It's dripping from their chins," said Jade. "I think..." Her gaze hardened as she looked at the faces of the creatures, trying to avoid actual eye contact. They all stared at her, but they never made another move. As if they were silent spectators, there to witness, not get involved.

"Jade? You still with me?"

"Oh god, Leela, it's their eyes. Blood's pouring from their eyes."

"Eeww!"

"I can hear them too. Sort of. They're not weeping like the other statues, not with poise and dignity. It's like a silent rage. This mute hissing and spitting. And they're just watching us, but their teeth, Leela, their teeth..."

"So, vampire angels then?" said Leela, forcing a smile. "Maybe banshee angels? Or Lamia angels? What horror movie she-creature cries blood tears?" Leela gave a timid little laugh, looking at Jade to see if she would find it funny.

Jade grabbed her sister by the elbows and pushed her back, slamming her against the tombstone. Leela lost her balance and fell on her butt on the grass.

"Ouch, Jade—"

"Keep your voice down!" Jade hissed under her breath. "And stay here, out of view of the lampposts *and* the church wall!"

"I don't like sitting on a grave, it's not right!" Leela said, trying to sit up to her knees, but Jade pushed her back down.

"One of them looked at you."

"What?" Leela stopped moving.

"They are staring at me only," Jade continued in an urgent whisper, "as if I'm, somehow, the only one here. But making jokes like that... they heard you! The one on that lamppost, it turned around and looked straight at you! So please hide! And stay quiet, until I figure this out!"

Leela hunched down, but a sigh of disgust escaped her lips.

"Calm down, you're sitting on a patch of grass, not a pile of bones!"

Leela shot her an angry look. Neither of them said that the pile of bones was not far under the grass; but they both thought it, because they looked away from each other uncomfortably.

"Ok, they seem to have forgotten about you again," said Jade, who was sitting up, peering over the tombstone. "They are all back staring *me* down. Which is fine, I can handle."

Jade was shaking. She coughed and pulled her sleeves to cover her freezing hands.

Leela studied her sister's face, and made one more valiant attempt to understand, speaking very gently.

"What do you think they want from you, Jade? Why would angels appear like that?"

"No, angels are benign. These things are fucking sinister," Jade said. A strange fervour gleamed in her eyes.

Leela's brows furrowed as she watched the beads of cold sweat form on Jade's forehead. Leela sighed with disappointment as her sister went on hoarsely, in a completely serious and urgent whisper.

"They are more like... Seraphs. Sombre, murdering saints. But also like a hybrid, between Seraphim, and, I don't know, gargoyle bats."

"Gargoyle bats!" Leela gave another, desperate try to lighten the mood. "Gargobats!"

Jade burst out laughing, and for a moment Leela sighed with relief.

"This has been fun. Shall we head to the car?" she asked softly.

But Jade was still laughing. It became louder, more breathless. She gasped for air and bellowed again with mirthless hilarity, compulsively, violently. Leela looked tired.

"Jade, there's no one here. Let's just go home, ok?" Leela's voice was firm now.

Jade's manic laughter slowly subsided. She wiped tears from her eyes.

"Come on, take my hand, let's get you up," said Leela.

Jade shook her head.

"Hellaphims," she said. Leela looked at her, confused, but Jade chortled to herself. "They're Hellaphims." Jade grabbed hold of the nearby tombstone and pulled herself to her feet. She slipped a folded piece of paper from her pocket and clutched it tightly in her shaking fist.

"What's that?" Leela asked, frowning.

"I think I know how to make them leave. Sit down. I need to do this alone."

"Do what, Jade?" Worry blanketed Leela's words.

Jade shook her head curtly and pointed to the grass. "Just look at your phone for five minutes. Find us somewhere to get breakfast. I promise I'll be right back."

"Okay," Leela said, slowly. She plopped back on the grass beside the grave. "So, I'm going to look up a nice breakfast spot nearby and you'll come with me and we can leave?"

"Yes." Jade waited until Leela began scrolling on the phone, then lifted her gaze to the shadows above the graves. Her chin thrust forwards. Her shoulders squared. She took a few steps forward, focused her vision on the tops of the lampposts, and walked with determination into the darkness.

She halted near the first dark lamppost. The shadow above it shifted, its head lowering toward her. Two heads. Three. God, there were so many of them up there, climbing on each other like insects. Clusters of limbs and leathery wings writhed from the lampposts down the path, as they all positioned their multiple heads in her direction.

"I know why you're here," Jade said quietly, "and I know you can hear me." She didn't need to shout. These beings would hear the slightest whisper. Maybe even her thoughts.

"I watched a man die." A knot jumped up her throat and blocked her voice. She had never before cried for him. But now her eyes were streaming, and she had to swallow a sob before she could continue.

"He was a good man. I wish this hadn't happened to him. He didn't deserve it." Jade looked around. Eyes blinked from the darkness above, like pairs of fireflies hanging still against the sky. They were listening.

"But I don't deserve this either. I didn't kill him. I was there, working *against* those who took his life." Jade continued to speak quietly as she unfolded the bit of paper. She held it up in front of her, turning around in full circle on the spot, so all of the glowing, bleeding eyes upon her could see it, even those on the church wall.

"You need proof, right? That I'm innocent? Here it is."

Laughter.

It was a scream at first, that trembled into a monstrous cackle. Then another screech tore into it, dropping to vibrate with dozens of voices merging together, a cacophony of mirth, a soul-wrenching hooting.

Jade's arm fell to her side; the paper crumpled in her closed fist.

"What?" she said, louder this time. "What do you want?"

There were words in the laughter. Strange, unfamiliar sounds. Jade brought her hands to cover her ears. The wailing drowned out her thoughts, the voices synchronised in a military cadence that echoed in her mind. But it wasn't a marching call she'd ever heard before.

The Law of men is blind.

Justice and vengeance, entwined.

Deaf is the Law of men,

blood calls for blood again.

Revenge is our eternal strife,

what's fair's a life for a life.

Jade fell to her knees. The screaming was no longer laughter. It was a raging lamentation. Sentiments that were not her own poured into her—a rampaging flood of furious anger, a call from the wronged for justice; excruciating pain that the call has gone unanswered.

"Nooo!" she yelled, "Get out of my head!"

Silence.

Cold.

So cold.

And then they were swooping down from the sky. Blasting icy wind at her with giant wings that batted overhead. She hunched into a ball. Why didn't it work? Hadn't Sarah said a legal verdict of innocence was what they needed? To turn from evil to good?

Jade peeked up from under her arms. They weren't touching her, but they kept diving for her, grazing her hair and flying on. The air thickened with the stench of rotting blood like festering wounds. Her hair kept blowing right and left as gusts of wind slapped her, with the *whoosh* of things zooming too close to her skin at the back of her neck.

"Stay back!"

"Jade who are you talking to?" Leela now stood beside her.

The attack ceased. Mists thickened above, black clouds slowly swirling. The things were still there, though. Hidden in the gloom. Biding their time.

"I... I did find us a breakfast place," Leela said, "it opens in fifteen minutes. Ready to go?"

Jade jumped to her feet, clasped her sister by the wrist and ran back to the grave with the violin. "Stay down, Leela," she said. "Sit still. Keep quiet. Please."

"Jade, that's enough!" Leela snapped.

"I need a weapon."

"You need a wha—Jade, this is too much. We're going!"

"My plan didn't work. I won't go down without a fight."

"A fight? No, we're leaving!"

"Exactly! I need to have something to keep them off us, they will descend the moment we start running for the gates. I need a weapon!" Jade launched herself at a grave two stones down.

"Jade, what the hell! That's someone's property!"

Jade didn't even register how the iron pole was suddenly in her hand. She had a vague idea of kicking something off the ground, sending flowers everywhere. Pain throbbed in the toes of her right foot. A funeral wreath formed of scuffed white lilies lay face down on a nearby grave, next to a little mount of disturbed earth.

"You ruined someone's wreath! These are expensive, Jade!"

Yes, the pole had a hook. A wreath stand. She must have kicked it loose so fast she didn't even see it happen. Good. It was heavy and long, with a sharp pointy tip covered in mud. A couple of brown, slithery coils dangled off it, trying to twist back up to the tip. Worms. She shook it till they all dropped to the ground.

"Put that back, right now!" Leela shouted.

Jade stumbled back to Leela, clutching the pole with both hands. She sank down on the ground, leaning back against her mum's tombstone, the iron rod held tight to her chest.

"Leela, listen carefully. We're surrounded. When we move, stay close behind me. Keep your head down. You can't see them, so don't *try* to. Just hold onto me and follow, like you're not even here. Okay?"

Leela furrowed her brow and shook her head, tightly. "Yeaaaah, no. I'm calling Dad. Jade, this is over the top, even for y—"

"What's Dad going to do!" Jade gave a dry laugh.

"You need help! It's either Dad or 999. Pick one."

"Police? Sure," Jade shrugged. "Let's see how *that* plays out."

"An *ambulance*, not the police," said Leela. "You're having a breakdown, Jade."

Jade wasn't paying attention. A strong metallic scent had begun to creep its way into her nostrils. Was it the iron pole?

She'd been gripping it so hard, the cuts in her hand had split open. A hideous gash gaped in the middle of her index finger and widened as she straightened her fingers. The flesh actually parted, red welling up. Quickly, Jade let her hand curve again to stop the hemorrhaging. And the blinding pain. The two sides of the wound squished together. A little yelp of agony escaped her lips. Instead of stopping the flow, the opposite happened. Squeezing it together, made it bleed more. Ripples of red streaked over the back of her hand and down her wrist.

"Jade! You're bleeding!" Leela cried, but Jade's gaze was fixed on a single streak of red. A blood drop had travelled down from her hand along the length of the rod.

Before she had time to do anything to stop it, the solitary drop fell off the iron tip to the ground.

Don't let...

But it was too late.

The breeze whooshed with the batting of wings.

Something moved overhead.

Shadows.

Landing soundlessly, falling from the sky.

Heavy, low-bearing clouds churned above, an angry storm spiraling rapidly over the treetops. A wind overhead picked up out of nowhere. Shadows skittered in the depths of the gloom.

Another figure dropped from above, and stood completely still, blending into the dark shapes of the trees.

A soft thud. Something had hit the ground behind Jade. She turned to look, but the outlines of the tombstones and willows concealed whatever might have landed there.

But she knew it: For the first time they were touching ground. There was no stopping it now, as the skies rained demons.

One by one, they descended. Some glided, wings spread out, the silken shreds of their ghostly gowns grazing the tombstones, until they found an empty patch of grass to pound on all fours; for those few moments Jade could see them clearly. She looked at their shoulders, her brain on autopilot trying to force this image her eyes were seeing to somehow match her existing knowledge of the natural world: how did the wings' bone structure connect to the skeleton of this woman-shaped organism? How did they all fly without crushing their shoulder blades? The grey skin changed smoothly into inky wing membrane with a neat line of cuticle, like nails come out of human fingers. But she couldn't figure out how those claw-like hands and feet had attached to the wall of the church like spiders. The creatures landed far too swiftly, obscured behind some statue, or looming Celtic cross, impossible to examine for too long.

"Don't worry Jade, I've got clean napkins, and we'll get you sorted in no time!" Leela returned at a run. She'd brought her backpack. She knelt beside her sister, with a bag labelled: 'This Pouch Contains My Face'. With a loud zipper noise, she produced a flurry of make-up removing wipes to clean the angry wounds. Jade winced against the sting but didn't complain.

"How did you do this?"

"It's nothing, just a bit of glass," Jade muttered, not paying much attention.

The were still coming.

Jade sat up, using her free hand to support her weight and bring herself to her knees, to see better.

Some of the flying creatures plummeted straight down from the night sky like solid statues, so fast and silently, that after a moment it was impossible to tell if the motionless silhouettes were grave markers, that had been there all along.

A slithering whisper made her skin crawl.

Desperately, she scanned the outlines of trees and graves.

The whisper surged like a wave.

It sounded like the chant of a mystic ritual, some magic beginning, an echoing invocation darker than death.

She glanced at Leela, who was busy creating make-shift bandages from a handful of tissues, with a waffle logo labelled 'Woofles', wrapping them around Jade's fingers to keep the cuts closed.

The noise intensified, as the last few shadows dropped from above.

The ritual fastened the thickening magic like hands closing around Jade's throat.

It sounded like an outraged crowd talking in breathy whispers. It came from left and right, from behind her as well.

She was in the centre of an invisible throng. Jade reached with her free hand and grabbed her iron pole again, holding it tight, ready to strike if any of the voices came nearer. And she finally started to see them.

A shape that repeated itself among the trees and graves: giant pairs of horns sticking out of the ground. But they weren't horns.

They were wings.

Stretched upwards, their wings pointed to the sky and stood still as the creatures crouched down on the ground. Their bodies hunched, knees askew like frogs, their hands flat on the earth between their feet.

Their cryptic whispering was unnerving.

What are they saying?

An undulating susurrus, a mysterious, suffocating sound of incessant spattering.

Concentrating hard, she tried to decipher it.

"Jjjjussssssssssstice-ssssssssh...!"

The blood drained from her face.

Justice?

The word echoed, relentless, all around her. Underneath it, something else, in another tongue... Or was it the same word? Chanted in the preternatural rhythm of some ancient, eternal incantation. Slowly bringing her to the precipice of insanity.

Jade wanted to yell, but it came out a croaky whisper. "Shut up!"

"What?" said Leela, crumpling a bunch of red stained wipes into a ball and sticking it in a side pocket of her backpack.

"Nothing," Jade muttered.

"Now I see what's going on! You were bleeding a lot, look at your sleeve! Blood loss causes hallucinations, doesn't it?"

"Leela shush!"

"No wonder you're seeing things! Can you stand up at all?"

"Keep your voice down!"

"Jade, stop it! I really think I should call an ambulance!"

"Sit the fuck down! I'm not playing with you right now! I'll *make* you if I have to!"

Jade had brought her face close to her sister's, who backed down in shock, tears welling up.

"Is that your 'thank you' for fixing up your hand?" Leela protested, but she kept her back flat against the tombstone, as Jade leaned into her, daring her to try to stand up again.

Jade was only vaguely aware that her hand was no longer bleeding, the pain dulled now that the wounds were clean. Comforting pressure was applied from, what appeared to be, several pink and stretchy hair bands glistening with purple glitter, holding the bandages together.

"Thanks, but if you try to get up again so help me, Leela! We are surrounded. They are watching from behind every headstone and statue, ok? And they are doing something-something... terrible!"

"I'm going to call the ambulance now," Leela said in a defiant little whisper.

"I don't care! Just keep it quiet! And don't move! Do *not* attract their attention!"

Leela wiped her eyes and shook her head angrily in mute disbelief.

Jade leaned away from her sister. She stabbed the rod on the ground and began heaving herself up to her feet.

"Where are you going?"

"Stay here! Don't move from my Mum's tombstone!"

Leela watched, mouth wide open, as Jade took a few cautious steps forward; then fumbled with her phone. Jade walked on.

A crowded circle of looming wings, eaten away and decayed at the edges, walled the two sisters in. Legions of them. Their hands vanished, wrist-deep in the ground between their feet. Their long, arachnid arms pulsed, in a bizarre, mechanical manner, reminding Jade of rusty pipe hoses sucking something from the ground or funnelling something down. Through those palms, buried in the earth. Jade shuddered. Why would anyone want to sink their hands in graveyard soil? Everything about them was disturbing.

And the worst part was, they suddenly went quiet.

As if they were done. As if they had finished something.

The world felt very, very wrong.

They watched. Hundreds of eyes, fixed ominously on Jade.

No. On something *behind* Jade.

Swerving around, she knew what she would see.

And yet, coming face to face with him, she froze.

"Jade, what are you looking at?"

"Leela?"

"What?"

"Run."

Chapter Twenty-One

United In Death

T he dead man had never been so close. She recognised the familiar silhouette, his height and general shape. The man she remembered bringing sweets, his radiant smile when holding up new pictures of his little girls. This spectre had his bearing.

She shuddered to notice one difference from the man she knew: something was off. His shoulders. Too narrow.

He had no arms. The dark silhouette had always been too narrow, too off. The ghost had kept this armless shape and she'd never realised till now. Now he was physically here, there was no mistaking it.

Flashing images of her nightmares assaulted her mind: the execution, how they mutilated him. How his arms had laid beside his torso.

He stood before her not the way he was in life, but as he looked while he died. His eye was a revolting bulge, swollen to the size of a plum, the flesh raw and glistening with dark red discharge. The other eye only a slit in the middle of a purple bruise, and the white of the eyeball burning orange with burst veins, no iris visible. A lock of matted hair, heavy with clotted blood, draped over half of what was left of his face.

Exactly as she remembered the victim of that murder. How could she possibly have recognised him like this?

The man turned his head and looked to the side.

Jade followed his gaze and saw her sister.

Leela had stayed hidden behind the tombstone. She hadn't left. Only the top of her head and tip of phone in her ear were visible. Urgent whispers came from the grave, the word 'ambulance' audible several times.

Jade stepped between her sister and him.

The apparition took a step towards her.

He was looking only at her now.

Then he stepped forward once again.

Jade backed away a little. Then more.

Do something! Snap out of it!

She couldn't shake the paralysing shock. Before, he'd been a shadow, no features, no details, a vague shape in the dark.

But this thing now?

This apparition was somehow fully corporeal. How was this possible? How could he have returned to walk the earth?

His beard was soiled with red desert mud, same as the sticky brown curls of his short hair. His ashen cheek bones weren't even, the shadow contours concave on one side, the bone cracked from a blow. The signs of torture evident all over him.

Jade's lungs constricted, making it hard to breathe. She looked away, she couldn't look at his face anymore.

The spectre twitched, swerved, and swung on its joints like a loosely assembled puppet to follow its feet. It propelled itself onwards causing the same frightful aftershocks.

And the winged sentries watched on, endless pairs of onyx eyes glimmering like hellish bloodstained gems in the darkness among the graves.

Jade walked backwards, her eyes drifting up his body but then jerking away when his shoulders and face came into view. The wounds on either side of his collar bone were preserved from the very moment the flesh was shredded apart, sinew torn out as the bones were ripped from their sockets.

He kept coming, and the silent horde crowded around them would never let her run away. They were everywhere. Watching. Witnessing. Her death.

Jade stopped retreating. She stood her ground.

"Malem?" she said softly. The spectre instantly stopped moving. "It *is* you, Malem!" She swallowed a knot in her throat. "I'm so sorry. It's so wrong, what's happened to you. So cruel."

The apparition was still. It was listening.

"You know it wasn't us who attacked your village. We were working together against those bastards. You know we didn't do this!" Jade pleaded, glancing behind him at the shadows to make sure they heard.

But there was no movement in the shadows. Their eyes bled in the darkness. They watched.

The apparition shuddered; its head cocked to the side. It looked like a metal puppet plugged to a faltering electric current.

Jade had been looking anywhere but this mangled visage, but she fortified her resolve to look into his face.

"Malem, that day on the road... All I could think was that... I wasn't allowed to confirm to you that the enemy was in the area! We knew there were rumours... that locals were getting tense. But we couldn't get involved! So, I thought you were panicking for no reason! That you worried they'd find out you worked for us. But I knew we had you covered, you see? They would never know you had a job on the base! I thought you'd be fine!"

She took a deep breath. It was so hard, looking into that tortured, corpse face. But there was more she wanted to tell him.

"I didn't for one moment imagine you were risking your life to give your daughters a better future, Malem. It wasn't helping *us* that made you a target. They didn't know about that. It was home-schooling your girls. That... That didn't even occur to me."

He didn't make a move.

She felt tears hot in her eyes and blinked them away.

"I get why you're angry with me. Should've told you they were coming, so you could hide or leave. At least give you a chance. I knew they wouldn't be able to figure out you were helping us. I didn't know that you were doing something they thought was even worse. I wasn't allowed, but I should've answered anyway. To me, it was my job; to you, it was your life. I'm sorry Malem."

For one moment it seemed the world stood still.

Just saying sorry felt like a weight lifted. She had not conveyed how guilty she had felt and how wretched she had been, but she was not good with words. The spectre was so still Jade thought it started to disappear.

That was it.

She had done it.

They were convinced of her innocence.

She let out a breath of relief. It was over.

Then it opened its eyes.

Jade gasped.

The bruised flesh bled as the eyelids parted; the swelling leaked black tears as the irises glowed beneath. The hazel with the green specks blazed against the dark mauve skies before dawn.

Jade stepped backwards, shocked.

She raised her iron hook, half in disbelief.

The hazel eyes burned with accusation that scorched. Jade felt her guilt swelling up to drown her.

"No!" she yelled. She wouldn't crumble in the weight of this guilt. She didn't owe him her life, making amends didn't mean dying.

The armless body lunged for her. Jaws first, open unnaturally wide; his face suddenly horrifically long. Insectile.

Jade swerved the rod across the shadow.

She braced herself for the squelching of torn flesh as the tip of the hook dug into the ribs of the armless torso. She even flinched at the thought of the hook lodging among the bones, and wondered if she would have the willpower to pull at the weapon and free it from the wound.

But none of it happened.

The hook went right through the apparition. It left nothing behind. Jade blinked.

The spectre was no longer there.

Then he flickered into existence where he had been before she sliced at him.

She took a few steps back, letting out a long breath.

The gravestones around her stood silently, as if nothing had happened.

She looked at the rod in complete bewilderment.

Ok, this funeral wreath hook could knock him out. For a moment, at least.

The spectre took another step.

Just keep him at bay, till sunrise. It's got to be less than ten minutes away. You got this.

He lunged at her so fast, she had no time to aim right, and her weapon missed him. At the last second, her body instinctively swung out of his way, like sparring in boxing class.

He sprang forth again with dizzying speed. Jaws open wider than a human mouth ever should.

Jade did a boxing slip and he brushed past her. A piercing ice sensation bit as she brushed against him. She ducked out of the way of his jaws shooting for her elbow, still stunned from the contact.

This time the pain shot through the bone into the marrow; Jade had a flashing image of the skeletal hand of death itself reaching at her from the abyss.

Eyes in the fight! Focus on the opponent dammit.

Jade swerved the iron pole with all the will she had left. If she missed, it was over.

Bang on!

Gone.

Won't let my guard down this time.

Rod raised, bouncing back and forth, boxing stance, she watched to see where he would re-appear.

The snap of teeth came from behind her head.

A strange chill travelled down the roots of her hair. The depths of her skull blasted with a frozen current, blossoming to a vicious brain freeze.

He's biting right into my skull?

Jade ducked and side stepped, sliding the iron rod beneath her underarm and pushing it behind her. That broke contact with him. The chill subsided a little, but still the world swam.

Keep that hook moving!

Jade let her brain go offline for a moment as she blindly swerved the iron rod around her body in stumbling circles.

But his ice touch on the back of her head, brief as it had been, was too potent. The freezing current washing over her wasn't spent yet. She tripped and fell on one knee on a grave plaque. Swishing the rod wildly right and left, even though she couldn't see much, Jade sensed him vanish from her left. She had saved herself one more time.

What am I going to do? He keeps coming back!

She rubbed her head with her bandaged hand, brushing the cold touch from her skin. The brain-fog subsided, and the blades of grass before her came into sharper focus: she'd regained the ability to see.

The creeping sensation down her spine warned her he was near. Clambering to her feet, she turned and stabbed.

Got him straight in the chest.

For a second he froze, staring at her.

He flickered and vanished right before her eyes.

She let out a breath of relief, but she was so, so very tired.

It's almost sunrise. Keep it together.

The breathy whispers from the dark chorus all around her erupted again, a cacophony of triumphant hissing.

"Jjjjjjjjjjjjjussssssssssssssssssitcccccccce-ssssssssh!"

"Back off!" Jade yelled at the top of her lungs.

"Jade? I can hear you! Where are you?" Leela's voice from somewhere in the distance.

"I'm fine! Do *not* come here!" Jade couldn't see her sister in the dark and didn't have time.

"Jade! There you are!"

Light blinded her.

The bright beam of a phone torch shone directly at Jade, and Leela's panting breath came steadily closer.

"No! Turn it off!" Jade yelled.

The ground around her acquired colour. Green lawn stretched empty, the newer marble tombstones nearest to her had coral pinkish hues shaded with brown, while some limestone graves were yellowish with veins of luminous green moss.

The dark angels were gone.

The spectre was no longer there.

Jade sighed with relief.

I did it!

"Justice-sssssssshhh!" hissed the breeze.

A crippling chill tickled up and down her spine.

Oh no.

Holding the rod with both hands, Jade blindly slashed the air around her, trying to cover every side.

"What are you... have you gone mad?"

"Leela switch off the damn..." the voice died in Jade's throat.

A bite burned the back of her left shoulder and hardened her flesh to stone. She heard the rod thump to the ground as her hand seized, her muscles freezing solid. Her heart pumped a million tiny, jagged shards of ice, tearing her veins up to her neck like razors in her blood.

"Fine! I just couldn't see where you were!" Leela said, and the light went out as suddenly as it had come.

Jade blinked, surrounded by darkness once again.

But it was too late. The very marrow of her bones was freezing over, these deathly throes surpassing any pain she had felt till now. She hit the ground with a soft thump, and finally saw him.

The spectre dropped with both his knees on her chest, and her lungs stopped. His insectile body folded over so his face was an inch away from hers.

Breathing in her last exhale.

Watching her die.

Somewhere out of view, Leela called her name.

The demonic flight spiralled in from above, observing, as Jade's eyes dried to frosty glass.

Their unforgiving gazes scorched her soul, sapping the last of her willpower, and the world collapsed to nothing.

Chapter Twenty-Two
A Parting In The Sunrise

Evelyn Palmer
Beloved Wife
and Mother

L eela didn't dare to switch her phone torch back on. The twilight got weaker every moment. She begun to discern outlines in the dark. She stood up carefully and held the top of the tombstone with both hands, her knuckles turning white, her brows rising to her hairline.

"Jade?'"

Leela's eyelids fluttered nervously. She shook her head.

Jade's fallen body was sprawled across the lawn.

"JADE!"

She wasn't moving.

Leela came out from behind the tombstone but hesitated. Her eyes darted left and right. She craned her neck to look behind her.

The graves stood solemn on the daisy strewn lawns in the twilight before dawn. A hint of silver glowed in the eastern horizon. The darkness was slowly fading away. There was no one there.

Leela took a deep breath, then ran around the tombstone, and came to kneel by her sister.

The fear subsided from her eyes, replaced by the weight of worry. She looked Jade up and down for blood or obvious injury. She found nothing. She felt gently with her fingers at the back of Jade's skull. No wounds or bumps.

"Jade! Please wake up!" Leela squeezed Jade's shoulders.

There was no response.

"Jade!"

She put her ear before her sister's lips and listened. Not a single breath.

Hands shaking, Leela took her sister's wrist and pressed her finger on her pulse. Her eyes glazed over as she concentrated.

"I can't find your heartbeat! Why!" Leela let go of Jade's hand and searched for a pulse on Jade's throat. Her fingers pressed, waited, pressed elsewhere, waited, pressed elsewhere, waited. She ran out of places a pulse could be.

Tears spilled down her cheeks as she blinked.

The buzz of a phone vibrating made Leela jump. She pulled out her phone and stared at it, silent in her hand. The buzzing came from her other pocket.

"Jade! I've still got your phone!" she said, pulling out the second device.

The screen showed no picture, but the name of the caller was *Ami's Parents!!!* with three exclamation marks at the end. Leela's shoulders hunched.

"Oh no," she muttered. "Jade! I can't pick up and speak to Ami's parents! *You* need to do that! Wake up, please!" Leela shook her sister's elbow. Jade's body limply swayed.

Leela rejected the call, almost about to break into sobs.

The roar of an engine made her look up.

An ambulance drove past the cemetery gates. It made its way slowly along the narrow path among the graves. Leela jumped up and waved her arm.

"Don't worry Jade, help is here! You will be fine!" Leela said, giving her sister's elbow a little reassuring shake.

The vehicle came to a smooth stop on the path nearest Leela.

"Thank God you're here!"

Two men in dark green uniforms jumped on the grass and came to kneel on either side of Jade's body. Leela watched their hands working fast. They checked her pulse, lifted Jade's eyelids to shine a light in the deep of her dark blue eyes.

"What happened to her?" asked the older man, in a deep fatherly voice.

"I think she had a panic attack!"

"Were you with her?"

"Yes!"

"What did she say?"

"She was afraid there was someone here. Someone was coming at her, but I swear it was just the two of us!"

"What is your name, miss?"

"Leela, I'm the one who called you," she replied, her eyes darting to his name tag that said, "Mr Daljit Varma".

"You are sure there was no one? Did you leave her alone at all?" said Daljit, quickly glancing around and making a note.

"No, I never left her alone, I was standing right here," Leela insisted. "No one attacked her. But she acted as if she could see somebody. I've never seen a panic attack like this. It was so intense!"

"No rigor mortis," said the younger paramedic, a slender black man in his early twenties, who looked up to Daljit often as if seeking confirmation.

"Too soon, it's been only a few minutes," Daljit said, indicating at the bulky green duffle bag they had placed beside Jade. The younger man dived to it, to fish out a piece of equipment, Leela saw his name was Kevin.

"What are you doing?" asked Leela. The words "rigor mortis" were ringing in her ears. Of course there was no rigor mortis, Jade wasn't dead.

"Assessing heart activity," Kevin replied, unbuttoning the top of Jade's shirt to stick some white circles on her sternum, as Daljit switched on the device the cables were attached to.

Leela looked from one to the other in terrified disbelief. She wrung the edge of her shirt with nervous fingers as she waited for them to speak again. They took their time, watching their portable monitors in silence.

Birdsong filled the little riverfront cemetery as the morning mists died away above the grass in the shadow corners along the wall. The sun touched the steeples and cast vivid long shadows on the church's roof.

"None," said Daljit, finally looking up.

"Do you mean no heartbeat?" said Leela.

Leela watched helplessly as Kevin pulled the stickers off Jade's skin. He bent into the duffle bag, now taking another, larger bit of equipment out of it.

"Can you please tell me what's happening?"

"We are going to cardiac arrest protocol," Daljit told her. "Please stand clear."

"Cardiac arrest?" Leela croaked. He didn't reply, busy wearing the pads on the palms of his hands. Leela wiped another silent tear and gulped down a sob. Daljit waited with both hands hovering over Jade, while Kevin applied much bigger stickers on Jade's chest and on her left ribcage.

They needed to hurry up and do it, so Jade could wake up. She looked so vulnerable, unconscious on the lawn, those horrid medical plasters stuck above and below her bra. Leela had never seen her sister look defenseless in all her life. She bit her lip to stop herself from yelling at them. They weren't paying attention to her at all, their eyes were fixed on the monitor. Ready for its signal.

Leela turned away from the unbearable sight for a second, her gaze catching the first sunbeams wilting a red rose high on the church's wall. Its petals rained down all the way to her feet. The sun reached lower along the wall; it ignited the stained-glass windows in their gothic arches. The cerise light of dawn turned the grey stone of the belltower to a muted purple.

The phone buzzed in her pocket. Leela pulled it out, staring helplessly at the screen.

Ami's Parents!!!

She shook her head dismally and rejected the call again.

Jade's body bounced up into an arch. The electricity made a thud as it drove through flesh and bone. Leela let out a tiny yelp.

In the silence that followed, everyone waited. Jade's eyes didn't open. Her chest didn't rise with the swelling of a new breath.

Leela brought her hands to her face, muffling into them a sob.

The men exchanged short, rehearsed commands, as they operated the defibrillator.

A second thud.

When it fell silent for the second time, Leela peeked behind her fingers.

Jade didn't move.

On the third time the paramedics engaged the machine, Leela watched through eyes streaming with tears. Her sobs were now coming loud, and she didn't try to hide them anymore.

Once the current running through her was spent, Jade's head dropped lifelessly to the side.

"Call it?"

"Yes."

"No! Don't stop! Keep going!" Leela shouted at them.

Daljit stood up to talk to her as Kevin pulled out the radio from his belt.

"Leela, is there anyone I can call for you?" he said.

"Is Kevin getting a doctor?" Leela said, trying to hear what the man by the ambulance was saying quietly into his radio.

"No, he is calling the police," said Daljit.

"Why, she needs a doctor!" Leela cried, hurrying around him towards her sister.

He put out his arm to block her way.

"We need to stay clear of the body, until the officers arrive," he said firmly.

"She is not dead!" said Leela between sobs.

"Leela this is your sister, right? Maybe we should call your parents. I can do it for you. Would you give me your phone to look at their number?"

"No, I'll call my Dad myself!" said Leela, taking a few steps back. Daljit gave her space and didn't press. He just watched her discreetly, hovering near Jade. Probably to stop her if she tried to approach her sister again.

She went behind the tombstone with the violin and stood there, phone in hand. Her other hand rested on the stone, as if she needed support to keep standing.

She scrolled to "Dad", looked at the number. She switched off the screen. No idea how to explain what was happening.

She glanced at Jade, her jaundiced cheeks, her closed eyes, her stiff limbs.

A blanket landed over Jade's face and Leela blinked in horror. Kevin had covered her sister's body.

"No, don't do that!" she shouted. "Can you please do the defibrillator thing again? One more time, please?"

"Let me call your parents, Leela," Daljit said.

"No! You have to try again!"

"Leela listen. It's been ten minutes since we arrived. Twenty minutes since your call. It's too long. The brain can't go without oxygen more than a few minutes. You must call your family."

Leela shook her head vigorously and turned her back to him. She rested her fists on the tombstone and took a deep breath. She squeezed her phone in the palm of her hand, tilting her head to the sky and steeling herself.

Spiderwebs sparkled silver on the arch of the church entrance doors, as the sunlight reached the lower level of the wall. Leela could almost see the line of light descending inch by inch, changing the colour of the ancient wall. Soon the golden rays would touch the first tips of the tallest gravestones. Leela could now see the sun playing among the leaves behind the treetops, but the ground was still in shadow.

"Jade is still in shadow," Leela thought, without knowing why. She pulled her hands off the tombstone, as if she'd been electrocuted. Her eyes darting around as if looking for someone, but there was no one near her. She folded her arms on her chest and shook her head.

For a second nobody moved. Leela's gaze was fixed on the blanket covering Jade. Her shoulders hunched, like someone had placed a heavy weight on her back.

Then Leela sprang forward. Before the paramedics could stop her, she had pulled the blanket off her sister.

"Please give me that!" said Daljit. Leela sped away from him, and he followed after her, looking peeved.

A ringtone and a dull buzz made everyone look around.

Leela pulled out Jade's phone.

"Is it your parents? You should speak with them," said Daljit. Then his gaze fell to the blanket Leela was still holding.

Leela stood there, with the body blanket in one hand and the phone in the other. Daljit made a step towards her, reaching for the blanket, and the phone kept vibrating loudly.

"We must cover the body," he said.

"No!" Leela couldn't take her eyes off of Jade. Her whole world seemed to be collapsing in on itself. Before she realised it she had brought the phone to her ear.

"Hello?" she said. Daljit glanced at Kevin and neither seemed inclined to wrestle the blanket from Leela while she was on a call.

"Jade!" said a woman's voice through the phone. Leela started to correct her but hesitated: The woman on the other end of the phone was crying.

"Jade, have you had any messages from Ami?"

"Ami?" said Leela.

"Yes, please check your messages! She may have gotten through to you, we have nothing from her!"

"Ok but..." Leela meant to explain the misunderstanding, but the woman interrupted her.

"The airport was bombed."

"Bombed?"

"Just as Ami was getting on a flight home. We're trying to reach her, it's impossible. The embassy has no staff or information. The military is saying nothing. Her father's contacts told us to wait a couple of hours and call again. They say she is down as MIA at the moment and to wait for updates. I can't wait! For two hours! Without knowing where my child is! Have you had any messages from her?"

Leela looked at Jade's pallid face, as if hoping for a clue.

This was a decision she had to make for herself. She took a deep breath.

"I will check for messages," she said to the woman, "give me one second." The notifications on the lock-screen didn't mention any new messages. "I'm so sorry, I don't think there are any," said Leela.

Crying erupted from the other end of the phone.

"She hasn't texted! Why? Where is she? Why hasn't she texted anyone?" the woman was telling someone else. Leela had no words to say.

The call was disconnected.

Leela was left holding the phone in one hand and keeping the blanket firmly tucked under the other arm.

She looked at Jade helplessly.

Jade's face was now drenched in sunlight. The sun was hovering, crimson-gold and huge above the treetops, cast against cerise skies. The lawn sparkled vivid green with twinkling dew drops, and Jade's ponytail was gloriously blonde with sun-bleached tips, while her ashen face was lit with a golden glow.

Kevin had got hold of a new blanket; he shook it out in the air above Jade, the shadow drenching her in grey. He let the fabric land softly over her. It covered her completely. Leela burst into tears. She let her own blanket drop on the grass.

Jade was gone and Leela didn't know what to do next.

The sunshine felt warm on her skin.

The two paramedics were packing away their gear and a stretcher was propped up already on the side. Their backs were both turned when it happened.

The body shaped blanket twitched.

Leela held her breath.

A hand rolled out of the side of the blanket and lay palm up on the lawn.

Leela glanced from the ambulance to Jade. They hadn't seen it! She tried to shout, but her voice wouldn't come.

A shiver ran through the fingertips that protruded from the blanket.

Leela's eyes widened, her mouth opened.

The top of the blanket rippled subtly. A breath, exhaled underneath the fabric?

Leela stilled herself, letting the constriction ease in her throat. Then she yelled to the top of her voice.

"She is alive!"

Daljit tried to intercept her as she headed for her sister. "It's time to call your parents."

"No look! She's waking up!" Leela ducked around him and ran to Jade.

Daljit and Kevin froze.

The blanket had formed a dome. The body under it sat upright.

Everyone was speechless as they took in the sight. Leela pulled the blanket off Jade's head.

Jade blinked in the sunlight, her eyes gleaming cobalt blue.

"Mum?"

"Jade! You're all right!" Leela fell into her sister's arms, squeezing her in a violent hug, all other thoughts forgotten.

"Mum!" Jade shouted, struggling to disengage herself to look around.

Leela studied her wearily, as Jade brought her hand to shade her eyes, still dazzled by the sunlight. Tears ran down her cheeks, as she urgently scanned around.

"Where did she go?"

"Who?"

"Mum! *My* Mum! Didn't you hear the music, the violin?"

"Jade, I'm so glad you're ok!"

"How could you not hear it? It came from right there!"

"Jade, you're pointing at..." Leela's voice faltered.

"It was pitch black, but I could see her! I saw her shadow as she played!"

"Jade..." Leela pleaded in a whisper. "Can you be spooky later? I'm so happy you're alive!"

"I couldn't reach her, I couldn't move!"

"Jade."

"She smiled, and she played for me, to keep me company! Because I was so scared! I couldn't move! She stayed with me, right there!" She pointed a shaking finger. "Like a goodbye, parting from her all over again..."

"Jade!"

"Yes!"

"You are pointing at your mother's grave."

The two sisters looked mutely at each other for a moment, as they sat huddled on the grass among the tombstones. A tear snaked down Jade's cheek.

"And it hasn't been *pitch-black* for a good forty minutes, so you must have dreamt it."

Jade bit her lip, noticing the paramedics for the first time. They were following the conversation and making notes on a little notebook. Her lips pressed tight in a thin line and her face became blank.

"Sure. I dreamt it. I'm fine now," she said, casting a sharp look at the paramedics—as if *that* would make them leave. Instead, they took a few steps closer.

"Just give us a moment," she went on in her on-duty voice, and the two men paused, tactfully looking away as Jade quickly buttoned her shirt.

Leela threw herself at her sister again. Jade hugged her back. She buried her face in Leela's silky hair and inhaled, holding that breath as if to preserve the moment for eternity.

Then she sighed, deeply, against her sister's shoulder, the last of the chills leaving her body with a final shudder. Leela squeezed her even tighter, beneath the warmth of the morning sun.

Chapter Twenty-Three

Touched by the Dead

I loved the Thames sunsets on the boat. Granny Tamsin's crochet cushions made her garden chairs so comfy I never wanted to get up.

My feet stretched on the empty chair across the bistro table, fluffy socks warming my toes. Enveloped in the late spring scents of the pots around me, I felt Gran's presence, like the soft caress of her hand on my face. The Lady Thomasine was a little heaven; and you know Mum, how your absence was a constant pain and gaping, aching void; but somehow Gran's memory was a salve and her boat a sanctuary. Like she hadn't left. Like being in her houseboat was being with her always. Like she was sitting beside me, among the cushions she'd made and the blankets she'd knitted and the flowers she'd grown. Gran was here, companion and protector, unseen and unheard but real as the air I breathed. It made me never want to leave the boat again.

Then I blinked.

Where on earth did that come from? I've never felt Grandma Tamsin's presence before.

I rubbed my eyes, trying to shake off the weird feeling. That's what happens when all I think about is ghosts.

I tried not to think about Grandma again and focus on my story. The words of Lovecraft came through my headphones, as my audiobook played on. The waters before me had become a glorious golden path through the trees to the endless horizon. I'd been blissfully listening to the final chapters as I finished a warm bowl of spicy barley and black bean bake, deliciously covered in thick, white sauce: cream of cauliflower, my favourite.

I know, very unlike me, lounging around, being lazy. But I did nothing much at all lately. I had no strength.

As light dwindled in the violet hues of dusk, I stood up and gathered my blanket and bowl to head inside. The houseboat was deliciously quiet, welcoming and peaceful. All I could handle right now was a cup of sweet tea, to sit steaming by the bedside table, and get the tablet ready to play my evening movies in bed. Cannelloni was belly up, asleep on my blanket, waiting for cuddles.

But then he opened one eye, ears prickled up, and he flipped into a crouch faster than I could look around. With a loud bark, he catapulted himself to the window, standing on his back legs to scratch at it, yelping the whole time.

There it is.

My bedroom window was too high for him to jump through, so I didn't bother closing it. I just sat with my face in my hands.

Something was going to happen, sooner or later. It had been great while it lasted, but too good to be true.

Seven whole nights without nightmares so far. I'd slept right through. Midnight till morning. Real sleep. Restful, restorative, night-long. And in my bed, not the roof of the boat after sunrise.

Nope. I wasn't going to survive this so easily. Let's face it, I've had too much sex in my life to be a final girl.

Cannelloni was about to break a toe the way he was scratching at the window, trying to climb up to it. I pulled my cargos back on, over my pyjama shorts, and took a deep breath.

Bracing myself, I peered out of the window.

The dusk cast the tree shadows long over the river path.

It was empty.

No. Someone had just turned around the bend...

You've got to be shitting me! No fucking way.

Irritated, I opened my cabin door, only to let out the dog. He shot through to the corridor, yelping with every step, and I closed the door after him, hearing him gallop to the lounge. I leaned with my back against my door. I was not ready for this.

I guess I'm the kind of final girl who survives only to go insane and be institutionalised in the sequel.

No, it was fine. I just needed to chill. I was in a good place. The nightmares were gone. And the shadow never returned. Not since That Night...

I locked the door and leaned my head against it once again, closing my eyes. I've been scared. That's why I never visited the cemetery again. I wanted to! I really wanted to. But I didn't dare.

Pounding. It came from the other side of the door. It reverberated through my body.

I flung myself to my bed, face dived into my pillow and yelled.

"Go away!"

The banging on the door stopped.

Then the handle turned violently. Once. Twice. I'd locked my door, but someone was trying to open it anyway. It rattled against its hinges.

"Leave me alone!"

The door went quiet.

I pulled myself up on my knees, and I punched my pillow, jab-cross-hook-hook, over and over, so fast I broke a sweat. I heard the seams of the pillowcase tear, and I kept going.

"Jade!" came a hushed whisper from the open window.

"No!" I grabbed the battered pillow and threw it at the window. It was only ajar, so the pillow bounced off the glass and slid to the floor.

I was so angry. I was done with this.

I've been a bag of raw, exposed nerves for a whole week. So much to process.

Malem. I *cannot* fucking believe it, even though I think about it every single moment of every single day. It was Malem. Can't come to terms with it. I don't know how I'm going to tell Ami.

And Ami! That's the worst thing. My brain goes blank. My thoughts switch off and I stare at the wall, like I'm going full catatonic. It's just too hard. Just the thought that she is... Nope. I just can't even *go* there.

Hands shaking, I tried to do what the therapist had told me and remember the good things I've got going for me right now.

I guess the spectre that was conjured here to kill me, hasn't come back. So that's a win.

I can't be happy about that, somehow. I still hope he is ok, wherever he is now. Maybe he is at peace. Maybe he thinks he killed me... Did I really die? The paramedics thought I died, although I'm not sure because... well, here I am. But maybe he thought I died as well— that he killed me— and maybe that gave him some peace. And I'm fine with that, if my death was what he needed to go to his rest. I have no hard feelings, how could I? After what was done to him! I'm just devastated to think that he had turned into something so heinous.

No, that wasn't him. He wasn't a creature of vengeance. He was a cook and pastry chef, so thoughtful and kind, good-natured and always making Ami laugh. He was the best father. Sacrificed everything for his little girls. I just don't see how he could have turned into that loathsome entity, driven only by hate and bloodthirst.

It's the other ones.

The flying ones. The way they dug their fingers in the graveyard dirt and their whole bodies pulsated, like sending a quake into the ground... And I still feel sick to remember it. How it looked like they were drawing something up, with those odd, synchronised vibrations. Raising something from the literal fucking grave. And that unearthly chant. My blood runs cold to remember it....

It was all *them*. The shadow with Malem's eyes became solid when they did that. I think, somehow, they turned him into a monster or outright created a monster in his name. I don't know. I don't know *what* they were. And I just can't begin to try to make sense of any of the whole, *I appear to have died at the hands of a ghoul* thing.

Although I did learn something. I have a newfound respect for darkness. I hardly switch any lights on anymore. That way I can *see* what's *there*. Once night falls, I sit in my room with the lights out and play games with my screen on the dimmest setting. So, my eyes are always able to adjust quickly. I have instant visibility even when I glance at the darkest corners of my cabin. Which I do often. Just checking.

Demons... I always thought demons were evil, but these... beings? They were the stuff of nightmares. And I *know* nightmares.

They weren't good or evil. They were just messed up.

They'd been there, on those lampposts, the entire time we were trying to leave the cemetery. I was right when I felt something there; I thought it was *him*. But it was the Hellaphims. The idea of Leela walking right under the lampposts, her face in the phone screen, completely oblivious to what was watching us from so close right above... I was so stupid not to look up. Even once I blew the lamps, I never looked up. We walked the path, and they hung right over our heads and I didn't know.

Probably for the better. At least I managed to burst all the lamps and plunge the whole cemetery into darkness *before* I saw them. If I'd logged those things earlier, I'd lose my mind and never finish the job. That means, when he appeared, I wouldn't be able to see him. And I wouldn't have been able to defend myself.

I think that helped, fighting him for so long. Keeping him at bay until it was almost daylight. Otherwise, I would have died instantly. The moment he appeared. But now I lived until right before sunrise. I don't know why, but I have a feeling that's important.

Anyway, that's why all my lights are off, all the time now.

So far there hasn't been anything. But I'm still not switching the big lights on.

And then there's the other thing. What happened to me? Did I really die? The paramedics insisted... but... how come it felt like sleep, like waking up from a dream? Oh God, *that* dream. Did I really hear that music? A violin playing from the tombstone?

So many questions, and it felt like the answers were waiting, back at the cemetery.

But I didn't dare return. What if the ghost came back?

All I did was hide away in my cabin and sleep the days away.

A foot in purple ballerina flats poked through the open window. I jumped to my feet, blinking wildly. The foot was followed by a leg in jeans with flowers embroidered along the side.

"Leela what are you doing?"

"I need to talk to you!" My sister was straddled on the window seal, half in half out of the boat.

Something crashed outside, behind her.

"What was that?" I said.

"Oh, no. The little chair I took from the garden... to step up here!" Leela said, her voice shaking. "It just... kinda... it just fell through the gap. Between the boat and the mooring. It's in the river."

"Grandad will kill you. Those are Grandma Tamsin's chairs."

"Jade, I'm stuck!"

Leela sat there frozen, holding on for dear life. The barge swayed gently with her antics, and I widened my stance to balance myself on the floor, the tea in my cup spilling a little in the saucer on the bedside table.

Leela held on to the window frame in panic.

"You didn't think this through, did you?" I asked.

"Can you please pull your chair over? It's too high for me to step down!"

"What if I don't?"

"Jade!"

"I asked you to leave me alone," I said. "Crawling through my window is not leaving me alone."

"I'm going to fall in the water!" she moaned, looking at the drop on the other side of the window.

"I've jumped in the river before, it's a bit cold, very smelly, but you'll survive."

"Jade why do you have to be like that?"

"You know why," I said, feeling the heat turning my cheeks and ears red. I folded my arms on my chest and stood my ground.

She tried to lift her leg that still dangled outside and bring it through the window, but she wasn't that bendy. Her calf got stuck between the frame and her chest, and she pushed her knee aside. Her foot went flying out of the window again and almost pulled the rest of her with it into the river.

"Jade, help!" she wailed, balanced very precariously now with one thigh on the windowsill and the rest of her body sliding slowly out of the window.

"Oh, for crying out loud,", I said. Grabbing my sister by the waist, I pulled her in. She wrapped her arms around my neck to lean her weight into me as I lowered her to the floor. "Why can't you take no for an answer? It's so fucking annoying."

We each took a step apart and stared daggers at each other.

"You blocked me?" she said.

"You told her mother you were me," I said.

"I'm sorry! But can you unblock my phone number? So, I can check you're alive?"

"Get out of here. I can't look at you." I unlocked the door and opened it. Leela slammed it shut without going through.

"Enough, Jade! I said I'm sorry every day this week and you blocked my number and all my social! You hung up on me when I call you from other phones! Isn't that a bit much?"

"I'll tell you what's a bit much. Me calling Ami's mother the day after her daughter had gone missing, asking if I can speak to Ami, and her mother, somehow, being under the impression that she had already told me. She started crying! And I didn't know what she was talking about. A bombing, Leela? How did you never think to tell me?

"I just forgot, ok?"

"How do you forget? The whole day we were at the hospital! Did it not cross your mind once on those eight hours you were sitting beside my bed?"

"Yeah, I don't know what distracted me. I'd had such a chill and peaceful night, nothing to worry about, certainly not that you refused to come to the car because you were seeing demons? Or that you were swinging around someone's funeral wreath pole like a demented Sith master on crack? Or that you woke up and just sat there, with the blanket over your head and didn't make a move, until I pulled it off you myself, your eyes wide, solid as stone, like the Rising of bloody Nosferatu? And not the whole –swearing that Evelyn was there playing her violin— thing."

I chewed on my lip. I wasn't going to confirm or deny, I'd just move on, like she never mentioned any of that.

"Ami's father had to explain to me what happened. And he insisted her mother had already told me. I contradicted him until I checked my phone and there it was. A call from Ami's parents that lasted several minutes that morning. Do you realise how you made me look?"

"I'm so sorry... I will call her mum myself and apologise..."

"And say what, hi I'm the maniac who impersonated your daughter's friend?"

"I didn't *impersonate* you! What do you think this is, identity theft? Ami's mum *assumed* I was you. I was standing next to your corpse, Jade! The paramedics had called your death! I just had no time to correct her. I was trying to get them to keep going with the defibrillator, because they were giving up, and she was calling nonstop, and I finally answered but I did not have the strength to interrupt her. What was I going to say? 'Sorry, my sister has just been pronounced dead so she can't come to the phone right now!' The paramedics covered you head to toe with the body blanket! Like you were heading straight for the morgue. Do you know what that felt like? I was suffocating, like someone had shut me in the body fridge in the autopsy room, and I was so cold, so cold! And I was starting to hear things. I did the best I could, ok?"

I frowned. That sounded oddly familiar.

"You were suddenly cold and hearing things?"

Leela was catching her breath and didn't answer.

"What did you hear?"

She looked up to me mutely.

"A man saying your name?" I pressed.

Leela cocked her head to the side, confused.

"What? No!"

"Then what?"

"I wasn't actually hearing things, just... I just had this thought in a loop, like it wouldn't stop. I couldn't stop thinking it."

"What did the thought say?" I asked, fear twisting my insides. Was he coming for Leela now? Was *that* why he had left *me* alone?

"I don't remember exactly..."

"Just try! Try to remember! What did it say?"

"Something about how you wouldn't see the sun again? Or maybe that you *should* see the sun... I don't know! I just had this sudden compulsion to pull that blanket off you. I can't explain it very well but, it was this insistent, urgent need... I couldn't stand the idea you were still in shadow when the sun was up. So, I took it."

"You took what?"

"The body blanket! I took it off you. So, the light touched your face, your skin, and somehow that made it so much better. Don't ask me why, I don't know what I was thinking!"

"Maybe I told you at some point that I had this thing about sunlight, it seemed to make the PTSD better? When I had the nightmares, I would only sleep in the daylight. Maybe that's why you did that."

"You never said that," Leela replied. "No, it was me, I was spinning out of control. You started that distorted reality thing, and I followed right after you."

"Distorted reality?"

"I saw that therapist a lot, used up all my visits in one week," she said sheepishly. "Told him everything that happened and we talked about you. He said your distorted reality episode was to be expected after the way I pushed you that night," she added, her eyes downcast.

"Oh, right."

"Anyway, it was insane, I wouldn't give the blanket back! I was convinced that hiding you under the blanket would stop you from turning out to be alive after all. The paramedics must have thought I was nuts. Mad lady stealing their ambulance equipment. And that's when the phone rang, just as I was having my own little breakdown."

I took a step back. Ok, that didn't sound like him. Relief washed over me. Leela had just been spooked from seeing me pass out that morning.

I examined her face, and for the first time I understood that it couldn't have been easy for her either. Her usually rosy cheeks were pale, her eyes brimmed with tears she was proudly holding back, her hands shaking as she remembered that morning. My anger melted away.

"I didn't know it was like that."

"No, you didn't! Because you blocked me so there was no way to explain!"

I let out a deep, long exhalation.

"Fine, I'll unblock you."

"How very gracious of you, after not talking to me for a week. Maybe I'll block *you* for a week first, just so you see what it's like."

"Leela, do you understand what's happening here? Amira is somewhere in religious extremist occupied territory, all alone. Everyone's left and she's stuck, with no way out! Maybe hiding, maybe hurt, maybe captured."

"Ami? You think that— that she's..."

"Of course she is alive."

"How do you..."

"I just know it." We locked eyes for a moment. I would not tolerate talk of Ami not being alive. If my sister even tried to argue *that*, I'd throw her into the river myself. She must have reckoned this from my face, because she swallowed whatever she had been about to say and nodded.

"Ok so if she's alive then that's great right? Now they only need to get her out."

"Who's they? Who's going to get her out?" I said, trying not to shout.

"The- the military, right? The military got everyone home. They will find her and bring her back, right?"

"Aren't you listening? The withdrawal has concluded!" I brushed a stray strand of hair from my eyes. "They had forty-eight hours left when Ami was boarding her plane. That's when the bomb went off. Forty-eight hours from the deadline. So, it was complete chaos in the last two days. They took everyone they could find and they're out. No more evacuations. People who are missing, are missing. The end."

"Are you saying that no one is looking for her?" My sister's eyes were wide like a child's.

The knot in my chest made it impossible to utter a word. I shook my head.

"Oh my god," said Leela. "What— what will happen to her?"

I had to take a moment, trying to swallow the knot to be able to speak. My voice was so hoarse, it was only a whisper.

"We can only hope she has found someone willing to hide her, until she can make contact safely. If they hear from her back home, they will ask her to cross the border to another country and plan an escape for her from there. Through the appropriate channels, which are very sparse at the moment."

"So, there is a way to get her back," Leela mumbled.

"It's not easy to get to a border, though. She'd have to walk for days, and it's not safe so she'll have to do it at night. And they'll be watching for people like her doing exactly that. The religious militia have completed their take over. They control the road infrastructure, and it's a mass scale purge. Hunting for anyone who helped fight against them."

We fell silent. We were thinking the same thing.

"If they were to catch her," I said, and paused again. "She is a British citizen, and an unaccompanied woman. The things they would do..."

Leela walked up to me and put her hand on my shoulder. Out of nowhere, my cheeks were wet. My chest was convulsing with sobs. I hated crying in front of my baby sister. She gently took both my hands in hers. We just held hands for a heartbeat, like we were both five years old. The knot in my chest loosened a little.

Then she was squeezing too hard.

"Ouch, Leela! My shoulder!"

"I'm not touching your shoulder!"

"Just let go of my hand, something's wrong with my arm."

She let go and pulled back, her gaze curious on my left shoulder.

"Oh yes, that burn. Are you ever going to tell me how you ended up with a frost bite on an early summer evening?"

I sighed. I couldn't exactly say 'a ghost bit me'.

"It's fine, it's almost gone now," I said instead. "Just don't touch it and it doesn't hurt."

"But you haven't removed the bandages yet?" she said, noticing the gauze peeking from under the neckline of my pyjama top. "Shouldn't you have done that by now?"

"I'm fine."

"Have you changed the bandages? No, you haven't, that's the spare ones the nurse gave us, there, on your desk."

"I said I'm fine!"

Voices out in the lounge made us both turn to look at my closed cabin door.

"Donovan?"

"Evening, Dad."

"Charleen?"

"How are you, Alan dear."

I stared at my sister, anger boiling up inside me. She shrugged.

"What are you all doing here? I wasn't expecting you!" said Grandpa's voice.

"We brought your favourite rhubarb pie."

"Is Jade here, Dad?"

"Yes, Jade hasn't been out for days! Showed up covered in bandages last week and won't tell me what happened. Is that from the Dutch bakery?"

"Why are Dad and Charleen here?" I asked my sister in a hushed tone.

"I didn't know what to do! I didn't know if you were alive! I had to tell them!"

"I asked you not to!"

"And I asked you to answer your phone, but you wouldn't!"

"Dad, I want to talk to Jade for a bit," my father said to Grandad. "Would you mind taking the dog for a walk?"

"What, right *now*? I'm about to put my evening shows on, Donovan!"

"Here, I'm heating up the pie in the meantime," Charleen said, and the sound of the old aga door squeaking open punctuated her words. "It will be ready when you're back."

"Fine! Make sure the kettle is on, Charleen, I'll be back in fifteen minutes. Come on, boy!"

"Look at this! The *dust* on your mother's gorgeous lampshades! Jade really has taken it too far this time, I'm so sorry darling."

"Just what I was looking forward to this evening," I said quietly to my sister, "Charleen inspecting my housekeeping efficiency. Why are they making Alan walk the dog?"

"They don't want Grandad to know you were in hospital and worry," said Leela. "They wanted to talk with you alone."

"Great, thanks for that."

"I *did* run ahead to warn you. But you wouldn't open the door!"

My door replied to this statement, with a loud knock. We stared at it.

It knocked again.

"Jade! May I come in," Dad demanded.

"Can't! Need to change my bandages," I said and fled to my bathroom. I went to close and lock the door, but Leela crammed in after me.

"What are you doing?"

"You didn't take your change of bandages," she said, holding up the bag the nurse had given me a week ago. Leela closed the bathroom door behind her and locked us both in.

"What change of bandages?" said Dad, and simultaneously:

"You'd think she would tell us she had an accident," said Charleen. They were inside my bedroom. Great.

"I didn't have an accident," I called. "I'm fine!"

"Leela said you got stitches in your hand? From broken glass? And antibiotics for an infected wound on your other hand..."

"That was just one of my nails that broke when I was walking Cannelloni..."

"Jade, I know you'd used skin adhesive to close another cut, along your arm," called Dad. "And you'd done such a bang up job it was infected, so they had to peel off the glue and do it over with sutures! How did you get all these injuries?"

"You had to tell them everything?" I hissed at my sister.

"If you won't tell me how you got hurt like that, maybe you'll tell Dad!"

I turned my back to her but there was nowhere to go, her face was glowering at me from the bathroom mirror.

"Jade, answer me!"

"It's fine, Dad, all healing perfectly now. Nothing to worry about!"

"What have you been doing?"

"Nothing just... the new boxing club I joined is a bit rough. Nothing I can't handle."

Leela rolled her eyes at me through the glass.

"Those are not boxing injuries, Jade!" Dad yelled.

"I'm fine!"

"There's no getting through to you," I heard Dad walk away from the door and the Stepmonster whispering angrily. I glowered at my sister. She looked back at me deadpan, clearly regretting nothing.

"Why did you have to go and tell them?" I hissed.

"You need to come up with better lies," Leela muttered, fiddling with the edges of the packet to rip it open. "The doctors didn't believe a word of it; I sure didn't buy it, and you'll never convince Dad you got mangled like that at boxing club."

Shut up, I mouthed.

Take that top off, she mouthed back, bandages in one hand, an oily burn gauze in the other.

"Can you please come out here, Jade? We can't talk through the door." Dad had returned.

"We are changing her bandages, Dad, she will be there in a second," said Leela. "*Are* we changing your bandages or are we going straight out?" she whispered to me, because I hadn't taken off my pyjama top.

I had no choice. I had to do this.

I had to look at that frost bite.

With shaking fingers, I undid the buttons and pulled off the top, standing in the strapless bra I had to wear since my shoulder and upper arm and top of my chest got covered in those bandages. Leela found the little clip and undid the end of the gauze, unwrapping it slowly.

What is it going to look like? I don't want to know! I wish I never had to see it!

The site of his bite had been a nasty white shade at the hospital, with several blisters. But that was a week ago. Online I'd found frostbites go completely black. I dreaded what I was about to see.

"No, Donovan, we are not leaving without talking to her! She can't just be vile to you and get her way. Jade, you can't just run away from this, okay sweetie?" Charleen's voice rang like a little annoying bell through the door. "She has a lot of explaining to do I'm afraid, darling, did you see the pile of dishes in the sink? The kitchen is a disaster!"

"Those aren't mine!" I called.

"Stand still!" Leela said, trying not to get tangled in the long gauze as she kept unwrapping it from my upper arm.

"You have not been looking after your Grandpapa, Jade, is this your new feminist outlook honey? Living in filth?" Charleen called back.

"Don't answer that right now," Leela whispered. I bit my lip.

The last of the bandage came off. My naked shoulders were fully displayed in the mirror.

Leela frowned, walking around me to see the back.

"Oh," was all she said.

"Huh!" I turned to see the back of my shoulder in the mirror too.

Nope. Nothing. There was nothing at all. The skin was just as pink and normal as it ever had been.

Like the frostbite never happened.

"It's healed well," said Leela. She binned the old gauze and stored the unused one in the cabinet under my sink. I was still staring at the mirror.

It didn't make sense. It hurt still, just as much as it did at first. It burned from time to time, the ache spreading. Sometimes it reached down to my elbow, and last night I was sure it made my fingers tingle. I had expected black flesh and rot setting into my nerves or veins or something. But I hadn't returned to the hospital, because they would start with the questions about how I got a frostbite in the first place. That's why I didn't dare look at it this whole time.

But it was completely gone.

"Aren't you going to get dressed? We should go talk to them," said Leela quietly, giving me my top.

"Right." I shrugged on the pyjama shirt and buttoned it up hastily. "Let's get this over with."

Leela unlocked the door and stepped out, switching off the light behind her.

"Jade is all good, isn't that great? She didn't need the extra bandages."

She had walked out into my cabin to talk to the parental units, but I was frozen on the spot. Standing alone in the dark bathroom.

She had switched the light off before I had time to do the three top buttons, and the fabric was off my shoulder a little.

And my shoulder was covered in a web of thread thin, white veins of pearly luminescence.

Instead of walking out into the light after my sister, I closed and locked the bathroom door. I stood in the dark, letting my half open top slide down to my left elbow.

Shimmering threads of silver on my skin. And I was right, it *had* spread down to my elbow. There it was, a pearly white glow, running in two separate veins—where no veins should anatomically be—

across my upper arm and past my elbow, stopping at the top of my forearm.

How far is it going to spread?

That was the first thought, but the second thought was even louder.

What is it?

A piercing pain skewered my skull. I shut my eyes tight and sat on the closed toilet lid, still holding on to the sink beside me. The pain was excruciating.

...Her body was covered in a web of fine silver chains, strewn with crystal gems. One moment the frail net of jewellery was translucent against her skin; the next, she ignited a mysterious light current with a sudden movement of her hands, and the whole lattice lit up...

I rubbed my forehead, trying to understand where the image came from. It was—

A memory?

A *hidden* memory.

Chapter Twenty-Four

Hidden Memories

M eanwhile outside the bathroom, Charlene was rapping at the door.

"Jade darling, I know you're so much cleverer than everyone else with all that tech know-how in that big brain of yours, but it's rude to ignore people when they are talking to you, ok sweetheart?"

"Mum, she's not ignoring you, she is probably using the loo! She'll be out in a second!"

I brought my hand, fingers trembling, to my shoulder. I wanted to touch the strange markings. I hesitated.

What harm can it do to touch it? It's already in my skin!

I ran my fingers softly over the strange shapes, tracing the mark down to my elbow. It was colder than my skin. But I felt it burn on my shoulder. And as I touched it, another wave of migraine coursed through my skull, rising from the back of my neck, and shooting behind my eyes.

...Lines of light pulsated along her skin... the mesmerising shimmer travelling from stone to stone along her body as she danced... writing invisible symbols in the air... a knife in her hand... slashing... screams?...

Where did I remember this from? When had I seen it? Who was this woman?

"Jade? Are you ok in there?" Leela's voice came quietly through the door. "Jade, can you hear me?"

"Yes, I'm fine! Just a bad headache."

Who was she? It felt like remembering a dream. Or had I been dreaming of things I'd forgotten in real life?

"Oh please! She is trying to avoid the consequences, darling. I peeked in Alan's cabin, the level of mess in there is *deranged*. His bedroom floor, the *hair*! Dog hair, Donovan! Your father's cabin has not seen a hoover since I last cleaned it. That was *weeks* ago my love. There's *nothing* more *mortifying* than walking on a carpet and feeling crumbs crunching under your feet. Your poor papa. She's just used to facing *no* consequences, it's incredible."

"Is that right?" I said, pushing myself up from the toilet lid. I steadied myself with a hand against the wall, buttoning up my pyjama with the other. Headache or not, there was no hiding in the loo while Charleen still needed to get this fight out of her system. I opened the door and leaned against the frame, glaring at Charleen, who stood beside Dad by the foot of my bed. "What consequences exactly, what will you do if I don't wash his dishes and scrub his cabin, you'll ground me? Cancel my allowance? What consequences am I avoiding exactly?"

"Oh honey, I think you'll find there *are* consequences, and by the way darling how lovely of you to grace us with your presence." This was the first time I was face to face with her in over a year; last time I saw Charleen was before the last tour to the desert. "Oh no, you must be devastated from all that sun damage on your hair my darling, how awful."

"Yes, utterly distraught, split ends are my biggest problem right now."

"I can imagine. And not to stress you out more but Donovan and I have discussed it a lot these last few weeks, and to be honest sweetheart we don't think this arrangement is working, you living here, I'm really sorry to say."

The world spun around me. For a moment I felt as completely alone as I used to feel when I was a teen, and Charleen had first showed up in our lives, mere months after the funeral. Her constant little changes and tweaks in our daily routines that pushed our family apart and, little by little, grouped me out. For a moment I thought I was going to collapse.

Leela caught me and steadied me.

"You mean I can't stay here anymore?" I looked at my father, but he turned away.

"It would be better for everyone if you found a place of your own, okay my darling?" said Charleen. "We'll help you of course, although I should hope you've saved enough for a rental deposit by now, and if you want to store anything in the basement again, we're happy to oblige. Family comes first, always my love."

"So, I come home after nearly two decades and not only I'm not allowed in my childhood room, in the house that *my* Mum and Dad bought when *I* was born," I said looking only at my father, "but now I'm not even allowed to stay in my grandma's empty cabin, while trying to save up to buy my own place. Fine," I interrupted my Dad who had opened his mouth for the first time to speak. "That's fine. Do you know what? Don't give me any handouts. I'll rent. It's all good."

I fought a fucking ghost last week. It kind of re-evaluates your bloody priorities.

I went to the wardrobe and pulled my suitcase out from the top of it. I unzipped it as my father looked on, stricken, and my sister watched with her bottom lip trembling, as if ready to burst into tears. I threw the open suitcase on my desk. Turning to the dresser, I opened the first drawer and began to empty its contents in the case.

"I'm glad you understand, it's gorgeous to see you've matured so much this last year," said Charleen with a smug smile, watching me pack with her arms folded on her chest. "This is best for both you and Alan, my darling."

"Mum!" said Leela. "Why can't Jade stay here! She has nowhere else to go!"

"I'm fine Leela. The world is full of rooms to rent and people looking for flatmates. You don't need to worry about me."

Theodora.

I stopped halfway while picking up my multiplug, charger and USB cables still hanging off it.

The name popped into existence like a balloon that burst to reveal a message inside. And suddenly I had the feeling I was surrounded by balloons exactly like it. Quietly floating in my head, carrying secrets concealed within. Memories that have been slipping through my thoughts these past few days, now I could feel them, hovering, just out of reach.

Who is Theodora?

"Jade, are you ok?" Leela sounded worried.

I realised I had been looking at the ceiling with my mouth half open. I tried to compose myself.

"I've got this... really strange headache," I said, rubbing my temples.

"I'm pretty sure she is faking it, Leela, it's quite obvious really," Charleen said.

"Mum! She's not! Just give her a second!"

He pointed at me with one hand and stirred in circles with the other, as the vapours surrounded me. The rings glimmered with foggy gems, some were even on his smaller knuckles just below his fingernails, which were painted white. Pearly threads of silver glistened, veined over the top of his hands, into rings in his fingers. A weapon that controls the mist?

It looks so similar... So similar to this thing on my—

"Come on, let's get you to sit down." A hand under my elbow, someone stirring me towards... my bed? I sat down and rubbed my eyes. The migraine was draining away as the room came back into focus. I blinked and saw all three of them standing around my cabin arguing over me. Well, Dad wasn't arguing. He doesn't like to get involved when Stepmonster is being awful to me. He was just supervising the conversation with a disaffected air of disapproval. Leela and Charleen *were* arguing over me.

"Leela, your Grandpapa needs proper care from someone who doesn't think looking after him goes against their political ideology. It's fine, I was expecting something like this, although I couldn't imagine this frightful situation!" She fluttered her fingertips towards the rest of the boat dramatically. "Not to worry my darling, I will get back to visiting Grandpapa every Monday and will have everything ship-shape in no time. And Jade can go do her own thing, like she wants. Embrace her freedom, yes? Why not Jade, honey, you do *you*, my love."

"Right," I said, "and I wasn't looking after Alan when I installed a satellite on the boat roof to increase broadband connectivity wherever he moors, then connected the dish to four mesh dots to boost signal across the boat, wall- mounted a tablet in each cabin and logged each tablet to a home network so he can have Alexa everywhere without using the mobile phone—because he complains his mobile's too small to read—, programmed notifications of his routine GP appointments to pop up and remind him on screeen, and routine prescription refills, got him an app with voice alerts so he takes the right pills at the right time, set up his weekly grocery shop on his favourite supermarket's app, so the shopping is delivered to the boat once a week without him needing to place an order, upgraded the fire safety system, replacing all smoke detectors and heat alarms which hadn't been changed since the eighties, and hooked him with a smart watch that monitors heart rate and blood pressure AND got it to email bi-monthly reports to his GP?"

The parental units' eyes had glazed over, like I'd just spoken to them in another language.

The multiplug was still in my hand. I wrapped the cables in a bundle and threw it across the room into my suitcase. It flew past Dad, standing by my desk, and he took a little startled step back.

"Yes, my darling, we all know you're very clever, Jade. But what good is any of that, sweetie, when Alan has no clothes? No food?"

I rolled my eyes and went to my wardrobe to get more stuff.

Why do I even bother talking to Charleen for fuck's sake. I've survived actual demons. With wings and shit. Flying bloody overhead. Why am I letting myself get dragged into this stupid conversation, when I need to think, I need to understand, no, I need to remember—

"I did offer to pay you for the smart watch, and I can cover some of the other stuff I guess..." Dad said.

"No need, Dad."

A migraine shot through my skull and the room blacked out for a moment. I turned my back to them and leaned against the open door of my wardrobe, images spilling before my eyes.

He lifted one arm to the sky as if supporting a great weight... something slimy sloshing beneath me, the white lake of vapours clotting in gooey spirals licking the graves... Climbing up to me... The entire body of this pearly grey gas was animated, using the stone statue to rise up to where I sat... He was sending the mist to attack me!

The pain subsided as the images died away. I was looking at the inside of my wardrobe, and Charlene was talking behind me. I had barely a moment to think how similar it was. The gear that man wore on his hands, and the one the woman wore all across her arms and upper body. How similar it looked to the web of glowing threads growing on my skin—

"We can reimburse you for all these things, of course, yes?" Charleen's voice drowned out my thoughts, as she came to stand before me. "If that's what you want darling. But your poor Grandpapa! While you've been here, he didn't get a single home cooked meal all week, sweetheart! Not until he'd come to us for Sunday dinner!"

"I don't want your money, thanks. I was happy to upgrade the boat. And I do offer to make him protein smoothies when I put the blender on. I don't mind sharing. But he says no."

"Oh no! Darling? You tried to feed the poor man your powder sludge drinks? What were you thinking, Jade?"

I didn't reply to her. I threw my biking helmet in my gym bag. Leela took it out and tried to put it back in my closet. I grabbed it from her, and she stood there, tears shimmering in her eyes, as I pummelled it back in my bag.

"What I don't understand," Dad said to his wife in a quietly tense voice, "is why can't you come look after my father while Jade still stays in my mother's old cabin?"

Charleen looked like she had swallowed a lemon slice.

"Donovan, what are you saying?" she said to him, looking truly hurt.

"Well, you've done it for years now, I don't see the problem."

"You want me to clean after Jade?" she said, eyes wide in complete mortification. "What am I? A *maid*?"

I couldn't help it, I burst out laughing. Finally, she gets what it feels like. I was holding my gym bag, and I dropped it on the bed as I sat beside it, doubled over with laughter.

"What's funny?" said Dad.

"It's just that Charleen thinks it's normal for a woman to clean after a man, but to clean after a woman makes her a maid. And also, you, Dad. You see nothing wrong with every woman in this family having to offer unpaid maid service to your father, but it's never you. No one talks about *you* coming to wash Alan's dishes. Hell, no one talks about getting Grandad to run his own dishwasher. And it's *not*!" I threw my boxing gloves in my gym bag. "*That*!" I threw my trainers next to them. "*Hard*!" I zipped it closed.

Do I talk to Dad like that? I guess I do, now. This is the new me. The Zero-Fucks-Were-Given-That-Evening Jade.

"No-no-no, sweetie! That's exactly the attitude we don't need in this family!" said Charleen. "Uncaring, thinking only about yourself, as always, and you know how much I hate to be the one to speak to you this way, but someone has to, ok darling? For your own good."

This time the migraine caught me by my chair, and I collapsed into it.

Theodora, drenched in moonlight, crossing a lake of grey, ankle-deep mists... Her mystifying, ice white gothic outfit, the long skirt that glimmered with pearl strings, as she glided like an apparition among the tombs.

And suddenly something else. The place where Ami last was, had a cemetery, and its name was written on a large label; on a pouch of dirt, kept inside a very strange box.

How could I forget this? How could I know such a thing, this whole week, and not remember it? When all I've done is try to figure out a way to find Ami?

My own voice answered back to me from a hidden memory, blasting to the surface like a hand tearing through a tissue paper screen to grab at me.

"Give me your mask, and boots, and goggles!" I'd shouted. All around the Celtic cross, the fog spun into a swelling vortex... I had to jump from tombstone to tombstone to escape it... They stood knee deep in the white lake of smoke, they tipped their tall hats... goggles and masks were lowered automatically... to fit on their faces by some invisible mechanism...

That was it. The fog was poison. So I must never let it touch me. But them? They had protection, to walk in it unharmed. Could I find gear like theirs? And no more rookie mistakes. I won't be letting them see me again. Those two won't be taking my memories away *ever* again.

The migraine was gone but I didn't stand up. If only all this family drama would be over so I could sit in peace and quiet and remember more...

"Mum, Jade is nothing like that," Leela was saying, torn as always between not wanting to displease her mother and not understanding why Charleen blames me for everything that goes wrong in her life. "Jade helps, she just does it in her own way!"

"Quiet, Leela!" Dad said and turned to me. "Is that what you have to say to me," he yelled, now starting to get flushed, "after I pay for your treatment to help you get better? You think it's cheap to get you weekly sessions with a top PTSD specialist in private care? It's not, it costs a fortune! And you speak to me like that, call me a bad father after all I do for you?"

"Want to stop my therapy?" I snapped.

"Technically, she didn't call you a bad father, Daddy, she called you a bad son," my sister said very quietly.

"Be my guest, cancel it, I don't need it," I spoke over her. "That counsellor did fuck-all for me. I almost died last week."

"Watch your language!" Dad bellowed, while Charleen at the same time cried: "How ungrateful, darling, not very classy!"

I marvelled, for a moment, at my complete lack of concern, even though I'd pissed them both off so bad.

But really, who cares? Who the hell cares about any of this bollocks when there's a woman out there... A woman who I'm pretty sure pulled out a knife... and cut some invisible fucking thread... and caused a whole arse legion of wing flapping fuckers to bugger off.

"Jade, will you quit pretending you have a headache, sweetie, stop rubbing your head like that! That's right, look up, we're all right here, it's not like we came all the way to see you now is it, oh wait a minute, yes, we did, darling. You owe your father an apology, don't you think?"

"Ok, sorry I'm not showing my gratitude by washing someone else's laundry. See you in seven months for Christmas, Dad," I said, zipping my suitcase.

"How did you almost die last week?"

Alan was standing at the door.

Everyone grew still, like children when an adult walks in. I sighed. I hated that Grandad had heard that.

"I'm moving out, Alan," I said and stuffed my toiletries in the first discarded shopping bag I could find. "Charleen will get back to visiting each week to get your things sorted. Thanks for letting me stay till now. I appreciate it."

"I *said*, how did you almost die last week?"

I shook my head. I wasn't going to answer that one.

I tied the top of the plastic bag in case my shampoo leaked, and I tucked it in the suitcase pocket. I looked around the bathroom for any other necessities I'd forgotten. I had to hold on to the sink when the next stab of migraine hit me.

A man coming towards me, the coat billowing around his long legs with every firm stride, taming the tentacles of mist that fumed from below.

Jeronymo.

What was it he said? Something important, really important... About Ami? No.

"This one has a bereaved daughter," he said. "She visits nearly every night..."

"Is that why the violin is playing? Pretty," said Theodora, a hint of sadness in her eyes.

"It's getting louder every time she returns," Jeronymo said. "I don't know what else to do!"

Oh my god! I'd heard it too! That morning, when I woke up. No, *before* I woke up!

I'd tried to convince myself I must have imagined this, it seemed such a small and inconsequential thing. But even if it was the tiniest of details, still— other people heard it too.

My heart warmed at the thought. It must be real. The music *must* be real.

"Jade had a panic attack when we were out last week Grandpa," said Leela, after a long pause where no one had answered Alan's question. "I— I stupidly forced her to watch a video from her service in the desert..."

"It's not your fault," I said, "and I'm fine now, Alan."

"You fainted from a video?" he asked.

"The doctors said it was probably a Post Traumatic stress episode," said Leela.

"What doctors? Jade had a doctor's appointment, and no one told me, Donovan?"

"It wasn't an appointment, she just had a quick trip to A&E, Dad," my father said. "She is better now, just needs some rest."

"What is a panic attack?" asked Alan.

"You know," Leela tried to explain, since no one else did. "Jade was worried something was going to attack us, it was very late, and the cemetery was rather spooky. Worked herself up so bad that she fainted."

"You were at the graveyard?"

"Yes, you know, visiting her mum, like usual."

"Leela that's enough," I said.

Alan looked at me and I looked away, busy putting Cannelloni's shampoo in with my own.

"Is that where you spent all those nights you were away? Evelyn's grave?" Alan asked me.

I didn't meet his eyes. I hated that everyone knew. I took the dog towel with me for Cannelloni but left all of my own towels behind. Hotel towels are too small, but somehow things that used to bother me, no longer seem to matter.

In a world where there's a man that remote controls the fog with a gauntlet of fucking crystals... and sends it at people... to knock them out... and wipe their memories... Bath towel size is somehow not that important.

"I've got everything I need for the next few days," I said. "I'll be back to pick up the rest of my stuff soon."

"You are not going anywhere," said Alan.

That surprised me. I stood there, staring at him.

"It's actually for the best, my dear," Charleen started, but Alan stopped her with a glower and turned to my father.

"Your woman's out of order!"

The cringe stabbed through me like a thousand needles. I don't like Charleen and yet I felt sorry for her. It sucked to be her right now.

"Grandpa, don't say things like that!" said Leela, "It sounds so sexist!"

Oh, poor Leela. This was probably her first family fight as an adult, and she clearly had no idea how things work around here.

"You keep your mouth shut," Alan barked at her, "or get out of my boat!"

My sister was so shocked she burst into actual sobs.

"See what you've done!" Charleen shouted at me, hugging Leela protectively.

"Don't worry, I'm out of here," I muttered, and shouldered my gym bag, pulling my suitcase to the floor to land on its wheels.

"I said you are not going anywhere!"

"It's fine, Alan, I'll come see you sometime," I said, rolling my suitcase to the door.

He positioned himself directly under the doorframe, blocking my way. His lined, round face set into a fire spewing grimace, daring me to defy him. He is taller than me, but I could still push him aside if I wanted.

I didn't dare.

I stopped awkwardly before him, suitcase in one hand, gym bag on the other, Cannelloni's bed tucked under my elbow.

Alan turned again to Dad and pointed a finger at him.

"You. Get your family back in line. This one," he pointed at me, "stays. She puts new shows on my television—"

"I can keep you on my streaming subscriptions," I said, but he spoke over me:

"...and the dog's a good chap. And I'm not throwing a child out in the street, with no place to stay. That's not what family does. That one," he pointed to Charleen, "stopped coming here when her stepdaughter moved in."

"But Alan—"

"Utter bollocks!" Grandad shouted over Chaleeen's objection. "You call yourself a mother? Or are you only mother to one of the two girls in this family?"

Charleen was flushed with anger, her lips pressed so tight together they turned white.

"And you sit back and let her kick your daughter out?" Alan turned back to Dad, and for a moment I thought maybe he's nicer than I thought, speaking up for me like that. But then he followed with: "Who's wearing the trousers in your marriage, son? Your wife better be back here once a week. Like always. Doing her job."

I flinched. Her job, really? I had to look away, seeing Dad's face souring into a grimace of humiliation at his father's complete rejection.

Welcome to the club, Dad. It stings, huh?

I glanced at Leela and her mum to see their reactions.

Leela's mouth had fallen open, her eyes narrowed in disbelief. She dried her tears on her sleeve, watching Grandad as if she was seeing him for the first time.

Her mother was now actually in the verge of tears herself, her eyes brimming even as they darkened under an angry frown. But she didn't talk back. I guess it's not easy having Alan for a father-in-law.

"And that one," Grandad pointed to Leela. "She better learn to control that lip when adults talk and go put the kettle on instead. What this family needs right now is a nice cup of tea. If I hear another word about this, you three are out of here. And I think my rhubarb pie is about to get burnt."

Alan turned around and sauntered back to the lounge, and his chair gave its usual creak as he sat.

I just couldn't help but note that he mentioned the pie getting burnt but didn't go do anything about it himself; just sat and waited for us to bring him his slice. I coughed into my hand to hide my amusement, while three sombre faces frowned around me.

"Yeah, Charleen, you heard him. His pie's about to burn."

Leela caught my eye.

"He is such a misogynist!" she mouthed.

"You don't know the half of it," I said, not wanting to shatter this already fragile conversation with the word 'homophobe'.

The parental units were ignoring us.

"After everything I do for this family," Charleen whispered, watery eyes fixed indignantly on my father, "To be spoken to like this. I told you Jade always causes problems, but you wanted her here on your parents' boat! I'm sorry darling, enough is enough. I won't! Simply not!" I found it funny they kept their voices low so Alan wouldn't hear them and return for round two.

"Why not?" Dad whispered back. "I really don't understand why you stopped coming when Jade moved in? It's not Jade you're looking after, it's my father!"

"I'm not dusting her furniture and cleaning her kitchen sink! If she lives here, she should do it herself!"

"I *am* doing those things." I was completely ignored.

"But you've been doing it since my mother passed. Nothing has changed!" Dad was now shouty-whispering at his wife.

"How about *you* do it then!"

My eyebrows shot up in shock. Charleen was shaking, and tears ran down her cheeks, but she had finally joined the gender revolution. Good for her.

Dad gaped at her, lost for words.

"Why is no one talking about Grandpa doing that stuff himself?" said Leela, desperately trying to diffuse the tension between her parents.

"Oh please, don't *you* start as well!" said her mother. "People his age need help around the house my darling!"

"Excuse me," said Leela, "Grandpa is perfectly capable. He sails his boat from one end of the country to the other, when he feels like a holiday."

This was new. In family arguments it's always been me against Charleen and Dad up till now. Which is why I lived as far away as possible these past twenty years.

"He is a tour guide," Leela continued, "and that's just for fun since he doesn't need it, not with *his* pension!"

Was she defending me? This sounded like she was defending me to her mother. I couldn't believe my ears.

"And talk about learning new things," she added, "he spends hours and hours researching history for his tours, travelling to every public library in a fifty-mile radius."

"I'm pretty sure he goes to senior swim in the community gym," I muttered.

"Yes, because like he says, 'no one likes a guide who can't keep up with their own group!'"

"So what?" said her mother.

"So, he can put his mugs in the dishwasher and switch it on! Grandma did it just fine!" I said. The headache had not been back for a while, but a little throbbing remained. It would happen again, soon enough. I felt the pressure of it in the back of my mind. Like my brain was a computer overdue for the next upgrade, going slow and crashing, with an enormous amount of downloads waiting to install.

Well great, I wanted to remember every moment I had spent with mist-rings dude and demon-knife chick. All I wanted to do was switch off all the lights, and sit in the dark. To remember.

"Alan will never think to put his mugs in the dishwasher," said Charleen. "And he shouldn't have to, darling. He's lived his life a certain way. You must respect that, okay my love? But I wouldn't expect you to understand, Jade, you've never thought of anyone else but yourself, I'm sorry to say!"

"Fine," I said, picking up my bag again. "I'll leave from the back door, so Alan doesn't stop me again. Good luck."

"Stop it, both of you!" Leela shouted, and I blinked.

Leela gave me a look and a nod, and I had no idea what it meant, but I had to stay and watch.

"Mum, you can't say these things about Jade! It's not nice, it's name-calling."

Wow.

"And besides, it's not even true! Jade's not selfish, she always brought us so many gifts, she's there when I need her, she likes helping out."

What's happening?

"And yes, I get that Jade doesn't do all the stuff you want, Mum! But she does other stuff! She's fine! And Dad," Leela did the unthinkable and turned around and faced our father. "Get involved already! Stop acting like this is all just the women in your life not getting along!"

"It *is* the women in my family not getting along," he said sternly.

"Not at all, Dad! These are actually *your* problems we are all trying to solve here! It's *your* father that my mum is looking after! And at first, I thought Jade was weird for refusing to do it, but I've done some research since, and did you know? Half of the women in the UK provide forty-five hours of unpaid care work per week. How insane is that? And apparently it happens partly because it's the women who are expected to care for the elderly, even if they have male siblings or even if it's their in-laws and not their blood relatives. So, Daddy, it's time for you to step in and do your part."

There was a pause where everyone, including myself, stared at my sister gobsmacked.

"And also, Daddy, it's *your* first wife that my sister is still grieving! That's your responsibility too, that Jade goes and talks to a tombstone instead of us, her actual living family! It's your job to be there for my sister!"

He tried to object, and I thought I heard the word 'therapy' being mentioned, but she spoke over him.

"No, Daddy, getting Jade a therapist isn't enough, you've got to talk with her about that stuff too! And you've got to stop treating my mum like your Personal Assistant. It's totally palaeolithic! If you don't change, Dad, you will turn into Grandpa!"

The silence continued.

I was speechless. I could not believe the balls on this kid. I would not speak to Dad like that unless I had a death wish. I expected him to explode in a bellowing diatribe of how ungrateful she is, tell her she is grounded, and threaten to remove any financial assistance she currently receives.

But that's *me*. Clearly Leela doesn't get any of that, when she stands her ground. Interesting.

The moment of stunned silence lingered.

Charleen was sobbing in the corner and wiping away tears, and Dad was gawking from me to Leela, then to his weeping wife. He stared at her the most. Then a shadow of sadness washed over his tired face. He walked up to Charleen.

"I'll get my father a cleaning lady," he told her.

I put my bag down.

"For real?" I said.

"Not for you," Dad told me. "Unless you want to chip in."

"No, I'm good," I said. "My dishes, my clothes, my room and bathroom; my responsibility. Like it's always been."

"Grand. I will look for a cleaning agency for my father tomorrow morning," he passed Charleen one of the tissues on my bedside table. "We will get this boat squeaky clean again, yes?"

"You will pay for someone else, Donovan?" said Charleen in disbelief, blowing her nose into the hanky.

"Well, my father is getting on a bit. I guess I shouldn't have left it to you and Jade to look after him. I'll do what's needed. I'll get somebody in every week."

The two of them looked at each other in the eyes, and I looked away. Charleen leaned into my Dad and gave him a little hug. Leela beamed brightly as she watched them.

"Thank you," said Charleen to Dad.

God, the eternal gratefulness of women. He should be thanking *her*, not the other way around. Instead, he patted her shoulder jovially like a dotting husband. Giving her the gracious gift of not having to be his father's carer.

"It's the girls you should thank," said Dad. "I wouldn't have seen how wrong this was if Jade hadn't been so obstinate. Pushing back every step of the way," he chuckled. "I guess we needed that, for once."

Charleen smiled to him but looked pained at the idea of thanking me for anything, so she just hid her face in Dad's shoulder. He wrapped his arms around her. I rolled my suitcase to the chair and unzipped it. Leela brought my gym bag and unzipped it too.

I glanced around at her as we stood shoulder to shoulder, looking at my stuff that now needed to be unpacked again.

"Thanks for standing up for me," I said quietly.

"I practiced it with my therapist," she whispered. "I felt so bad after I made you so unwell that night—"

"Leela it wasn't *you*, I was very unwell all on my own and you mustn't..."

But she spoke over me.

"I had a sister home from the war with PTSD and instead of being mindful, instead of holding a safe space for you, while you were trying to get better, I was stupid and nosey and stubborn and acted like a total child."

"I'm sure the nosey wasn't all you," I said, hushed, so the parental units wouldn't hear.

"Well yes, it started with my mum asking me to find out why you were back, but Jade, it hurts her feelings when Dad refuses to tell her what's happening with you."

I wasn't angry with her for pushing me that night; I *had* been at first, but not anymore. Let's face it; it was because of my little sister's mission to discover my secret, that I had to confront reality. She made me *see* Malem.

Ever since I got home and sent to live with Grandad I was irritated at how women are expected to help everyone out all the time: how incredibly sexist it is to call us selfish for not looking after other people, when men are not held to the same standard. But at the same time I must never forget: the complete opposite is also true. Helping another human being is a fucking moral imperative. It's a duty that transcends all layers of reality and bleeds into some deeper, darker level of existence. A duty which in one moment in time, I miserably failed. And sure, knowing the ghost's identity didn't make a difference; it didn't stop the shadow from coming to take my life in the end. I'd have to fight him even if I had no clue who he was.

But I felt so much better, knowing. Talking to him. Apologizing. I'm so grateful I got the chance to speak to Malem. Even if I wasn't granted forgiveness; still, I feel I can finally let go, and live to do better next time.

"Leela I swear, it's fine."

"Well, I wanted to make it up to you so I saw the therapist a lot this last week and we talked about ways I could do that. You're an awesome big sister and I want us to be friends. Real, grown-up friends."

"You're my baby sister and you don't have to be anything else. Luvya, kid," I said, giving her a little nudge with my elbow.

Leela fell into me with arms wide and squeezed me in a hug. I laughed in surprise. Then I hugged her back.

"That still leaves my shirts, for my tours," Alan called from the lounge. Leela and I broke apart, startled.

"You got half the bills paid now that Jade lives here, Dad," my father called back, gently disentangling himself from his wife. "You can afford to have the ladies at the dry cleaners come pick up your laundry at the end of each week. They'll drop it off when it's ready. I'll set it up for you."

There was no reply from the living room.

Then the high-pitched scratch of tape being torn off, followed by the rustling noise of paper being torn in half.

"What is he doing?" Leela whispered.

"He is binning the washing machine and dishwasher instructions I taped for him on the appliances," I said, amused. "I guess he won. He will not have to use them now that he gets a cleaning lady."

Then a sound no one expected. Leela and Charleen, Dad and I looked at each other and smiled.

The low buzzing of the heater and the bubbling of water: The kettle was on.

"No way!" I mouthed. And yet, the clinking of mugs, being set on the counter, was unmistakable. "Grandad is making us tea!"

Chapter Twenty-Five

The Spirit Fleet

"So actually, Mum, that evening turned out better than I expected."

Jade gave a little chuckle and rested her chin on her knees. The summer evening breeze carried the playful rushing of the Thames, ever sweeping by, behind the cemetery wall. The western skies were blazing orange and lavender in the sunset. The last bumblebees of the day buzzed around the dandelions, that dotted the green tufts at the roots of the tombstones.

"Stepmonster was civil for the rest of the evening and didn't bring up my shortcomings and life choices at all. And Dad walked Cannelloni with me before they left, and we had a good chat, he and I." Jade paused, a reminiscent smile twitching on her lips. "About you."

Her eyes glimmered with a hint of tears, but her smile didn't waver.

"He said he misses you too. It was good to hear, but at first, I didn't believe him. So, he said he would like for the two of us to go out and celebrate your birthday every year from now on. Actually, Grandad told him to do that. Alan apparently takes them all out to eat at Grandma Tamsin's favourite restaurant every year on her birthday, same as when she was alive. So, he told Dad the two of us should do the same for you. Somehow it changes from the saddest day of the year to one I will look forward to. Now I can't wait for your birthday, to spend it remembering you, with Dad. Who'd have thunk it, huh."

"I'm sorry it took a week to come back and see you, Mum. I really wanted to. But I was terrified after what happened. I thought it might happen again. But after what I remembered, I don't think Malem will be back. I think there are rules to this thing, and there are people out there who *know* the rules. And I will find out, if I can. For you, and for Ami."

The river breeze whistled gently through the willows.

She shivered at the sound.

She scanned around the empty cemetery, her eyes weary, but her chin held high, ready to fight back.

"Getting a bit spooked, Mum," she said to the tombstone. "Last time when I woke up here, I thought I heard— I thought I heard—"

Her gaze fixed on the violin, cast in steel in the middle of the headstone. She sighed.

"Well, I thought I heard you play."

The sun must be setting somewhere over the ancient oaks outside the wall, because the Celtic crosses and weeping angels all around her were turning crimson. The blackened headstones on the ancient burial ground were now a deep violet.

"I heard it clearly, you were playing the violin," she said, wrapping her arms around her waist as if to keep herself warm. "I was standing right here, you know, and I had passed out- well Leela said I was dead, but she freaks out easily. And in the complete darkness, you were playing right beside me, Mum. I couldn't see you. But I'd know your music anywhere."

The violin on the headstone was now glowing with crimson sunset hues. She glanced up at the sky, streaked with dusky cerise and lilac to the west, while already dark blue to the east, from where the night was swiftly approaching.

"So, I thought I'd come again and check." She shook her head. Disappointment furrowed her brow, a glint of frustration in her cobalt eyes.

"I need to get going. I can't let those two—" she faltered, as if forcing herself to speak the names aloud. "Jeronymo and Theodora. I can't let them see me here again, or they will take my memories again. I won't let it happen. I need to learn more, much more. So much to be done." She stood up quickly, blew a kiss to the tombstone and headed to the path.

The evening dew glistened on the lawn among the graves. It looked like emeralds as she passed. She wiped tears from her eyes as she walked.

Why is there no music? Why? And what does it mean if there really was music before? Is Mum here? Why doesn't she appear? If Malem could do it, why not my mother?

By the time she had reached the wrought iron gates of the little riverside churchyard, the tombstones around her were no longer crimson.

The sun had set.

The twilight gave a sense of gloom and eeriness, that made her shudder, as she was about to cross the gates and leave the cemetery.

And then she froze.

Somewhere behind her, in the heart of the silent graveyard, a violin was playing.

Jade ran back up the path. Her gaze was fixed on the little tombstone in the distance, where the music came from, straining to see the violinist.

There was no one there.

The music was constant, sweet and welcoming.

Her heart pounded painfully against her ribcage, her footfalls loud on the gravel, but as she cleared the curve of the path, she shivered. The closer she got, the more the music seemed to come from the grave itself. The ancient side of the graveyard appeared, just behind the whispering curtain of the willows. A gust of cold wind hit her.

Jade's head snapped around, her feet coming to a halt, her chest heaving as she panted hard from the sprint. She scanned the cracked and lopsided ancient tombstones for any sign of people, but no one was there.

Not yet.

The unmistakable mist made everything in that side seem hazy.

Jade hesitated. She glanced from her mother's grave, still some distance down the path, to the ancient graveyard, where something was stirring.

She is playing her violin! She is calling to me!

Smoky grey tentacles fumed from the ground.

Jade started to back away, eyes never leaving the rising fog. She had never watched it from the start, or seen it form into veils that hovered, gently swaying over the grass.

I can't be here right now.

The milky lake of vapours quickly swallowed the ancient tombstones, reaching the leafy drapes of the willows and heading for the cemetery path.

It's them. They will be here soon.

She turned and ran.

When she reached the cemetery gates, she stopped and turned to look back one last time.

The smoky tide pulsated gently at the edge of the path, just where she had been standing, like the waves on a lake shore.

The violin was still playing.

Sorry Mum. I can't risk losing my memory of your music again. But I promise, I'll be back.

Jade fled.

She ran to the cemetery gates. She reached them and accelerated. She ran straight through the wrought iron arch, as the two Georgian lamps came on for the evening. She was out of the cemetery.

But she didn't leave.

Instead of taking the village road, she turned right along the river path. She followed the curve of the footpath and soon found herself walking between the dark waters of the Thames on her left hand, and the cemetery wall on her right.

The outside of the wall, for once. I'm safe on the outside.

She walked with purpose. She knew exactly where she was going. Some distance away, she stopped and found an opening into the bushes along the wall.

There it is!

Jade's bike had been concealed in the shrubs, and now she grabbed her water bottle and drank half of it. Tearing open a protein bar she took a bite. Then she tucked herself in the tight space beside the bike and the wall and slid down to the ground. Sitting with her legs crossed, she propped several devices open on her lap, water bottle and snack at hand, ready for a long session.

She clearly remembered it now. The box with the pouches marked with names of burial grounds from all around the globe. The name of the graveyard in the city, in the desert, where Jade had served. By the base where Jade and Ami had first met. Jeronymo and Theodora might hold the key to saving Ami.

Jade leaned her back against the cemetery wall, and pulled out Ami's compact mirror, balancing it on her leg beside her devices:

A tablet, and a transistor radio. And her little tattered Goals journal.

Ha! I see you! Hidden camera, baby!

The screen showed the old part of the cemetery, where the lakes of fog were quickly spreading.

It was just so very odd that the mist rose inside the wall, when out here by the river, it was clear. Jade had always thought the fog came from the Thames. But it was coming from the old graveyard itself.

The image flickered but returned.

Jade kept her eyes on the screen as she opened her journal to the last page she'd written. It was last week, when she'd only been writing: Stay Alive every day.

Then after that night, she'd stopped.

Today, she started a new page:

Today's Goal: Find A Way To Ami.

She looked at her screen because the image of the cemetery rippled and pixelized again for a brief moment.

You're going to die, aren't you? My phone died every time. It's ok, let's check plan B.

Swiping at a button at the bottom of her screen, Jade made the image zoom to the side, on the dense foliage of a willow at the thickest part of the fog. Another flicker, and the image came back grainy. A little transistor radio was barely visible, hooked among the leaves. The image broke into pixels, got distorted and then returned, even more hazy than before. Zooming several times more, Jade checked on several more audio surveillance devices concealed around the area. They were all in place and switched on.

The screen went blank.

Dead. It's fine. Analogue should work. Their stuff looked analogue. I'm sure I'll be able to listen in, at least.

Jade put the screen back in her backpack and held the little radio with both hands. She pulled a little cable and plugged it into the device, hooking the earbud end to her ear.

Hey Mum!

Violin played in her ear. Jade sighed, leaning her head against the wall, closing her eyes. Lost in the soothing melody.

So, you only play after nightfall, Mum. Not in the daytime. Cool. Only problem is, the fog comes in the nightfall as well. How will I be able to go looking for you while they are there? I need to figure something out.

"Jade!" said Theodora's voice in her ear.

Jade froze.

How could they know she was there?

"She isn't here," said Jeronymo.

"But she must have been here," Theodora's voice came into her ear again. "It doesn't do this unless Jade visits."

They do hear the music. They've heard it all along, even before I ever did.

"I've not heard Evelyn's song since that night, so Jade hasn't been back for a week."

"Jeronymo, it's playing right now. She's been here." Something about her tone sounded like a continuation of a disagreement they've been having.

"Or she hasn't," Jeronymo said quickly, "and her mother is singing because she's missing her."

Jade's shoulders were tense, the veins on her neck were throbbing with contained emotion. Singing because she's missing her?

"If you say so," Theodora said, but sounded suspicious. Jade wasn't sure of what.

Their footsteps were gravelly on the path. Then they thudded on the lawn. They were walking to her mother's tombstone.

Jade took a note in her Goals journal: 'Search for hidden passage, underground? How do they appear so suddenly? What are these Gates?'

Sounds of a backpack opening. Jade remembered that strange bag Jeronymo carried, with the dancing symbols. And the candles with the purple flame.

Is he using those candles on Mum's grave again? What do they do?

It wasn't a long pause, before Jeronymo said: "Rest peacefully now, Evelyn."

And the music stopped coming out of her earbud.

Jade's hands balled into fists.

He stops her! Why does he do that? I want her to play forever. I want her to speak!

"So?" asked Theodora.

"So what?" said Jeronymo.

"What happened? You've been avoiding me last week and not answered any of my messages. What's going on? What happened with your gorgeous soldier lady?"

Jade blinked in surprise and quietly took a bite off her bar.

Jeronymo sighed.

"I left. Just like you said I should. I didn't see what happened."

"Yes, I know you made sure to be home all night. But you've done something. I know you have."

"What could I do? Without your help? I had to run away."

"Did you see the shadow?"

"Yes. It was a man. He hadn't materialised so I don't know what he looked like. He watched her."

"I expect so. And the Erinyae? Did they return?"

"I felt them there." His voice shook. "I didn't stop to look. But I'm sure they were gathering as I stepped through the Gates."

Jade made another note: 'He says he 'steps through' the Gates, like a door? Maybe look for an actual trap door?'

"So then, she died? You should be able to procure an obituary by now. And yet, there isn't one. I looked."

"How did you look?"

"I got her surname from the tombstone, and I know she lives nearby. She hasn't died yet, Jeronymo. So, what are you hiding?"

"Did you want her to die?"

"Of course not, but what we want in this work is not relevant. That's something you need to start getting used to. Now. Tell me what you know."

"That night, she put up a fight," Jeronymo said. "The lamps were smashed all over the grounds. So, she was able to *see* them."

"She's brilliant," said Theodora. "She figures things out so fast! But that alone would not have been enough for her to survive."

"And you won't believe this. An iron wreath stand was missing, and I found it a good distance away. I think she procured herself a weapon."

"Unbelievable! Both iron *and* a funerary object? That would have been most effective. But even if she survived till the morning, she can't possibly be doing this for seven nights and still win."

"I don't know what to tell you. Because every day since then all I can think of is I really wish I had stayed," said Jeronymo.

"No. You did well to leave."

"It doesn't feel that way."

"You would have gotten hurt, like last time you were stupid about it."

"There still was one simple, decent thing to do."

Jade's eyebrows rose in surprise. He sounded really upset for her. It was rather cute.

"And what's that?" said Theodora.

"We should have told her."

"Told her." She said it as if that confirmed he had indeed lost his mind.

He exploded, speaking so fast, Jade had to press the earbud into her ear canal, to discern all the words.

"We should have told her she had been marked for death! That she had only a few nights left to live, we should have told her that!"

"She would have forgotten!"

"You know what I mean," said Jeronymo. "We should have given her something she wouldn't forget. A note. A message. There are ways."

"But. We *can't*," Theodora said, her voice heavy with meaning she didn't expand on.

"I *know*. But it feels so awful. I feel like I should have. I feel like it was the right thing to do. Give her the information she needed to do the best she could!"

Jade shuddered. She'd been there, she knew how that felt. She didn't blame him, he was clearly following some code of conduct, some duty of silence. And at the same time, she remembered how she'd almost hated them both the night they refused to answer any of her questions. She was still a bit angry with them for that. It was just so unfair they hadn't helped her. For them it was their job, for her it was her *life*.

She sighed.

You're probably out there, Malem, laughing at me right now.

"And how do we explain it? Hey gorgeous, you're about to die, a ghost is after you? She wouldn't have believed it."

Jade's mouth twitched into a little playful grin.

Classy lady likes me!

"First of all, those targeted by a shadow can see it," Jeronymo argued. "I imagine she was going mad trying to understand what was happening to her. Someone telling her it's real might have actually given her some peace of mind."

"And what good would it do? If it can't prevent her death?"

"I don't know, it might make her passing less traumatic, if she knows what's going on. She might feel less alone."

Jeronymo you big softie. I was fine on my own, but you're a good kid after all.

"The opposite. First thing she'd do, if she had concrete information, is she'd reach out to friends and family. However, vengeance spirits are entirely imperceptible to everyone apart from the afflicted. Her loved ones can't see the invisible. They wouldn't believe her; they would commit her. How would that be any less traumatic?"

"Do you realise," he said, "they are not as clueless as they used to be. They know dark matter is 93% of the universe, they even have pie charts about it. Any idiot can run a search. They will find it staring them in the face. 73% of the world is dark energy and only 4% is visible. Their own scientists know this now."

Jade pulled out her phone and typed those claims into the web search.

"A pie?" Theodora's voice was blank. "A pie that is also a chart?"

"What I mean to say is they *know*. They call it particle physics or quantum something, someone called haggis..."

"Is that the five-legged, hill-dwelling Scottish rodent?" She laughed.

"What? No—"

"You hang out too much with young MacAvoy from the Necropolis, Jeronymo."

"Sorry no, I meant Higgis."

"Higgins?" said Theodora with barely hidden sarcasm. "Of Henry Higgins and Eliza Doolittle? Did you mean physicist or phoneticist?"

"Can you just *not*."

Jade swallowed a chuckle. Her Mum loved that movie. She used to put it on and try to teach Jade to sing. That endeavour had failed, Jade danced instead. Bouncing around the room in marsupial macropod frenzy, as her Mum, snuggled up in her fluffy blanket on the couch, sang along the songs, her voice perfectly in sync with Audrey Hepburn's.

Theodora chuckled at the same time as Jade. She had such a lovely, tittering laugh.

I wish I could meet her. But she'll just wipe my memories again.

"Invisible no longer means imaginary," Jeronymo continued. "They have established the existence of dark matter with all kinds of indisputable evidence. And they keep building telescopes. And accelerator machines as big as entire underground cities. To try and find it."

"Find it?" She outright laughed. "Moronic."

"But you see, it is now possible to explain, if we only tried. They have already discovered the invisible exists."

There was a pause. Jade was researching on her phone, many pages opened over each other.

The things he says are true, but on particle level. Particles being invisible is not the same as demons being real.

"I didn't realise all this had happened. No one talks about it," said Theodora at last.

"Their cosmologists do. Their astrophysicists do. They even named Dark Matter Day, the 31st of October."

"Halloween?"

"Yes! They call it the hunt for the unseen."

"Extraordinary. Can you imagine the day their scientists will walk out of the labs and announce to the world, hey, we found ghosts."

He chortled. She didn't.

"Enough of your changing the subject," she said. He stopped laughing.

They were walking on gravel again. Heading back to the old part of the cemetery again? They always came and went from the thick of the mists. It grew practically solid, right on the other side of the wall where Jade sat right now.

She could actually hear their footfalls over the wall now, not only through the earphone. She hunched, even though there was no chance they could see her behind the wall; she held her breath.

"Jeronymo, I know she is alive," said Theodora.

"How?"

"You know there are ways."

"No, you would need something of hers."

"Well, there were a couple of blonde strands of hair left on my sleeve from the night we met her."

"And you kept that?"

"I wanted to *know* when she was gone. I wanted to say a prayer for her. So, I've been checking." Theodora's voice was soft when she said that. "I liked her. I agree with you that she didn't seem to deserve what was after her."

Jade was lost for words.

Jeronymo must have been too, because there was a pause.

"And even though I'm very glad Jade still lives, I also know it's not possible. You've done something. And at this point, you can either tell me out of your own free will, or I will have to *make* you. I'm sorry. But this is serious."

"Look, she was innocent, ok? I saw that document Jade talked about. From the military. It described the incident, and she told the truth. She wasn't involved in the killing."

"You don't have to *commit* a killing to be involved in it," said Theodora. "Even bystanders are not innocent, by virtue of not stepping in. The Furies need two things to manifest: blood spilled in an act of murder, and for the victim's spirit to linger, seeking revenge. If the dead man held her responsible for his murder, then that's enough."

Jade stopped looking at her screen and her eyes glazed over as she listened in.

"There are some other factors that are relevant to when they rise," Jeronymo said. "Sometimes murder on holy ground will do it, right? Like blood spilled in or near a temple of any kind."

"I'm impressed you'd know that."

"I did some reading. So maybe they didn't come for her..."

"Yes, they did. I saw the binding threads. I cut off three of them. Jeronymo, what have you done?"

"Maybe they acquitted her! She had proof she was innocent."

"That can't happen."

"Can't the Erinyae turn to Eumenidae?" said Jeronymo.

"How do you know about that?" Theodora sounded surprised. "We can hardly get you to read your own manual, and suddenly you've memorised ancient source material? I'll ask you again. What have you done?"

"I went and looked it up in the bibliotheca. Well, Jade told me about it, so I knew what I was searching for."

"She did?"

"Yup."

Theodora sighed.

"That's ancient literature. It would never work on the field."

"Why not?"

"Demons don't willingly switch to Patrons Hallow. From simply, what? Reading a bit of paper? No. They are potent entities, consumed by raw emotion, thirsting for human conduits to pour it all into. What did you think, they'd act like judges? Consider the evidence and deliver a verdict based on logic and reason? These beings *burn* with wrath."

"But it's been done before, if it's been documented, so it *can* happen."

"You're missing an important detail. There was a higher divinity in *that* story. And there isn't one here. I can tell you that for certain."

"What? You mean a God?"

"Goddess. What did you think, Jade could, all on her own, just *compel* demons to reverse their moral alignment? Daemons are lesser deities, Gods of dead religions. Only Greater Gods can command Daemons."

"I didn't know a Goddess was involved in that story…"

"Now you do. So, for the last time, what did you do? How come the Furies are no longer after Jade?"

"Fine. I did do something I wasn't supposed to. But I'm allowed to do it. I'm the Gate keeper."

"What did you do?"

"I sealed my Gates that night."

"How is that relevant?"

Buckles clinked, popping open. He was rummaging in that weird bag of his.

"It was just an experiment; I have no idea if it worked."

"You're not making sense!"

A slapping rustle of pages turning. He had his book out again.

"See here, where it says a soul won't cross over when the gates are closed?"

"Yes."

"So, if they *did* kill her, she lingered."

"But then she'd be dead, and she'd have an obituary." Theodora sounded frustrated.

"Well, it says here that the sunlight brings back those who died from the Erinys Curse."

"No one can come back to life once they cross the Styx, Jeronymo."

"But Jade's spirit wouldn't have crossed over. She'd be trapped here. I shut the Gates."

There was a pause.

"Wait… are you actually telling me there's a chance Jade died that night, got trapped in your section, and the sunrise brought her back to life the next morning?"

"Yes!"

"And the Curse would be fulfilled with her death. The Furies would return to the Underworld and the shadow would move on… so she'd be clear. She'd wake up normal, like it never happened."

"Exactly! Wouldn't it be brilliant?"

"You absolutely *must* report this, Jeronymo. The Inquisitors will want to know. I don't think the Academy has a single historical record of something of this magnitude! This is terrible."

"Terrible? Why? I found a loophole and saved her life! Pretty cool for a newbie, wouldn't you say?"

Easy there, Sherlock. It was me who wrote down all those notes in your book. I found your loophole.

Jade remembered writing that question on the pages, because it had seemed inconsistent at the time. "What if the Gates are closed? What if the sun comes out just then?" Because she'd wondered, still thinking this was a video game, if a lingering soul, trapped between worlds, might not return to its body in the daylight.

And she'd been right.

She had no idea that little note would save her life in the end. But she'd figured it out and nodded to herself with a smile. Although, she couldn't take all the credit.

Everyone helped. They'd all done a small thing each. Every step proved crucial to the outcome.

Jeronymo had said: "I'll close the Gates to protect you." And so, he had. That haunting sound of giant doors shutting. It had shaken her to the marrow of her bones. She'd never seen any gates, but she know now she'd heard them. They had to be here, somewhere. And she was going to find them.

And Leela had pulled off the body blanket. So, the sun touched Jade's skin and broke the curse.

Jade couldn't begin to think what would have happened if she'd just been shoved in the ambulance under that blanket. Ended up in a body bag, in a drawer at the morgue. Then in some basement in a funeral home. Never seeing the sun again. Never waking up.

And Leela had said something about a voice? No, just an urgent feeling, some imperative need to make sure her sister wasn't in the dark. How curious.

Could that have been Mum?

Had Evelyn led Leela to do this, somehow? If one bitter ghost had inflicted thoughts of self-destruction and pushed Jade out of her mind, could a spirit with good intentions put *helpful* feelings in someone's heart? Was Jade's Mum guiding her sister's hand in that crucial moment?

But Jade was pulled out of her reverie as the voices in her ear became louder. Jeronymo and Theodora were arguing.

"I can't believe this!" Theodora sounded shaken.

"You're about to get philosophical right now, aren't you," said Jeronymo. "You will tell me that no one knows how primeval deities pass their judgment on mortals. And that if they found her guilty and killed her, by making sure she didn't die I subverted Daemonic retribution..."

"Jeronymo..."

"...and something dreadful will happen to me, and her, and everyone involved, and—"

"Jeronymo!"

"I don't care! Theory of Theology in Primordial Powers was not my favourite subject in the Grove of the Academias. All I care for is that an innocent person didn't die in my cemetery. No one dies on my watch if I have anyth—"

"JERONYMO!"

"What?"

"If she came back to life after being killed by a curse, that is Dark Serendipity."

The river rustled, agitated, as it swept by. Crickets chirped manically from the wet reeds. Somewhere on a bed of waterlilies in the shallows, a toad croaked a long, rough, quirky trill.

"I didn't think of that."

"Clearly."

"Which one is that, again?" Jeronymo sounded weary. "Sorry," he said, all the hype gone from his tone. "I don't remember all the Metamorphosis Singularities."

"You may have just enlisted someone in the Spirit Fleet, and you're not a Recruitment Selector.

Dark Serendipity is where she becomes one of *us*."

Acknowledgements

Rayne's class. My first ever writing class, a decision in a parallel reality, in the strange days of the pandemic. Because, why not? Take Gothic Horror lessons, sure. The world was about to end, and that ultimate silence outside: no cars driving down the road, no planes flying to Heathrow overhead- never before had I heard that complete, deathly quiet. So eerie. Started the Horror lectures and loved every minute. And then the teacher set a short story competition, which prompted: Write a story entirely in a cemetery... I never submitted it— I never stopped writing it. Here's the first part. Thanks, Rayne, you helped me shape something tangible out of decades' worth of unusable drafts. Thanks for getting me to finish a book for real.

Then came Daniel, fantasy coach extraordinaire. The most amazing developmental editor I could have ever hoped for. You read every single draft, you probably know this story better than anyone. If someone listened in on our meetings they'd think Jade, Leela, Jeronymo and Theodora were the rest of our chat group and we were gossiping about them behind their back; that's how real my characters became when you read them. "But what do you think Leela would say to that?" And "No, Jade would never do it!" And "Do you know what I thought about Jeronymo's options the other day?" You corrected all the silly stuff without making me feel bad. You made me believe it was possible every time I doubted myself, and I doubt myself several times an hour, so really your reservoir of positive energy is inexhaustible. You tidied up each chapter, watching for inconsistencies in every detail, and you edited half of this book sitting in some part of Disneyland or adjacent to it, which is the most spectacular quality of your editing process. There are no words big enough to thank you.

Third came Magdalena, because the more I wrote, the more I drew, and those paper illustrations had to enter the screen somehow. You sure don't scare easy, girl. I pulled out sketches with actual grave dirt rolling off them on to my desk, holding them up to the camera for advice— the weirdo who takes her audiobook headphones to quiet countryside cemeteries and sits and sketches in the shado ws... You just laughed. Hundreds of hours together, me with stylus in hand, you listening carefully to all my wild ideas: here's a photo of my old garden brolly, mossy and moulding, can we make green, fungus ridden demon wings out of this? You nodded and grinned: Yup, we can! Right, here's my photos of five church elements from old towns up and down the country, can we please Frankenstein them all into my original medieval cemetery sketch? Yup, let's do it. Magdalena, thank you so much, for always finding a way so I can bring my nightmares to life.

Chris was actually the very first editor I've worked with, but in this book they came in half way, as a professional beta reader. The book they edited before comes after, because prequels are the bane of my existence- they suck me in like black holes, but that's another story for another Acknowledgements Section. Chris, you should be doing reaction videos because watching your face, when you read my chapters, is the best feedback I've ever had. You convey exactly what worked, and you pick up on all the stuff that need revisited—which somehow I never notice until *you* do, but then it's blatantly obvious. Also, killer dialogue teaks. Your witty comebacks granted my characters some fabulous conversation moments, much cooler than this ghoul of an introvert and social anxiety disaster could ever come up with. Thanks for holding safe space for my frequent feminist rants. Editors who are also gender equality advocates are a rare and beautiful thing. When I hesitate, I think, would Chris go there? And if you would, I will too, because we need to be talking about this shit.

Jocelyn runs a gorgeous writers' space, where everyone is welcome: The gory goths smashing watermelons to come up with accurate descriptions of brain-splatter, the fantasy geeks with week long geopolitical ravings about what con-stitutes sufficient worldbuilding, the sassy lady folk exploring new styles of witty, girl-power romance. Who ever you are, that's where your magic happens. It is an online haven for all things authorly, the good days with big wins, the bad days with zero word count, the weird days with cutting locks straight off my head to set on fire and time how fast human hair burns. Thank you for the excellent classes, the fun writing challenges, the workshops where several of my chapter drafts were shaped by the feedback of my classmates... The writing sprints, where some of my settings descriptions emerged, because I'm a skip-the-scenic-paragraphs kind of reader and wouldn't have the patience for them otherwise. And no one would know what anything looked like around Jade. Thanks, Jocelyn, for giving me a place to go and write, when I had to stay at home; as the midnight moon rose outside my window, my cats curled up to sleep around my desk, my open word document waited at the ready, and a side screen with thirty authors from all over America talked on and on in the lecture chat. I couldn't have done it any other way.

Sarah is the only one who read the whole manuscript start to finish, and she did it in 30 days. The line edits bled into every page and it took me many months to get through; what surfaced on the other side was a drastically changed document. Same story, but better told. Thank you for sharing your thoughts so frankly, and giving me a good impression of what it felt like joining Jade for the first time- I've been Groundhog-Day-ing this story in a loop for two years and I'd lost all perspective. Your trad-pub take was useful to hear, even though it's not for those of us indies-by-choice. I felt a bit of a rogue writer, reading your email advice on the industry's inner workings, because I value my creative autonomy more than any flashy book deal; but I'm grateful that an author I much admired has left her mark on my first published piece.

Gareth is the horror master who I had to wear down with my constant requests for ghost scene edits, till he gave in and accepted to have a look. That was five years ago, and ever since, he's been rendering Jade's twisted nightmares more perverse, and her gloomy nights even more traumatizing. You have no qualms about chopping my wordcount mercilessly ("Ditch the adjectives please!") to spare the unsuspecting reader my random ramblings (concise is not a word in my vocabulary). Thanks for making the suspense edgier and the scares screamier. You're the only one of my editors I don't have to apologize to, for the blood scenes coming up; you're most likely to find it insufficient: "This hardly qualifies as gore. Send it over again when it's got some actual injury detail." Gareth, I'm so glad to have your sinister guidance on the spoopy, the sticky and the squirmy, and for all the dark ways you inspire me to sharpen the horror in this cozy.

My Pet Gamer has been in his mancave, that shares a wall with my booknook, for over twenty years. He doesn't much notice the artistic endeavours on my side of the house, but he observes the angst and tries to alleviate it by luring the dog to sleep under my desk (her twitchy dreams of running are the most soothing thing to watch). When he wakes up at 5.30am to get ready for work and finds me with hair like a spider's nest, eyes practically bleeding and claws shaking from the caffeine overdose, still typing away since the night before, he does back away in fear- but he then orders breakfast pastries to be delivered to the door. He can be heard telling the cats, "The sugar will finally knock it out and it will sleep, and it will transform back into your mum by early afternoon." Honey, I forgive you for never reading any of the chapters I sent you for feedback. I didn't, for the longest time, but now I think it's cute you take my manuscript printouts to your desk, and to your bedside table, and to our holidays, and still have never opened any of them. Good news, you're off the hook, it's now got published, no further changes can be made. It's ok; you water the pots outside my desk window so I have sunflowers growing behind my screen, and you hold the fort while I book myself to remote sea side cottages for week long writing retreats. Thanks for never refusing to watch one more horror film. And for nodding understandingly at the ensuing angry tangent, that invariably follows, about sexism in horror movies. And for still watching another horror movie with me the following night. There's no one else I'd rather be with in a zombie apocalypse, but you.

Printed in Dunstable, United Kingdom

66716409R00218